ANDOLFO · GOY · BROCCARDO · NOSENZO

Deep Beyond

VOLUME 01

DEEP BEYOND, VOL. 1. First printing. September 2021. Published by Image Comics, Inc. Office of publication: PO BOX 14457, Portland, OR 97293. "Deep Beyond" is created by Mirka Andolfo, David Goy, Andrea Broccardo, and Barbara Nosenzo. Copyright © 2021 Arancia Studio s.n.c. All rights reserved. Contains material originally published in single magazine form as DEEP BEYOND #1-6. "Deep Beyond," its logos, and the likenesses of all characters herein are trademarks of Arancia Studio s.n.c., unless otherwise noted. "Image" and the Image Comics logos are registered trademarks of Image Comics, Inc. No part of this publication may be reproduced or transmitted, in any form or by any means (except for short excerpts for journalistic or review purposes), without the express written permission of Arancia Studio s.n.c., or Image Comics, Inc. All names, characters, events, and locales in this publication are entirely fictional. Any resemblance to actual persons (living or dead), events, or places, without satiric intent, is coincidental. Printed in the USA. For international rights, contact: licensing@aranciastudio.com. ISBN: 978-1-5343-2071-0.

DEEP BEYOND

created by
MIRKA ANDOLFO - DAVID GOY
ANDREA BROCCARDO - BARBARA NOSENZO

MIRKA ANDOLFO and **DAVID GOY** writers

ANDREA BROCCARDO artist   **BARBARA NOSENZO** colorist

FABIO AMELIA and **MAURIZIO CLAUSI** letterers - **ROSSANO BRUNO** editor

ANTONIO SOLINAS associate editor - **ANDREA MELONI** color editor

DAMIANO TESSAROLO editor assistant - **FABRIZIO VERROCCHI** designer

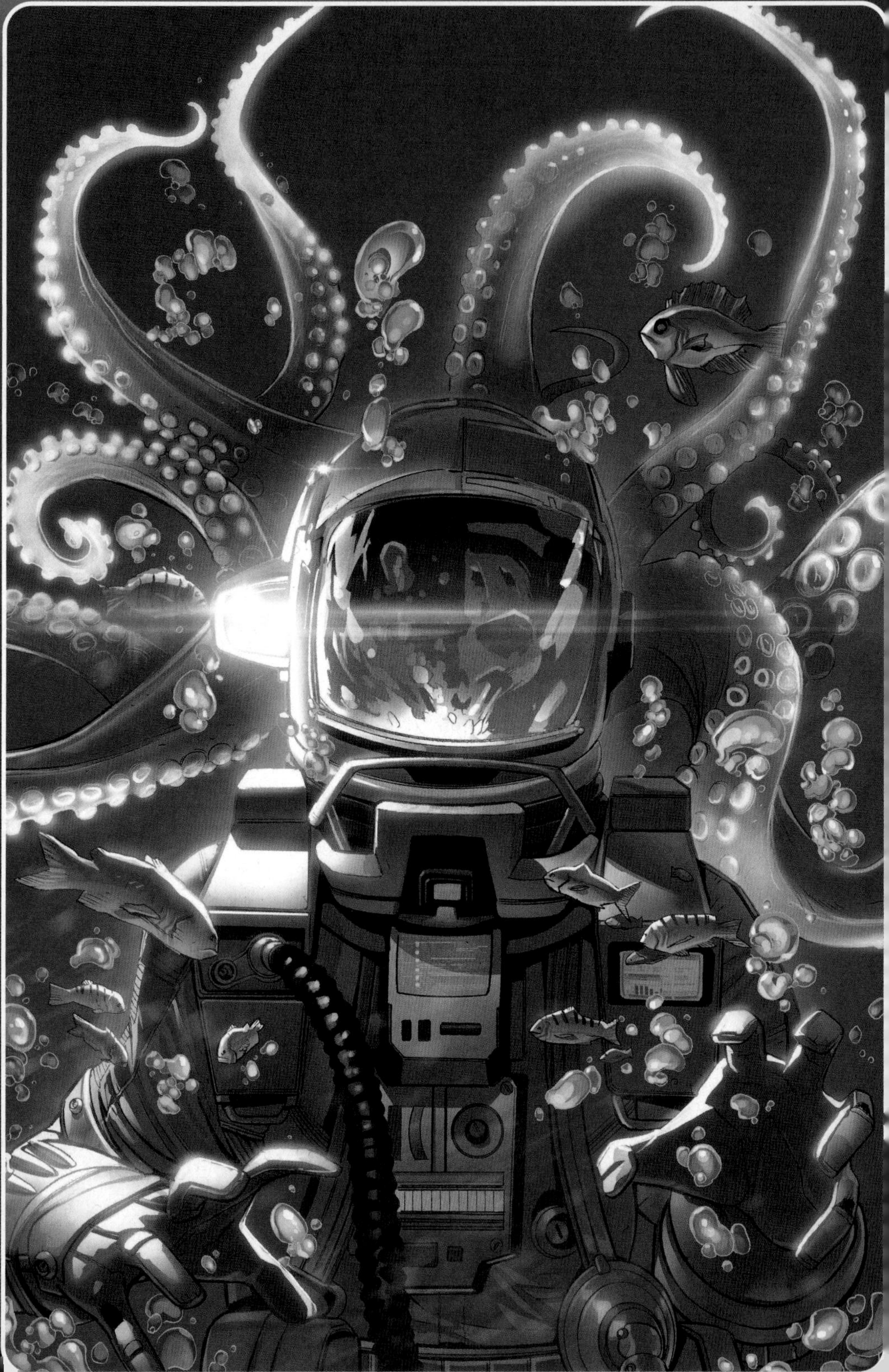

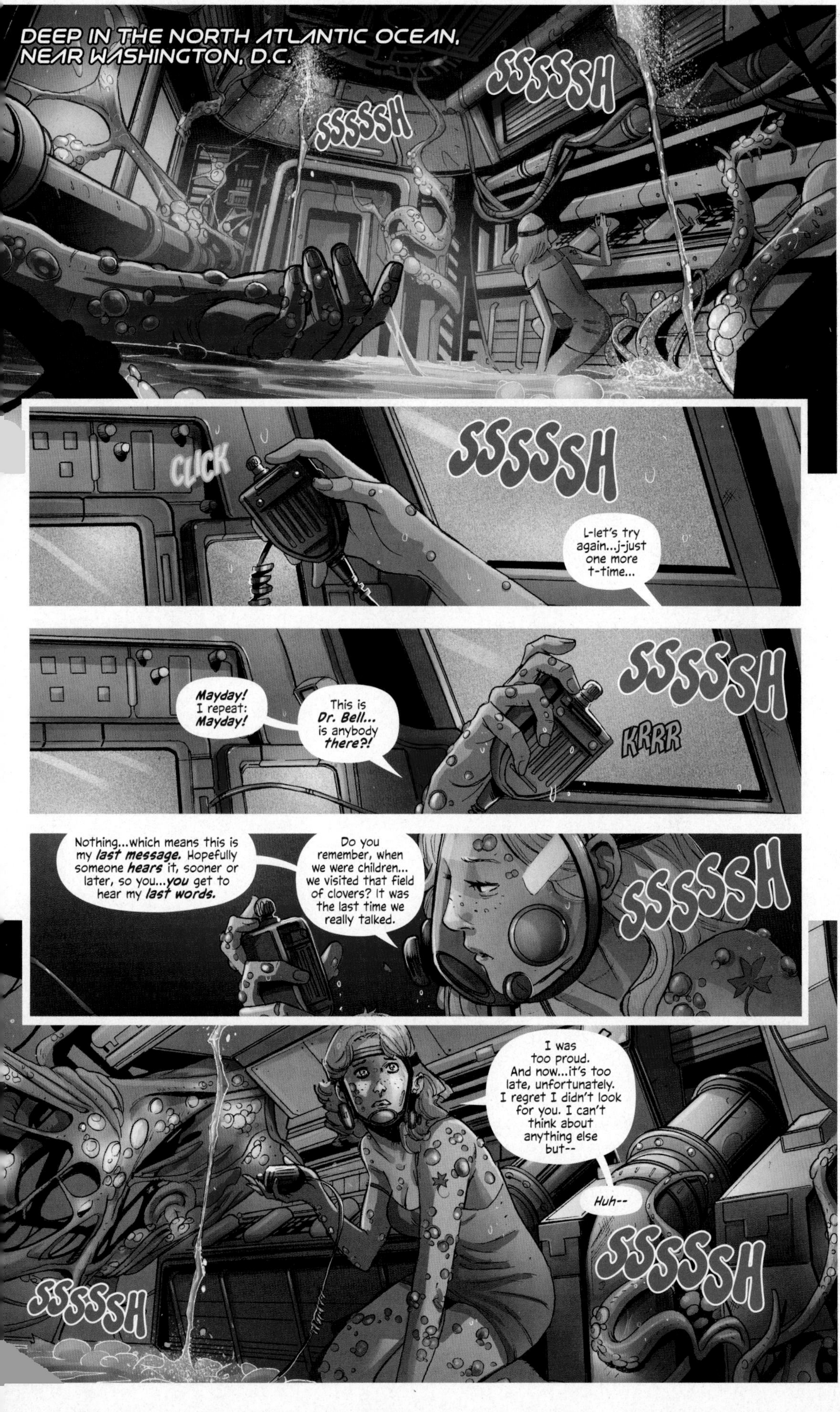
DEEP IN THE NORTH ATLANTIC OCEAN, NEAR WASHINGTON, D.C.
SSSSSH
SSSSSH
CLICK
SSSSSH
L-let's try again...j-just one more t-time...
Mayday! I repeat: Mayday!
This is Dr. Bell... is anybody there?!
SSSSSH
KRRR
Nothing...which means this is my last message. Hopefully someone hears it, sooner or later, so you...you get to hear my last words.
Do you remember, when we were children... we visited that field of clovers? It was the last time we really talked.
SSSSSH
I was too proud. And now...it's too late, unfortunately. I regret I didn't look for you. I can't think about anything else but--
Huh--
SSSSSH
SSSSSH

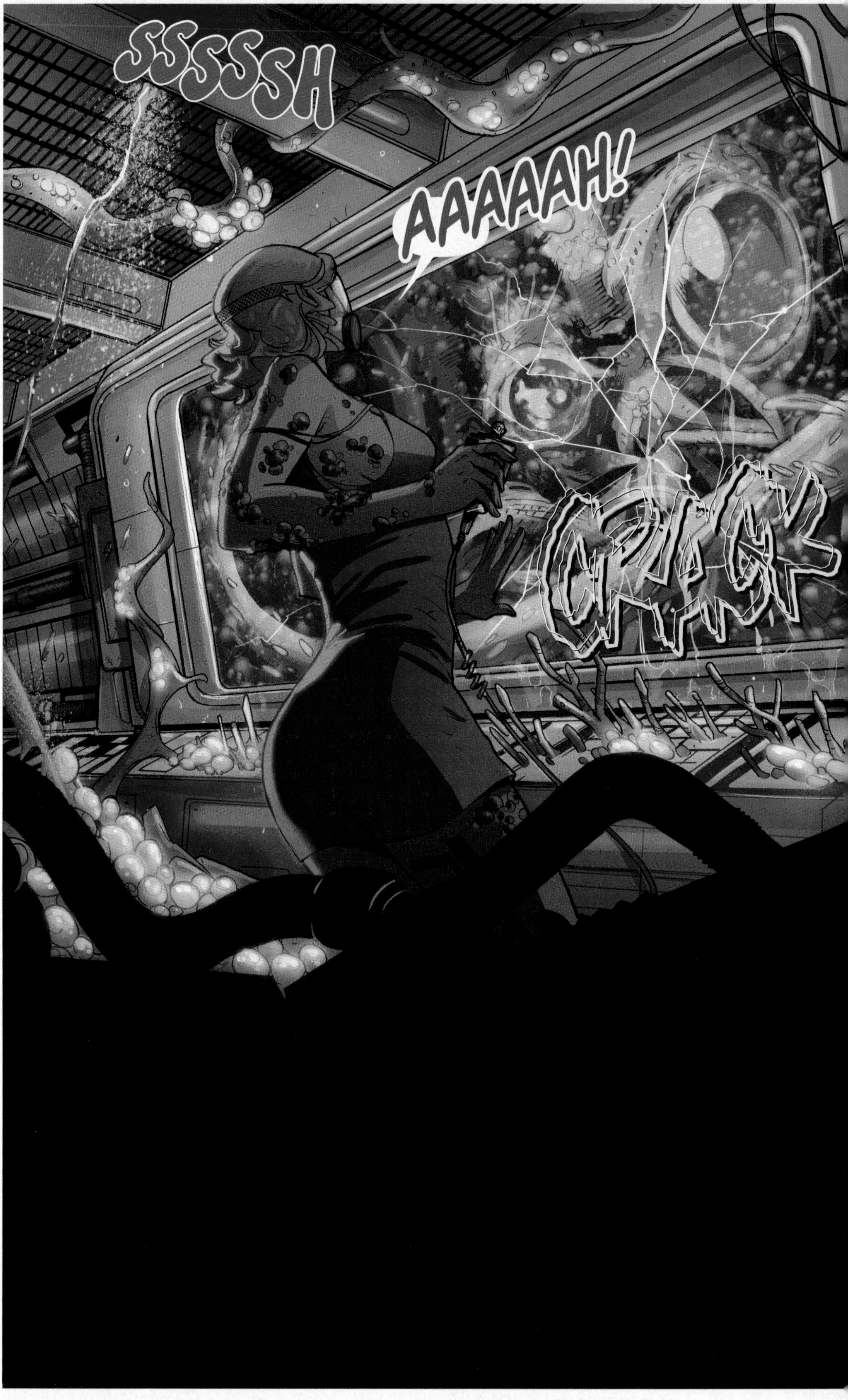
SSSSSH
AAAAAH!
CRACK

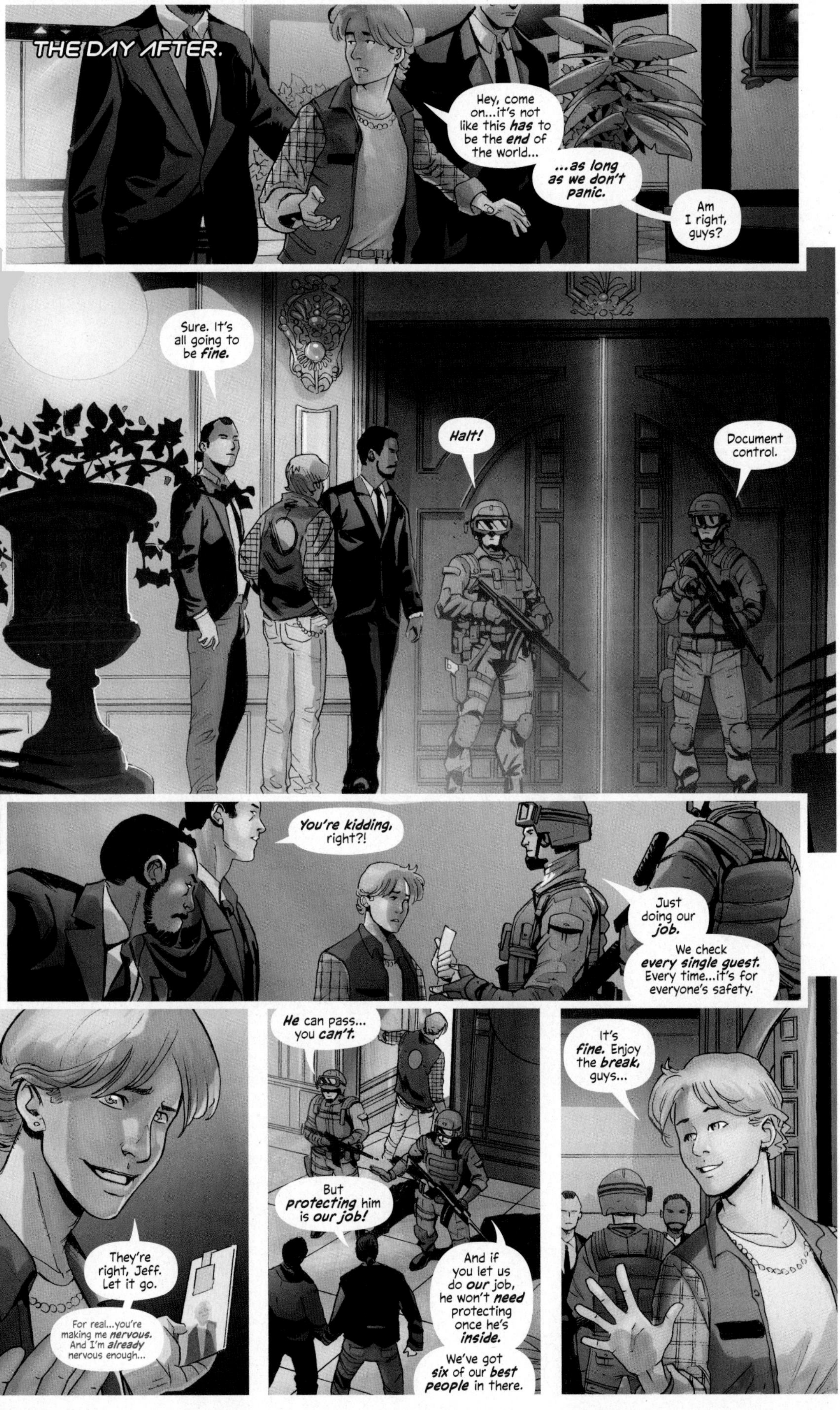
THE DAY AFTER.
Hey, come on...it's not like this *has* to be the *end* of the world...
...as long as we don't panic.
Am I right, guys?
Sure. It's all going to be *fine.*
Halt!
Document control.
You're kidding, right?!
Just doing our *job.*
We check *every single guest.* Every time...it's for everyone's safety.
They're right, Jeff. Let it go.
For real...you're making me *nervous.* And I'm *already* nervous enough...
He can pass... you *can't.*
But *protecting* him is *our job!*
And if you let us do *our* job, he won't *need* protecting once he's *inside.*
We've got *six* of our *best people* in there.
It's *fine.* Enjoy the *break,* guys...

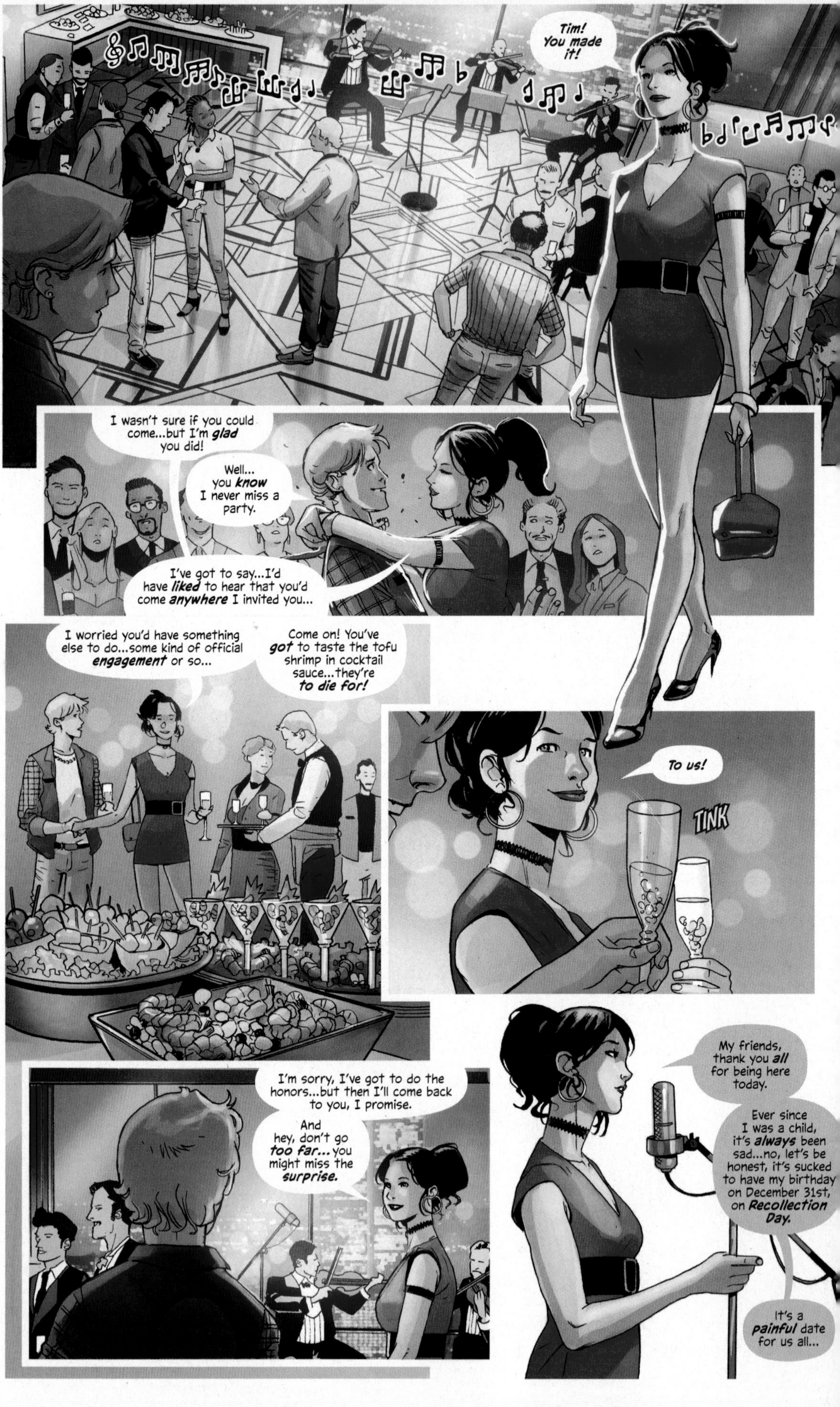
Tim! You made it!
I wasn't sure if you could come...but I'm glad you did!
Well... you know I never miss a party.
I've got to say...I'd have liked to hear that you'd come anywhere I invited you...
I worried you'd have something else to do...some kind of official engagement or so...
Come on! You've got to taste the tofu shrimp in cocktail sauce...they're to die for!
To us!
TINK
I'm sorry, I've got to do the honors...but then I'll come back to you, I promise.
And hey, don't go too far... you might miss the surprise.
My friends, thank you all for being here today.
Ever since I was a child, it's always been sad...no, let's be honest, it's sucked to have my birthday on December 31st, on Recollection Day.
It's a painful date for us all...

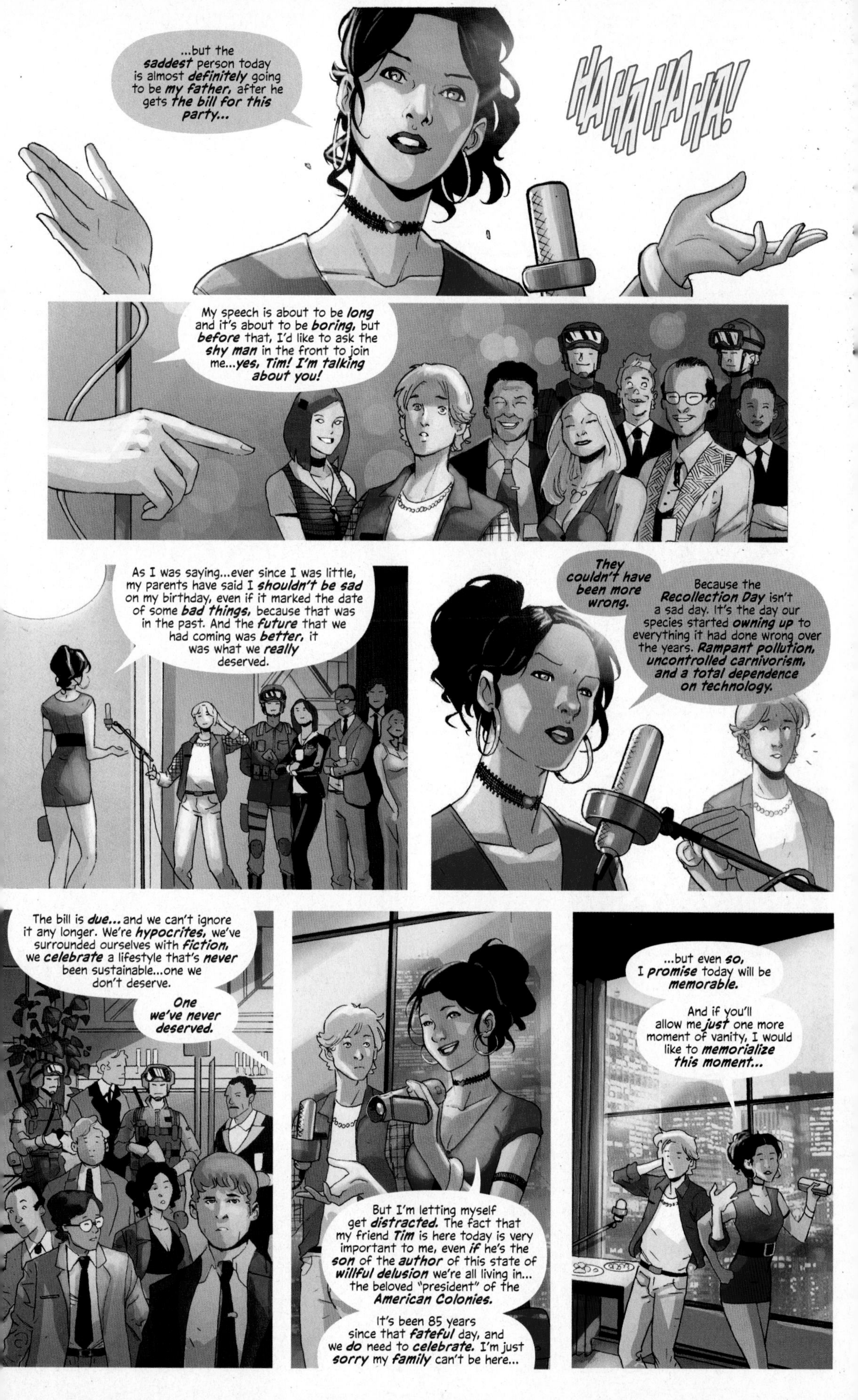
...but the saddest person today is almost definitely going to be my father, after he gets the bill for this party...
HAHAHAHA!
My speech is about to be long and it's about to be boring, but before that, I'd like to ask the shy man in the front to join me...yes, Tim! I'm talking about you!
As I was saying...ever since I was little, my parents have said I shouldn't be sad on my birthday, even if it marked the date of some bad things, because that was in the past. And the future that we had coming was better, it was what we really deserved.
They couldn't have been more wrong.
Because the Recollection Day isn't a sad day. It's the day our species started owning up to everything it had done wrong over the years. Rampant pollution, uncontrolled carnivorism, and a total dependence on technology.
The bill is due... and we can't ignore it any longer. We're hypocrites, we've surrounded ourselves with fiction, we celebrate a lifestyle that's never been sustainable...one we don't deserve.
One we've never deserved.
But I'm letting myself get distracted. The fact that my friend Tim is here today is very important to me, even if he's the son of the author of this state of willful delusion we're all living in... the beloved "president" of the American Colonies.
It's been 85 years since that fateful day, and we do need to celebrate. I'm just sorry my family can't be here...
...but even so, I promise today will be memorable.
And if you'll allow me just one more moment of vanity, I would like to memorialize this moment...

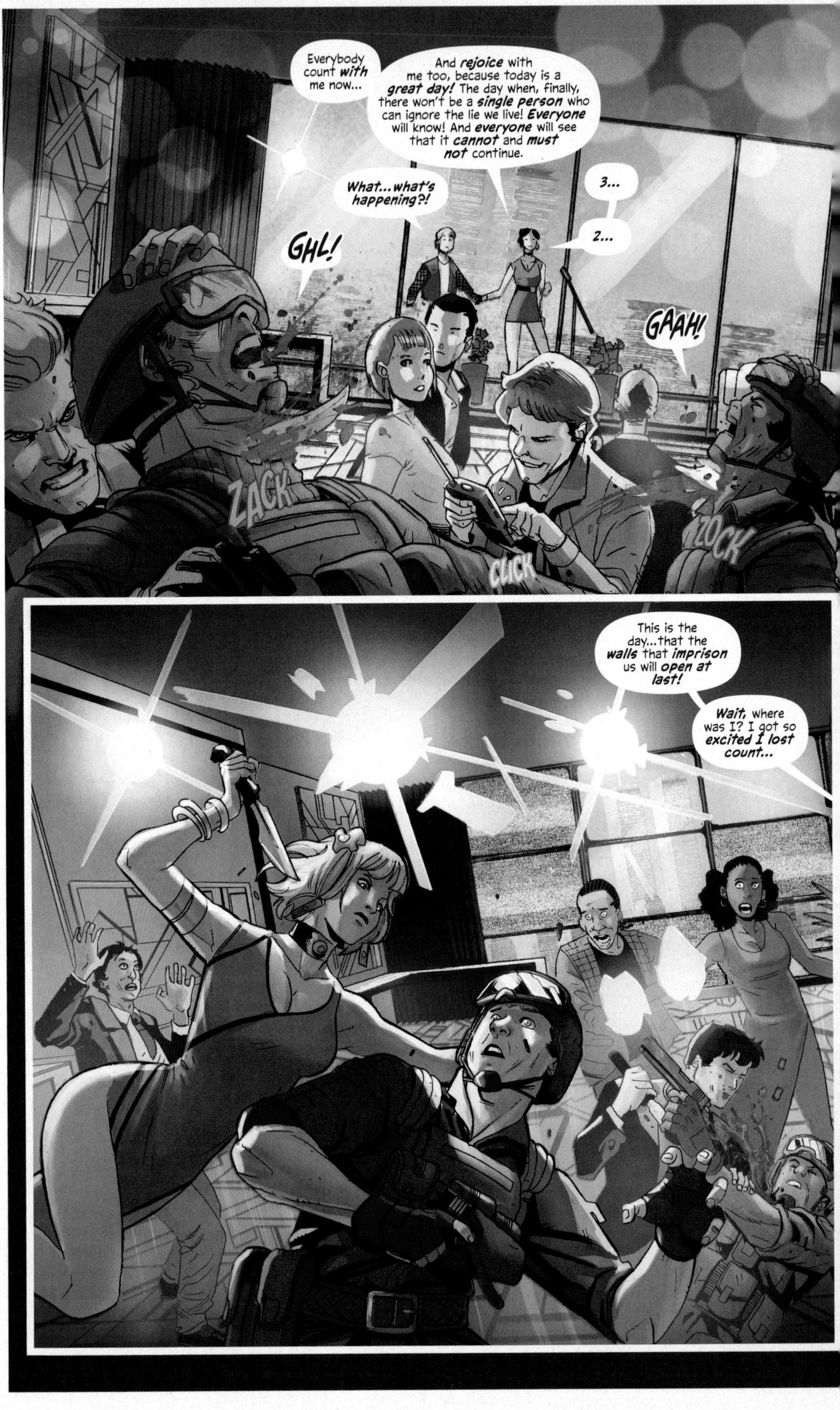

Everybody count with me now...
And rejoice with me too, because today is a great day! The day when, finally, there won't be a single person who can ignore the lie we live! Everyone will know! And everyone will see that it cannot and must not continue.
What...what's happening?!
3...
2...
GHL!
GAAH!
ZACK
ZOCK
CLICK
This is the day...that the walls that imprison us will open at last!
Wait, where was I? I got so excited I lost count...

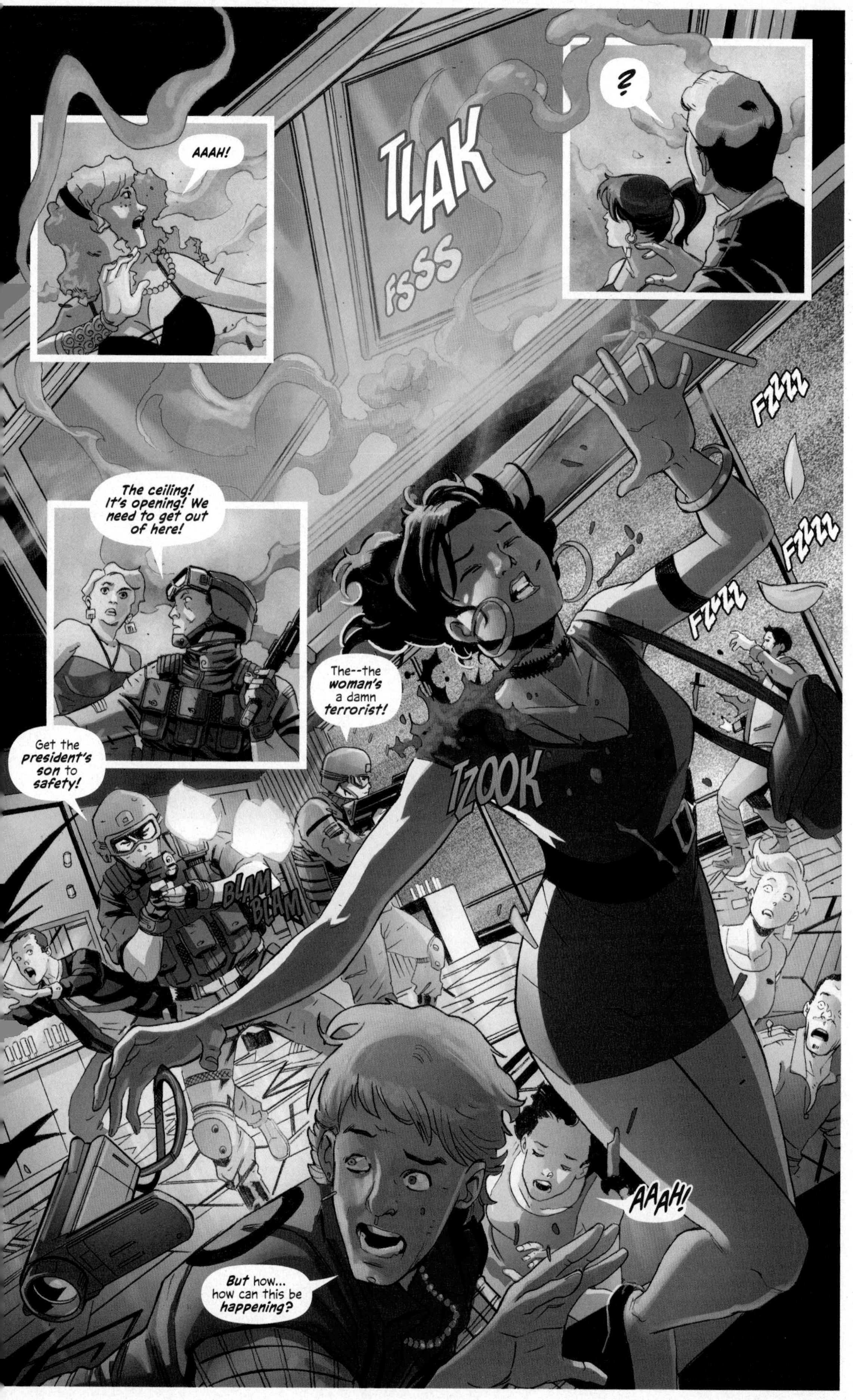
AAAH!
TLAK
FSSS
?
The ceiling! It's opening! We need to get out of here!
The--the woman's a damn terrorist!
Get the president's son to safety!
FZZZZ
FZZZZ
FZZZZ
TZOOK
BLAM BLAM
AAAH!
But how... how can this be happening?

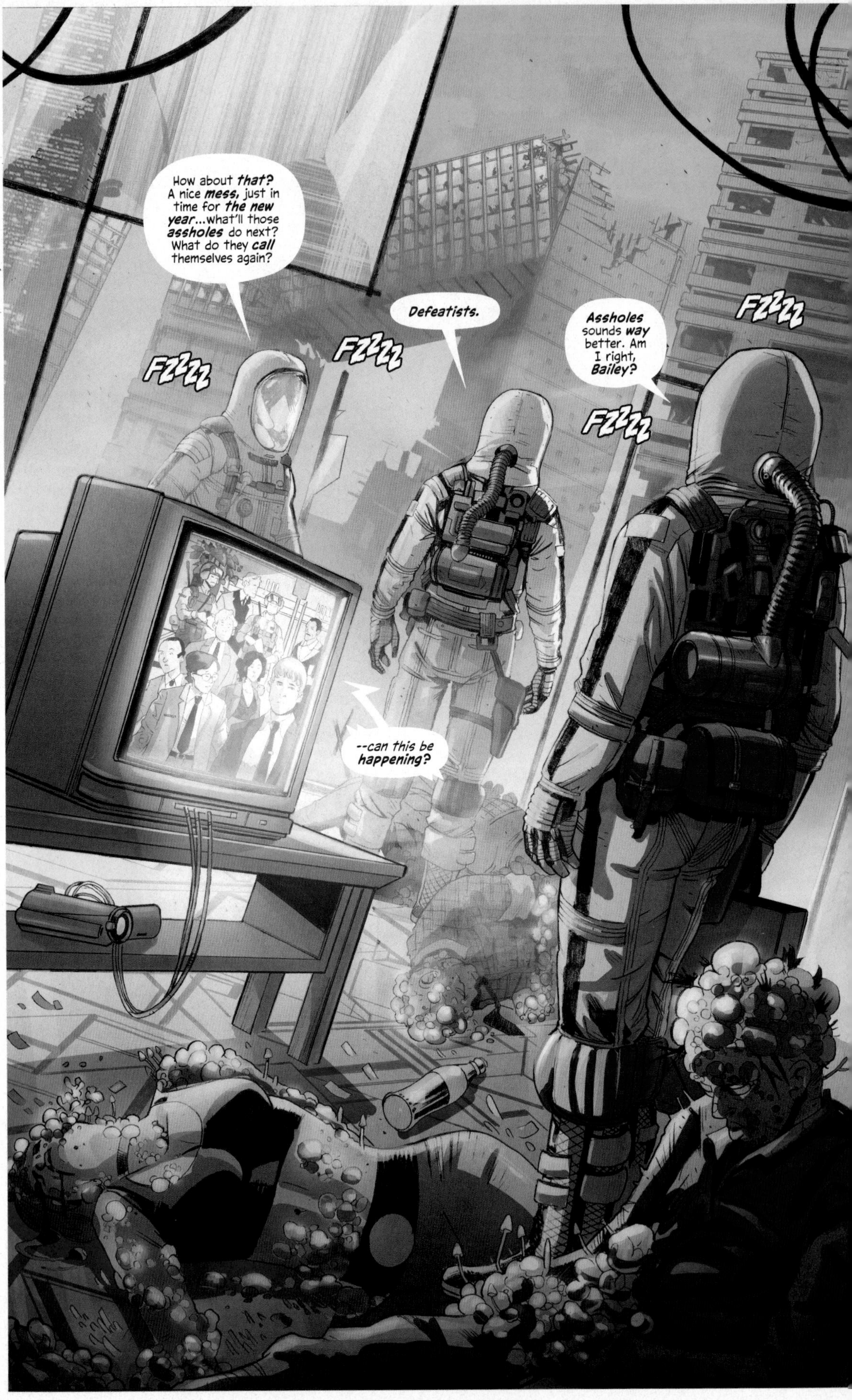

How about that? A nice mess, just in time for the new year...what'll those assholes do next? What do they call themselves again?
FZZZZZ
FZZZZZ
Defeatists.
Assholes sounds way better. Am I right, Bailey?
FZZZZZ
FZZZZZ
--can this be happening?

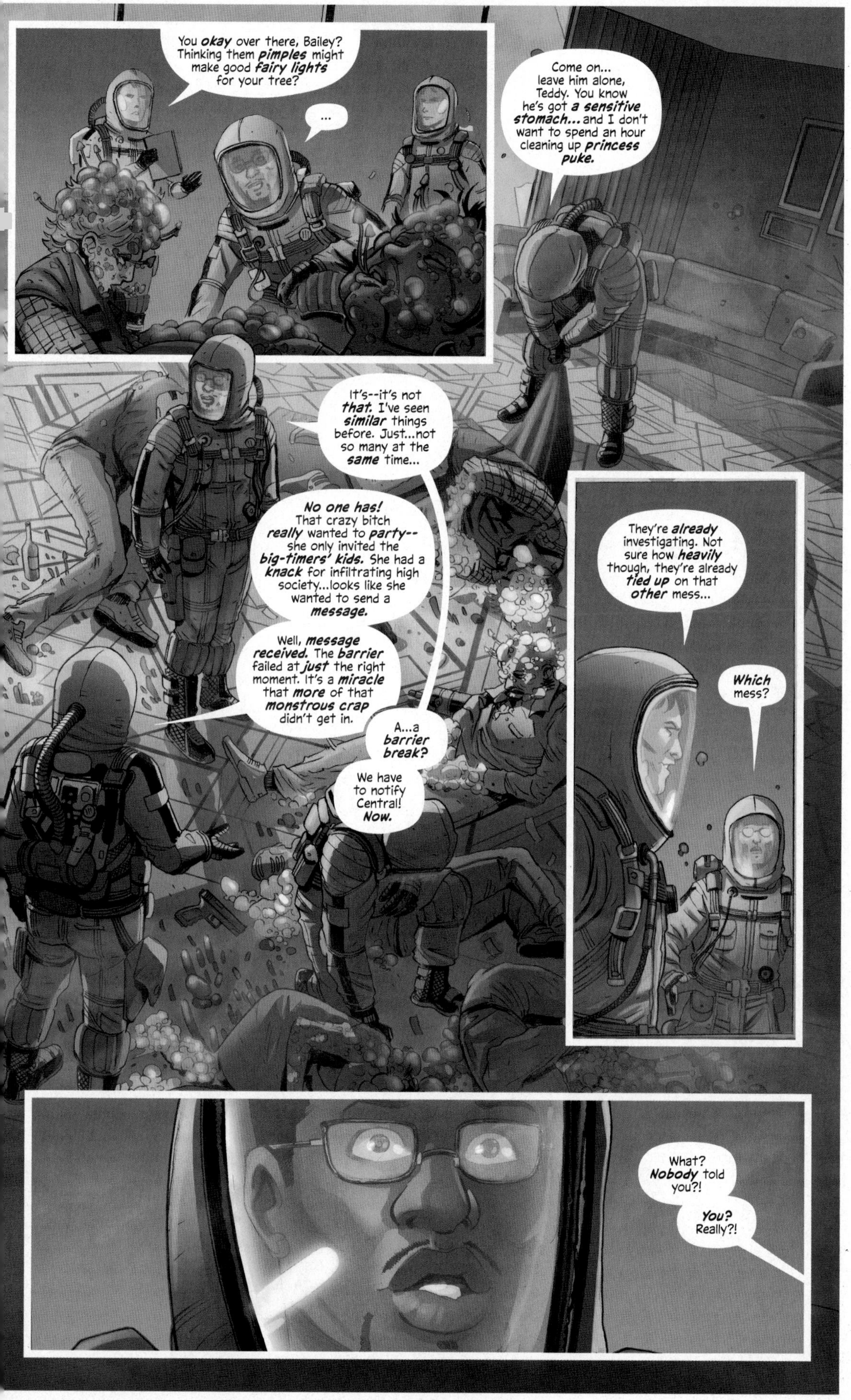
You okay over there, Bailey? Thinking them pimples might make good fairy lights for your tree?
...
Come on... leave him alone, Teddy. You know he's got a sensitive stomach... and I don't want to spend an hour cleaning up princess puke.
It's--it's not that. I've seen similar things before. Just...not so many at the same time...
No one has! That crazy bitch really wanted to party-- she only invited the big-timers' kids. She had a knack for infiltrating high society...looks like she wanted to send a message.
Well, message received. The barrier failed at just the right moment. It's a miracle that more of that monstrous crap didn't get in.
A...a barrier break?
We have to notify Central! Now.
They're already investigating. Not sure how heavily though, they're already tied up on that other mess...
Which mess?
What? Nobody told you?!
You? Really?!

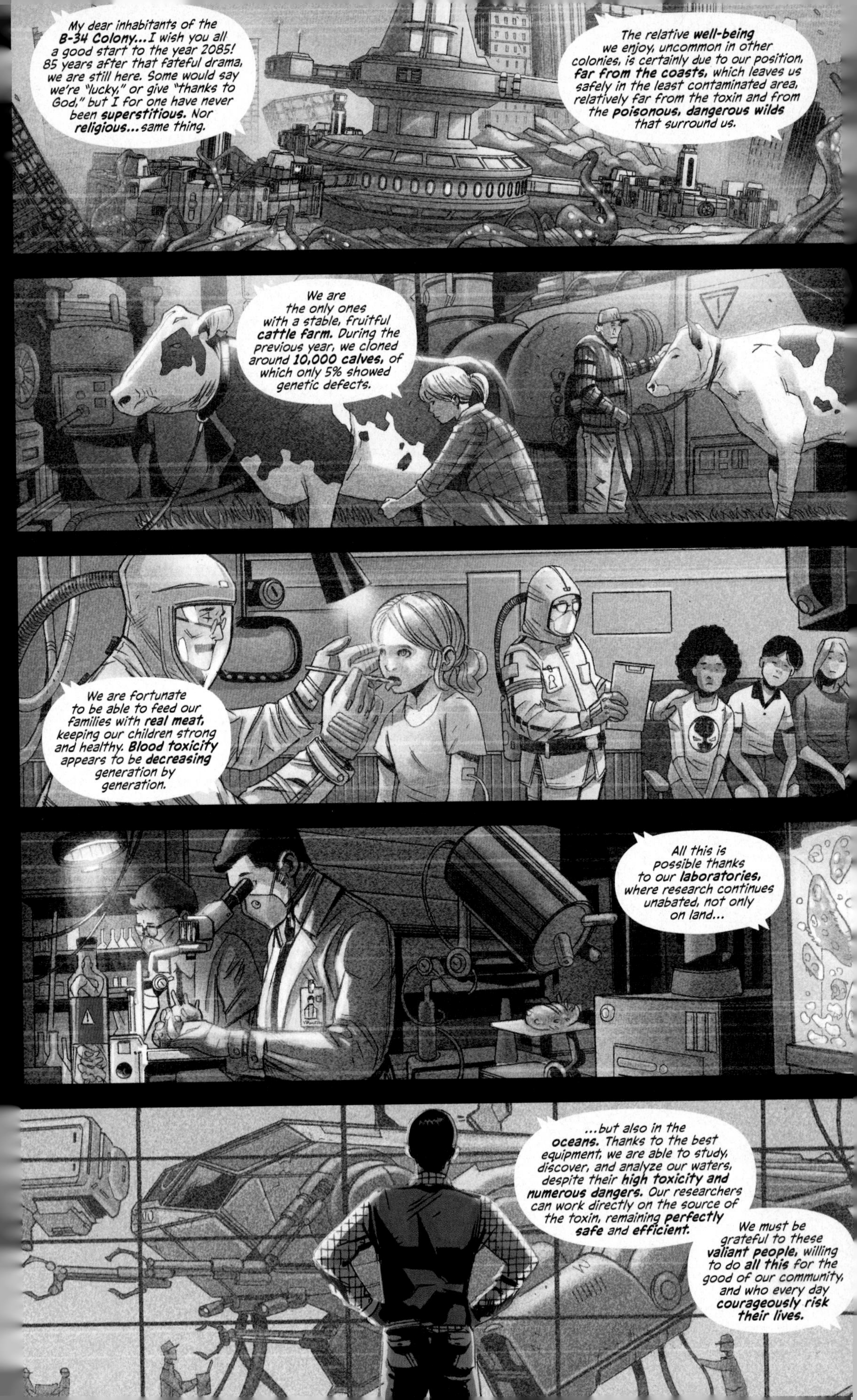

My dear inhabitants of the B-34 Colony... I wish you all a good start to the year 2085! 85 years after that fateful drama, we are still here. Some would say we're "lucky," or give "thanks to God," but I for one have never been superstitious. Nor religious... same thing.
The relative well-being we enjoy, uncommon in other colonies, is certainly due to our position, far from the coasts, which leaves us safely in the least contaminated area, relatively far from the toxin and from the poisonous, dangerous wilds that surround us.
We are the only ones with a stable, fruitful cattle farm. During the previous year, we cloned around 10,000 calves, of which only 5% showed genetic defects.
We are fortunate to be able to feed our families with real meat, keeping our children strong and healthy. Blood toxicity appears to be decreasing generation by generation.
All this is possible thanks to our laboratories, where research continues unabated, not only on land...
...but also in the oceans. Thanks to the best equipment, we are able to study, discover, and analyze our waters, despite their high toxicity and numerous dangers. Our researchers can work directly on the source of the toxin, remaining perfectly safe and efficient.
We must be grateful to these valiant people, willing to do all this for the good of our community, and who every day courageously risk their lives.

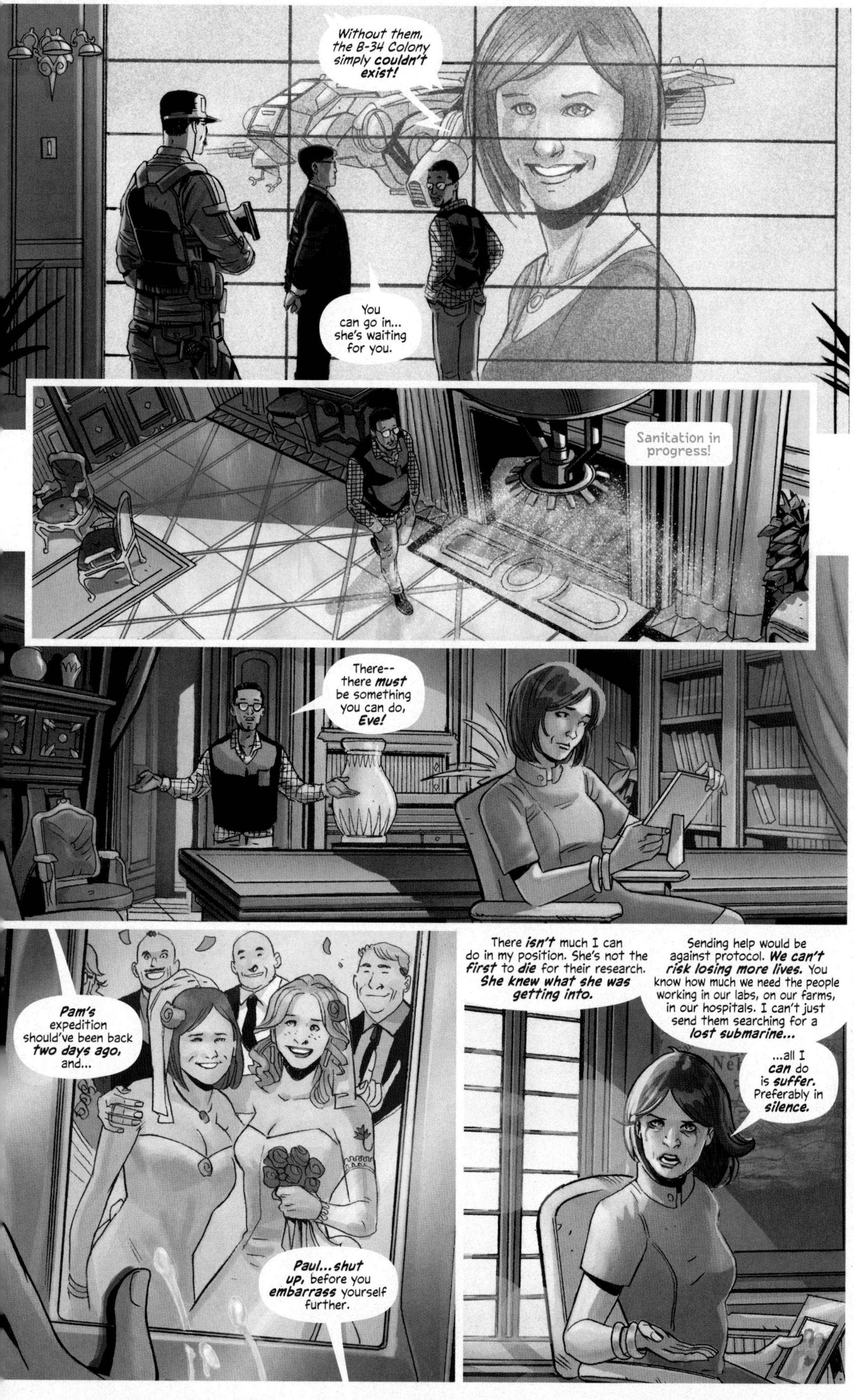

Without them, the B-34 Colony simply couldn't exist!
You can go in... she's waiting for you.
Sanitation in progress!
There--there must be something you can do, Eve!
Pam's expedition should've been back two days ago, and...
Paul...shut up, before you embarrass yourself further.
There isn't much I can do in my position. She's not the first to die for their research. She knew what she was getting into.
Sending help would be against protocol. We can't risk losing more lives. You know how much we need the people working in our labs, on our farms, in our hospitals. I can't just send them searching for a lost submarine...
...all I can do is suffer. Preferably in silence.

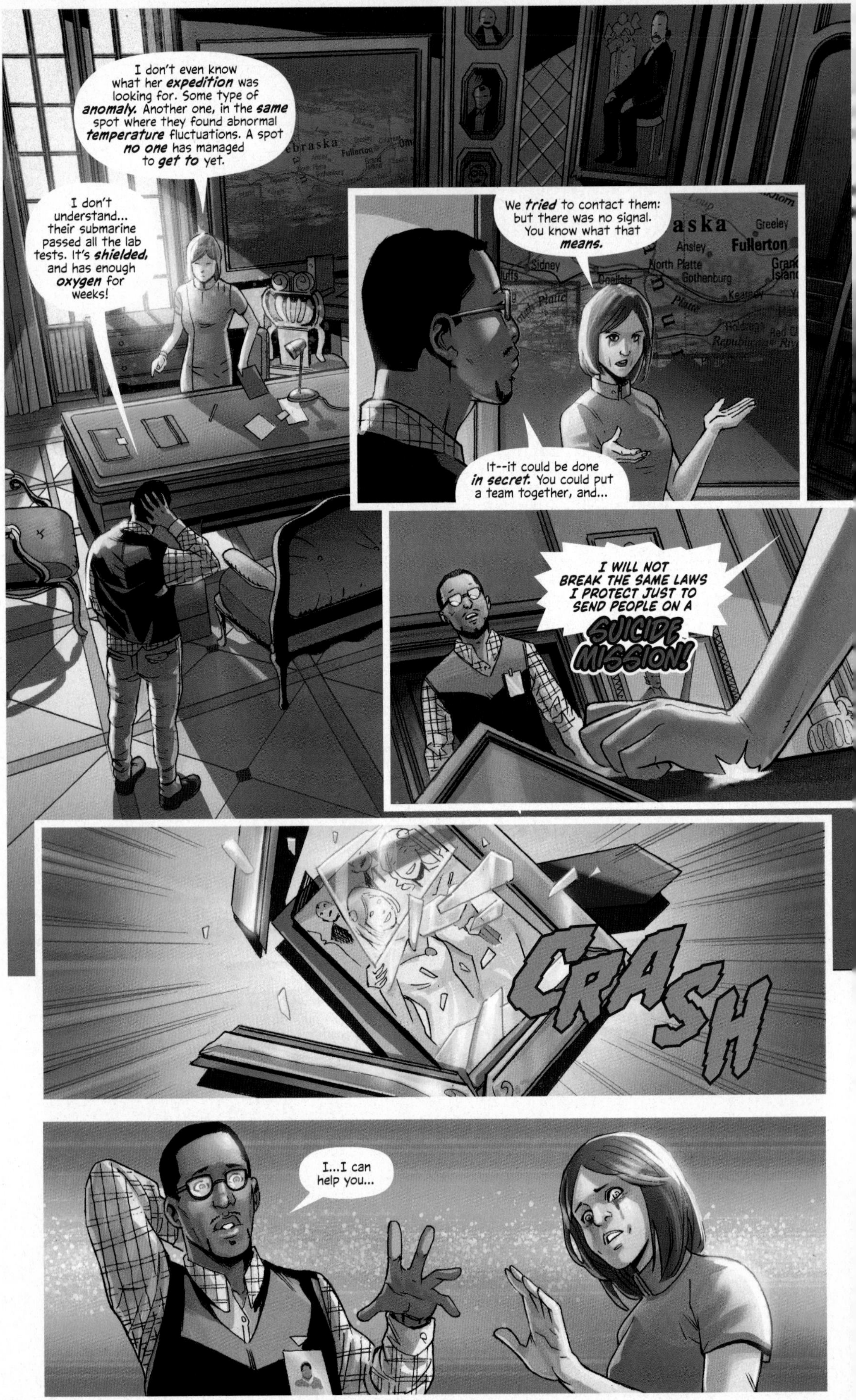
I don't even know what her expedition was looking for. Some type of anomaly. Another one, in the same spot where they found abnormal temperature fluctuations. A spot no one has managed to get to yet.
I don't understand... their submarine passed all the lab tests. It's shielded, and has enough oxygen for weeks!
We tried to contact them: but there was no signal. You know what that means.
It--it could be done in secret. You could put a team together, and...
I WILL NOT BREAK THE SAME LAWS I PROTECT JUST TO SEND PEOPLE ON A SUICIDE MISSION!
CRASH
I...I can help you...

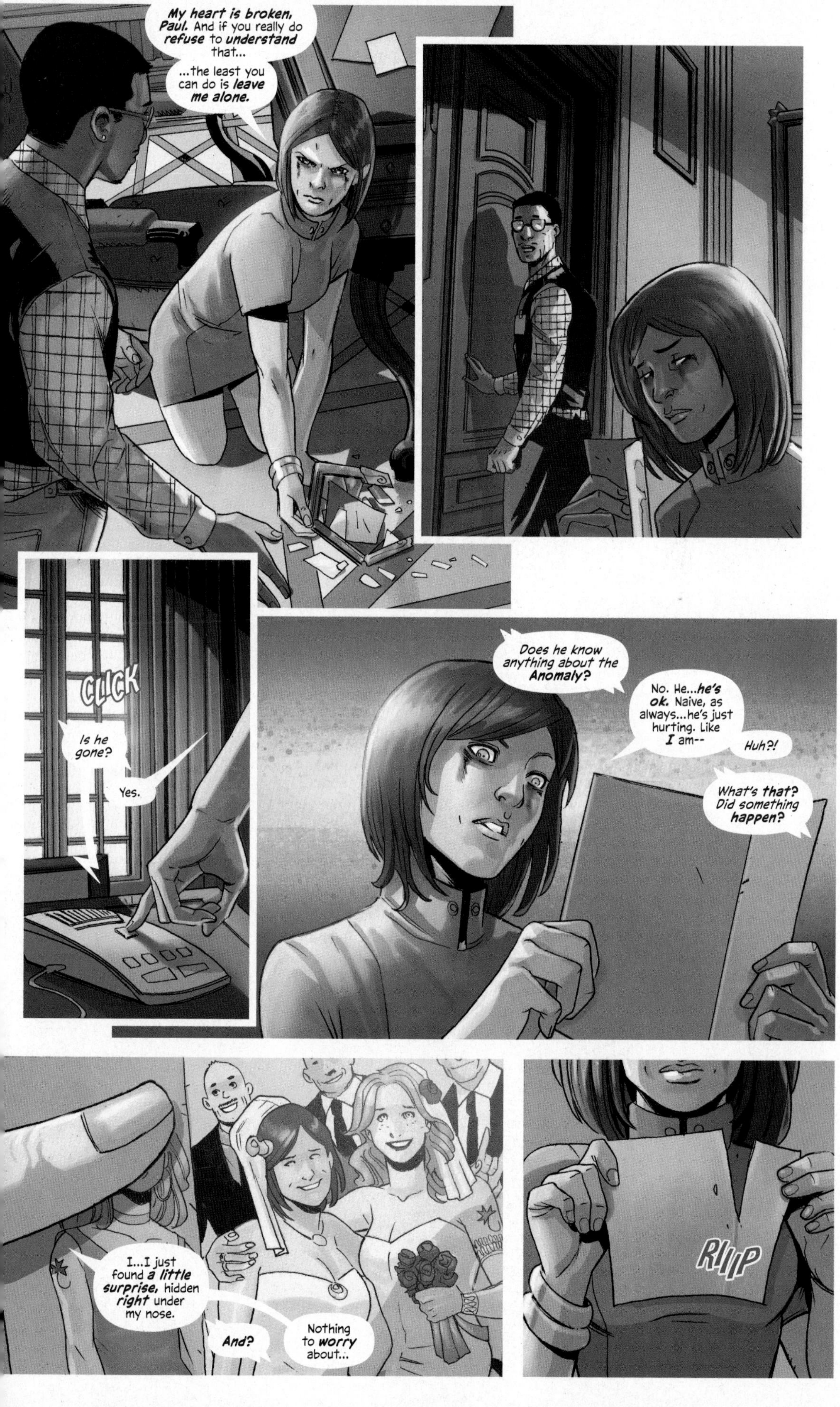
My heart is broken, Paul. And if you really do refuse to understand that...
...the least you can do is leave me alone.
CLICK
Is he gone?
Yes.
Does he know anything about the Anomaly?
No. He...he's ok. Naive, as always...he's just hurting. Like I am--
Huh?!
What's that? Did something happen?
I...I just found a little surprise, hidden right under my nose.
And?
Nothing to worry about...
RIIIP

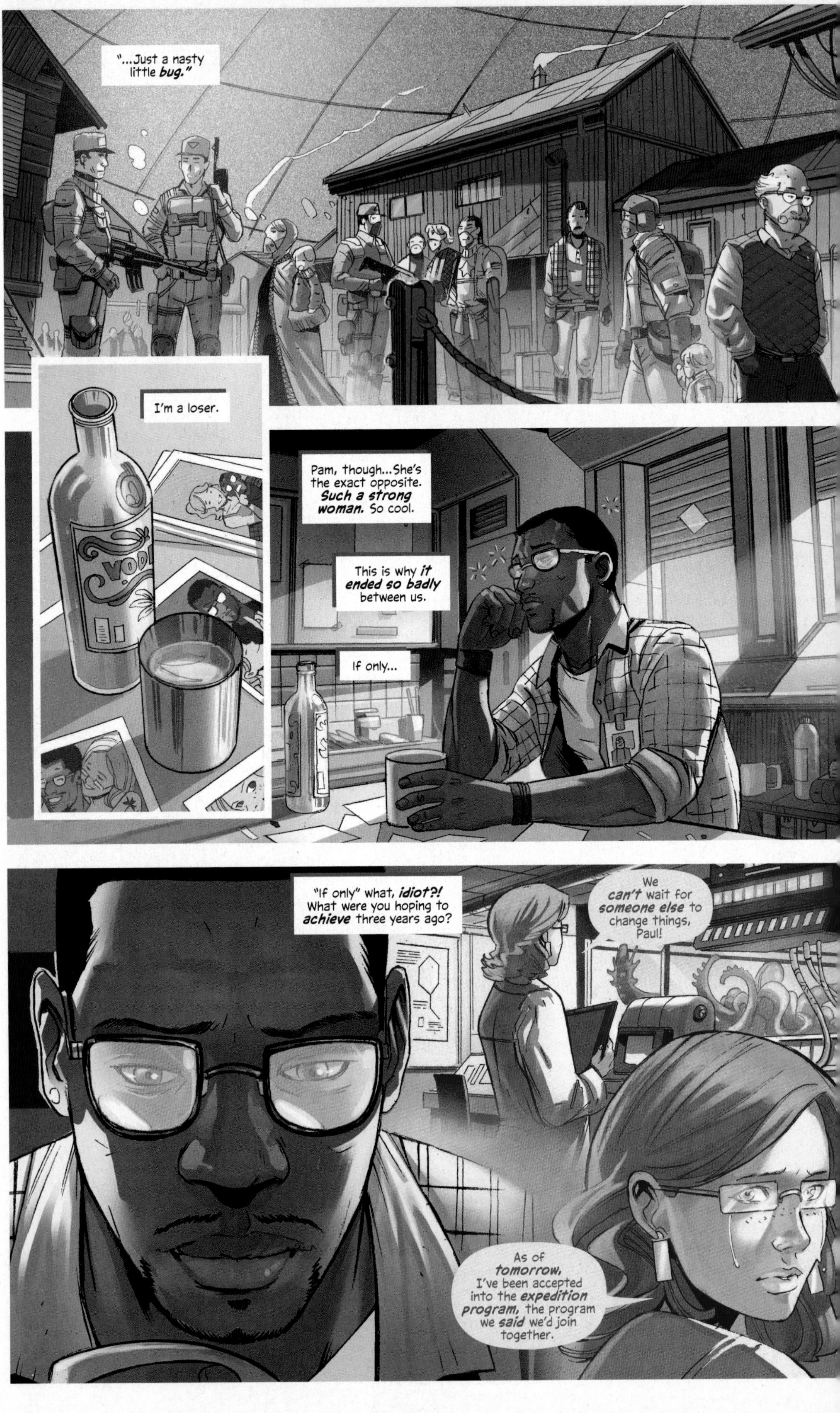
"...Just a nasty little *bug.*"
I'm a loser.
Pam, though...She's the exact opposite. ***Such a strong woman.*** So cool.
This is why ***it ended so badly*** between us.
If only...
"If only" what, ***idiot?!*** What were you hoping to ***achieve*** three years ago?
We ***can't*** wait for ***someone else*** to change things, Paul!
As of ***tomorrow,*** I've been accepted into the ***expedition program,*** the program we ***said*** we'd join together.

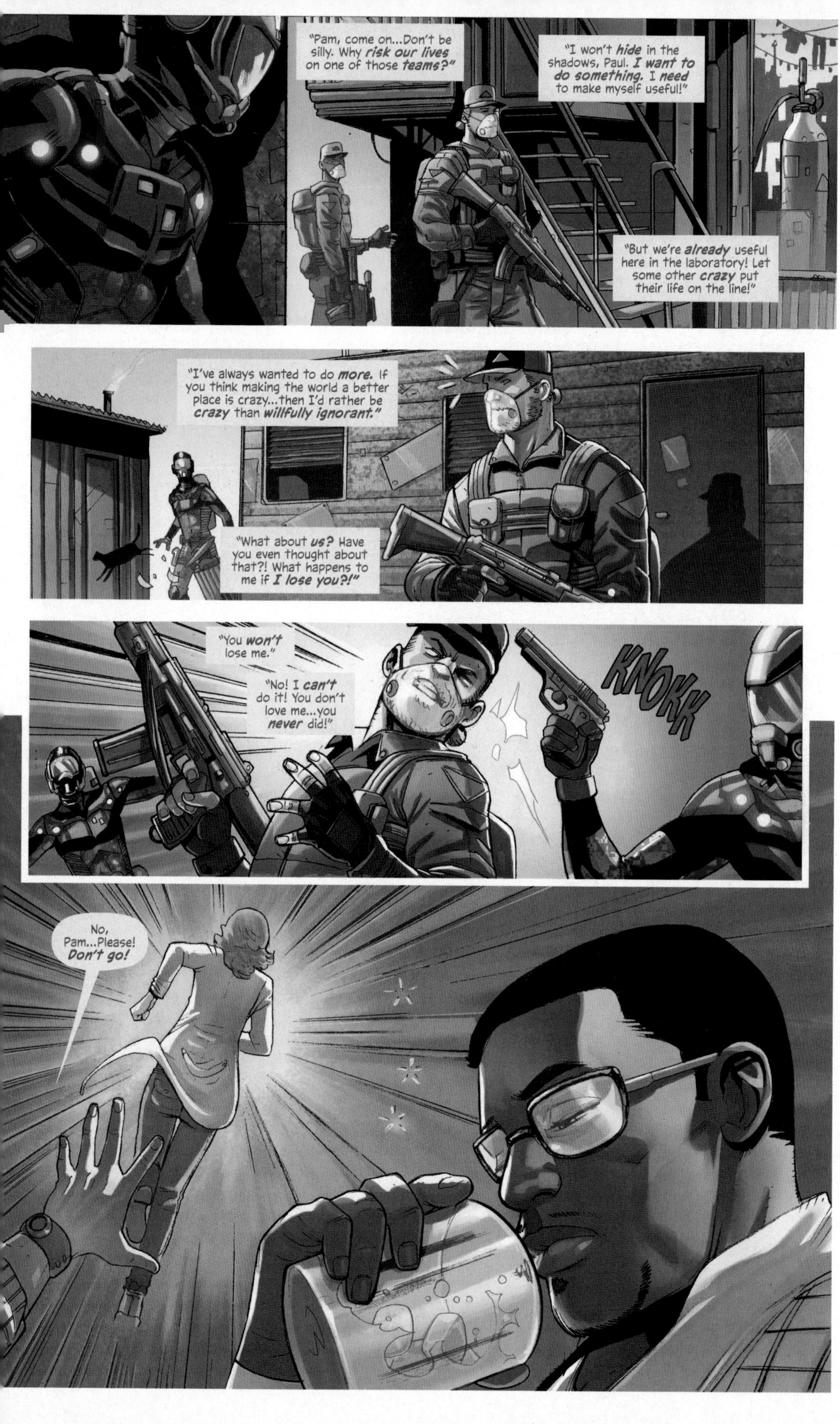

"Pam, come on...Don't be silly. Why *risk our lives* on one of those *teams?*"
"I won't *hide* in the shadows, Paul. *I want to do something.* I need to make myself useful!"
"But we're *already* useful here in the laboratory! Let some other *crazy* put their life on the line!"
"I've always wanted to do *more.* If you think making the world a better place is crazy...then I'd rather be *crazy* than *willfully ignorant.*"
"What about *us?* Have you even thought about that?! What happens to me if *I lose you?!*"
"You *won't* lose me."
"No! I *can't* do it! You don't love me...you *never* did!"
KNOKK
No, Pam...Please! *Don't go!*

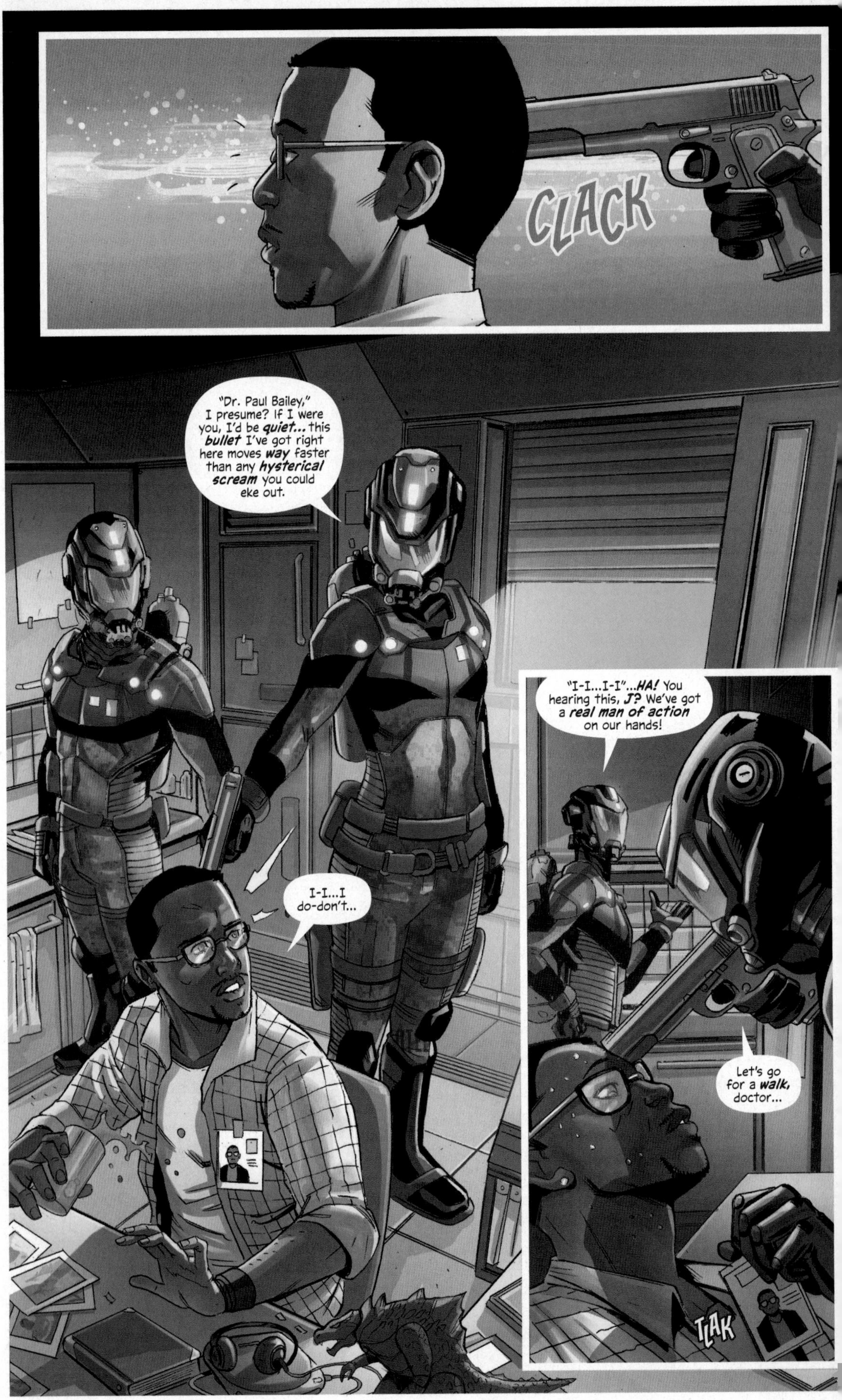
CLACK
"Dr. Paul Bailey," I presume? If I were you, I'd be quiet... this bullet I've got right here moves way faster than any hysterical scream you could eke out.
I-I...I do-don't...
"I-I...I-I"...HA! You hearing this, J? We've got a real man of action on our hands!
Let's go for a walk, doctor...
TLAK

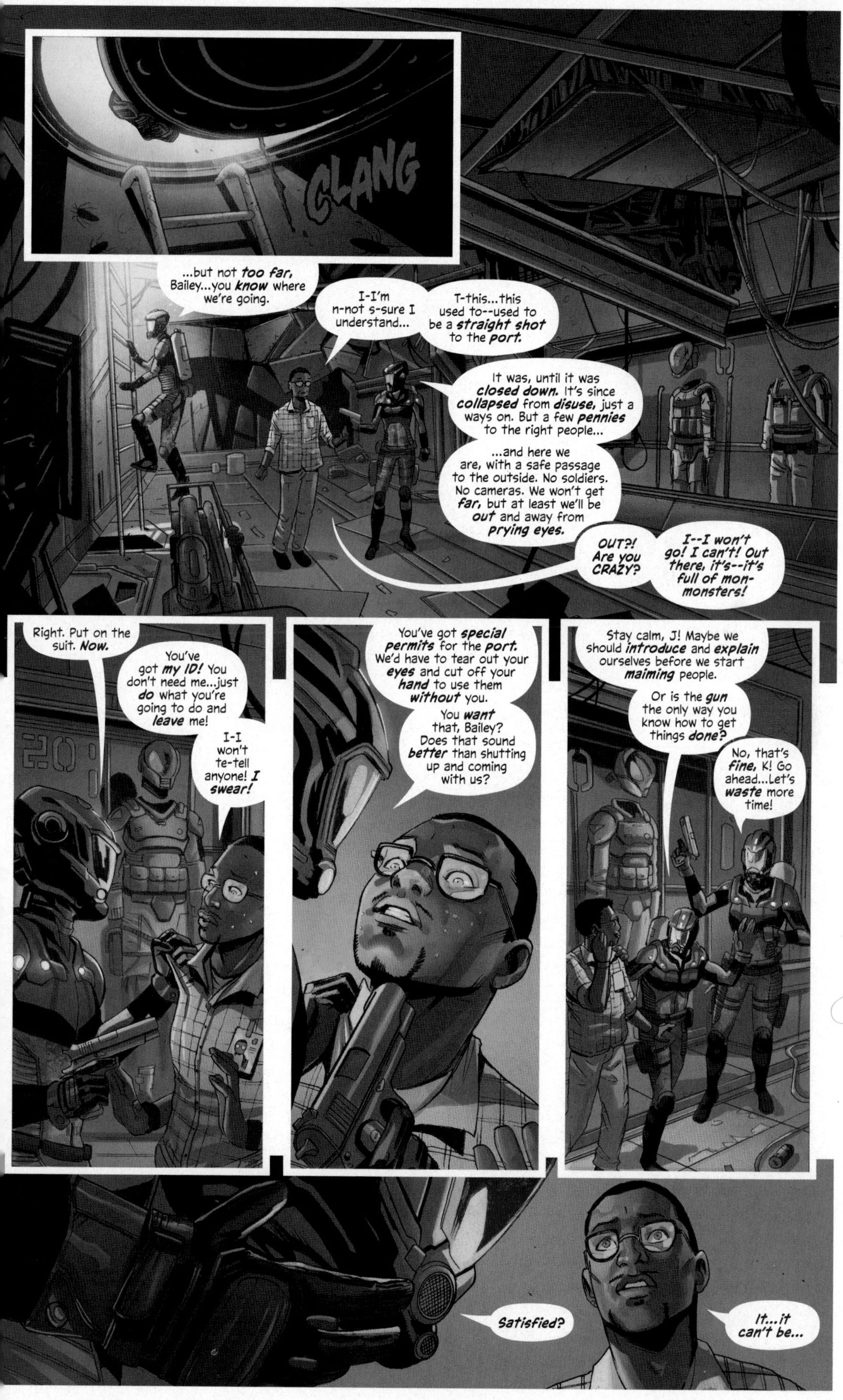
CLANG
...but not too far, Bailey...you know where we're going.
I-I'm n-not s-sure I understand...
T-this...this used to--used to be a straight shot to the port.
It was, until it was closed down. It's since collapsed from disuse, just a ways on. But a few pennies to the right people...
...and here we are, with a safe passage to the outside. No soldiers. No cameras. We won't get far, but at least we'll be out and away from prying eyes.
OUT?! Are you CRAZY?
I--I won't go! I can't! Out there, it's--it's full of mon-monsters!
Right. Put on the suit. Now.
You've got my ID! You don't need me...just do what you're going to do and leave me!
I-I won't te-tell anyone! I swear!
You've got special permits for the port. We'd have to tear out your eyes and cut off your hand to use them without you.
You want that, Bailey? Does that sound better than shutting up and coming with us?
Stay calm, J! Maybe we should introduce and explain ourselves before we start maiming people.
Or is the gun the only way you know how to get things done?
No, that's fine, K! Go ahead...Let's waste more time!
Satisfied?
It...it can't be...

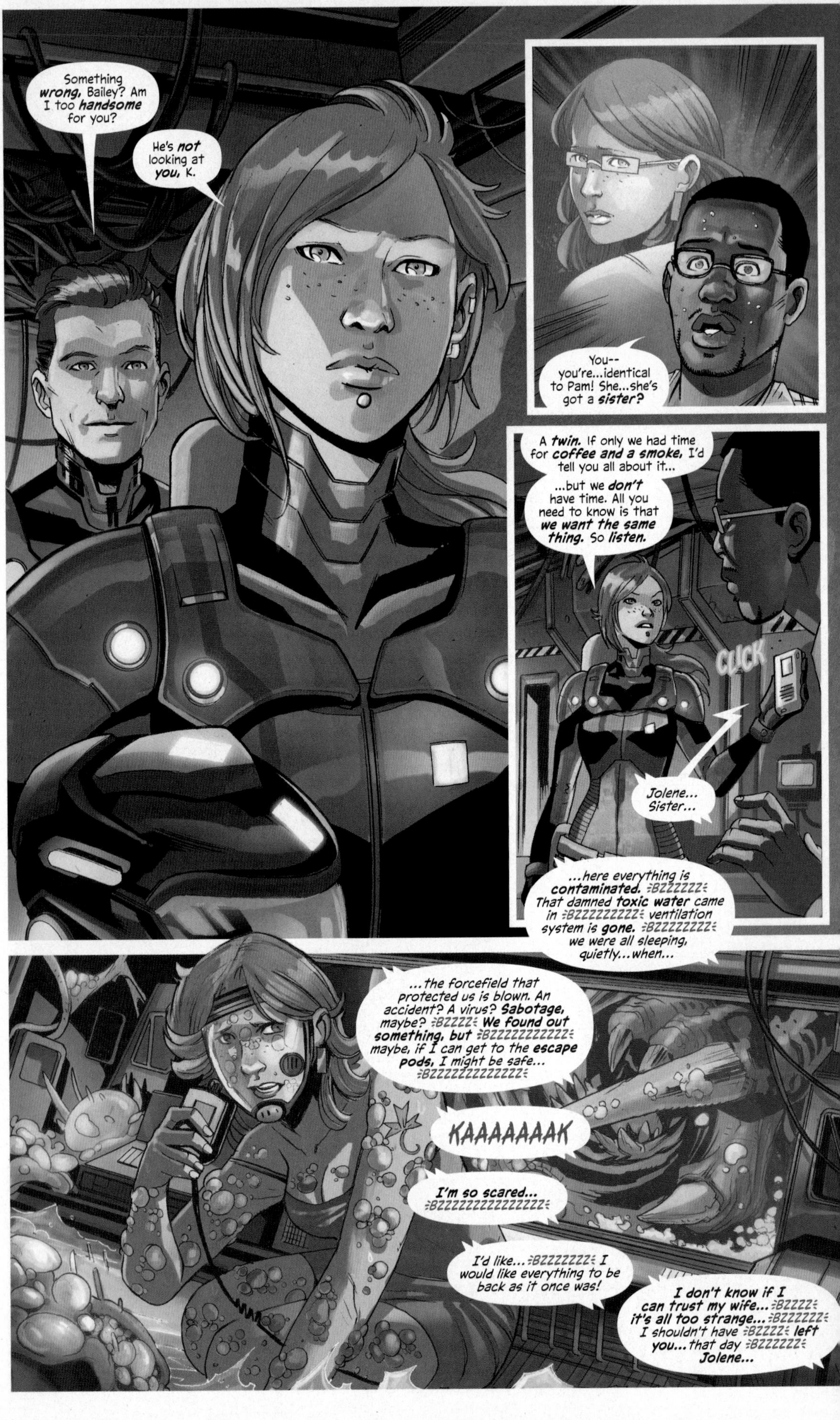

Something wrong, Bailey? Am I too handsome for you?
He's not looking at you, K.
You-- you're...identical to Pam! She...she's got a sister?
A twin. If only we had time for coffee and a smoke, I'd tell you all about it...
...but we don't have time. All you need to know is that we want the same thing. So listen.
CLICK
Jolene... Sister...
...here everything is contaminated. BZZZZZZ That damned toxic water came in BZZZZZZZZZ ventilation system is gone. BZZZZZZZZ we were all sleeping, quietly...when...
...the forcefield that protected us is blown. An accident? A virus? Sabotage, maybe? BZZZZ We found out something, but BZZZZZZZZZZZ maybe, if I can get to the escape pods, I might be safe... BZZZZZZZZZZZZZ
KAAAAAAAK
I'm so scared... BZZZZZZZZZZZZZZ
I'd like... BZZZZZZZ I would like everything to be back as it once was!
I don't know if I can trust my wife... BZZZZ it's all too strange... BZZZZZZ I shouldn't have BZZZZ left you...that day BZZZZZZ Jolene...

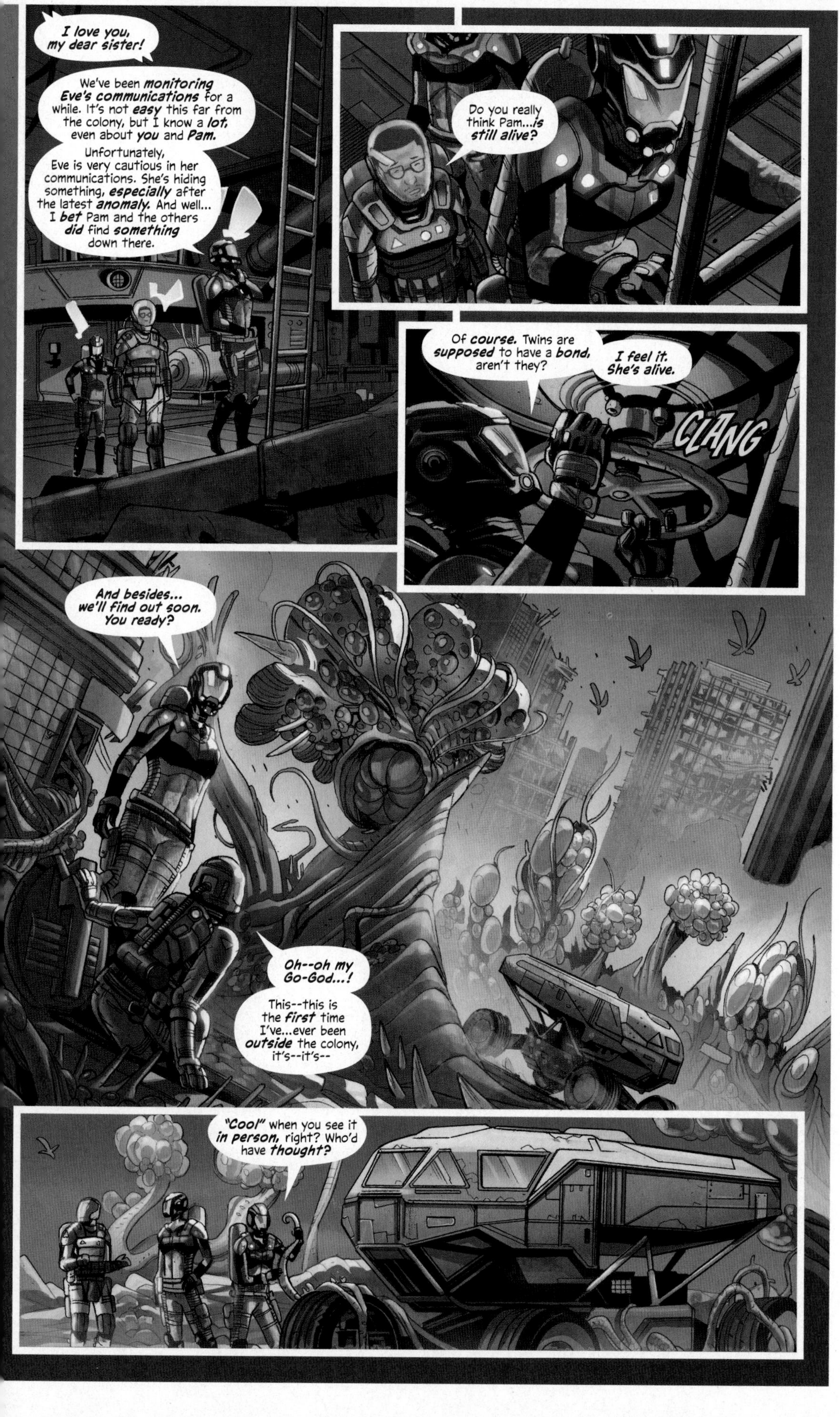
I love you, my dear sister!
We've been monitoring Eve's communications for a while. It's not easy this far from the colony, but I know a lot, even about you and Pam.
Unfortunately, Eve is very cautious in her communications. She's hiding something, especially after the latest anomaly. And well... I bet Pam and the others did find something down there.
Do you really think Pam...is still alive?
Of course. Twins are supposed to have a bond, aren't they?
I feel it. She's alive.
CLANG
And besides... we'll find out soon. You ready?
Oh--oh my Go-God...!
This--this is the first time I've...ever been outside the colony, it's--it's--
"Cool" when you see it in person, right? Who'd have thought?

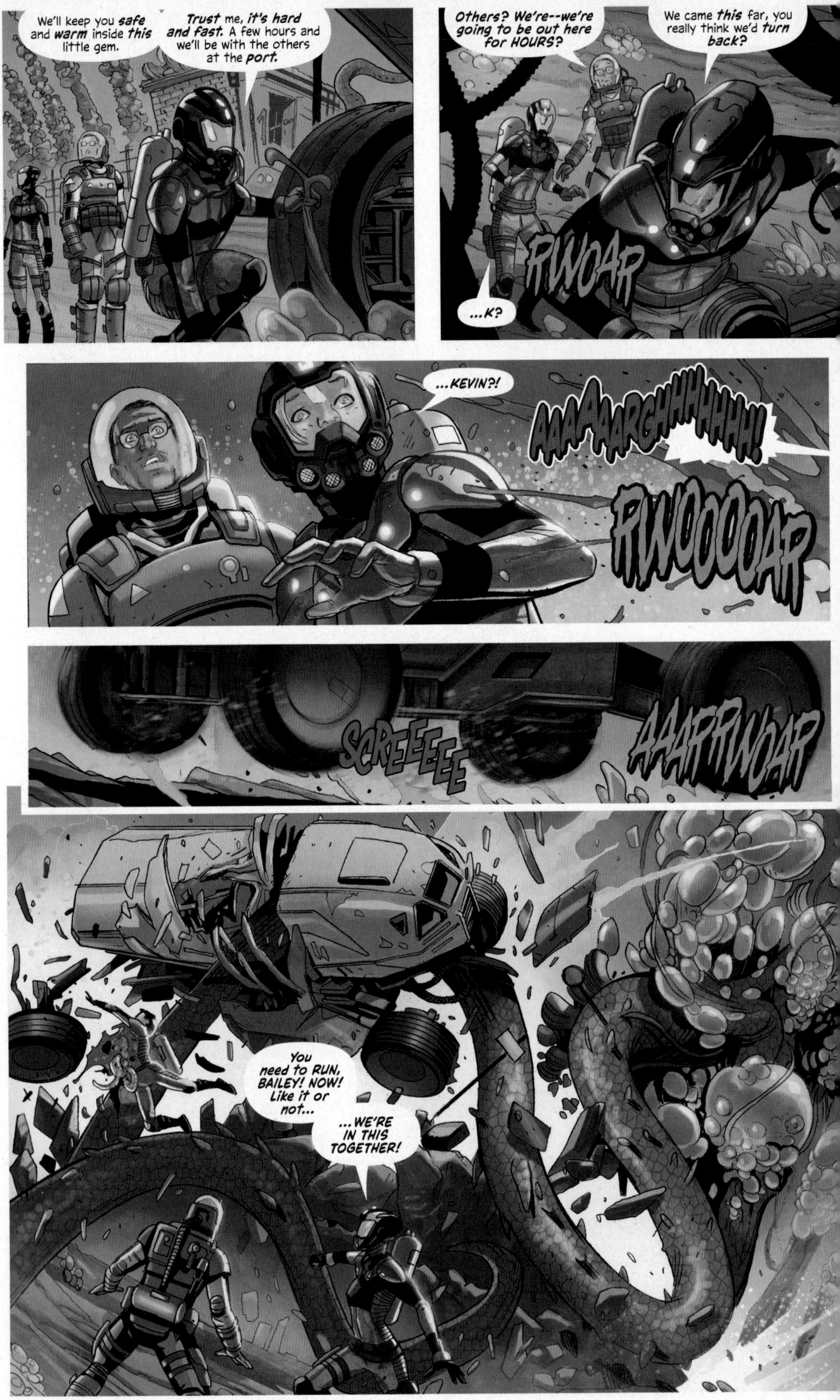
We'll keep you safe and warm inside this little gem.
Trust me, it's hard and fast. A few hours and we'll be with the others at the port.
Others? We're--we're going to be out here for HOURS?
We came this far, you really think we'd turn back?
RWOAR
...K?
...KEVIN?!
AAAAAARGHHHHHHH!
RWOOOOAR
SCREEEEEE
AAARWOAR
You need to RUN, BAILEY! NOW! Like it or not...
...WE'RE IN THIS TOGETHER!

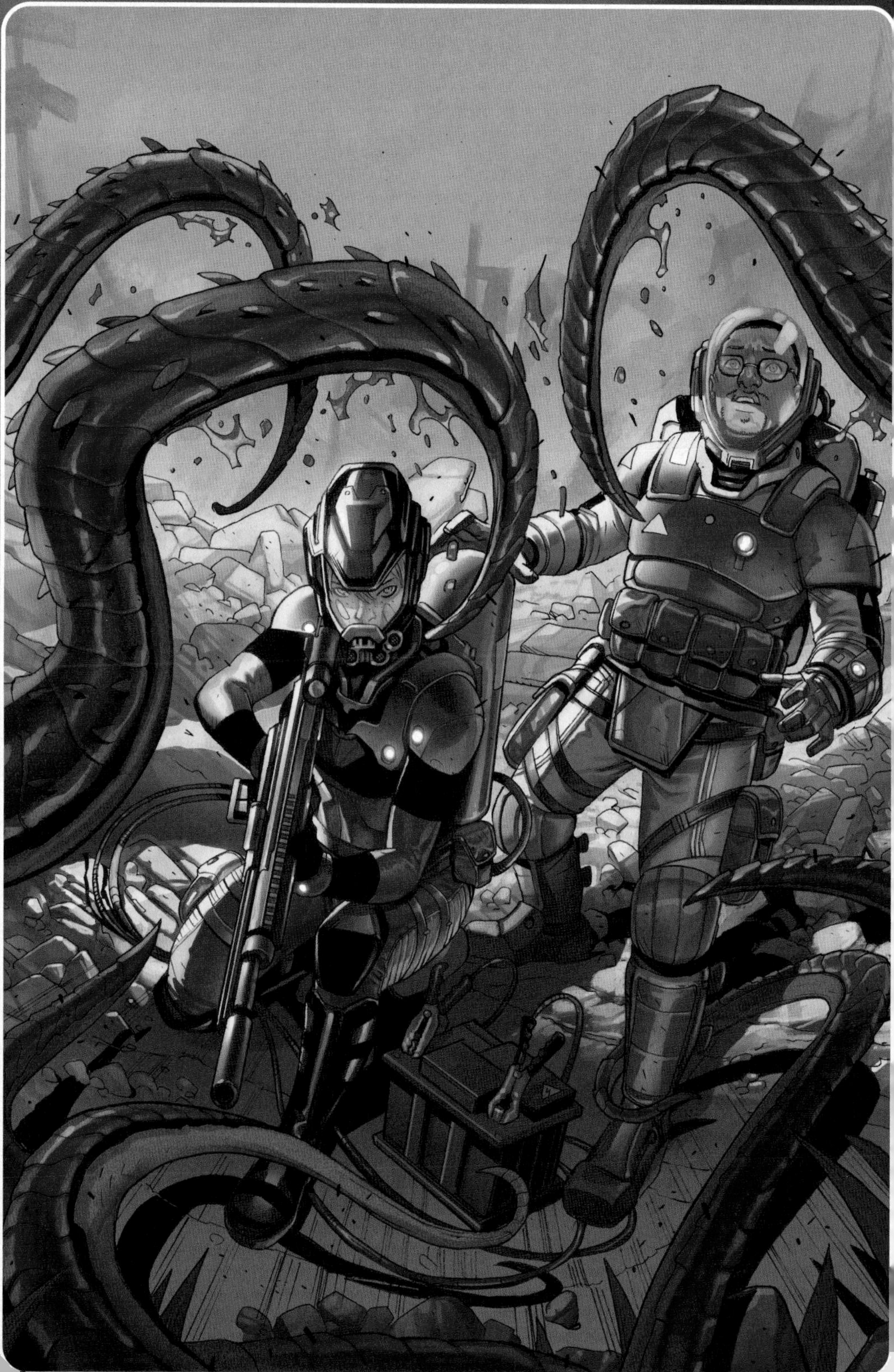

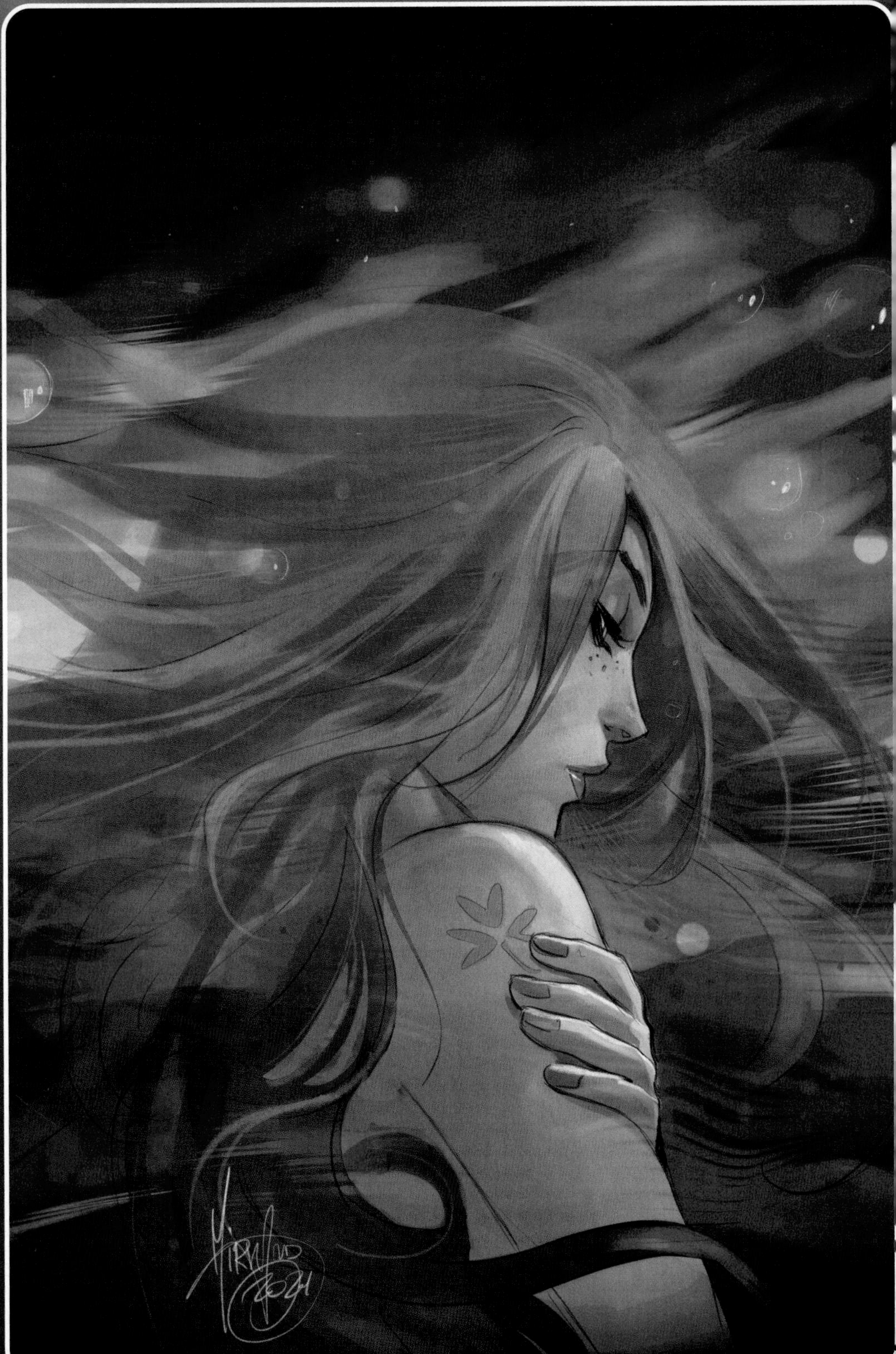

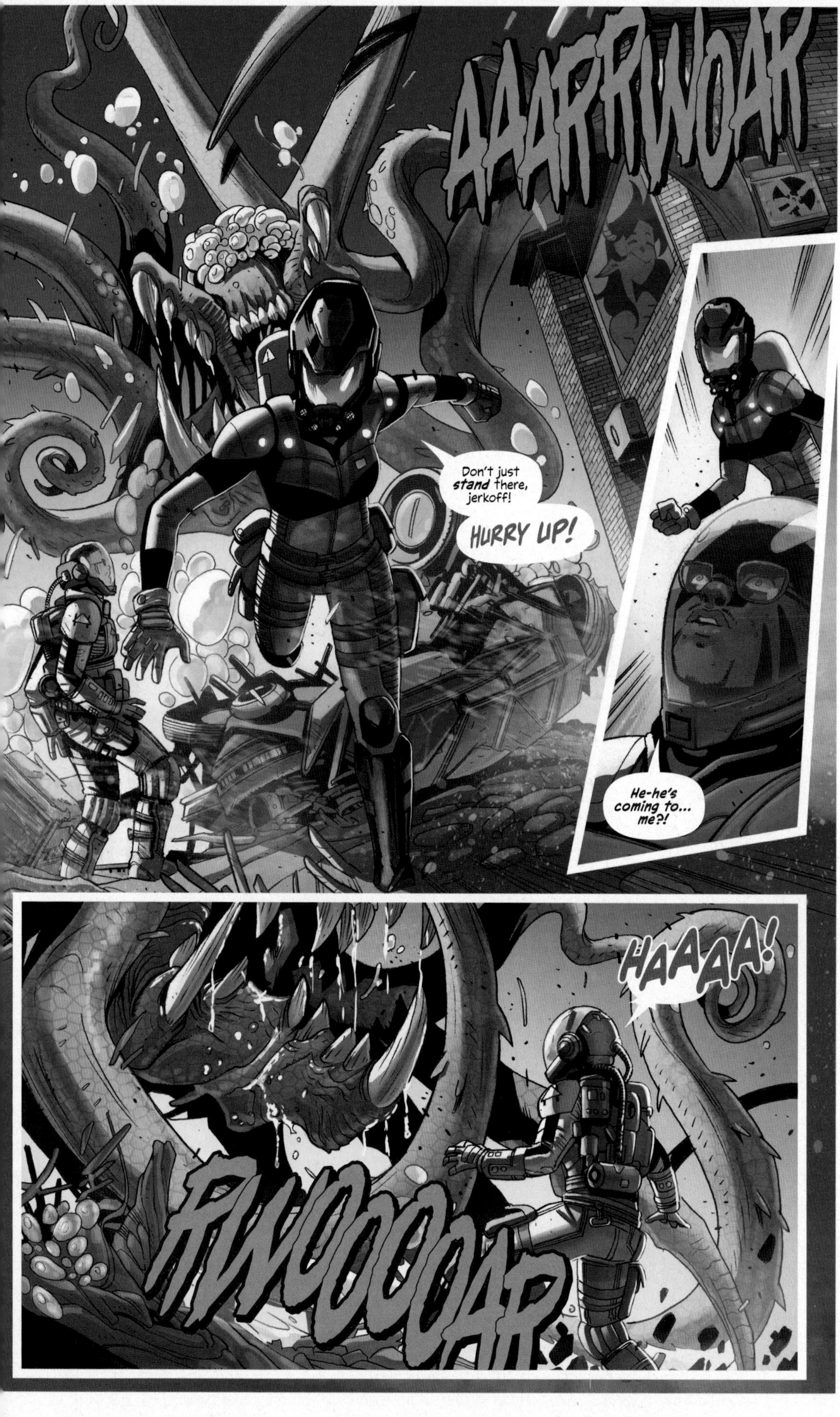
AAARRWOAR
Don't just *stand* there, jerkoff!
HURRY UP!
He-he's coming to... me?!
HAAAA!
RWOOOOAR

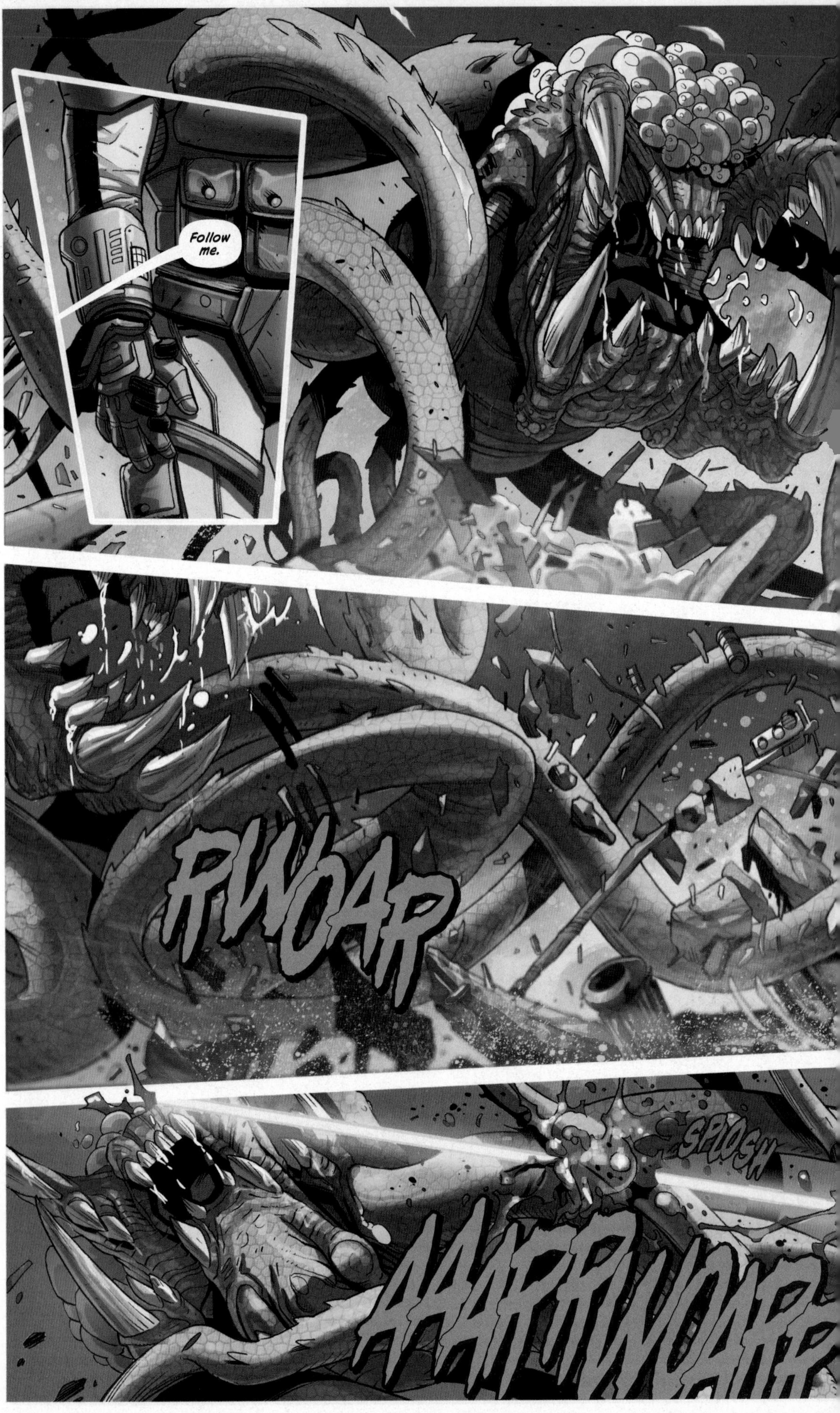

Follow me.
RWOAR
SPLOSH
AAARRWOARR

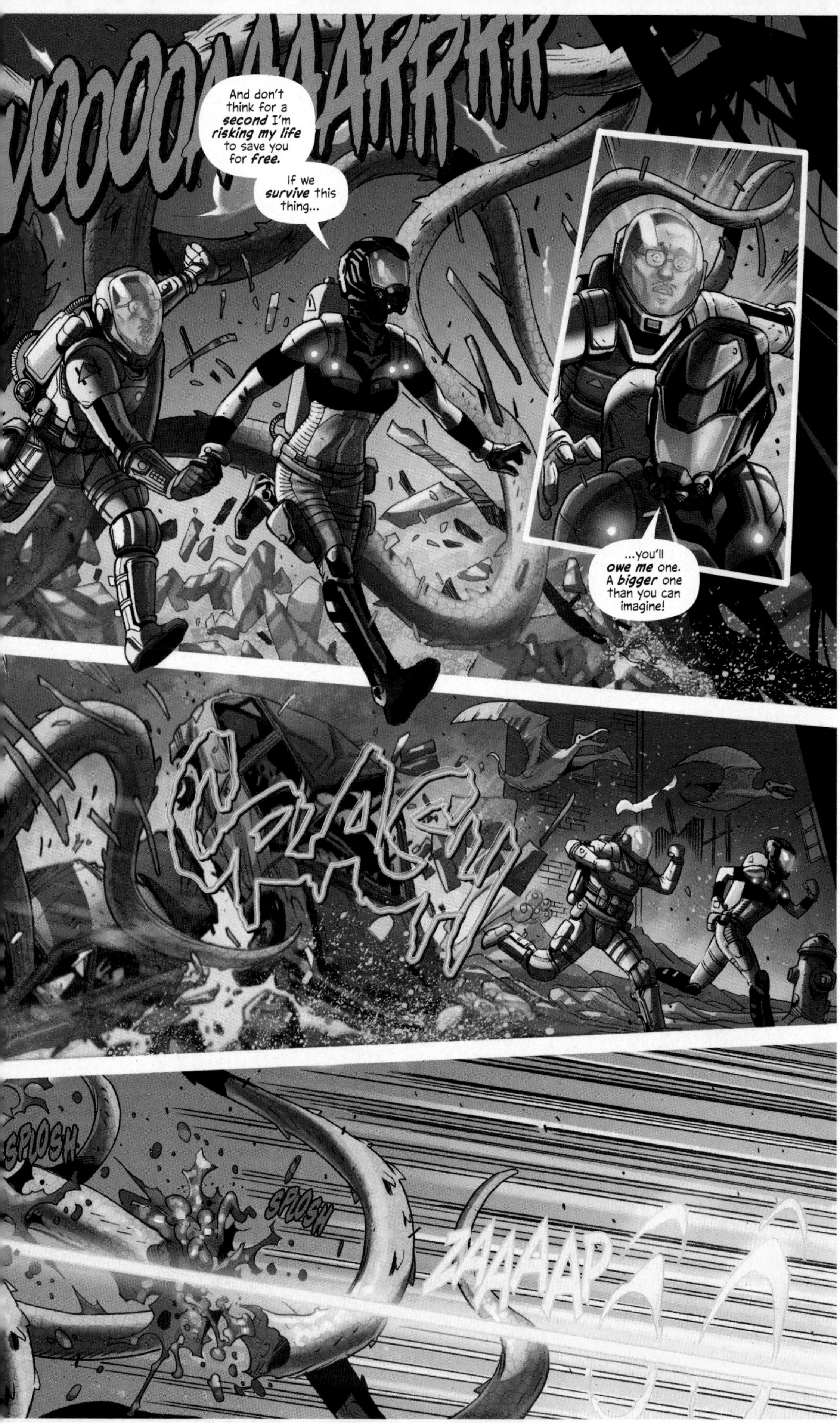
And don't think for a *second* I'm *risking my life* to save you for *free.*
If we *survive* this thing...
...you'll *owe me* one. A *bigger* one than you can imagine!
SPLOSH
SPLOSH
ZAAAAP

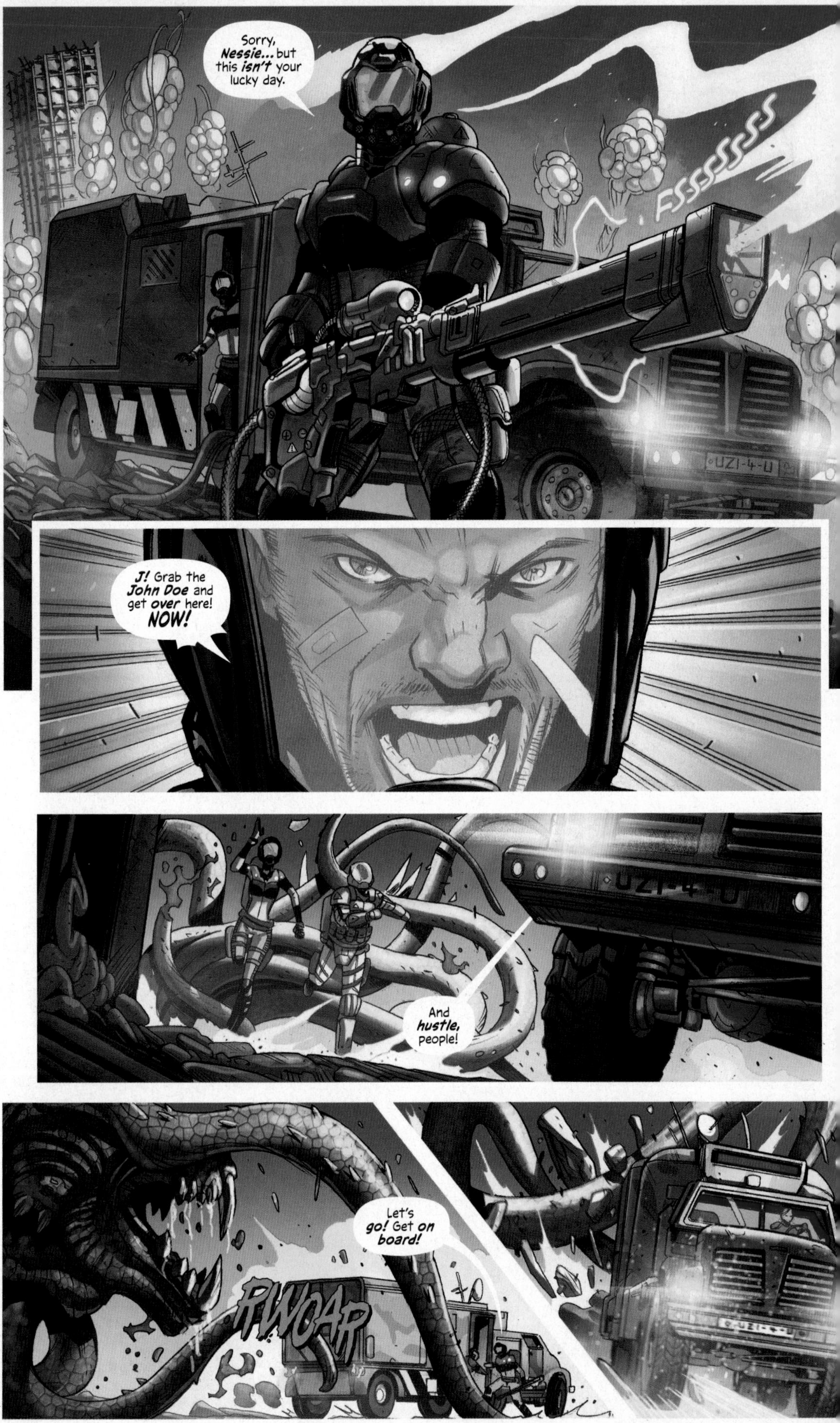

Sorry, Nessie... but this isn't your lucky day.
FSSSSSSSS
UZI-4-U
J! Grab the John Doe and get over here! NOW!
UZI-4-U
And hustle, people!
Let's go! Get on board!
RWOAR

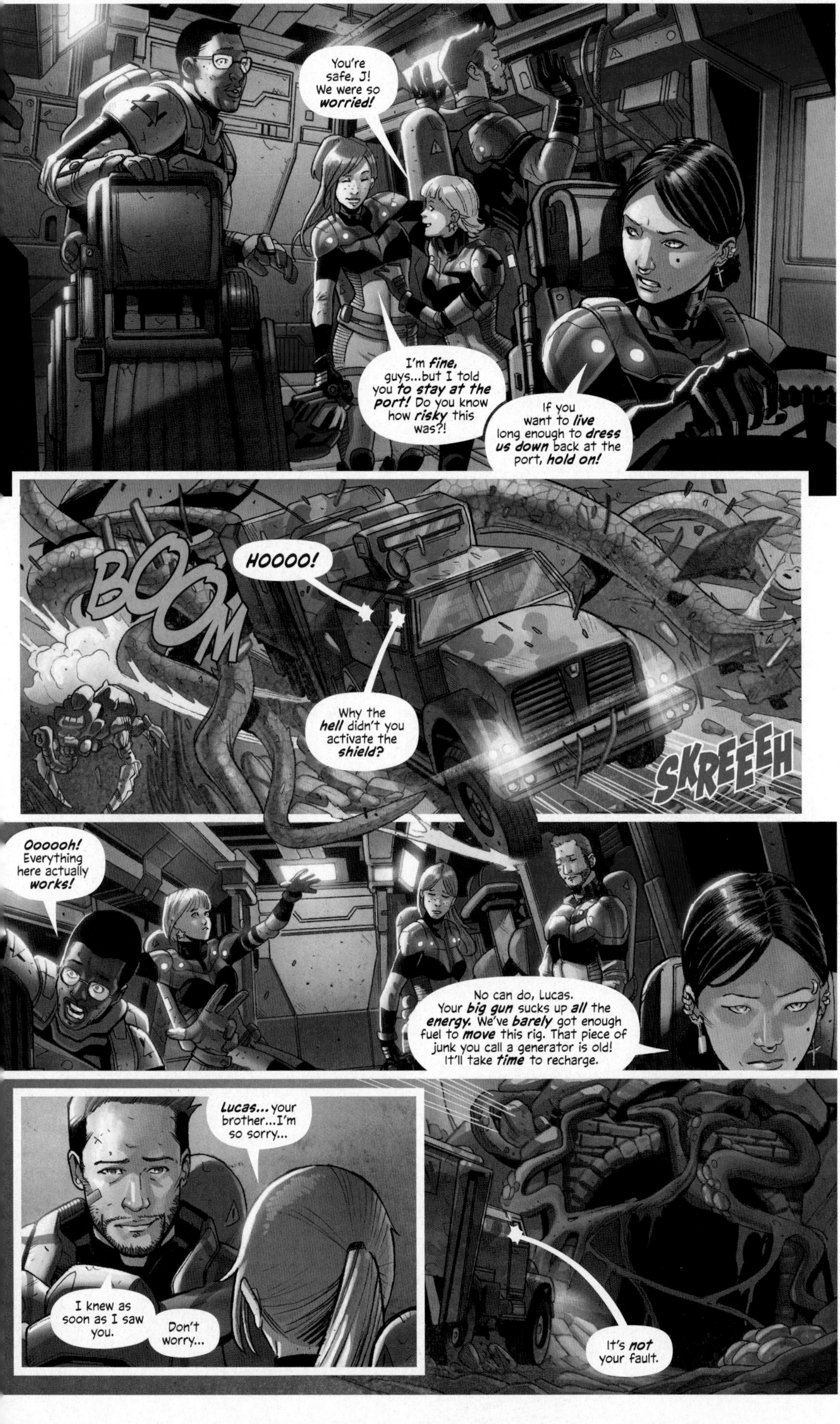
You're safe, J! We were so worried!
I'm fine, guys...but I told you to stay at the port! Do you know how risky this was?!
If you want to live long enough to dress us down back at the port, hold on!
BOOM
HOOOO!
Why the hell didn't you activate the shield?
SKREEEH
Oooooh! Everything here actually works!
No can do, Lucas. Your big gun sucks up all the energy. We've barely got enough fuel to move this rig. That piece of junk you call a generator is old! It'll take time to recharge.
Lucas... your brother...I'm so sorry...
I knew as soon as I saw you.
Don't worry...
It's not your fault.

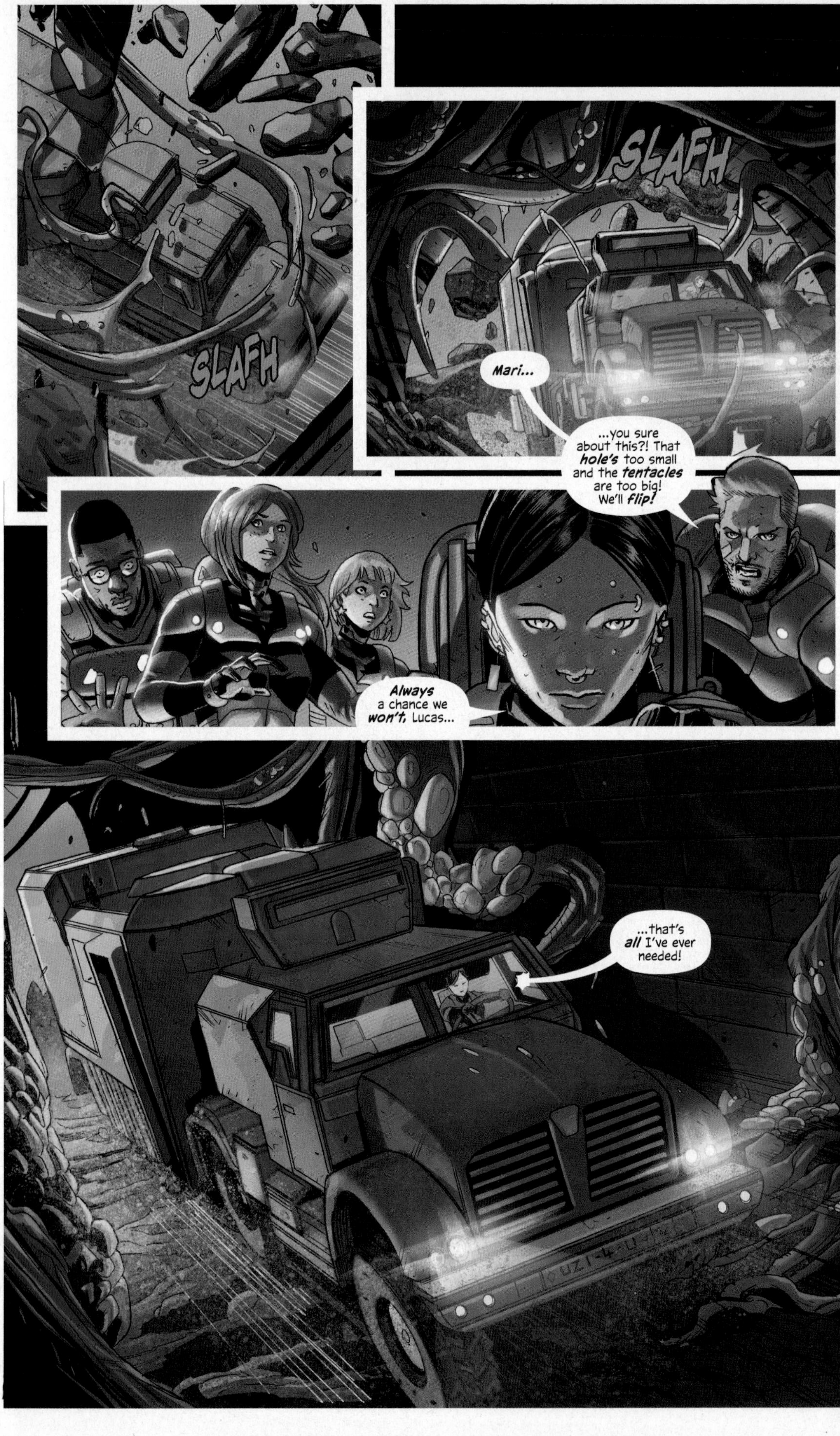
SLAFH
SLAFH
Mari...
...you sure about this?! That hole's too small and the tentacles are too big! We'll flip!
Always a chance we won't, Lucas...
...that's all I've ever needed!

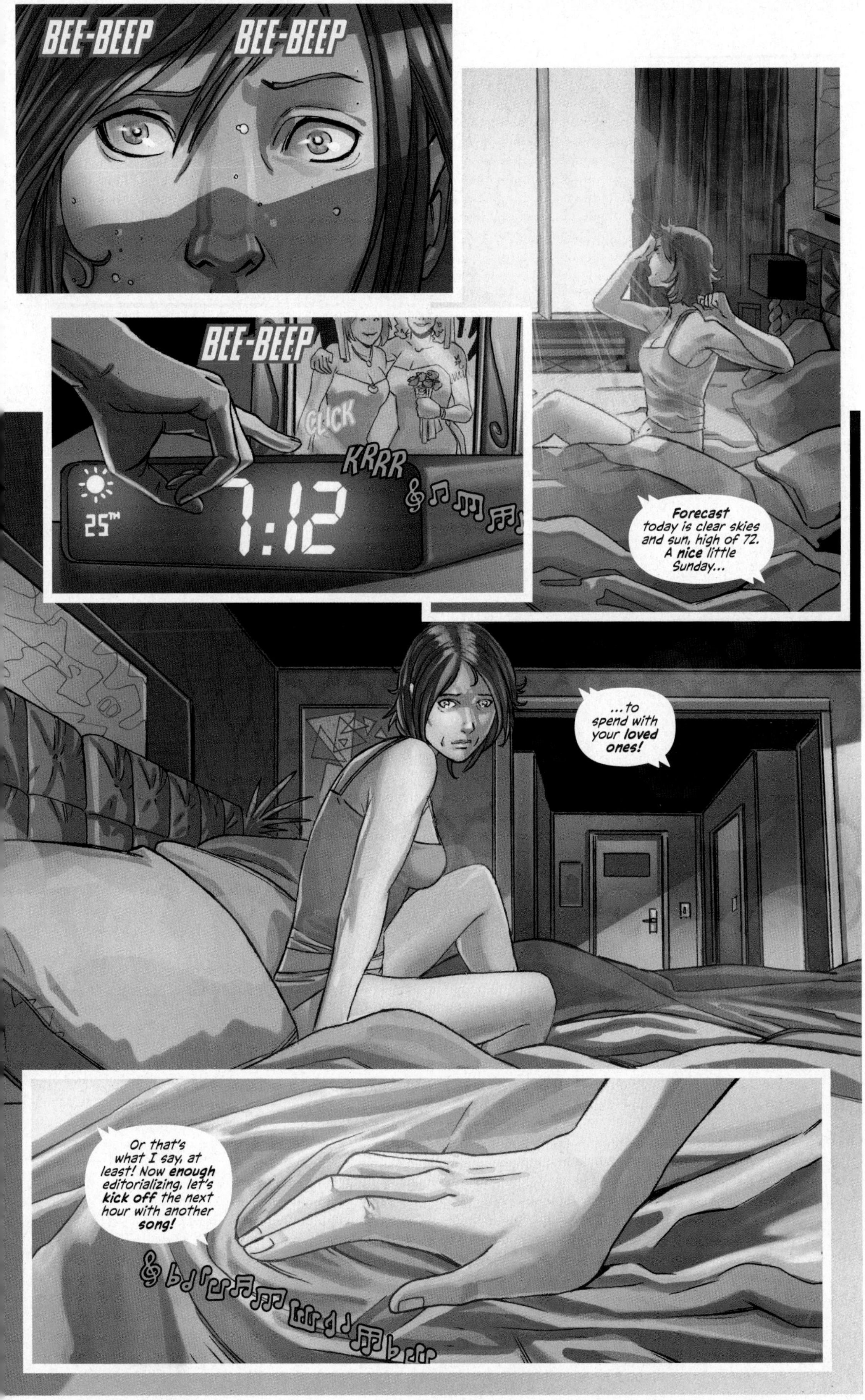
BEE-BEEP
BEE-BEEP
BEE-BEEP
CLICK
KRRR
25TH
7:12
Forecast today is clear skies and sun, high of 72. A nice little Sunday...
...to spend with your loved ones!
Or that's what I say, at least! Now enough editorializing, let's kick off the next hour with another song!

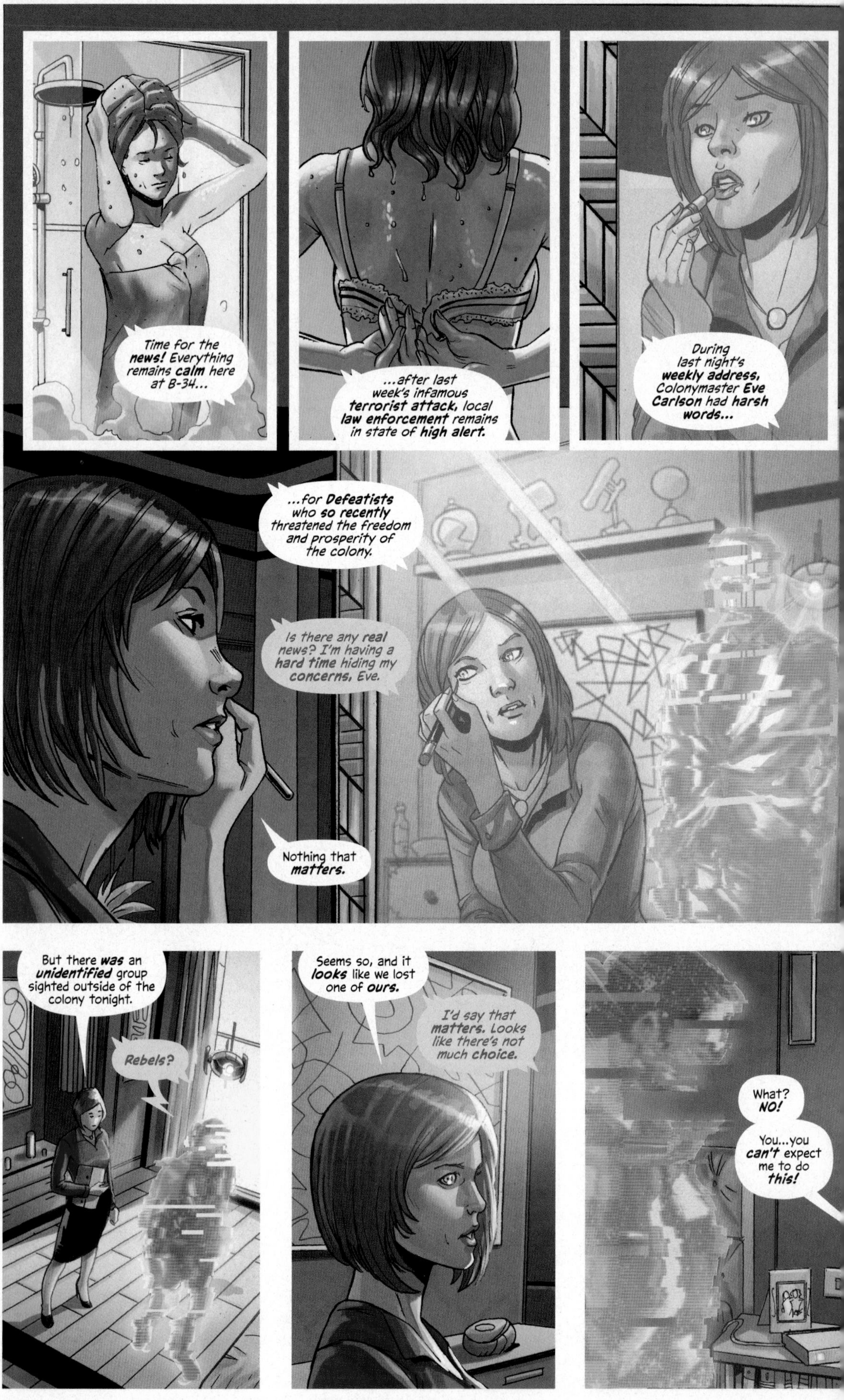

Time for the news! Everything remains calm here at B-34...
...after last week's infamous terrorist attack, local law enforcement remains in state of high alert.
During last night's weekly address, Colonymaster Eve Carlson had harsh words...
...for Defeatists who so recently threatened the freedom and prosperity of the colony.
Is there any real news? I'm having a hard time hiding my concerns, Eve.
Nothing that matters.
But there was an unidentified group sighted outside of the colony tonight.
Rebels?
Seems so, and it looks like we lost one of ours.
I'd say that matters. Looks like there's not much choice.
What? NO!
You...you can't expect me to do this!

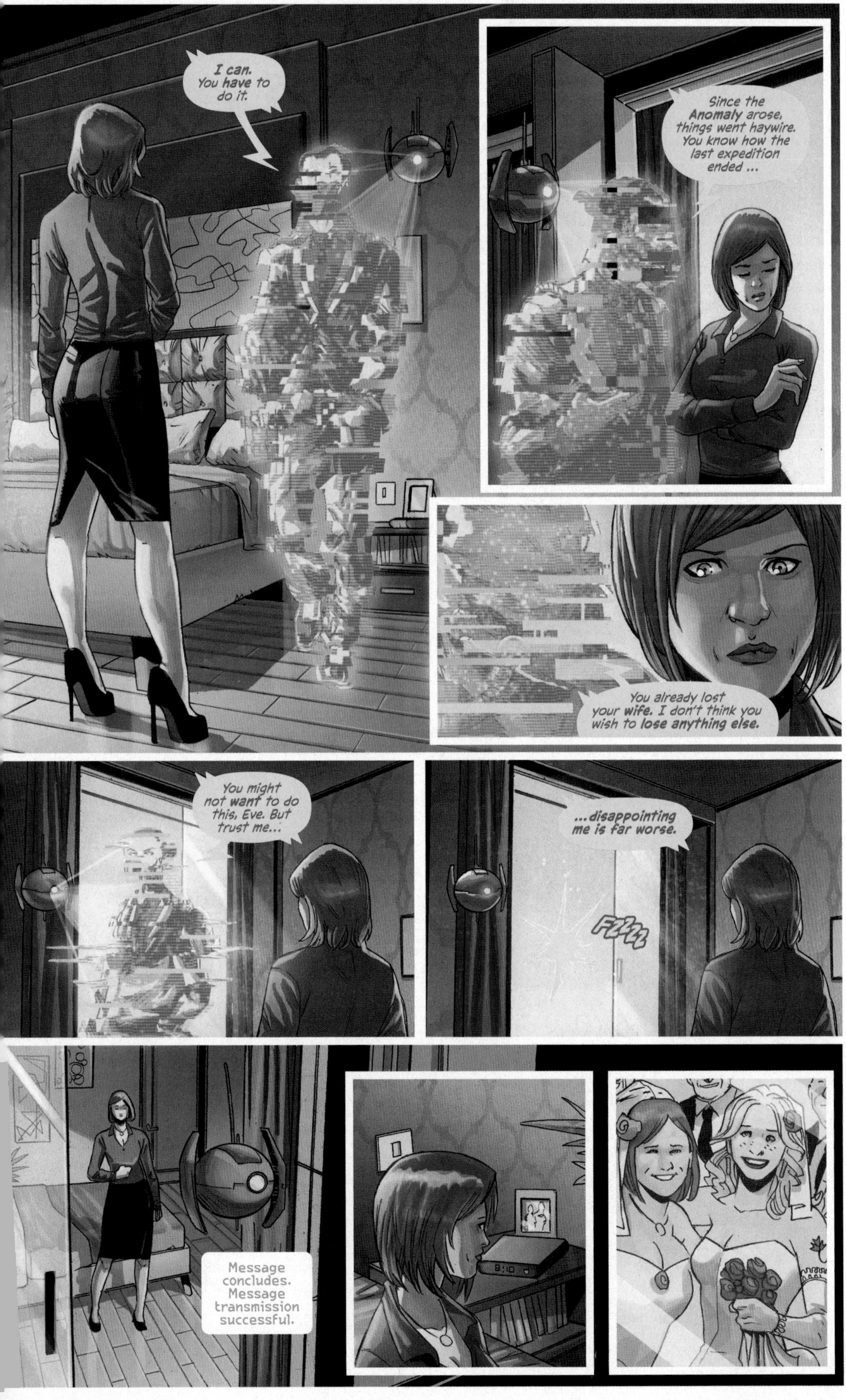
I can. You have to do it.
Since the Anomaly arose, things went haywire. You know how the last expedition ended ...
You already lost your wife. I don't think you wish to lose anything else.
You might not want to do this, Eve. But trust me...
...disappointing me is far worse.
FZZZZ
Message concludes. Message transmission successful.

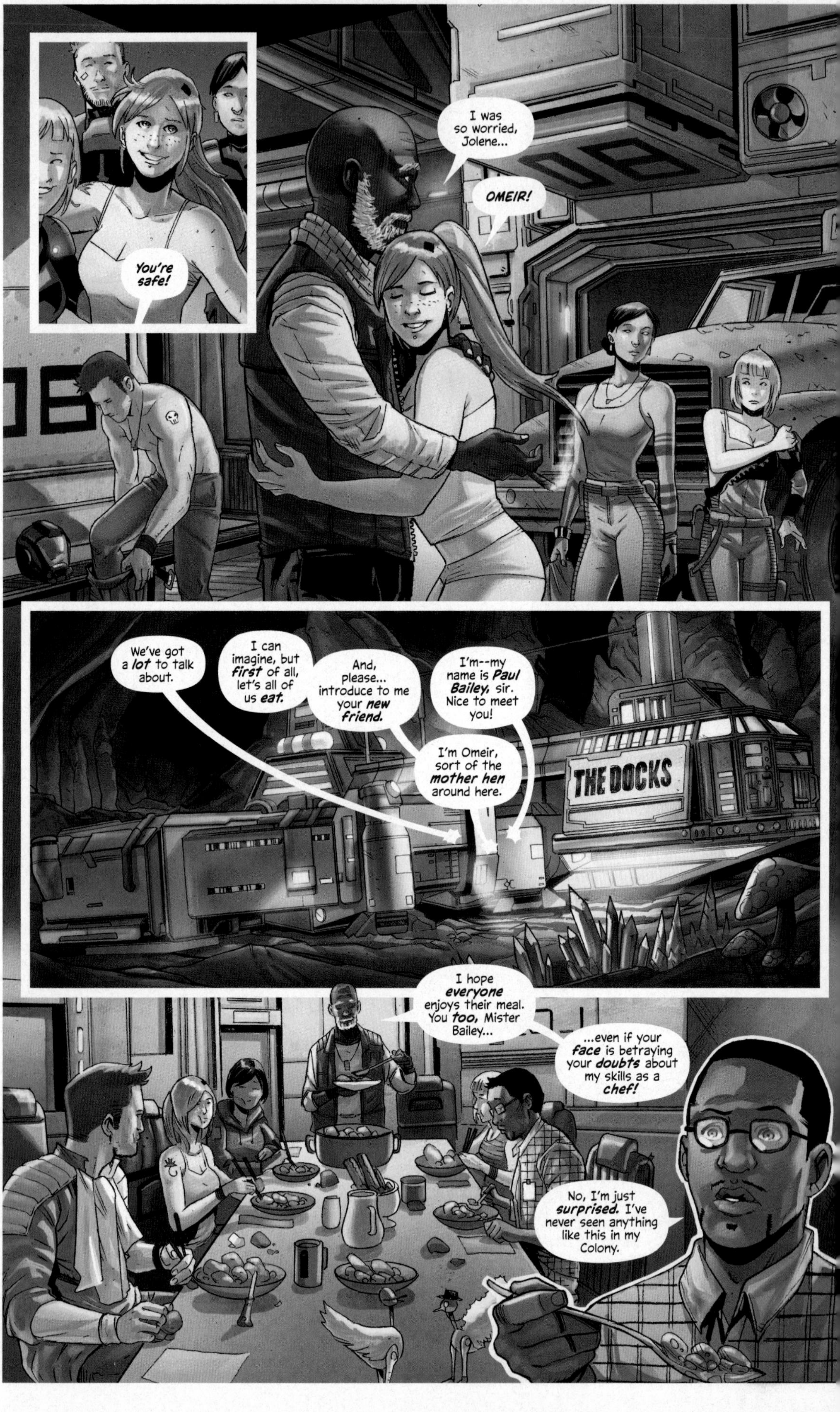
You're safe!
I was so worried, Jolene...
OMEIR!
We've got a lot to talk about.
I can imagine, but first of all, let's all of us eat.
And, please... introduce to me your new friend.
I'm--my name is Paul Bailey, sir. Nice to meet you!
I'm Omeir, sort of the mother hen around here.
THE DOCKS
I hope everyone enjoys their meal. You too, Mister Bailey...
...even if your face is betraying your doubts about my skills as a chef!
No, I'm just surprised. I've never seen anything like this in my Colony.

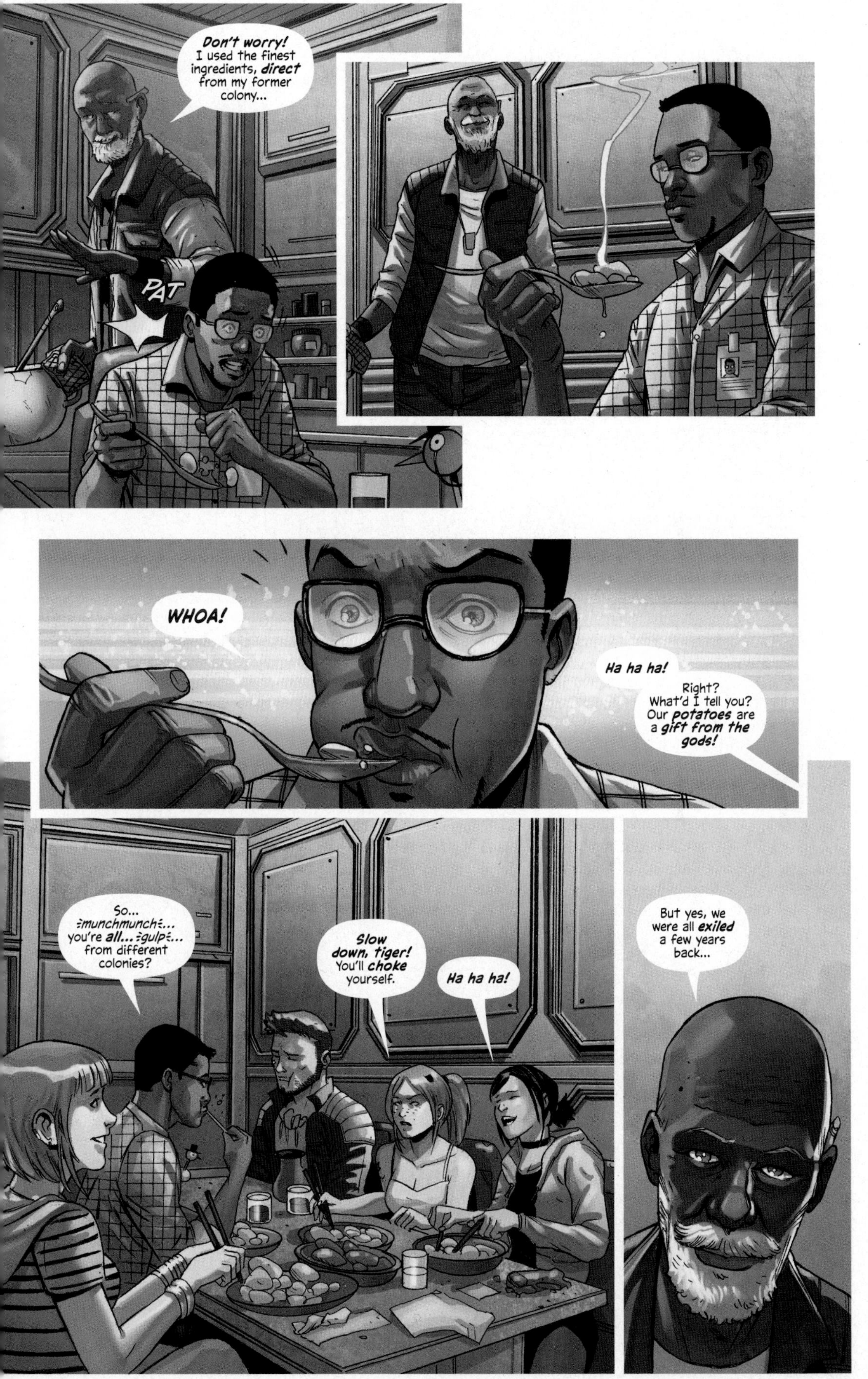

Don't worry! I used the finest ingredients, direct from my former colony...
PAT
WHOA!
Ha ha ha!
Right? What'd I tell you? Our potatoes are a gift from the gods!
So... ≈munchmunch≈... you're all... ≈gulp≈... from different colonies?
Slow down, tiger! You'll choke yourself.
Ha ha ha!
But yes, we were all exiled a few years back...

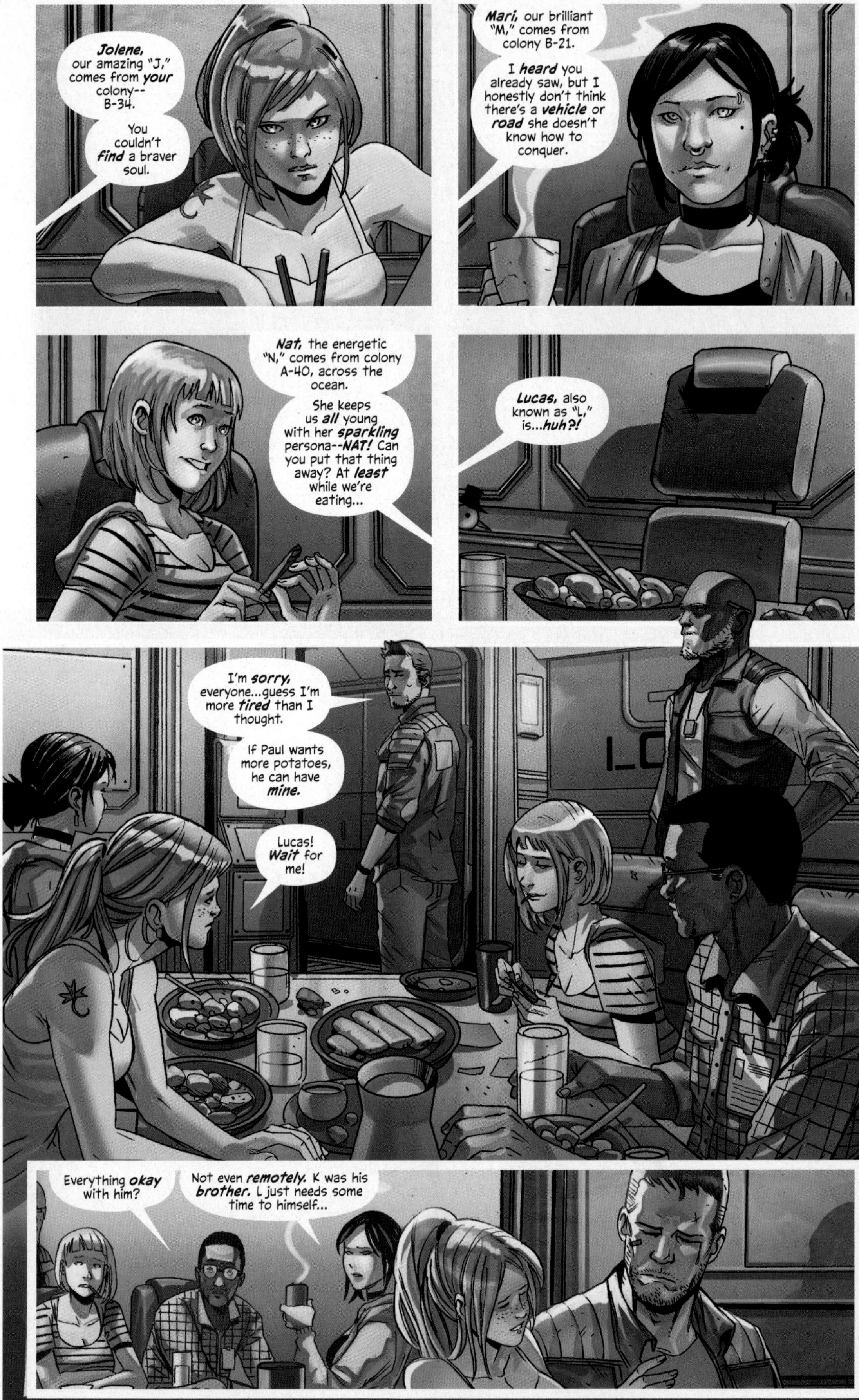
Jolene, our amazing "J," comes from your colony-- B-34.
You couldn't find a braver soul.
Mari, our brilliant "M," comes from colony B-21.
I heard you already saw, but I honestly don't think there's a vehicle or road she doesn't know how to conquer.
Nat, the energetic "N," comes from colony A-40, across the ocean.
She keeps us all young with her sparkling persona--NAT! Can you put that thing away? At least while we're eating...
Lucas, also known as "L," is...huh?!
I'm sorry, everyone...guess I'm more tired than I thought.
If Paul wants more potatoes, he can have mine.
Lucas! Wait for me!
LO
Everything okay with him?
Not even remotely. K was his brother. L just needs some time to himself...

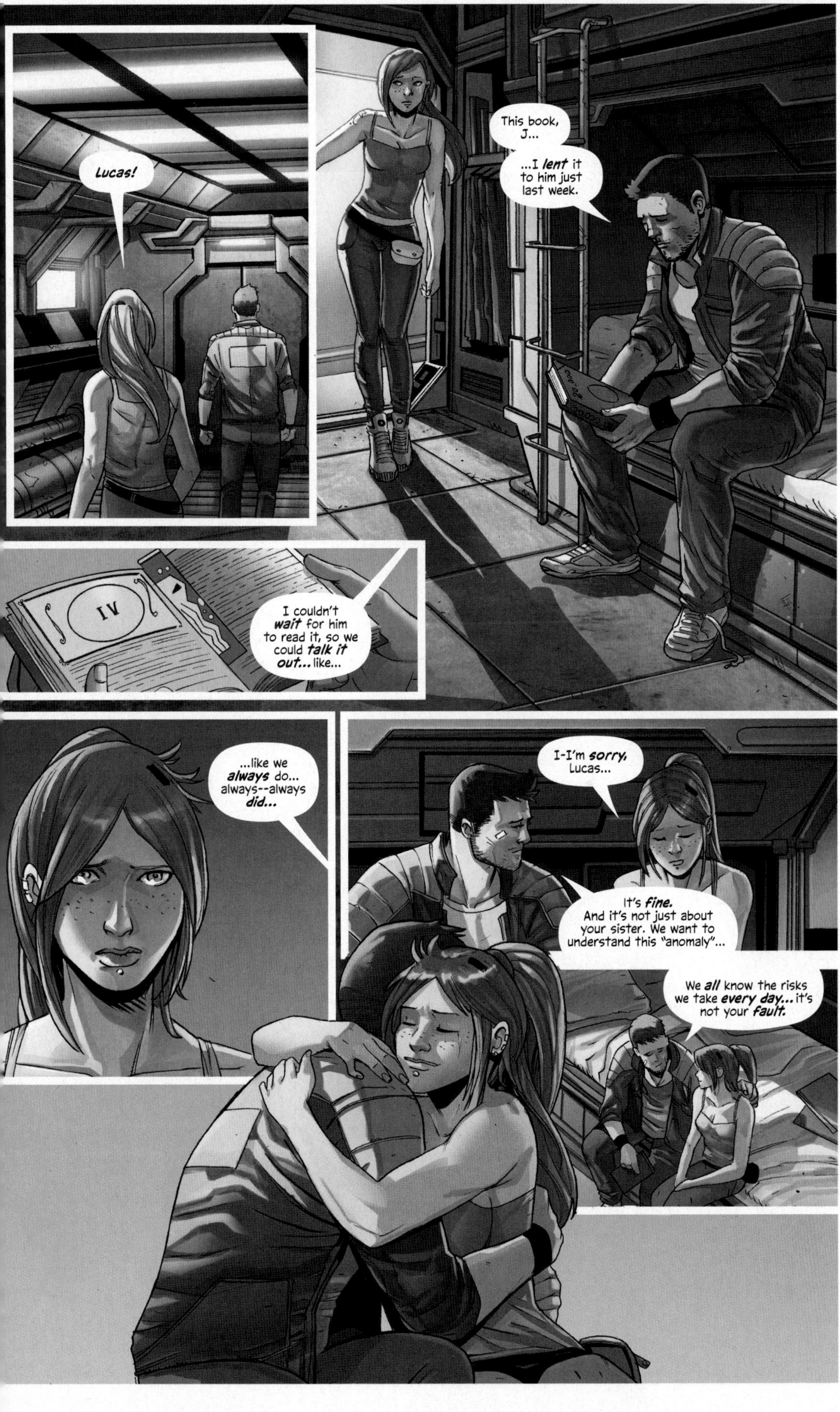
Lucas!
This book, J...
...I lent it to him just last week.
I couldn't wait for him to read it, so we could talk it out... like...
...like we always do... always--always did...
I-I'm sorry, Lucas...
It's fine. And it's not just about your sister. We want to understand this "anomaly"...
We all know the risks we take every day... it's not your fault.

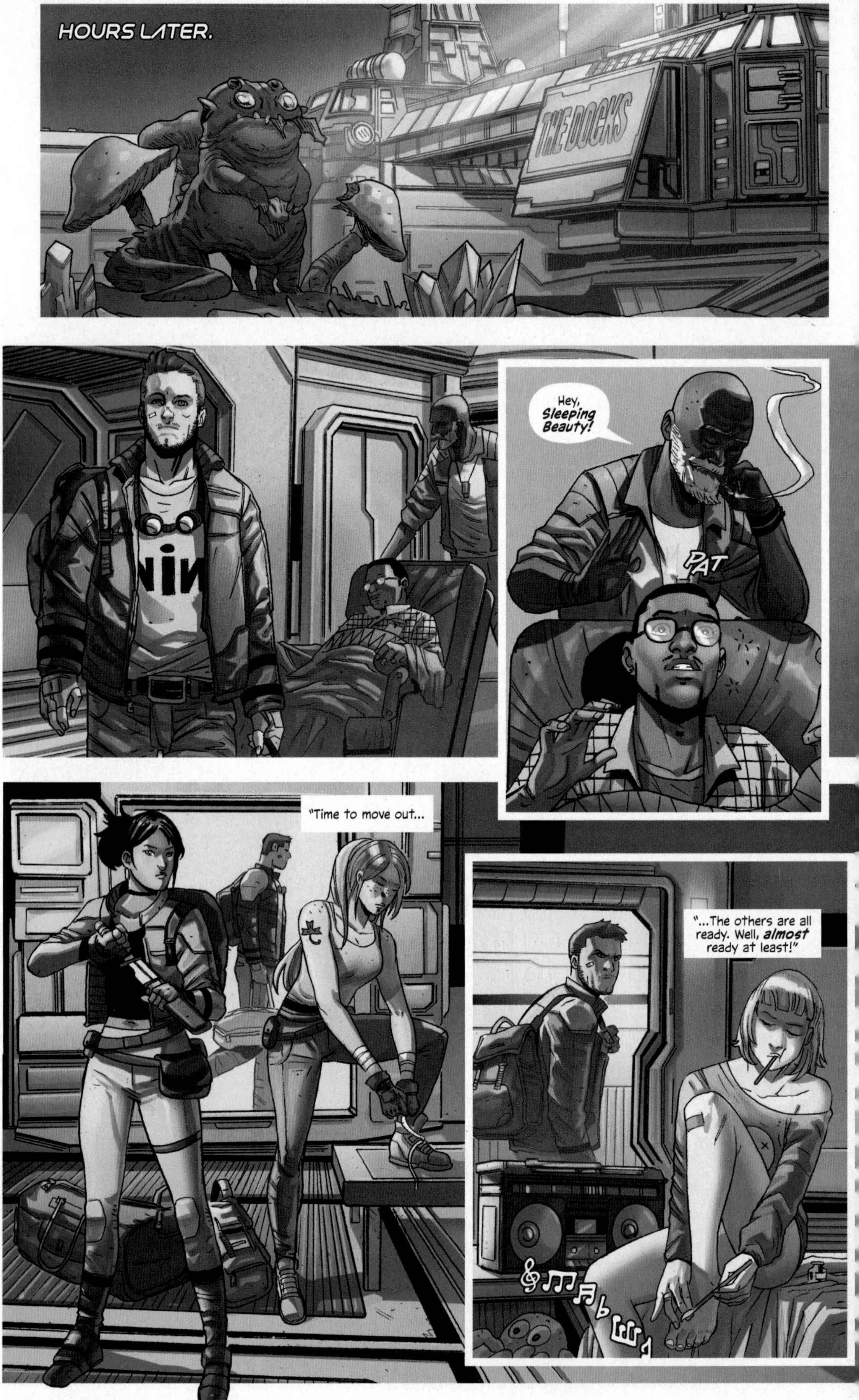
HOURS LATER.
THE DOCKS
Hey, Sleeping Beauty!
PAT
"Time to move out...
"...The others are all ready. Well, *almost* ready at least!"

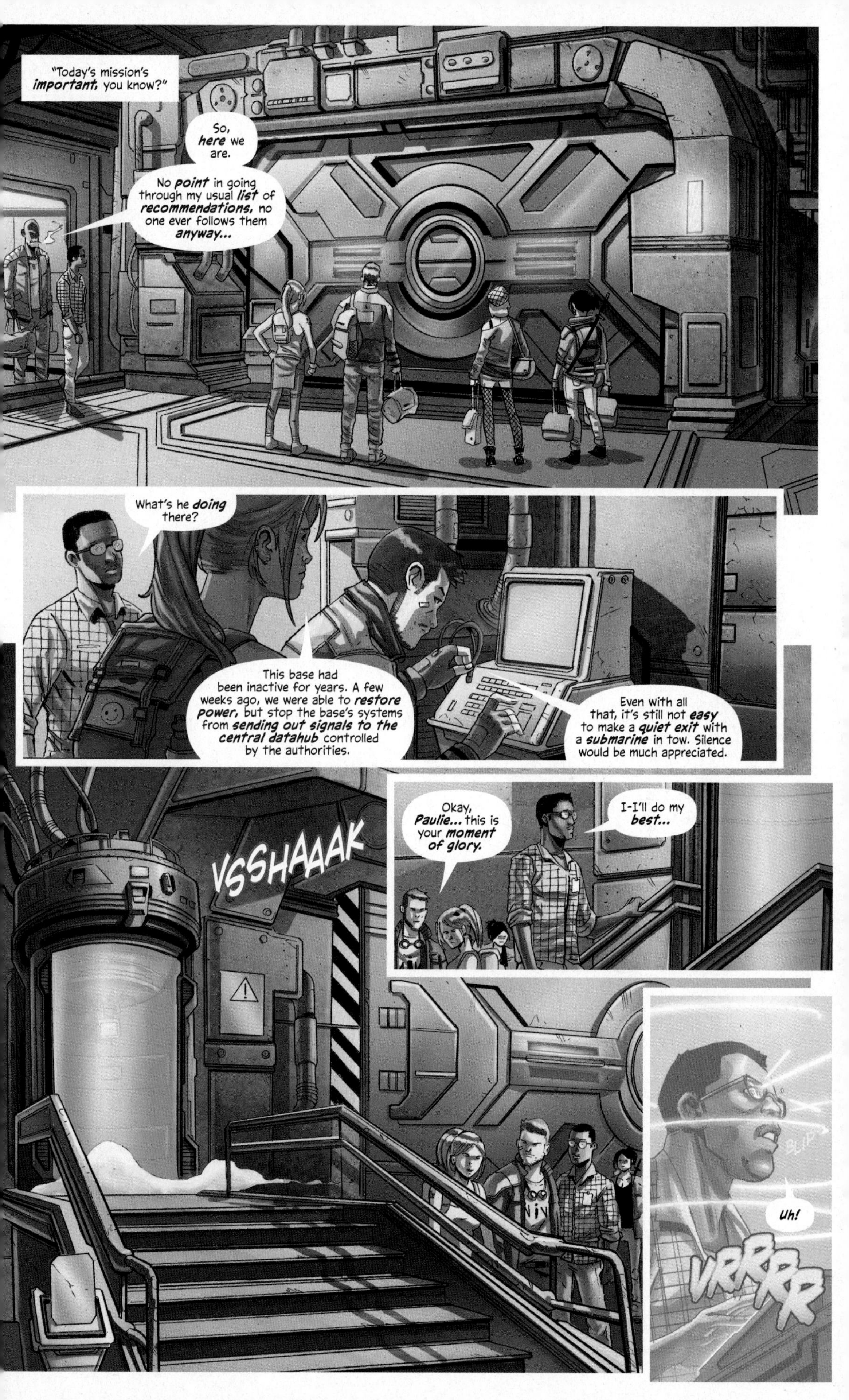

"Today's mission's *important*, you know?"
So, *here* we are.
No *point* in going through my usual *list* of *recommendations*, no one ever follows them *anyway...*
What's he *doing* there?
This base had been inactive for years. A few weeks ago, we were able to *restore power*, but stop the base's systems from *sending out signals to the central datahub* controlled by the authorities.
Even with all that, it's still not *easy* to make a *quiet exit* with a *submarine* in tow. Silence would be much appreciated.
VSSHAAAK
Okay, *Paulie...* this is your *moment of glory.*
I-I'll do my *best...*
BLIP
Uh!
VRRRR

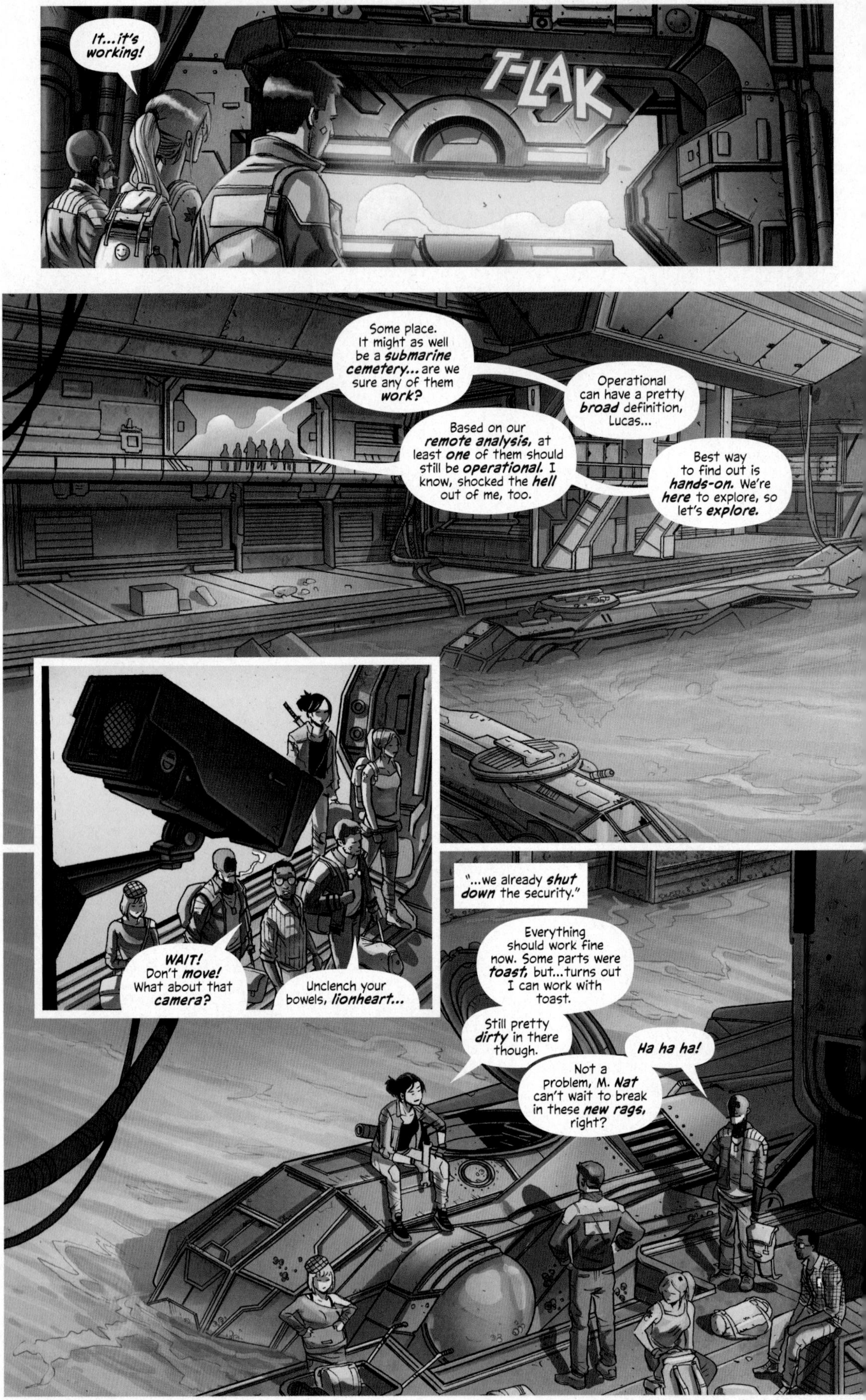

It...it's working!
T-LAK
Some place. It might as well be a submarine cemetery... are we sure any of them work?
Based on our remote analysis, at least one of them should still be operational. I know, shocked the hell out of me, too.
Operational can have a pretty broad definition, Lucas...
Best way to find out is hands-on. We're here to explore, so let's explore.
WAIT! Don't move! What about that camera?
Unclench your bowels, lionheart...
"...we already shut down the security."
Everything should work fine now. Some parts were toast, but...turns out I can work with toast.
Still pretty dirty in there though.
Not a problem, M. Nat can't wait to break in these new rags, right?
Ha ha ha!

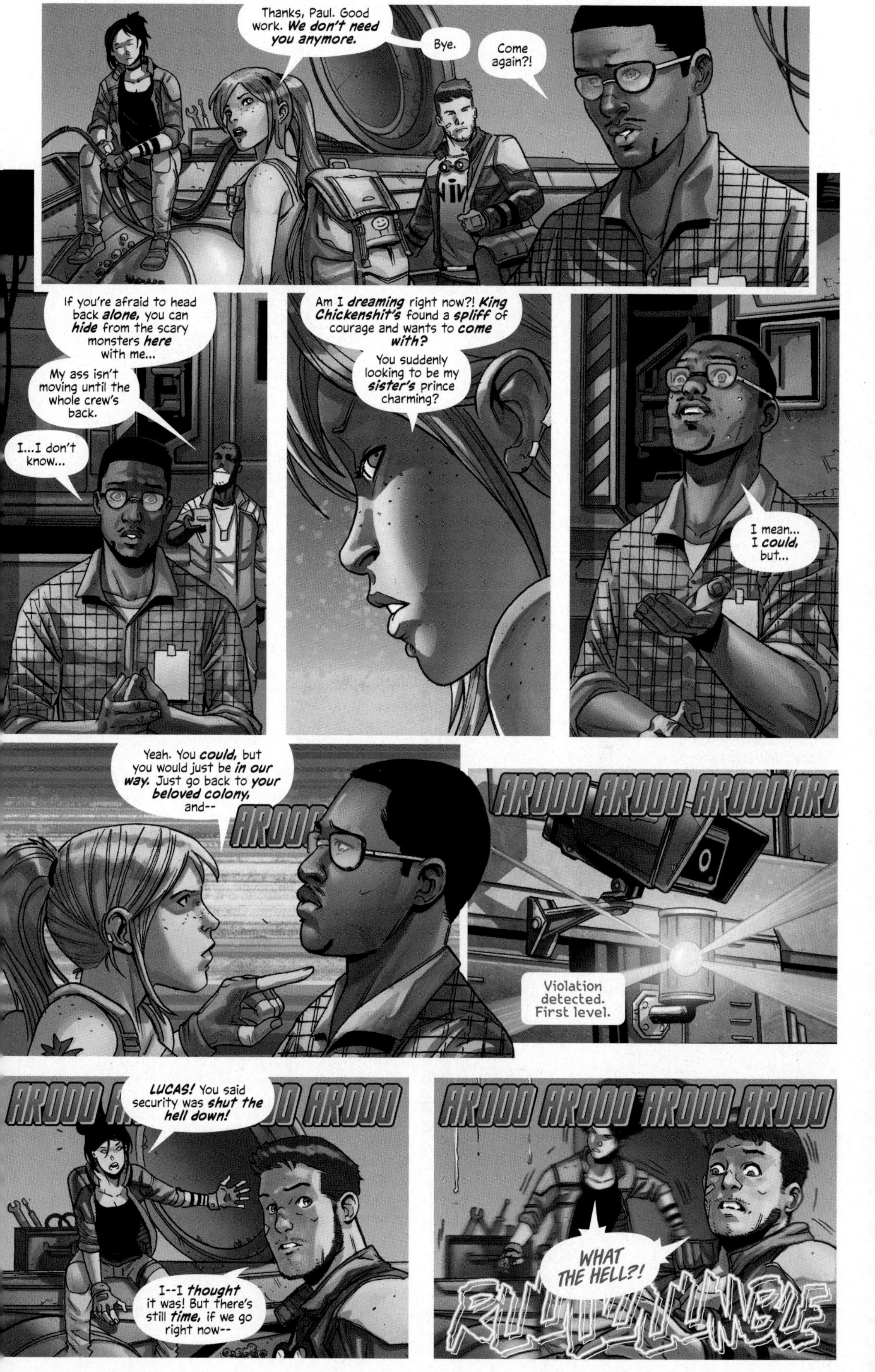

Thanks, Paul. Good work. We don't need you anymore.
Bye.
Come again?!
If you're afraid to head back alone, you can hide from the scary monsters here with me...
My ass isn't moving until the whole crew's back.
I...I don't know...
Am I dreaming right now?! King Chickenshit's found a spliff of courage and wants to come with?
You suddenly looking to be my sister's prince charming?
I mean... I could, but...
Yeah. You could, but you would just be in our way. Just go back to your beloved colony, and--
AROOO
AROOO AROOO AROOO ARO
Violation detected. First level.
AROOO A OO AROOO
LUCAS! You said security was shut the hell down!
I--I thought it was! But there's still time, if we go right now--
AROOO AROOO AROOO AROOO
WHAT THE HELL?!
RUMMMMMBLE

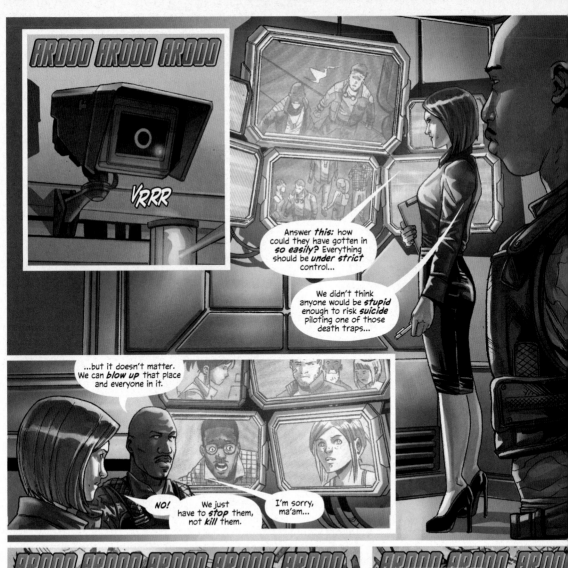

AROOO AROOO AROOO

VRRR

Answer **this:** how could they have gotten in **so easily?** Everything should be **under strict** control...

We didn't think anyone would be **stupid** enough to risk **suicide** piloting one of those death traps...

...but it doesn't matter. We can **blow up** that place and everyone in it.

NO! We just have to **stop** them, not **kill** them.

I'm sorry, ma'am...

AROOO AROOO AROOO AROOO AROOO

"...but you know our **common friend.** His orders are clear."

Haa!

RUUUUUMBLE

Self-destruct protocol activated.

AROOO AROOO AROOO

Self-destruct protocol activated.

There!

RUUUUUMBLE

We're **in!**

Go! GO!

HURRY, Mari!

These old **boys** take a **second** to submerge...

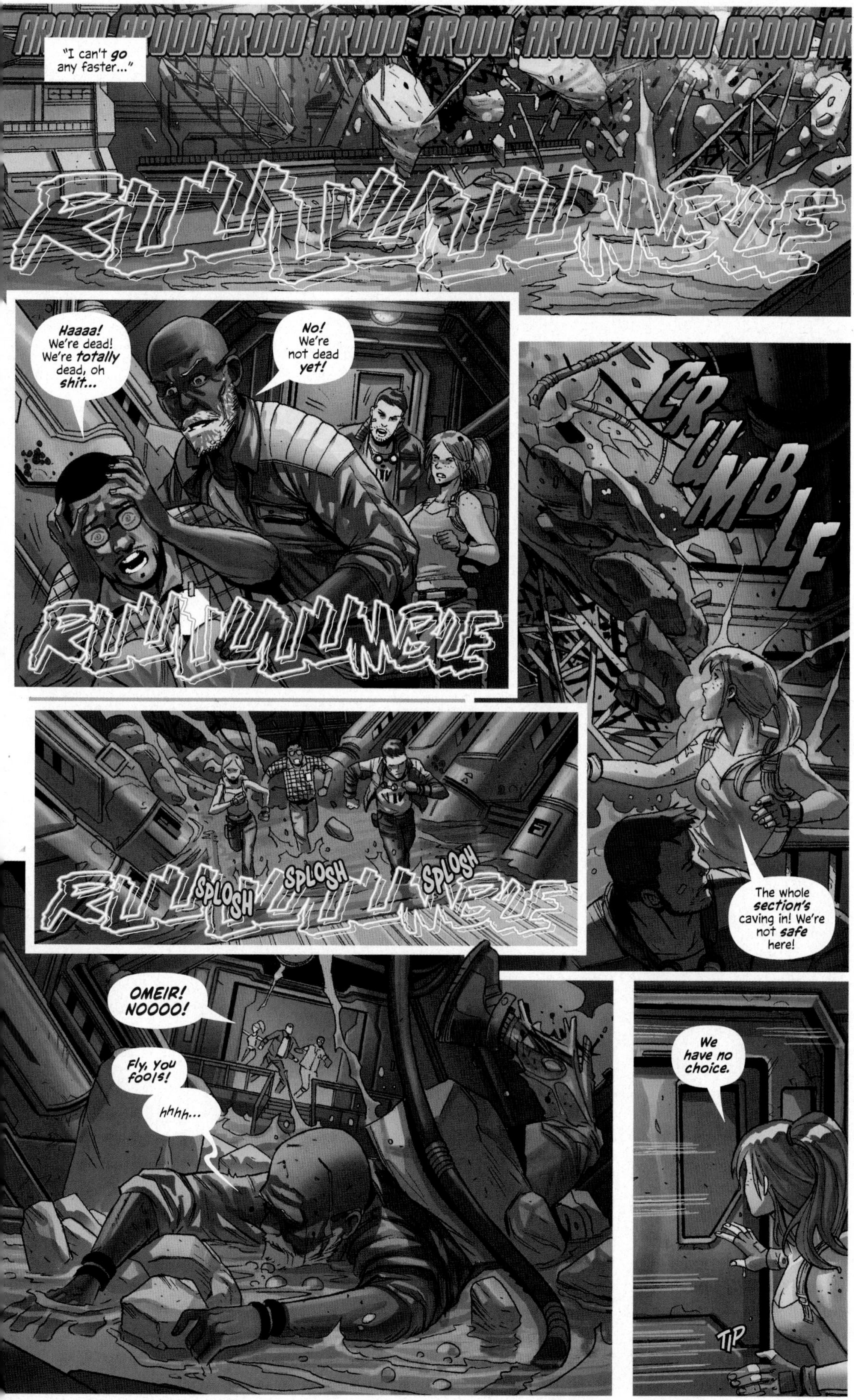
AROOO AROOO AROOO AROOO AROOO AROOO AROOO AROOO
"I can't go any faster..."
Haaaa! We're dead! We're totally dead, oh shit...
No! We're not dead yet!
CRUMBLE
SPLOSH
SPLOSH
SPLOSH
The whole section's caving in! We're not safe here!
OMEIR! NOOOO!
Fly, you fools!
hhhh...
We have no choice.
TIP

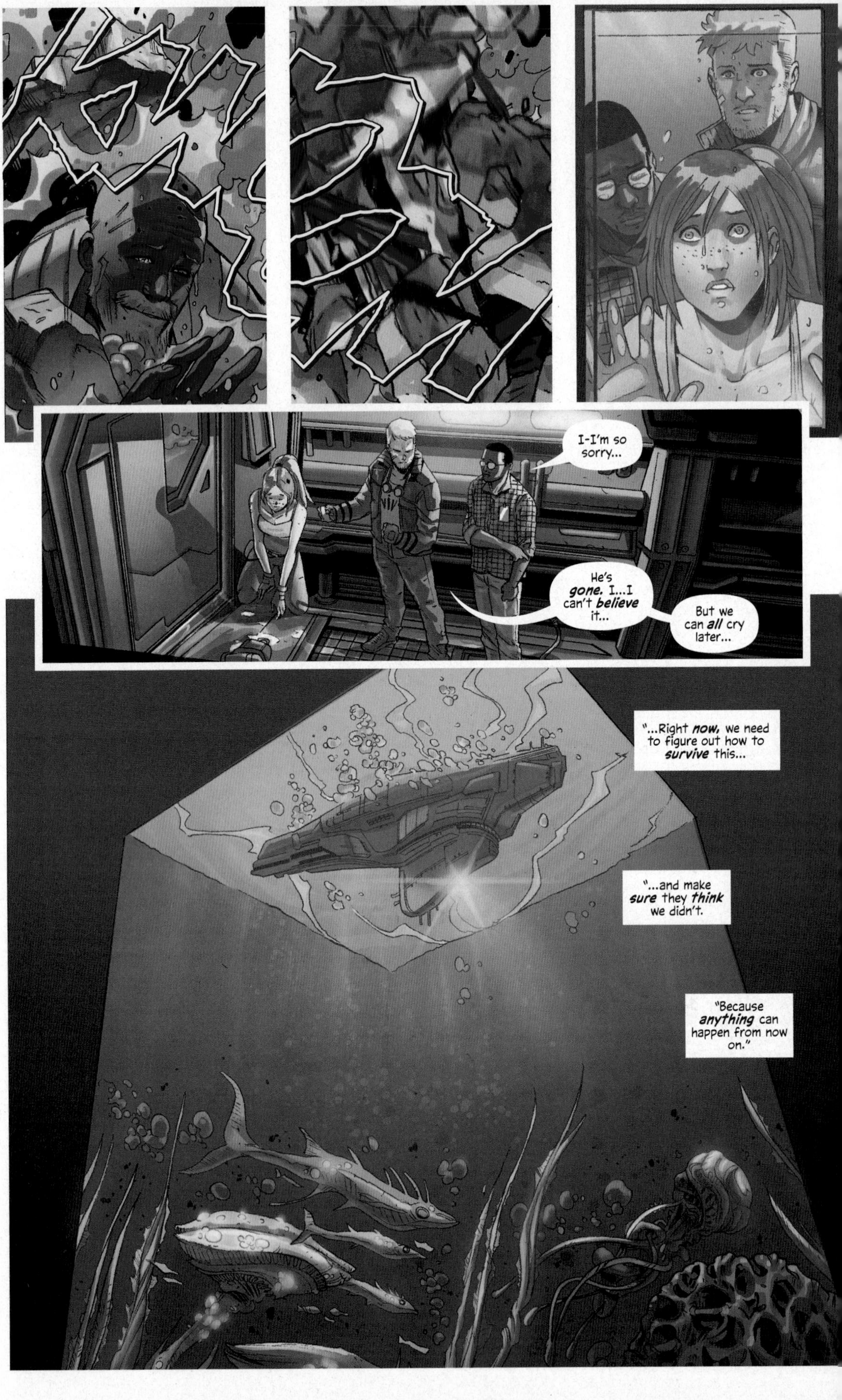
I-I'm so sorry...
He's *gone.* I...I can't *believe* it...
But we can *all* cry later...
"...Right *now,* we need to figure out how to *survive* this...
"...and make *sure* they *think* we didn't.
"Because *anything* can happen from now on."

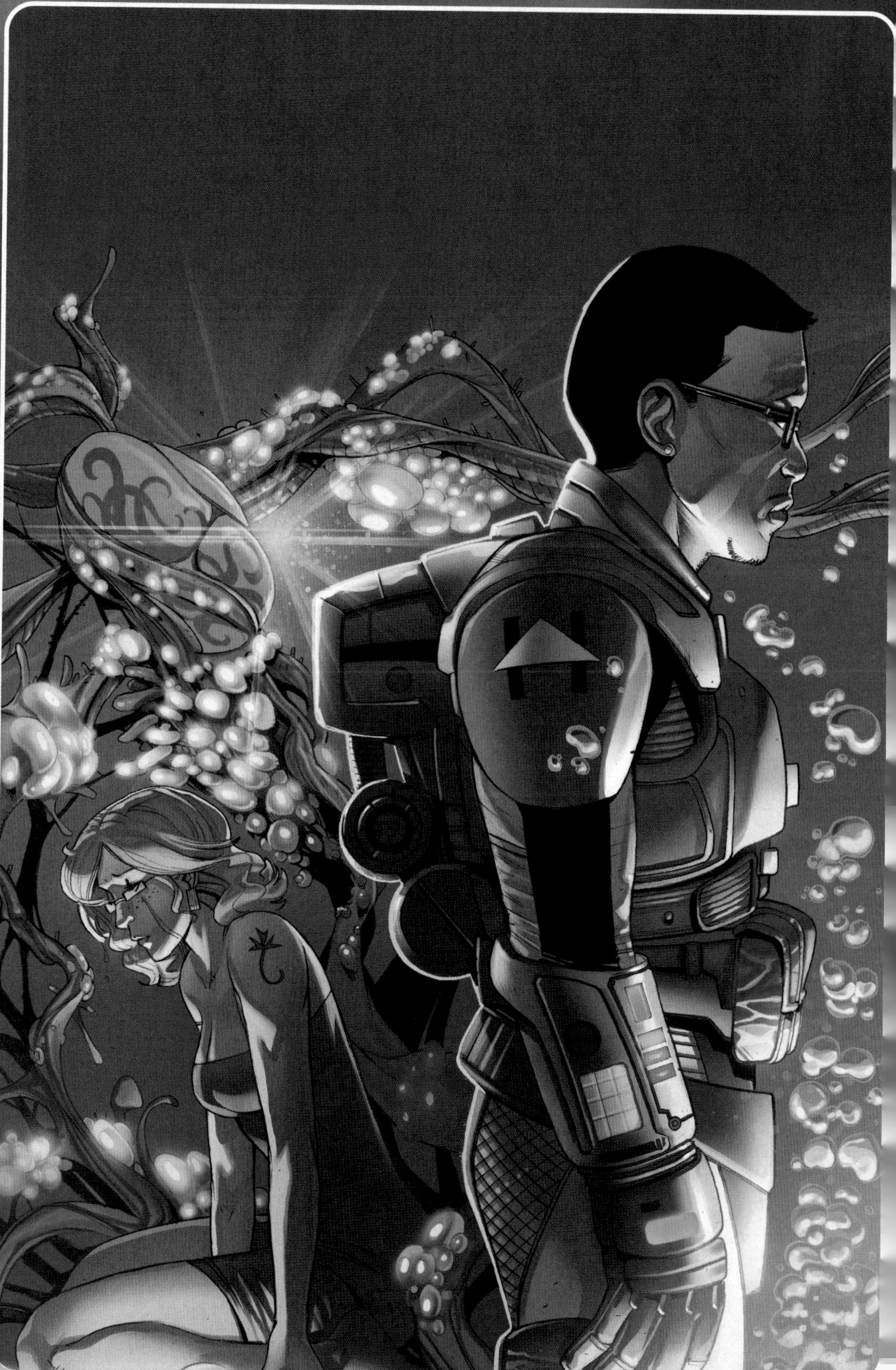

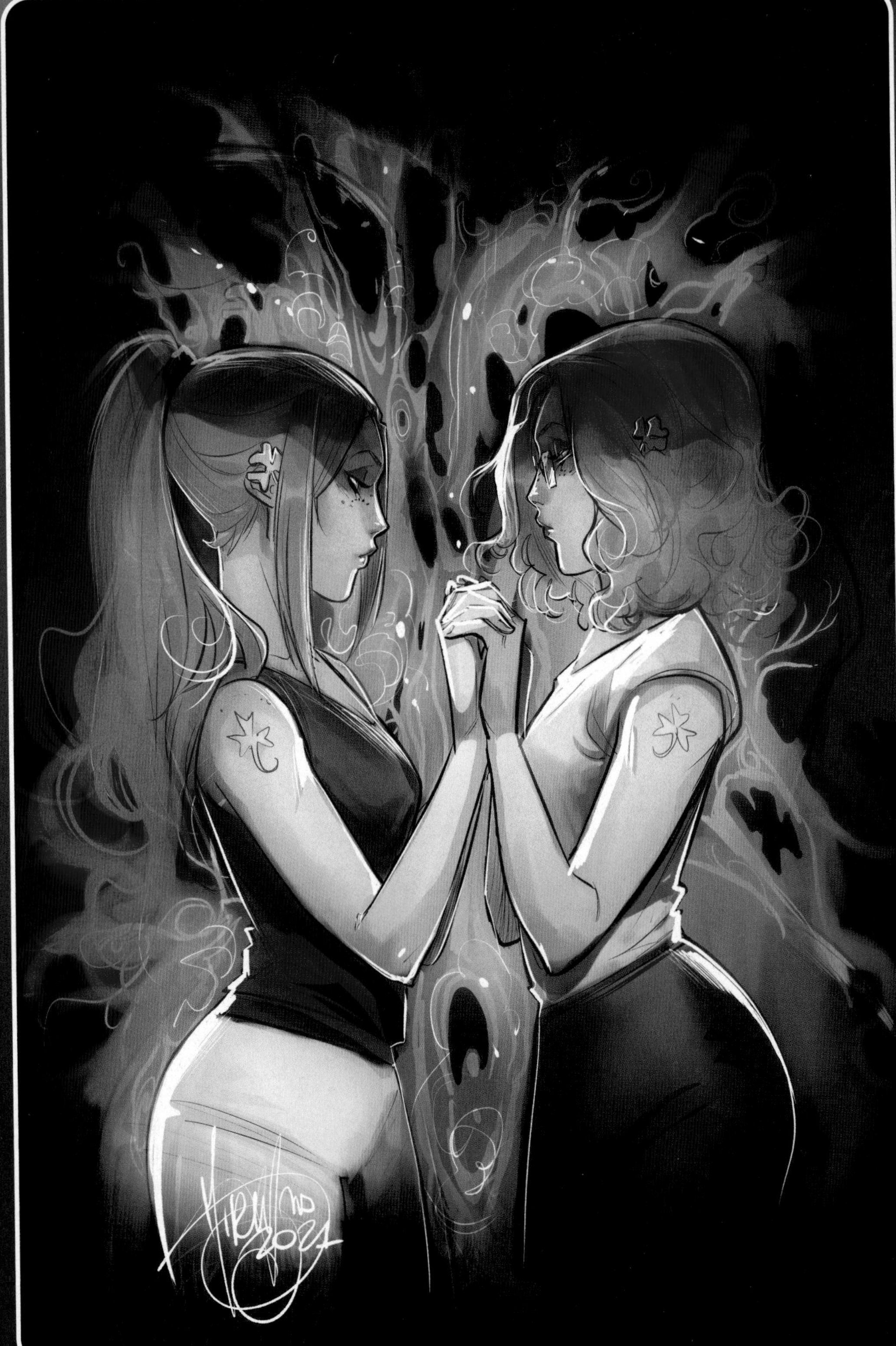

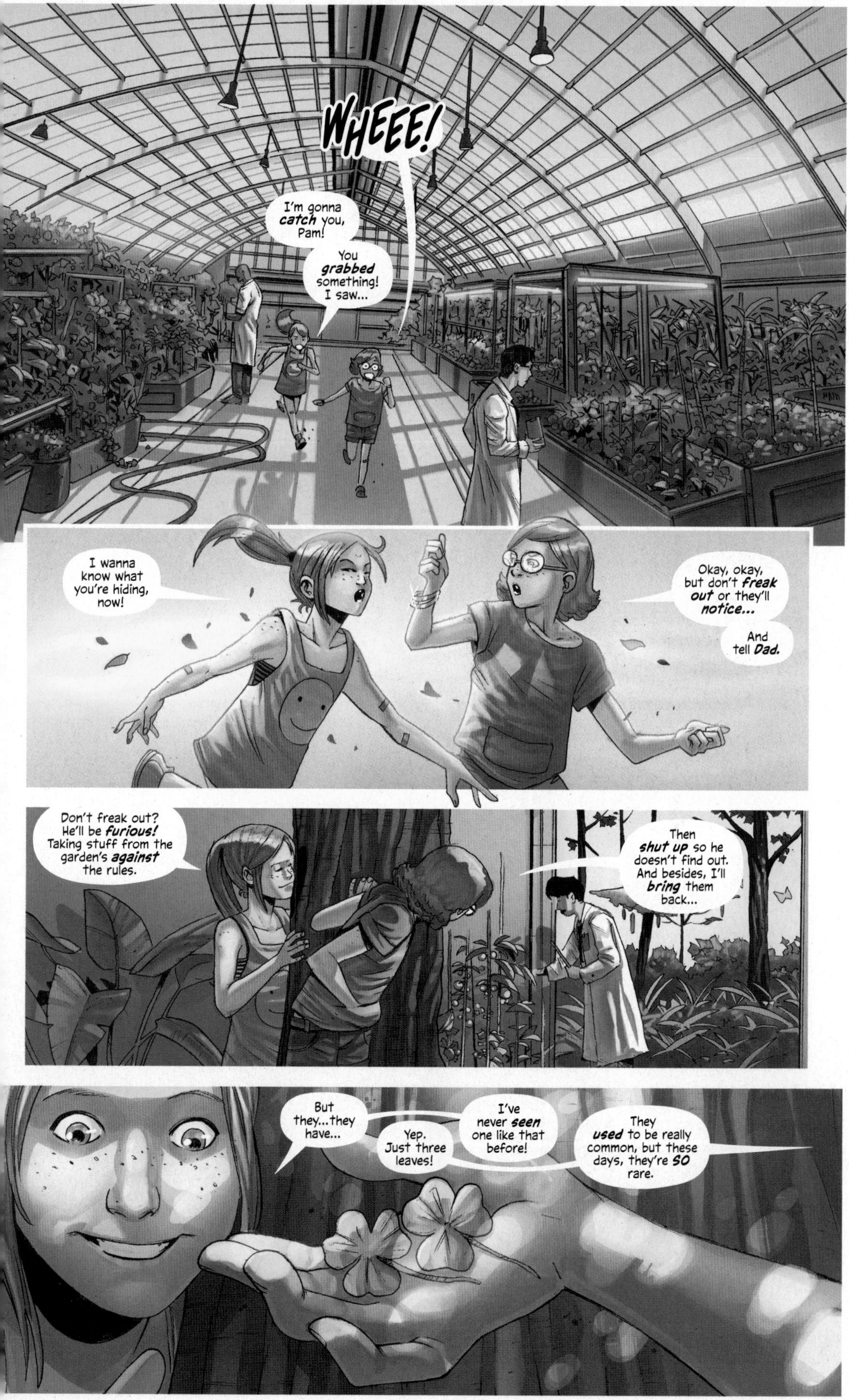
WHEEE!
I'm gonna catch you, Pam!
You grabbed something! I saw...
I wanna know what you're hiding, now!
Okay, okay, but don't freak out or they'll notice...
And tell Dad.
Don't freak out? He'll be furious! Taking stuff from the garden's against the rules.
Then shut up so he doesn't find out. And besides, I'll bring them back...
But they...they have...
Yep. Just three leaves!
I've never seen one like that before!
They used to be really common, but these days, they're SO rare.

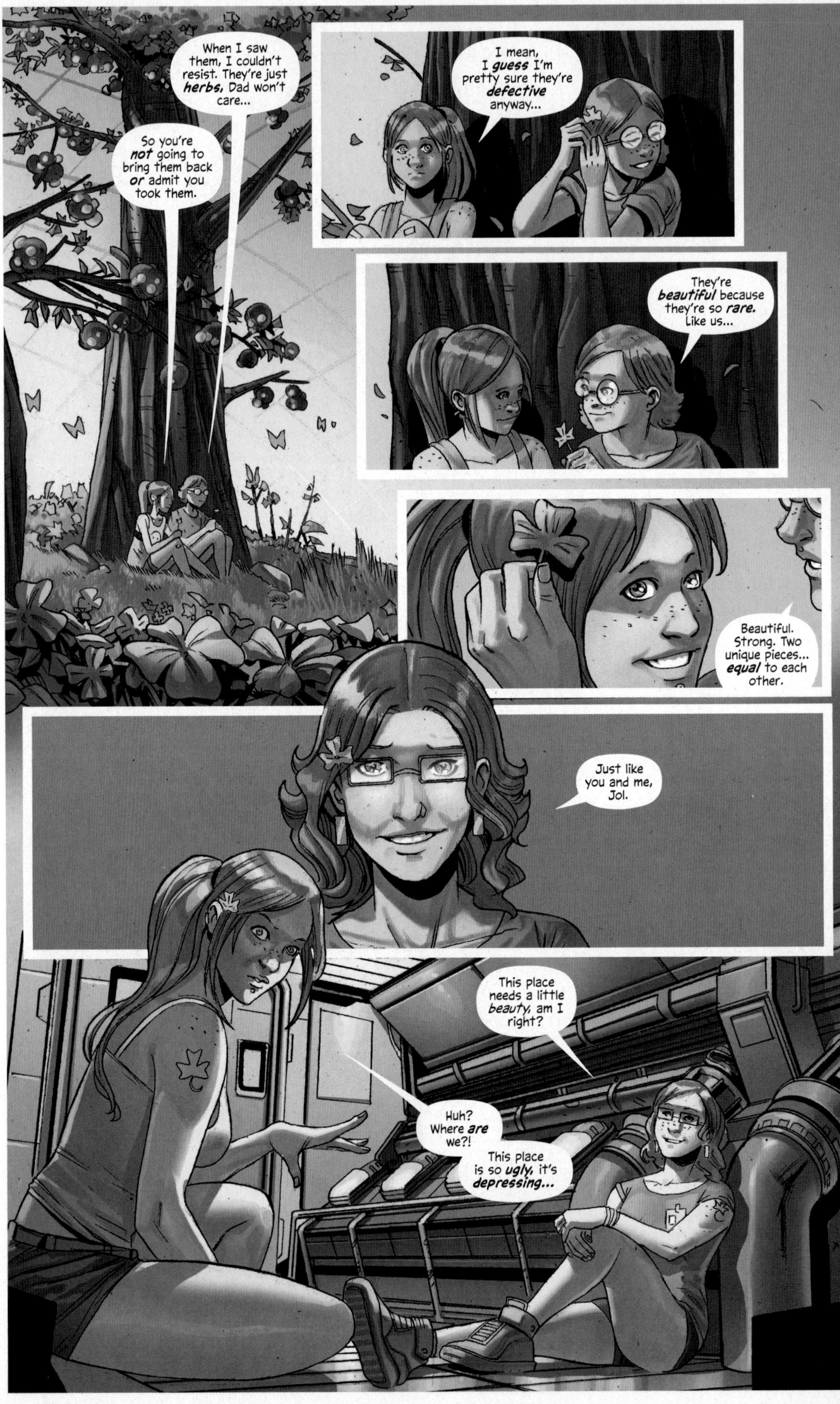

So you're **not** going to bring them back **or** admit you took them.
When I saw them, I couldn't resist. They're just **herbs,** Dad won't care...
I mean, I **guess** I'm pretty sure they're **defective** anyway...
They're **beautiful** because they're so **rare.** Like us...
Beautiful. Strong. Two unique pieces... **equal** to each other.
Just like you and me, Jol.
This place needs a little *beauty,* am I right?
Huh? Where **are** we?!
This place is so **ugly,** it's **depressing...**

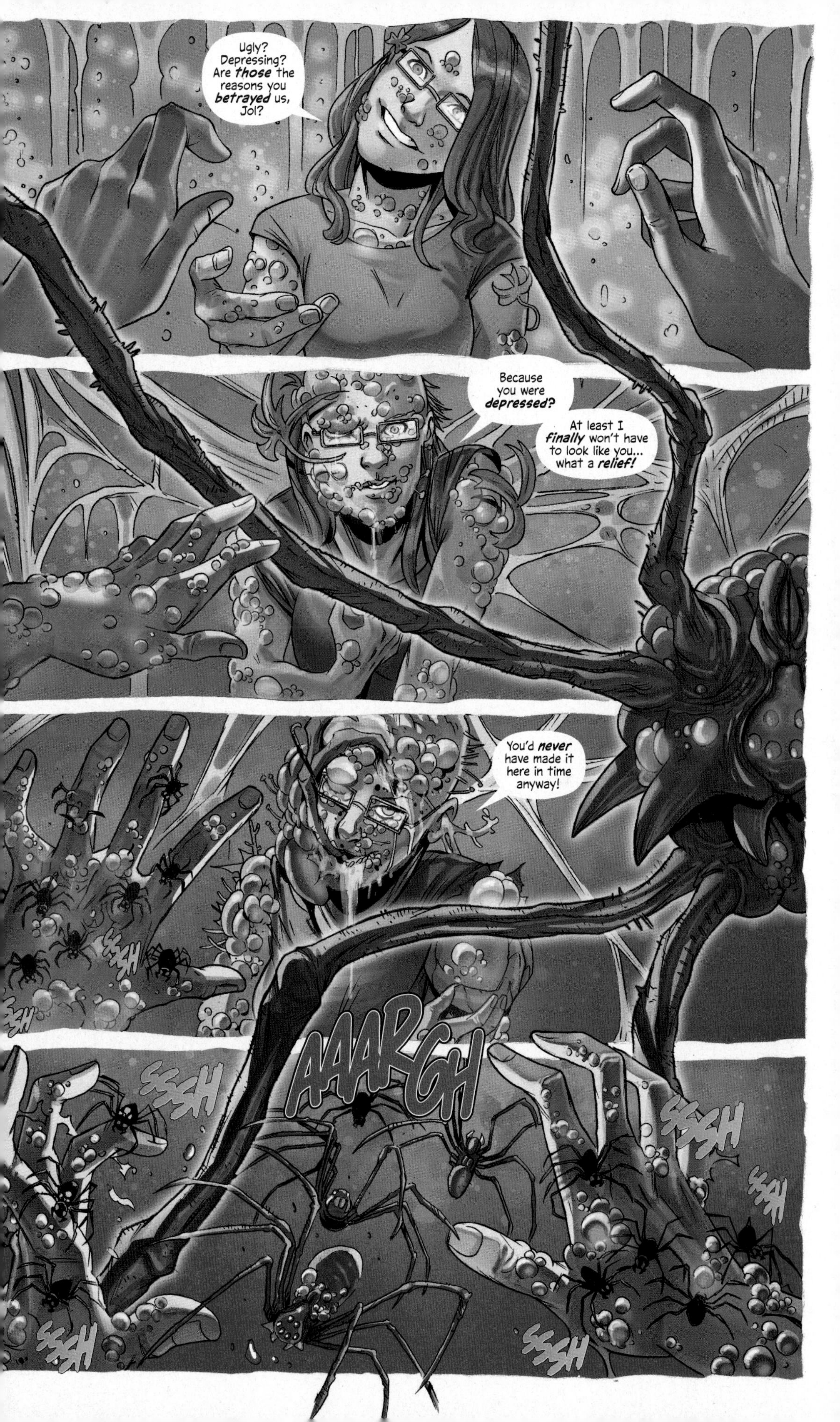
Ugly? Depressing? Are *those* the reasons you *betrayed* us, Jol?
Because you were *depressed?*
At least I *finally* won't have to look like you... what a *relief!*
You'd *never* have made it here in time anyway!
SSSH
SSH
AAARGH
SSSH
SSSH
SSSH
SSSH
SSSH

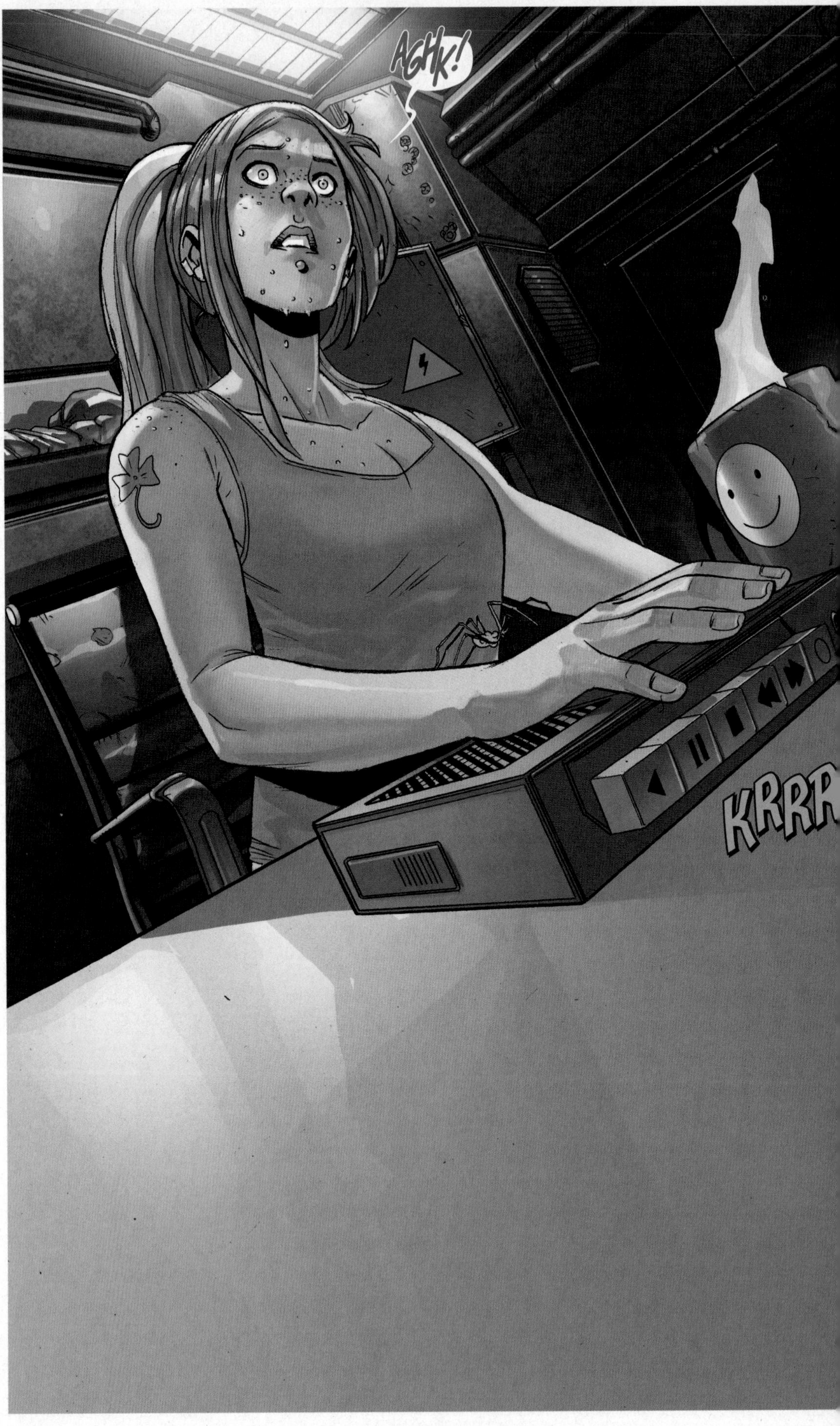
AGHK!
KRRR

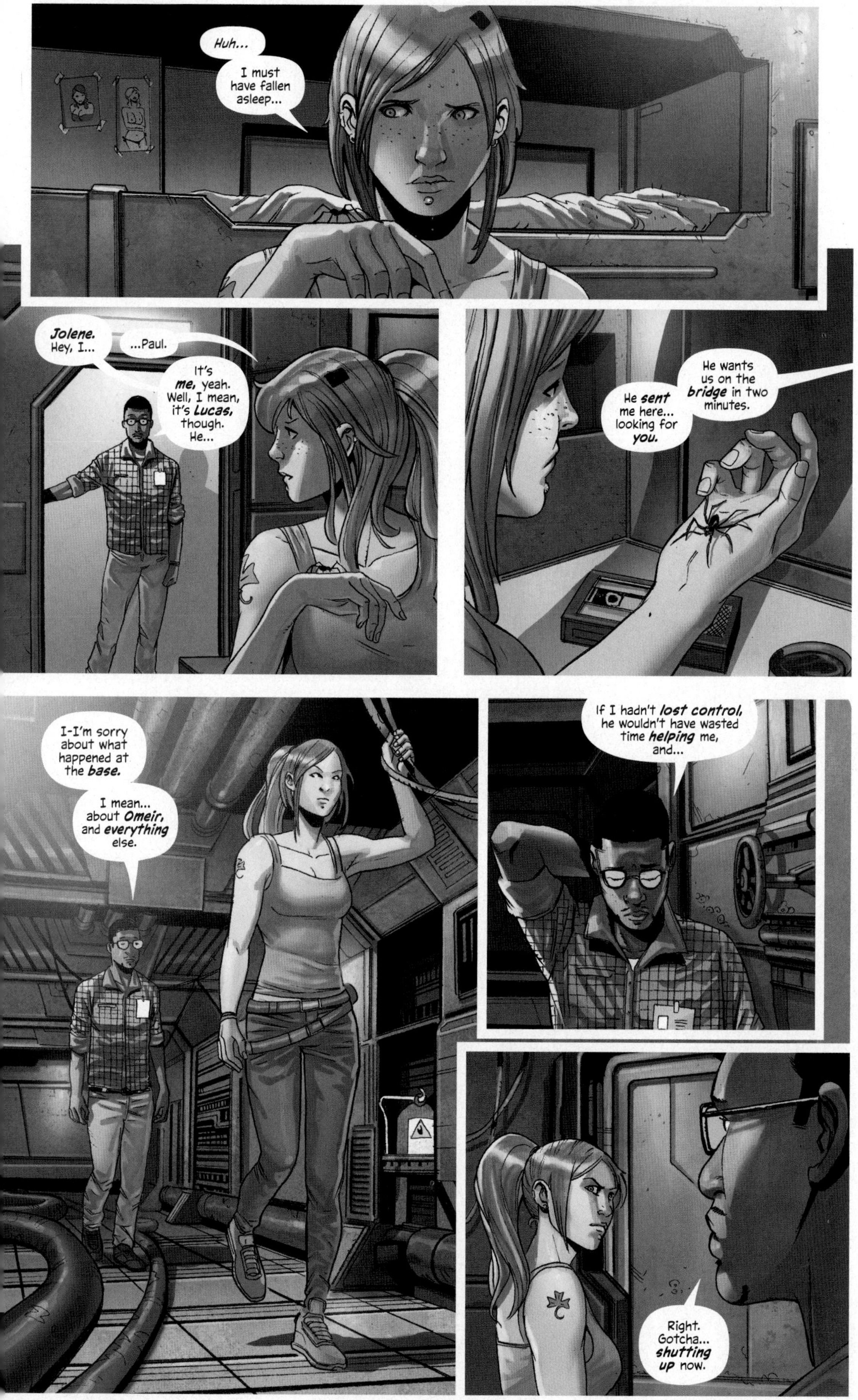
Huh...
I must have fallen asleep...
Jolene. Hey, I...
...Paul.
It's me, yeah. Well, I mean, it's Lucas, though. He...
He sent me here... looking for you.
He wants us on the bridge in two minutes.
I-I'm sorry about what happened at the base.
I mean... about Omeir, and everything else.
If I hadn't lost control, he wouldn't have wasted time helping me, and...
Right. Gotcha... shutting up now.

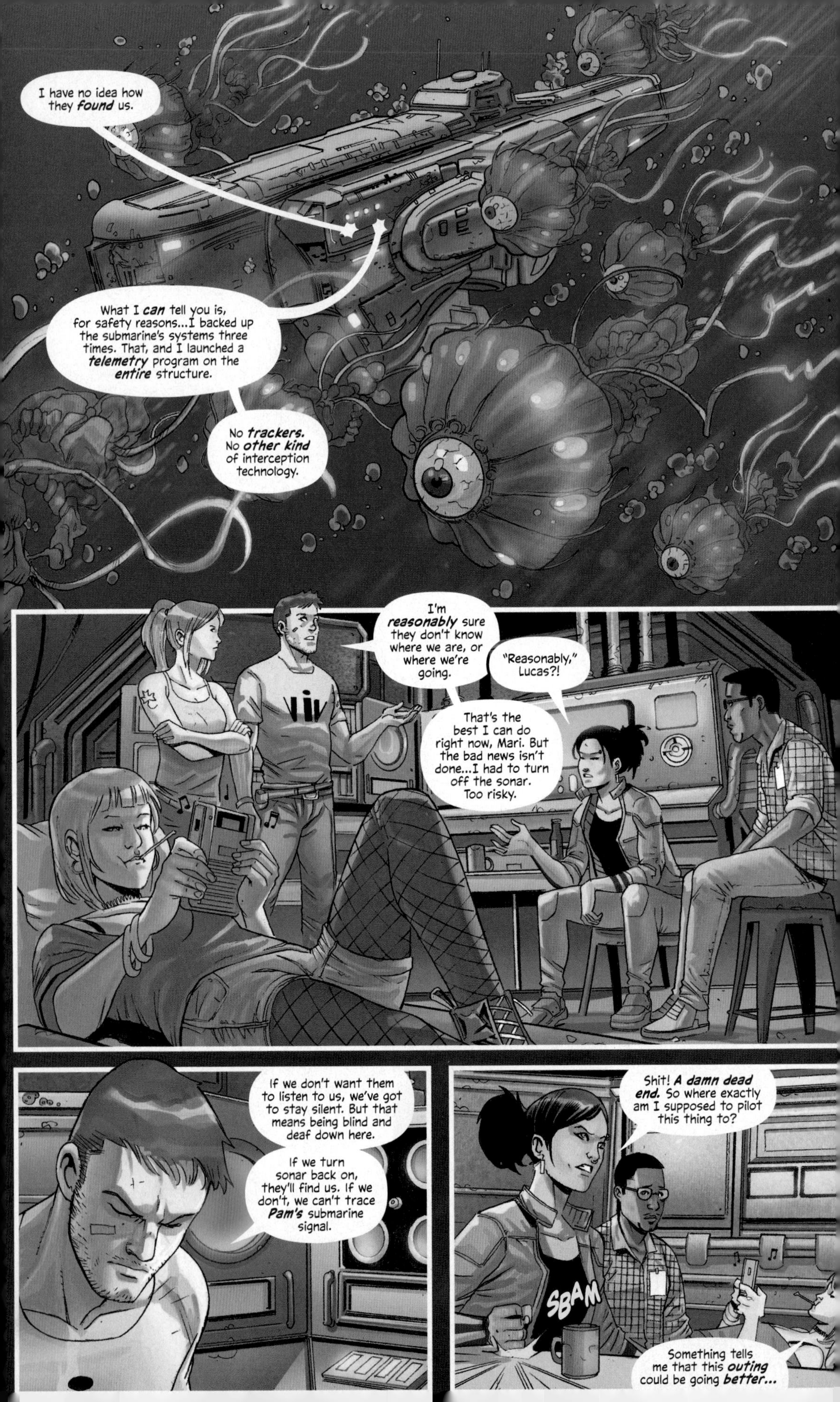
I have no idea how they found us.
What I can tell you is, for safety reasons...I backed up the submarine's systems three times. That, and I launched a telemetry program on the entire structure.
No trackers. No other kind of interception technology.
I'm reasonably sure they don't know where we are, or where we're going.
"Reasonably," Lucas?!
That's the best I can do right now, Mari. But the bad news isn't done...I had to turn off the sonar. Too risky.
If we don't want them to listen to us, we've got to stay silent. But that means being blind and deaf down here.
If we turn sonar back on, they'll find us. If we don't, we can't trace Pam's submarine signal.
Shit! A damn dead end. So where exactly am I supposed to pilot this thing to?
SBAM
Something tells me that this outing could be going better...

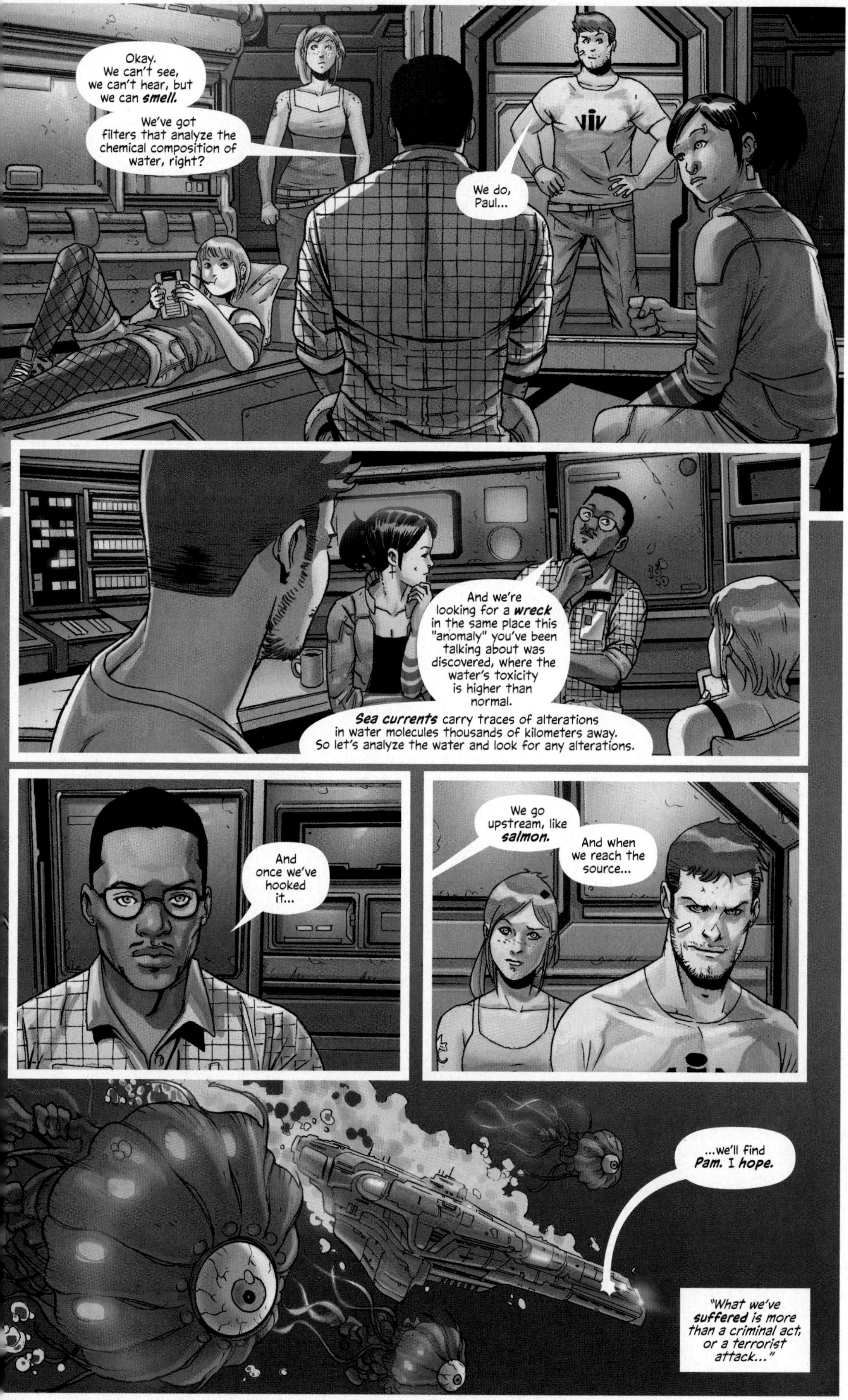

Okay. We can't see, we can't hear, but we can **smell.**
We've got filters that analyze the chemical composition of water, right?
We do, Paul...
And we're looking for a **wreck** in the same place this "anomaly" you've been talking about was discovered, where the water's toxicity is higher than normal.
Sea currents carry traces of alterations in water molecules thousands of kilometers away. So let's analyze the water and look for any alterations.
And once we've hooked it...
We go upstream, like **salmon.**
And when we reach the source...
...we'll find **Pam.** I **hope.**
"What we've **suffered** is more than a criminal act, or a terrorist attack..."

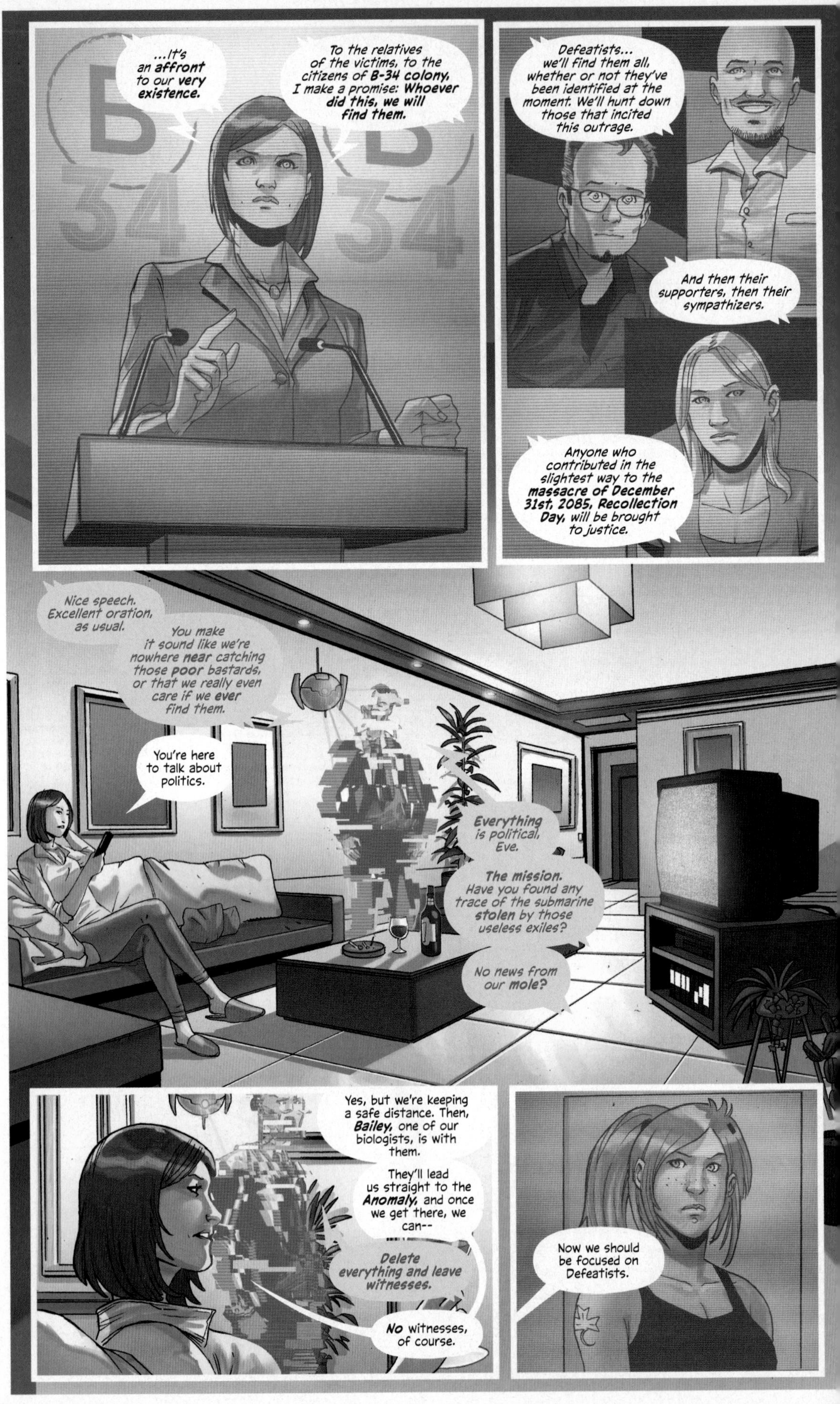

...It's an affront to our very existence.
To the relatives of the victims, to the citizens of B-34 colony, I make a promise: Whoever did this, we will find them.
Defeatists... we'll find them all, whether or not they've been identified at the moment. We'll hunt down those that incited this outrage.
And then their supporters, then their sympathizers.
Anyone who contributed in the slightest way to the massacre of December 31st, 2085, Recollection Day, will be brought to justice.
Nice speech. Excellent oration, as usual.
You make it sound like we're nowhere near catching those poor bastards, or that we really even care if we ever find them.
You're here to talk about politics.
Everything is political, Eve.
The mission. Have you found any trace of the submarine stolen by those useless exiles?
No news from our mole?
Yes, but we're keeping a safe distance. Then, Bailey, one of our biologists, is with them.
They'll lead us straight to the Anomaly, and once we get there, we can--
Delete everything and leave witnesses.
No witnesses, of course.
Now we should be focused on Defeatists.

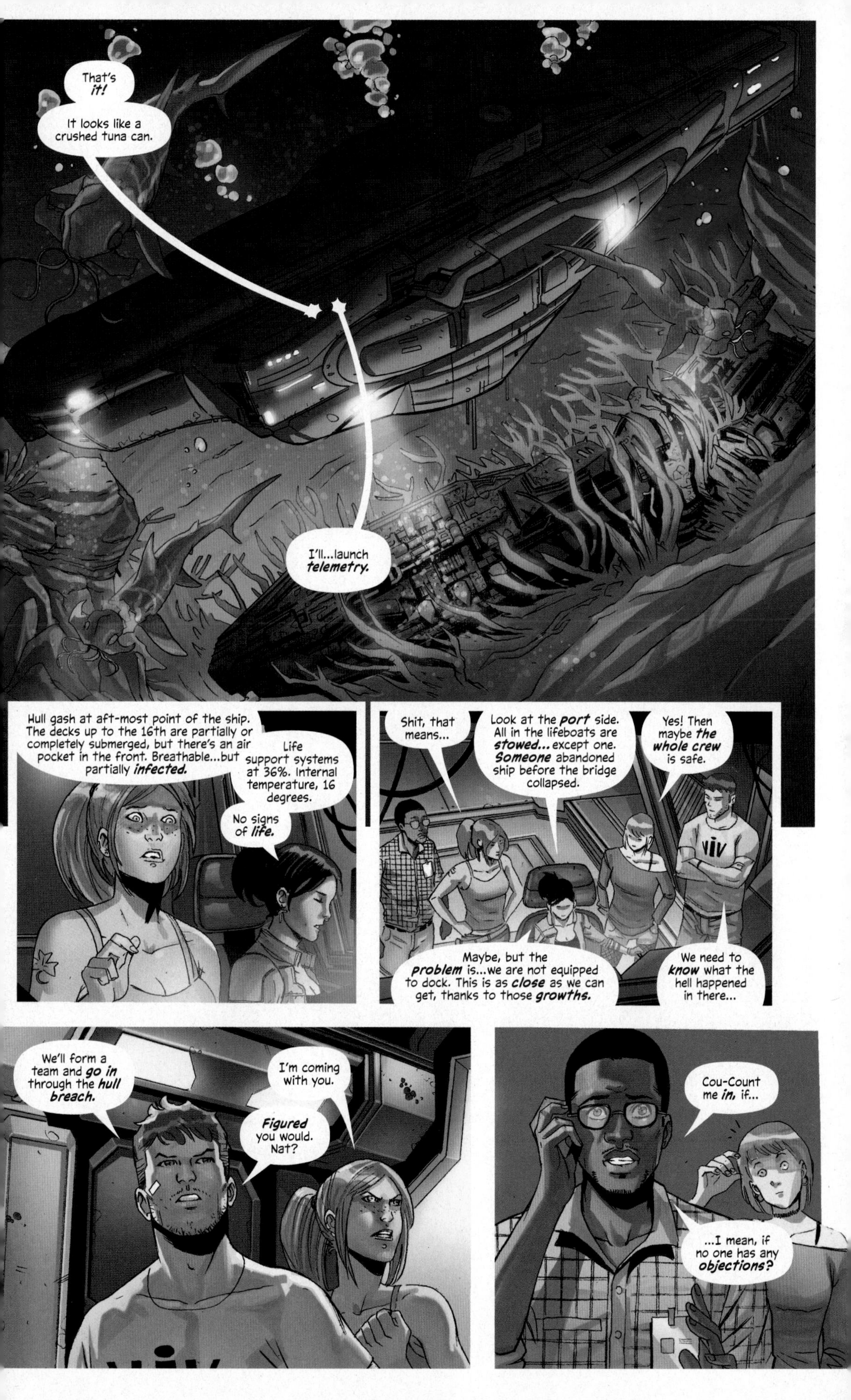
That's it!
It looks like a crushed tuna can.
I'll...launch telemetry.
Hull gash at aft-most point of the ship. The decks up to the 16th are partially or completely submerged, but there's an air pocket in the front. Breathable...but partially infected.
Life support systems at 36%. Internal temperature, 16 degrees.
No signs of life.
Shit, that means...
Look at the port side. All in the lifeboats are stowed... except one. Someone abandoned ship before the bridge collapsed.
Yes! Then maybe the whole crew is safe.
Maybe, but the problem is...we are not equipped to dock. This is as close as we can get, thanks to those growths.
We need to know what the hell happened in there...
We'll form a team and go in through the hull breach.
I'm coming with you.
Figured you would. Nat?
Cou-Count me in, if...
...I mean, if no one has any objections?

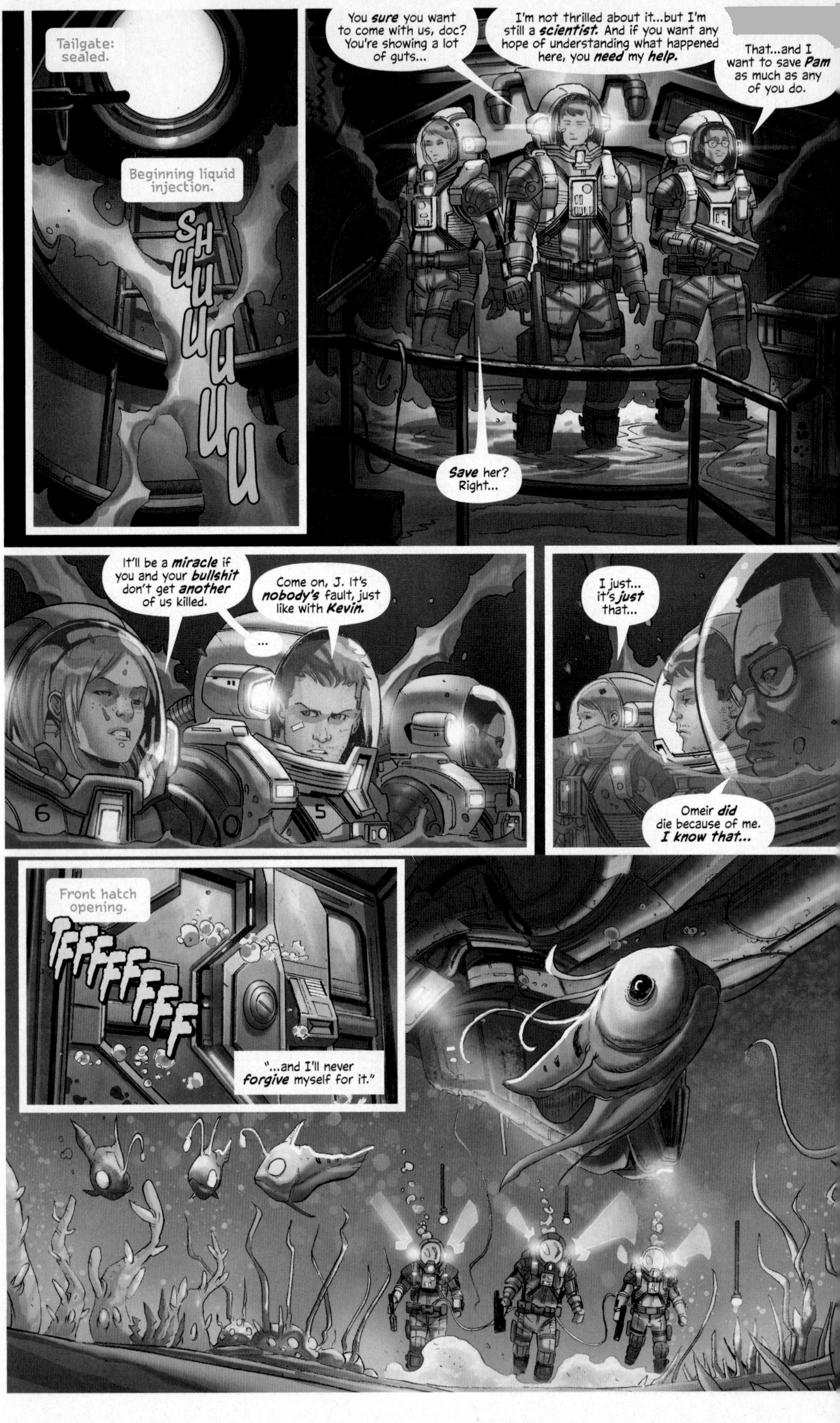

Tailgate: sealed.
Beginning liquid injection.
SHUUUUUUU
You sure you want to come with us, doc? You're showing a lot of guts...
I'm not thrilled about it...but I'm still a scientist. And if you want any hope of understanding what happened here, you need my help.
That...and I want to save Pam as much as any of you do.
Save her? Right...
It'll be a miracle if you and your bullshit don't get another of us killed.
...
Come on, J. It's nobody's fault, just like with Kevin.
6
5
I just... it's just that...
Omeir did die because of me. I know that...
Front hatch opening.
TFFFFFFFFF
"...and I'll never forgive myself for it."

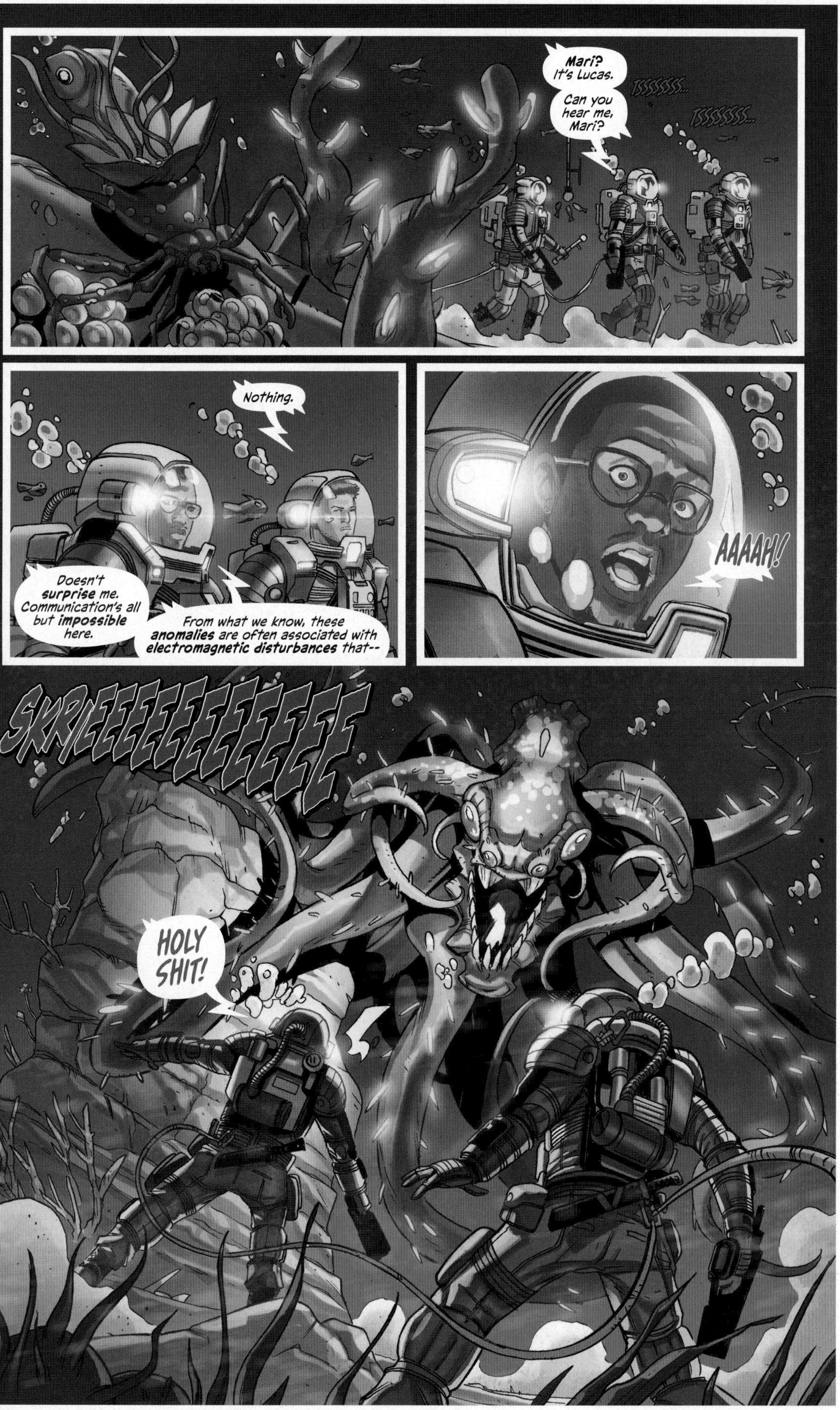
Mari?
It's Lucas.
Can you hear me, Mari?
TSSSSSSS...
TSSSSSSS...
Nothing.
Doesn't surprise me. Communication's all but impossible here.
From what we know, these anomalies are often associated with electromagnetic disturbances that--
AAAAH!
SKRIEEEEEEEEEEEEE
HOLY SHIT!

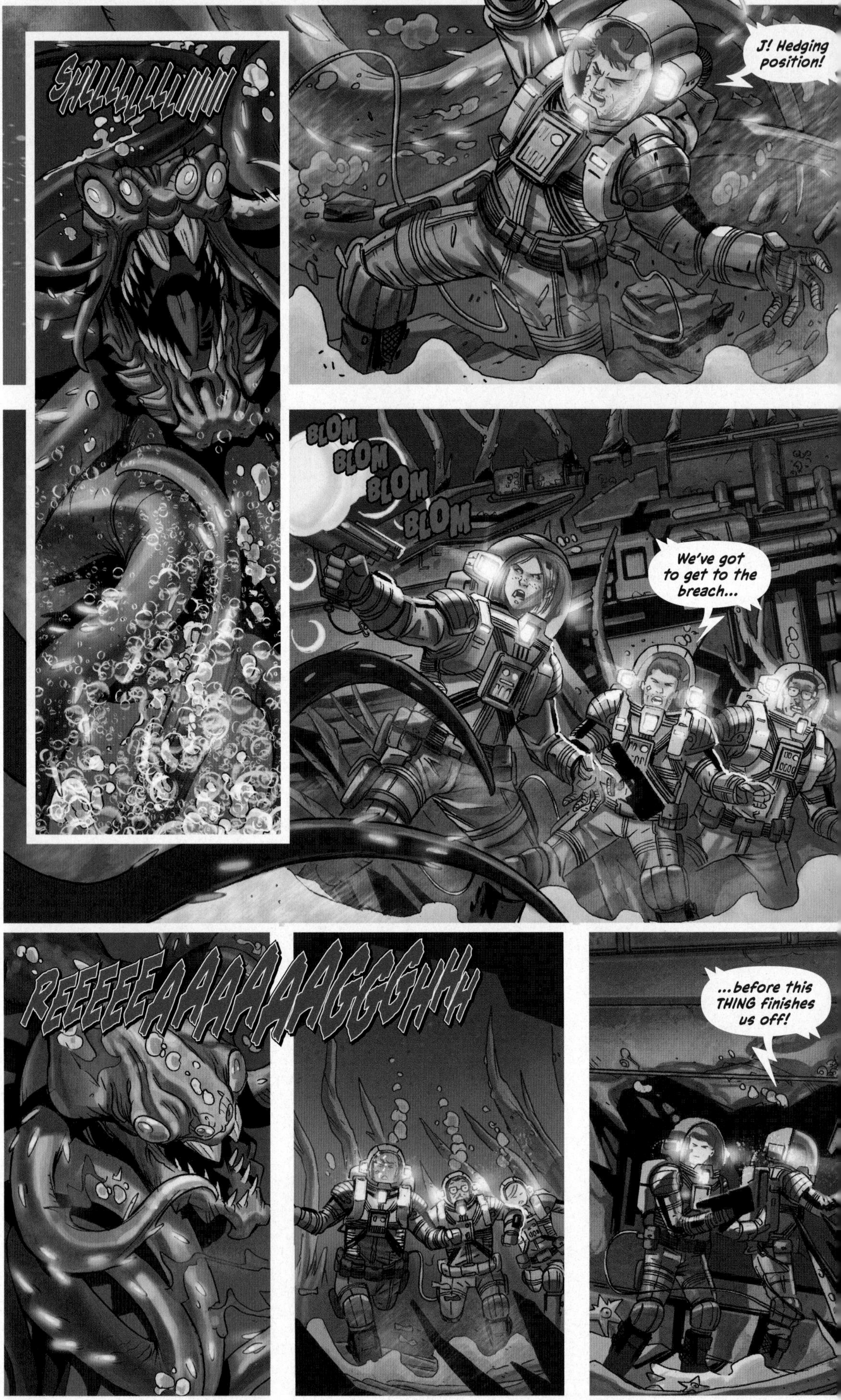
SHLLLLLLLLIIIIIII
J! Hedging position!
BLOM
BLOM
BLOM
BLOM
We've got to get to the breach...
REEEEEAAAAAAAGGGGHHH
...before this THING finishes us off!

The *crew* consisted of *seven* members, but I only see *six* bodies here.

Then *Mari* was *right.* Someone got to a lifeboat and *escaped.*

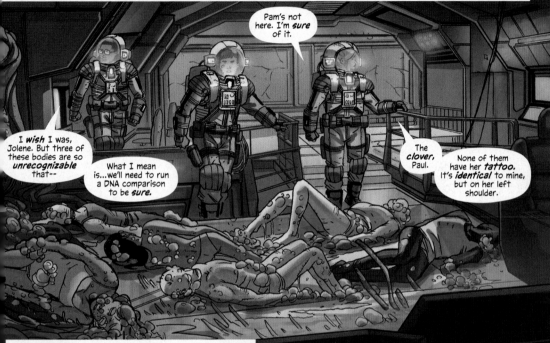

Pam's not here. I'm *sure* of it.

I *wish* I was, Jolene. But three of these bodies are so *unrecognizable* that--

What I mean is...we'll need to run a DNA comparison to be *sure.*

The *clover,* Paul.

None of them have her *tattoo.* It's *identical* to mine, but on her left shoulder.

She got *out* before this place collapsed. She would've tried to get to wherever the crew meant to go. Want to know where *she* is? Find out where *that* is.

And on the way...find out *exactly* what happened.

I've got *coordinates.* Jolene programmed all the lifeboats for the same destination. Maybe she *thought...* maybe she *hoped* her crew would catch up with her.

Eighty-eight nautical miles from here, north-northeast. But as far as we *know,* there's nothing there. And *that's* not even the *weirdest* thing...

The *Anomaly Detector* is out of order.

This is like...the computer equivalent of an *Egyptian tomb.* The file formats here were current a *century* ago. This is *Pre-catastrophe stuff.* You know how *rare* documents from that time are?

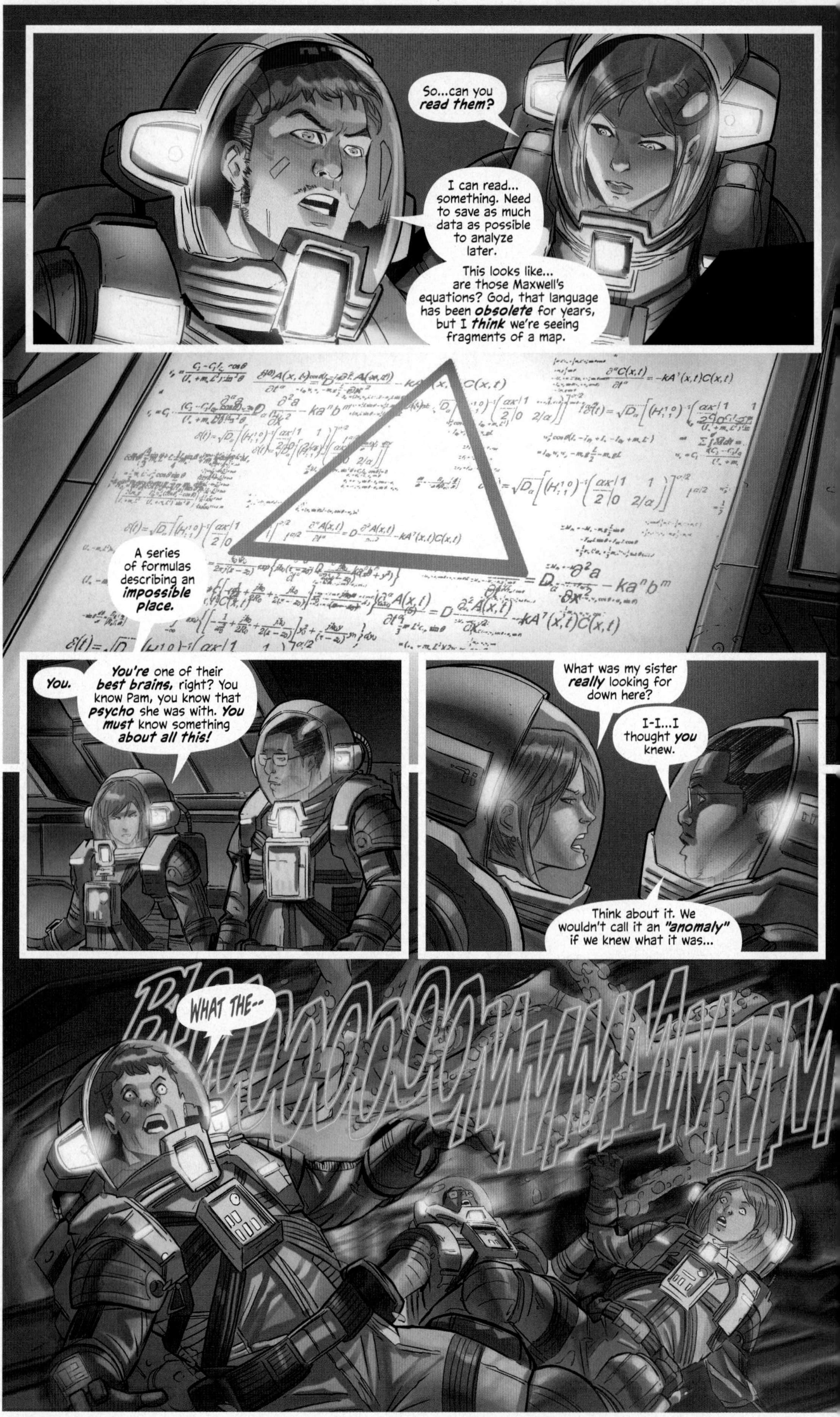
So...can you *read them?*
I can read... something. Need to save as much data as possible to analyze later.
This looks like... are those Maxwell's equations? God, that language has been *obsolete* for years, but I *think* we're seeing fragments of a map.
A series of formulas describing an *impossible place.*
You.
You're one of their *best brains,* right? You know Pam, you know that *psycho* she was with. *You must* know something *about all this!*
What was my sister *really* looking for down here?
I-I...I thought *you* knew.
Think about it. We wouldn't call it an *"anomaly"* if we knew what it was...
WHAT THE--

Is that... that *beast* again?

Uhhnn... no. That was *metal* on metal, rang like a damn *bell.*

"That's no *beast* that's *hooked* us."

CRREEEAKKLEEE

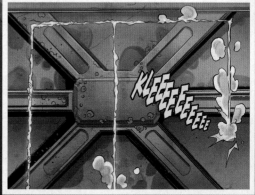

KLEEEEEEEEE

BAM

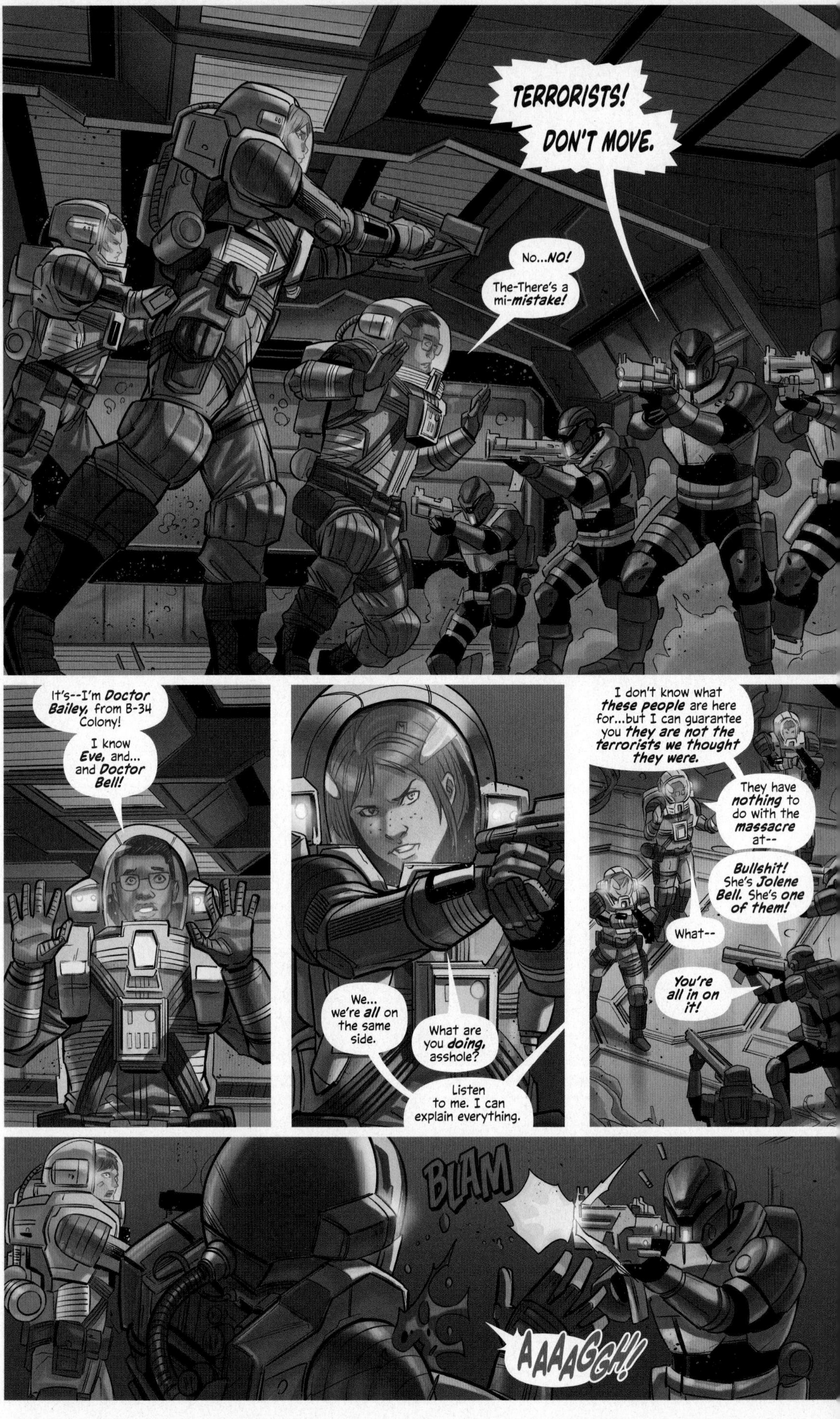
TERRORISTS!
DON'T MOVE.
No...NO!
The-There's a mi-mistake!
It's--I'm Doctor Bailey, from B-34 Colony!
I know Eve, and... and Doctor Bell!
We... we're all on the same side.
What are you doing, asshole?
Listen to me. I can explain everything.
I don't know what these people are here for...but I can guarantee you they are not the terrorists we thought they were.
They have nothing to do with the massacre at--
Bullshit! She's Jolene Bell. She's one of them!
What--
You're all in on it!
BLAM
AAAAGGH!

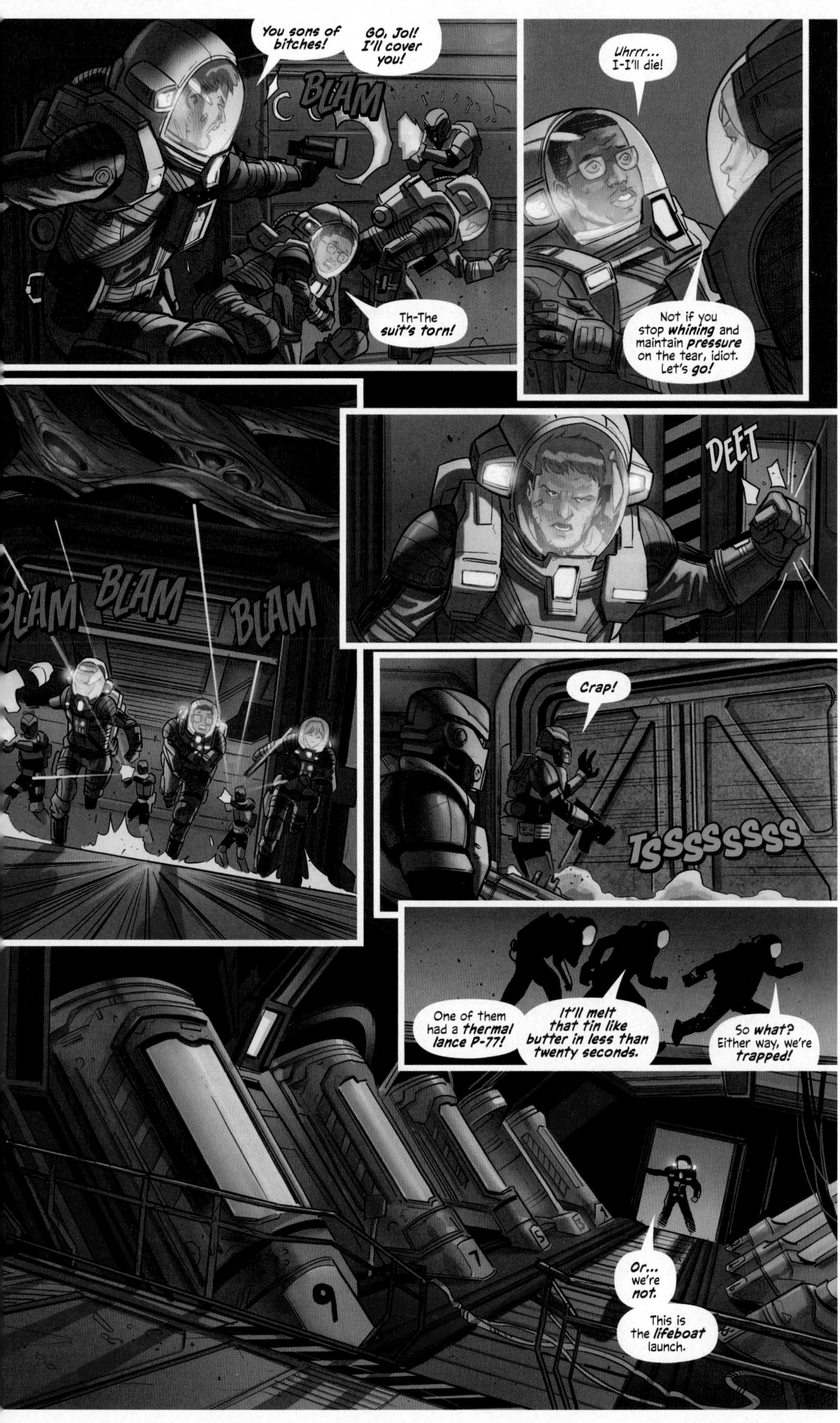
You sons of bitches!
GO, Jol! I'll cover you!
BLAM
Th-The suit's torn!
Uhrrr... I-I'll die!
Not if you stop whining and maintain pressure on the tear, idiot. Let's go!
BLAM
BLAM
BLAM
DEET
Crap!
TSSSSSSSS
One of them had a thermal lance P-77!
It'll melt that tin like butter in less than twenty seconds.
So what? Either way, we're trapped!
Or... we're not.
This is the lifeboat launch.

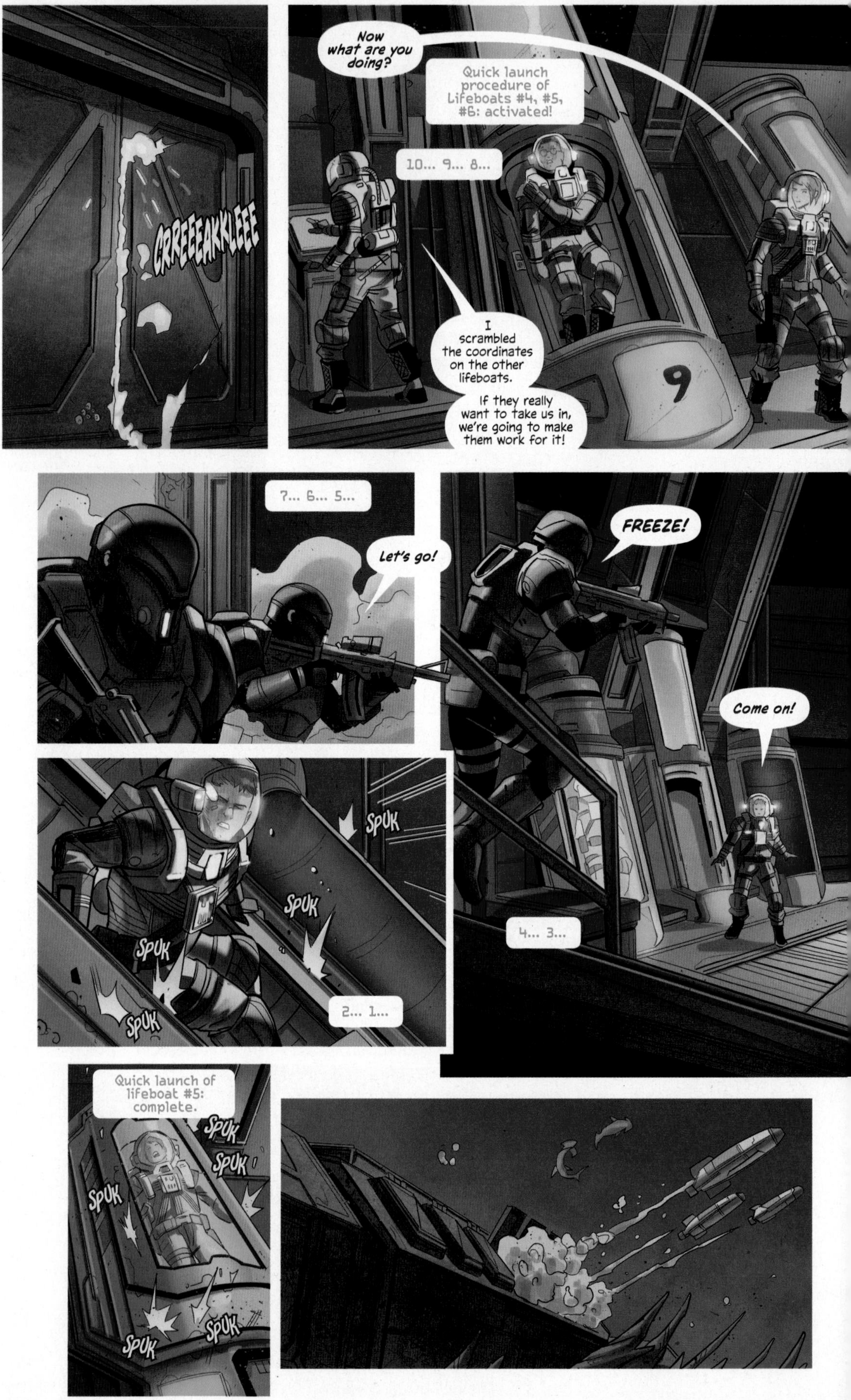
CRREEEAKKLEEE
Now what are you doing?
Quick launch procedure of Lifeboats #4, #5, #6: activated!
10... 9... 8...
I scrambled the coordinates on the other lifeboats.
If they really want to take us in, we're going to make them work for it!
9
7... 6... 5...
Let's go!
FREEZE!
Come on!
SPUK
SPUK
SPUK
SPUK
4... 3...
2... 1...
Quick launch of lifeboat #5: complete.
SPUK
SPUK
SPUK
SPUK
SPUK

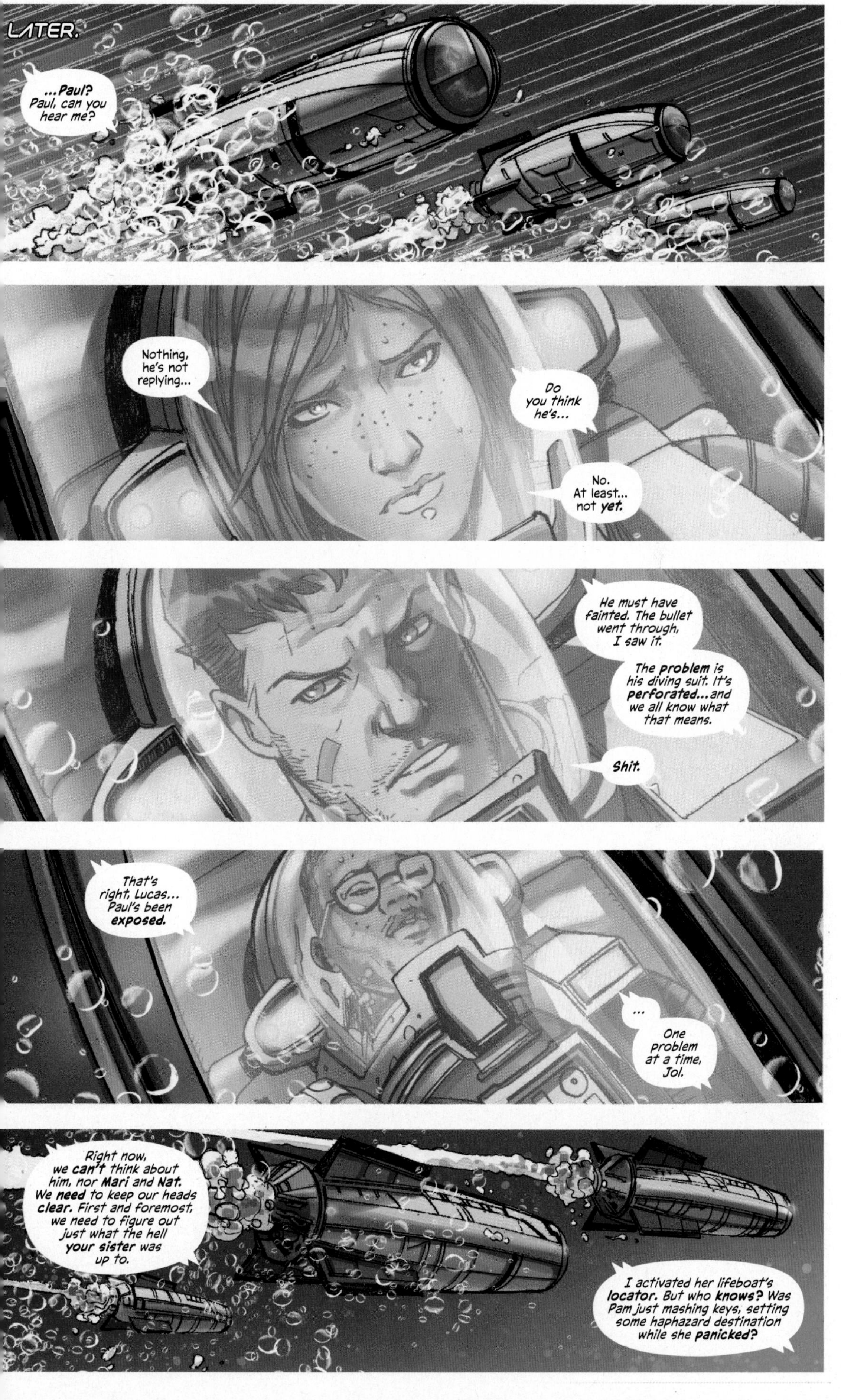
LATER.
...Paul? Paul, can you hear me?
Nothing, he's not replying...
Do you think he's...
No. At least... not yet.
He must have fainted. The bullet went through, I saw it.
The problem is his diving suit. It's perforated...and we all know what that means.
Shit.
That's right, Lucas... Paul's been exposed.
...
One problem at a time, Jol.
Right now, we can't think about him, nor Mari and Nat. We need to keep our heads clear. First and foremost, we need to figure out just what the hell your sister was up to.
I activated her lifeboat's locator. But who knows? Was Pam just mashing keys, setting some haphazard destination while she panicked?

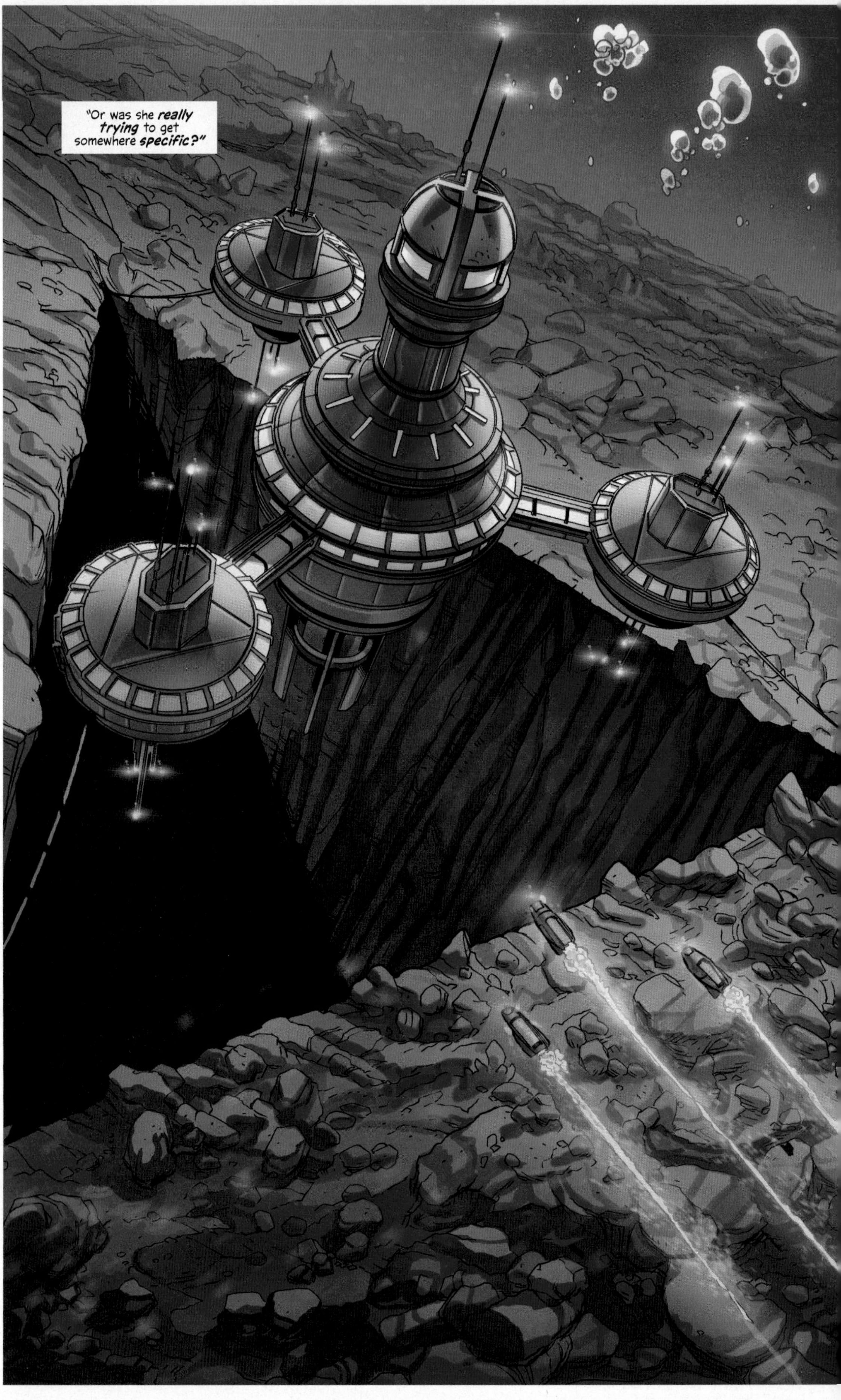
"Or was she *really* *trying* to get somewhere *specific?*"

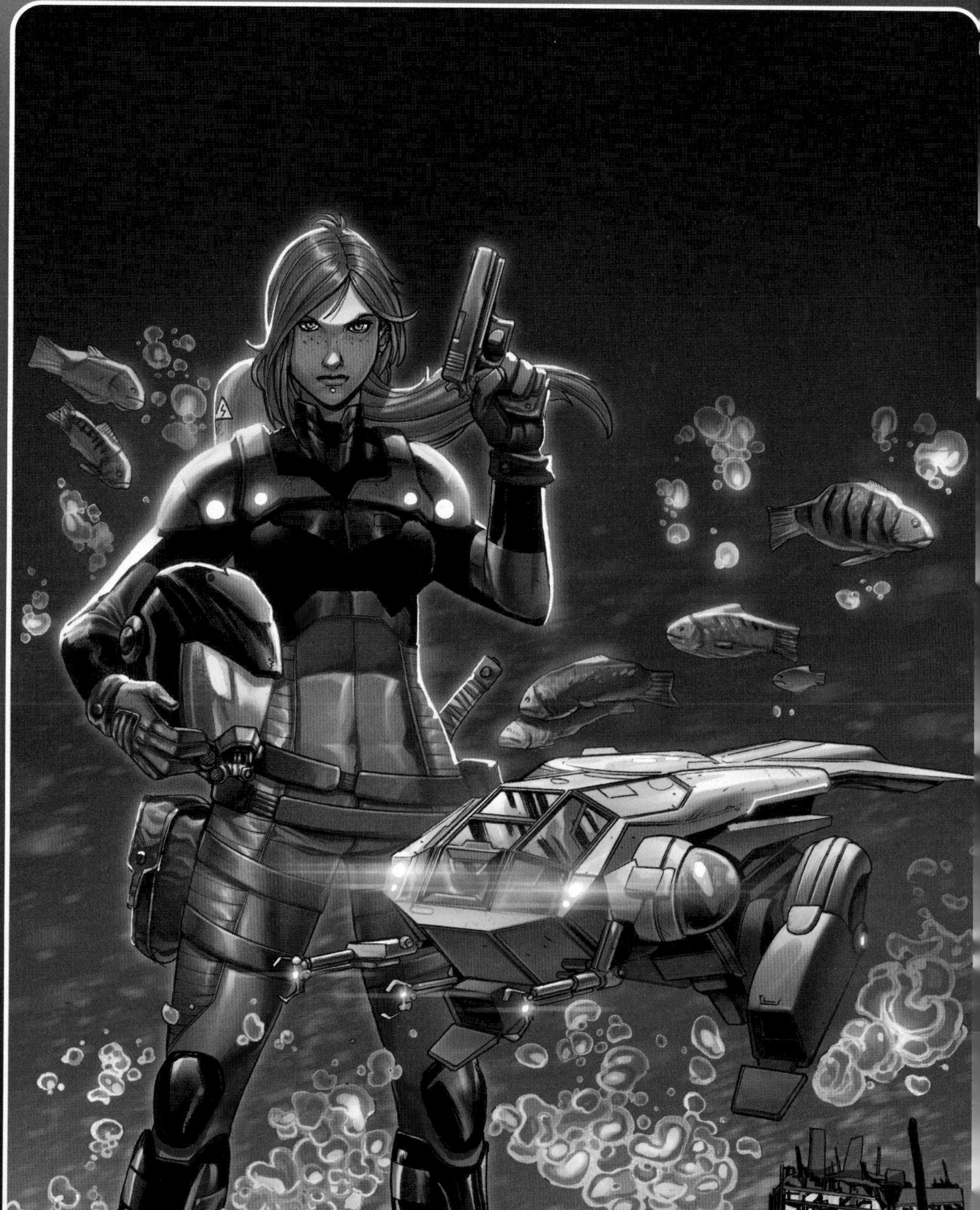

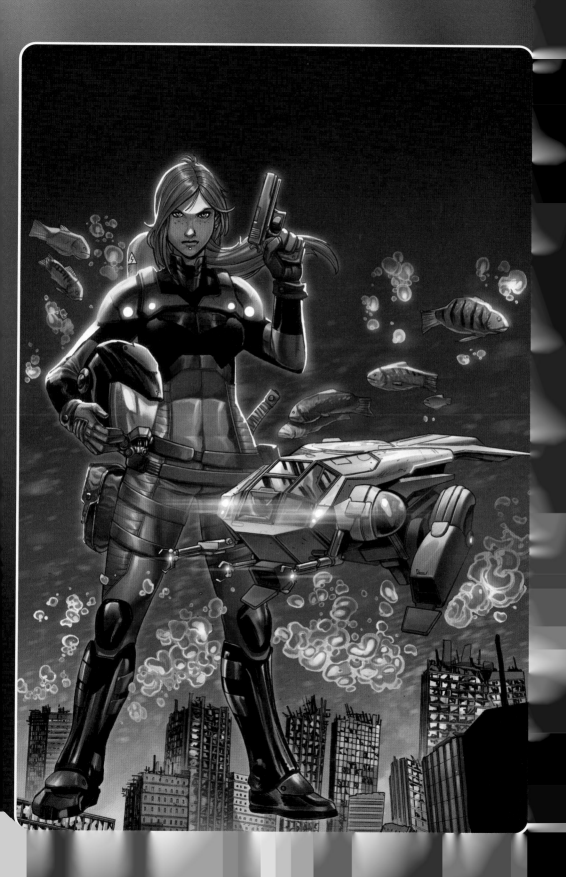

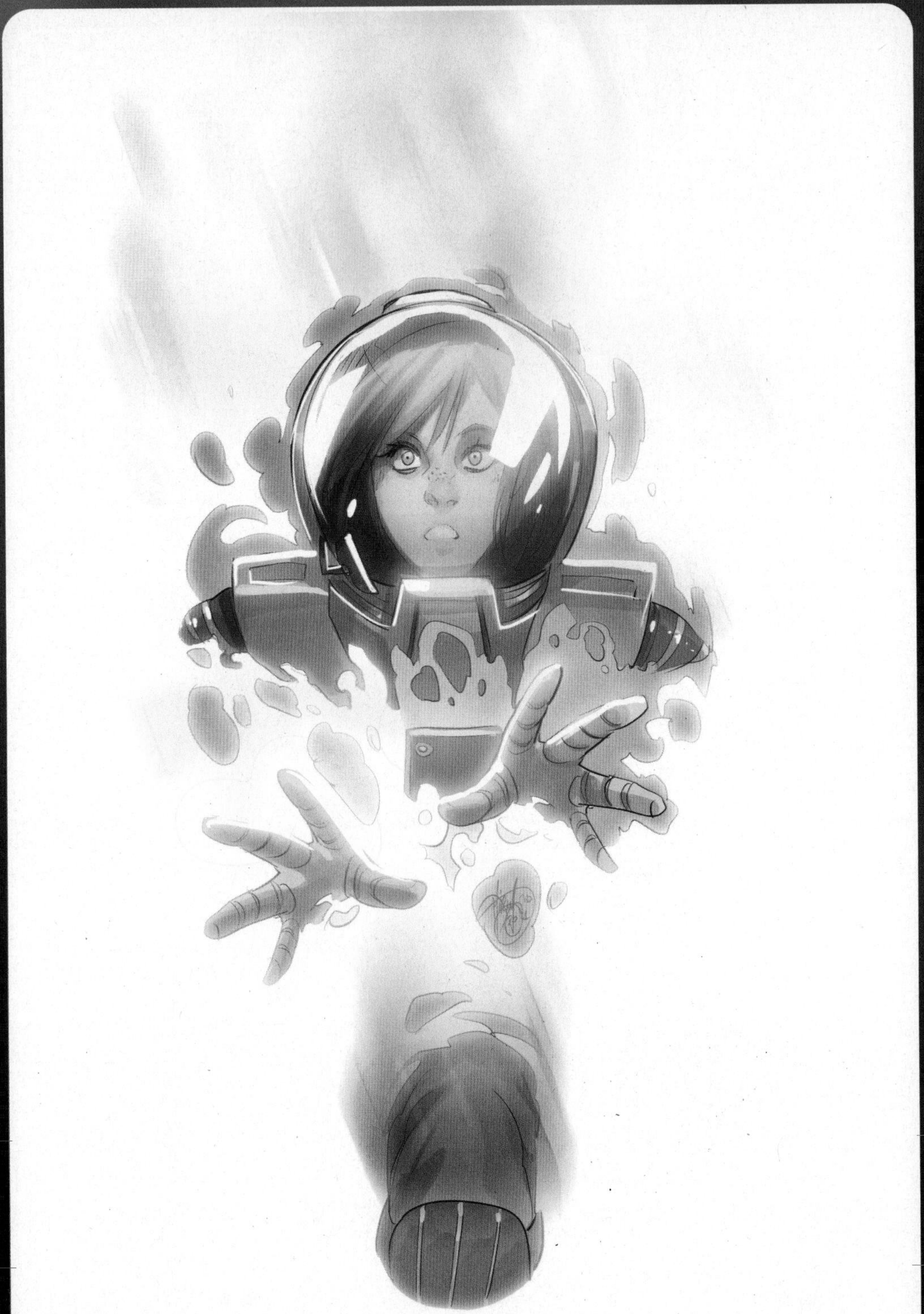

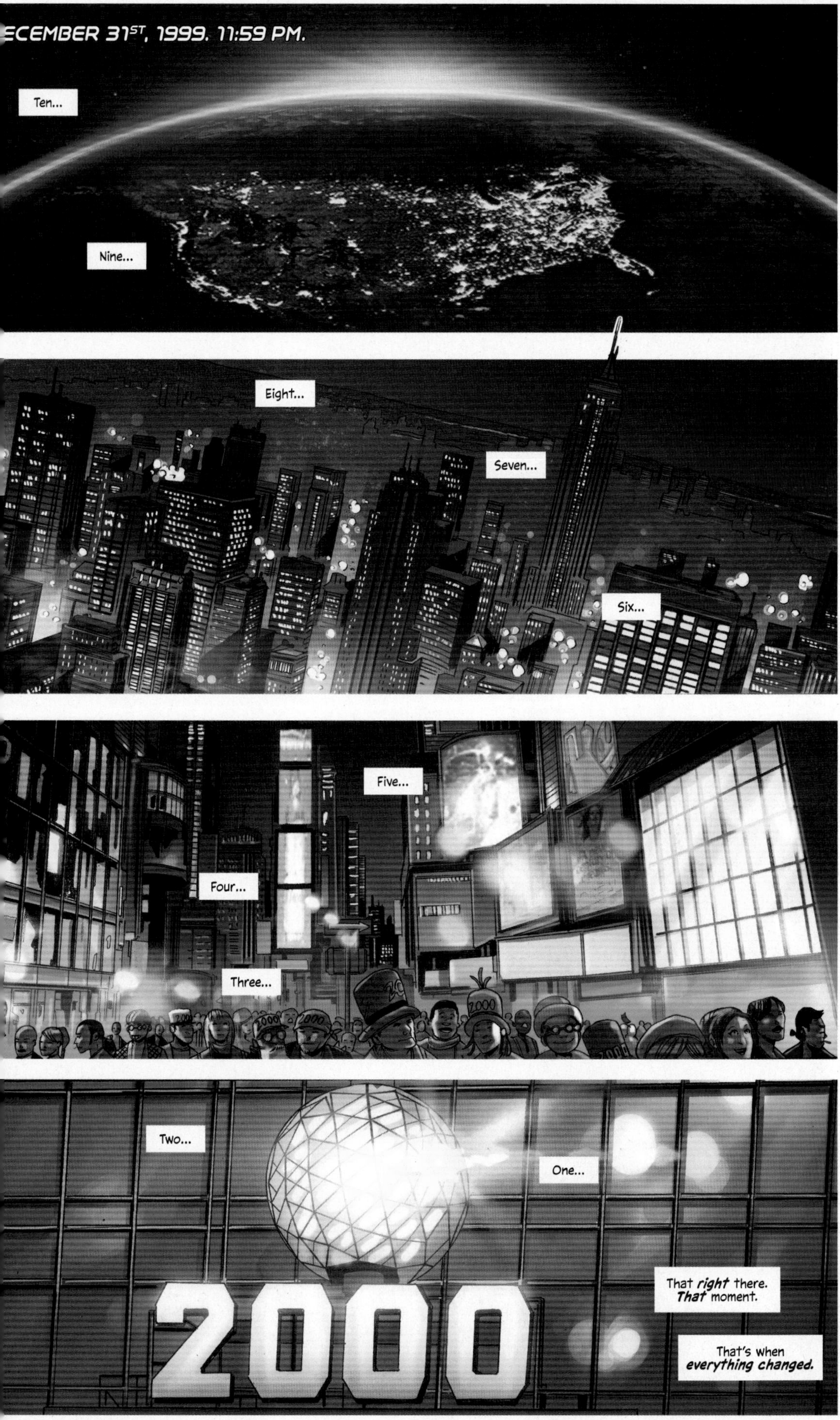
ECEMBER 31ST, 1999. 11:59 PM.
Ten...
Nine...
Eight...
Seven...
Six...
Five...
Four...
Three...
2000
2000
2000
Two...
One...
2000
That right there. That moment.
That's when everything changed.

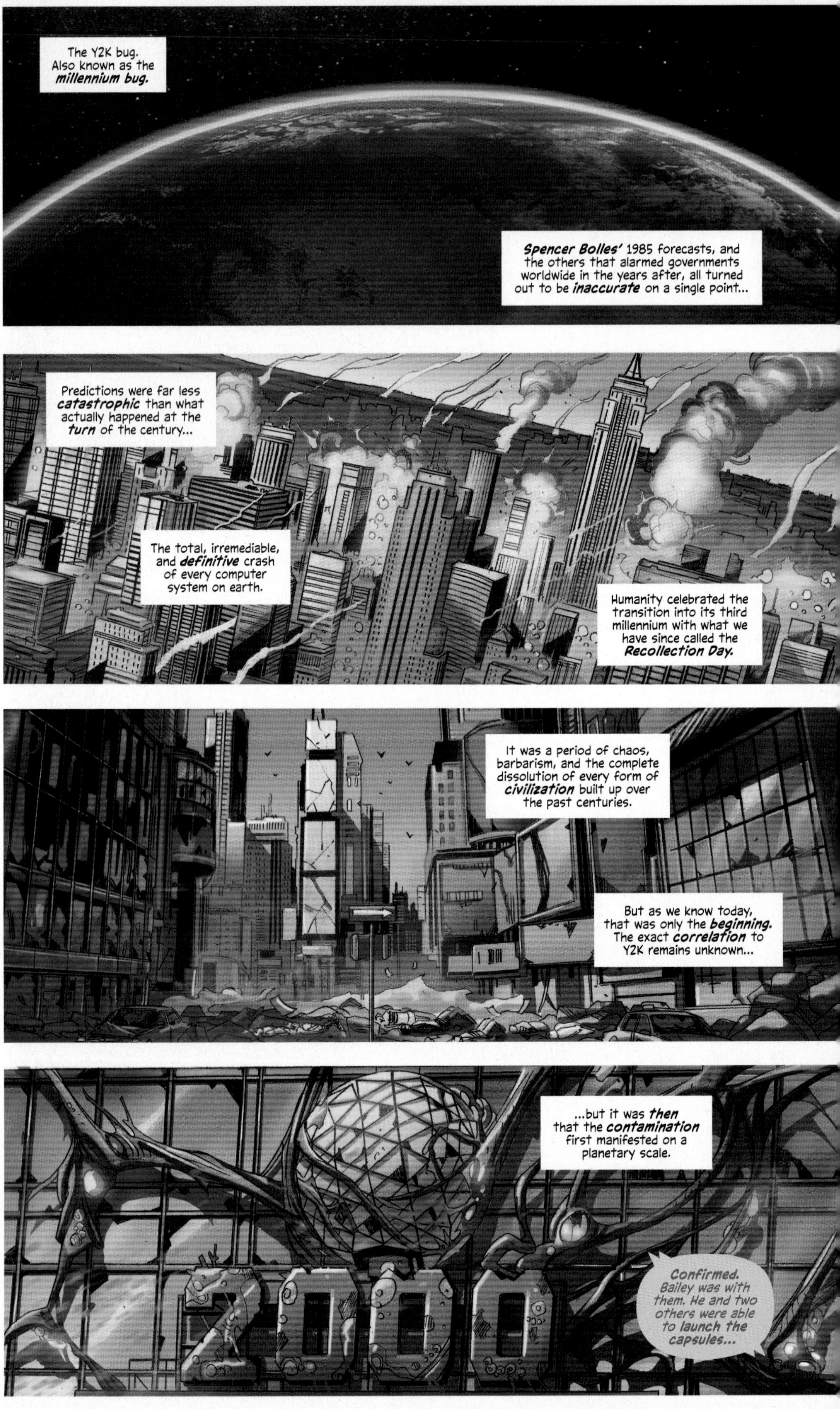
The Y2K bug.
Also known as the *millennium bug.*
Spencer Bolles' 1985 forecasts, and the others that alarmed governments worldwide in the years after, all turned out to be *inaccurate* on a single point...
Predictions were far less *catastrophic* than what actually happened at the *turn* of the century...
The total, irremediable, and *definitive* crash of every computer system on earth.
Humanity celebrated the transition into its third millennium with what we have since called the *Recollection Day.*
It was a period of chaos, barbarism, and the complete dissolution of every form of *civilization* built up over the past centuries.
But as we know today, that was only the *beginning.* The exact *correlation* to Y2K remains unknown...
...but it was *then* that the *contamination* first manifested on a planetary scale.
2000
Confirmed. Baily was with them. He and two others were able to launch the capsules...

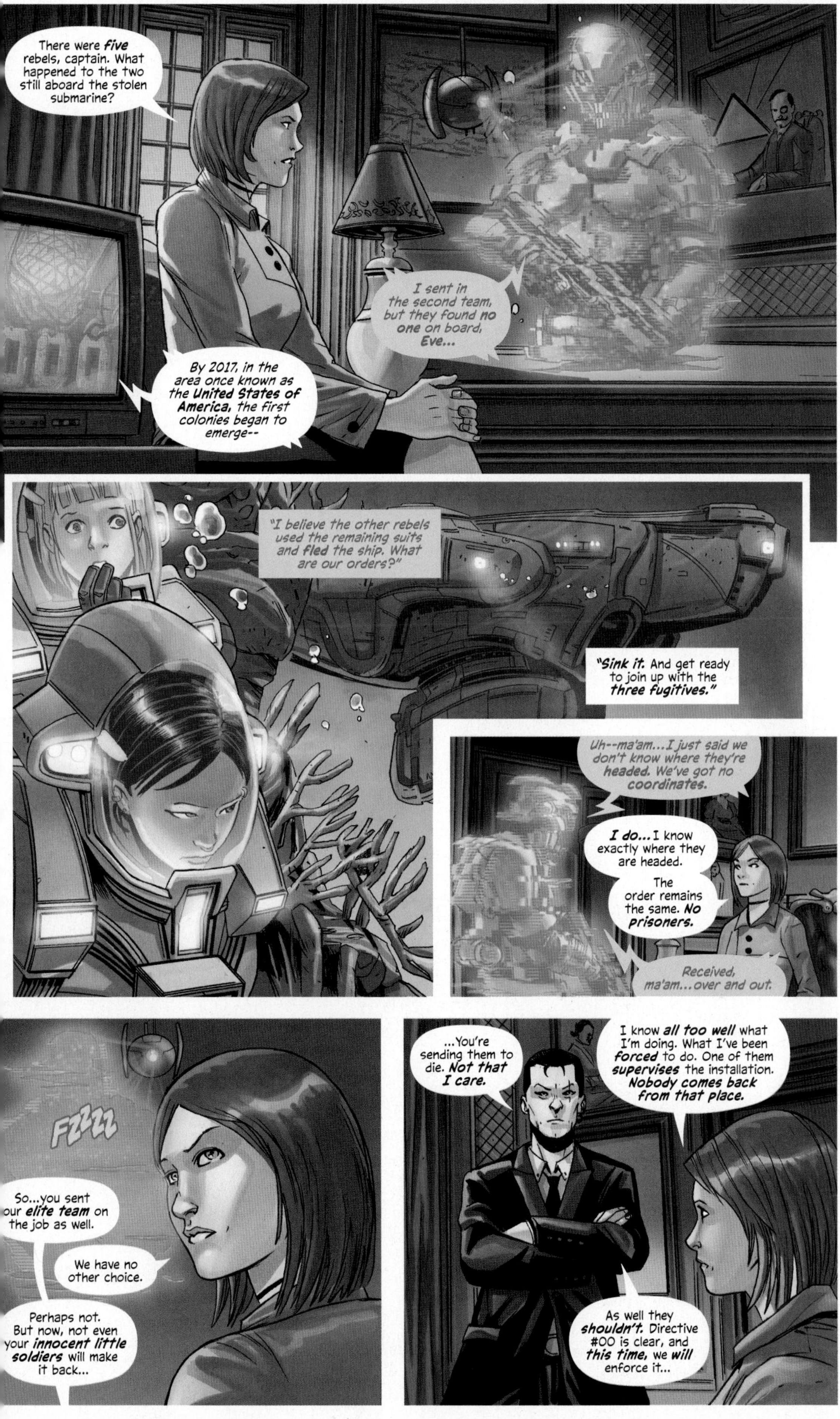
There were *five* rebels, captain. What happened to the two still aboard the stolen submarine?
I sent in the second team, but they found **no one** on board, **Eve...**
By 2017, in the area once known as the **United States of America**, the first colonies began to emerge--
"I believe the other rebels used the remaining suits and **fled** the ship. What are our orders?"
"**Sink it.** And get ready to join up with the **three fugitives.**"
Uh--ma'am...I just said we don't know where they're headed. We've got no coordinates.
I do... I know exactly where they are headed.
The order remains the same. **No prisoners.**
Received, ma'am...over and out.
FZZZZ
So...you sent our **elite team** on the job as well.
We have no other choice.
Perhaps not. But now, not even your **innocent little soldiers** will make it back...
...You're sending them to die. **Not that I care.**
I know **all too well** what I'm doing. What I've been **forced** to do. One of them **supervises** the installation. **Nobody comes back from that place.**
As well they **shouldn't.** Directive #00 is clear, and **this time,** we **will** enforce it...

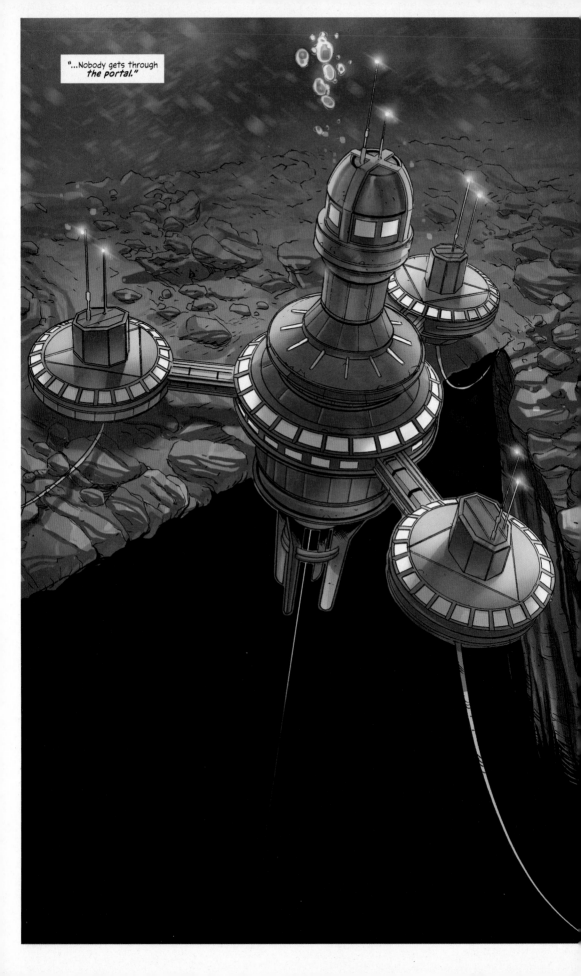
"...Nobody gets through *the portal.*"

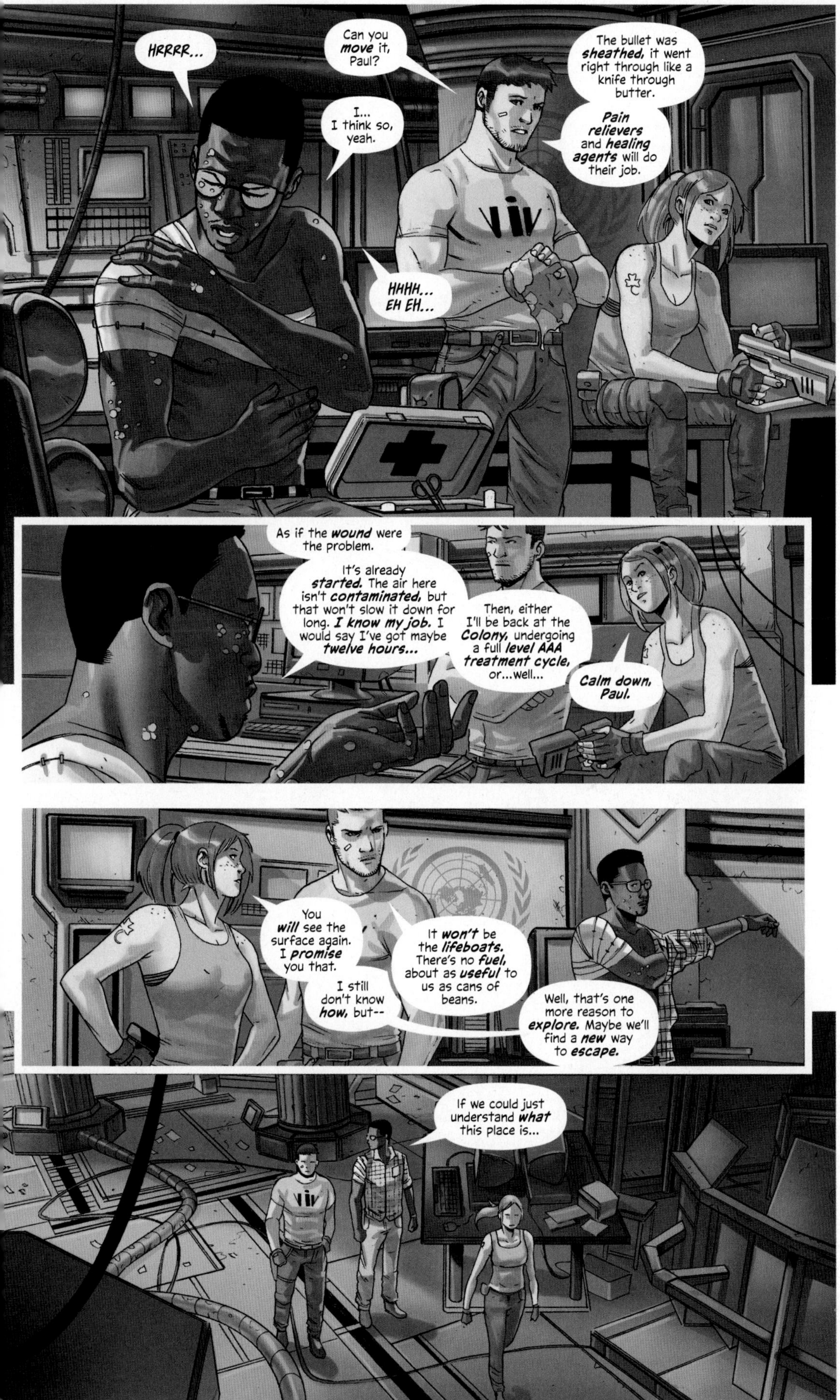
HRRRR...
Can you move it, Paul?
I... I think so, yeah.
The bullet was sheathed, it went right through like a knife through butter.
Pain relievers and healing agents will do their job.
HHHH... EH EH...
As if the wound were the problem.
It's already started. The air here isn't contaminated, but that won't slow it down for long. I know my job. I would say I've got maybe twelve hours...
Then, either I'll be back at the Colony, undergoing a full level AAA treatment cycle, or...well...
Calm down, Paul.
You will see the surface again. I promise you that.
I still don't know how, but--
It won't be the lifeboats. There's no fuel, about as useful to us as cans of beans.
Well, that's one more reason to explore. Maybe we'll find a new way to escape.
If we could just understand what this place is...

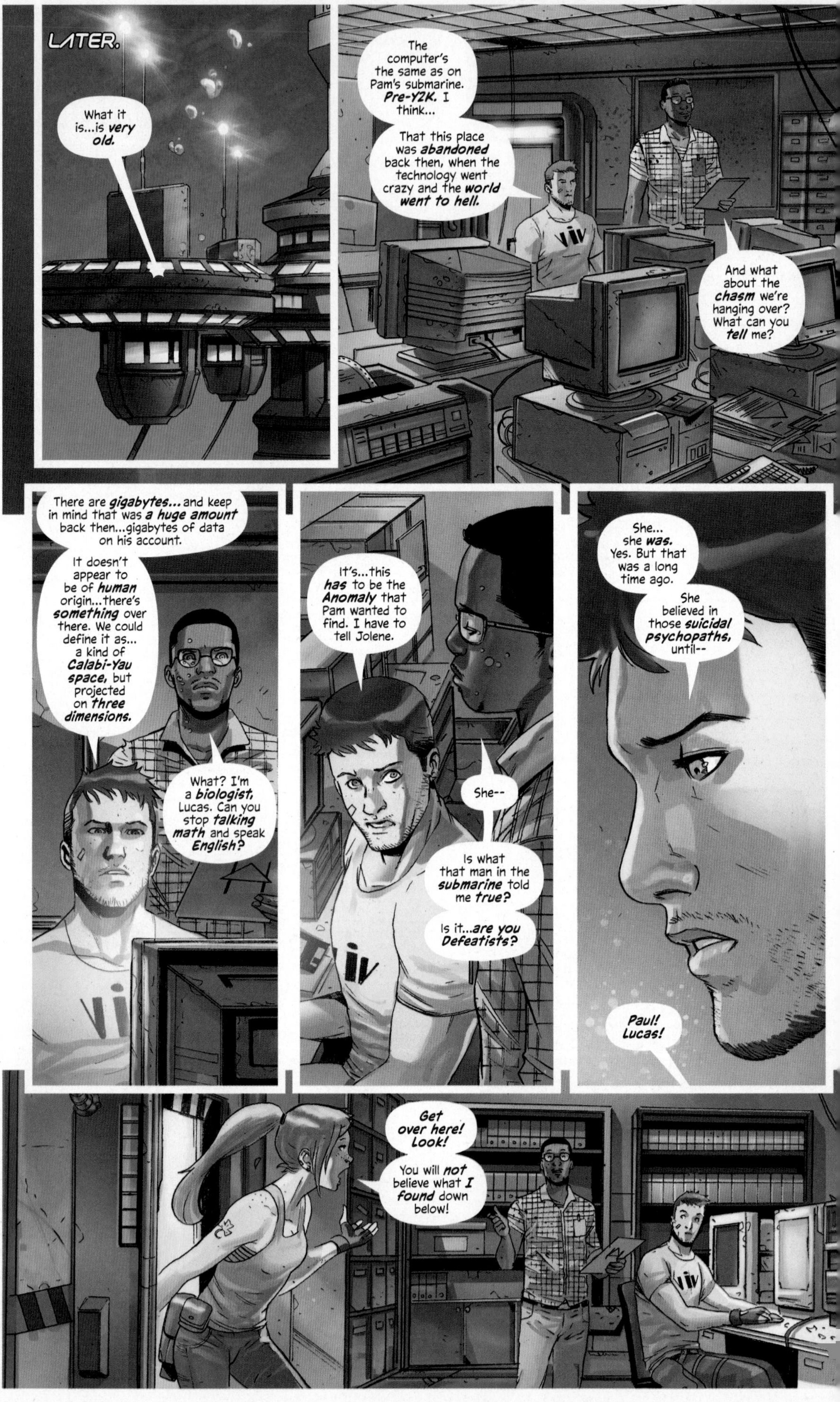
LATER.
What it is...is very old.
The computer's the same as on Pam's submarine. Pre-Y2K. I think...
That this place was abandoned back then, when the technology went crazy and the world went to hell.
And what about the chasm we're hanging over? What can you tell me?
There are gigabytes... and keep in mind that was a huge amount back then...gigabytes of data on his account.
It doesn't appear to be of human origin...there's something over there. We could define it as... a kind of Calabi-Yau space, but projected on three dimensions.
What? I'm a biologist, Lucas. Can you stop talking math and speak English?
It's...this has to be the Anomaly that Pam wanted to find. I have to tell Jolene.
She--
Is what that man in the submarine told me true?
Is it...are you Defeatists?
She... she was. Yes. But that was a long time ago.
She believed in those suicidal psychopaths, until--
Paul! Lucas!
Get over here! Look!
You will not believe what I found down below!

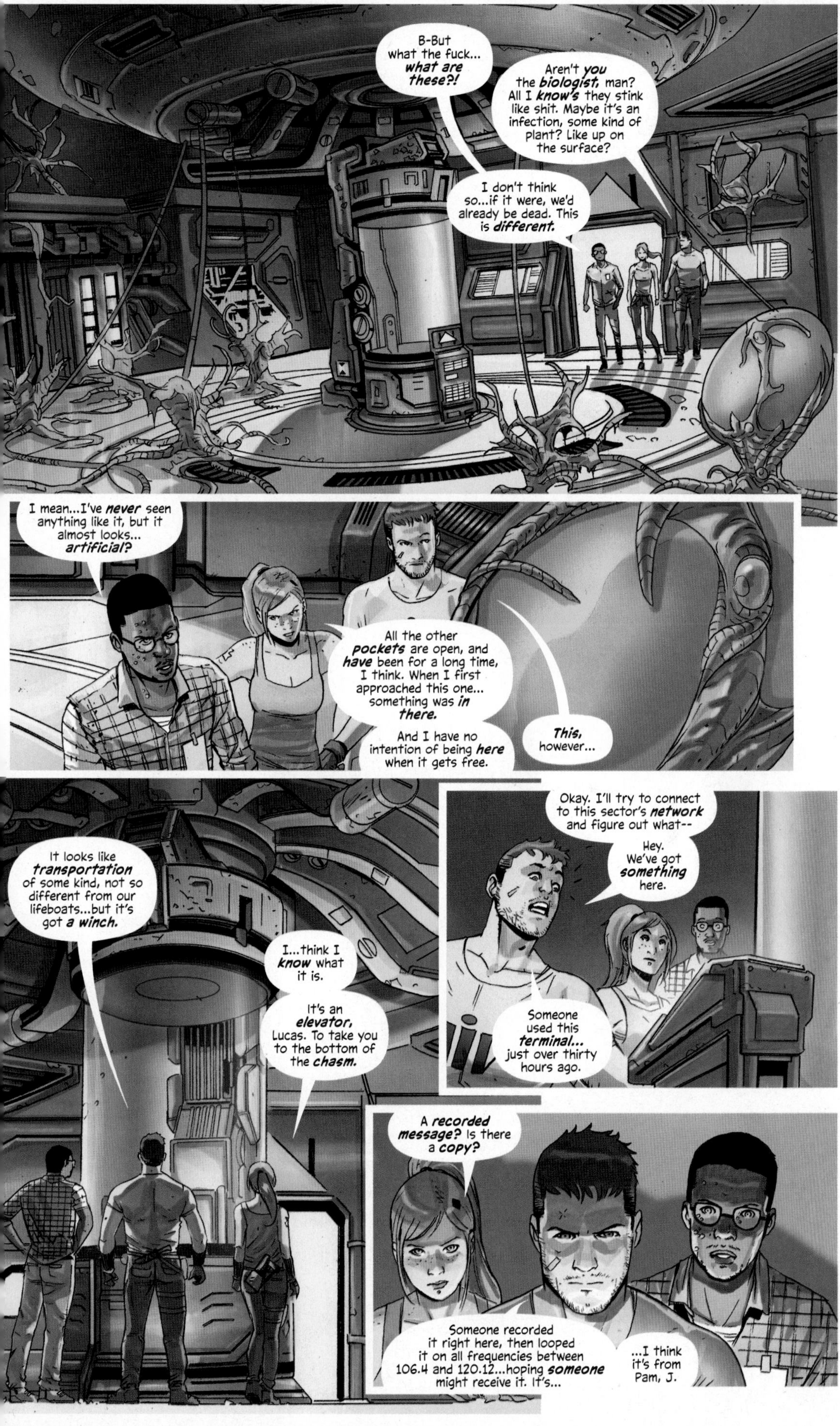
B-But what the fuck... what are these?!
Aren't you the biologist, man? All I know's they stink like shit. Maybe it's an infection, some kind of plant? Like up on the surface?
I don't think so...if it were, we'd already be dead. This is different.
I mean...I've never seen anything like it, but it almost looks... artificial?
All the other pockets are open, and have been for a long time, I think. When I first approached this one... something was in there.
This, however...
And I have no intention of being here when it gets free.
It looks like transportation of some kind, not so different from our lifeboats...but it's got a winch.
I...think I know what it is.
It's an elevator, Lucas. To take you to the bottom of the chasm.
Okay. I'll try to connect to this sector's network and figure out what--
Hey. We've got something here.
Someone used this terminal... just over thirty hours ago.
A recorded message? Is there a copy?
Someone recorded it right here, then looped it on all frequencies between 106.4 and 120.12...hoping someone might receive it. It's...
...I think it's from Pam, J.

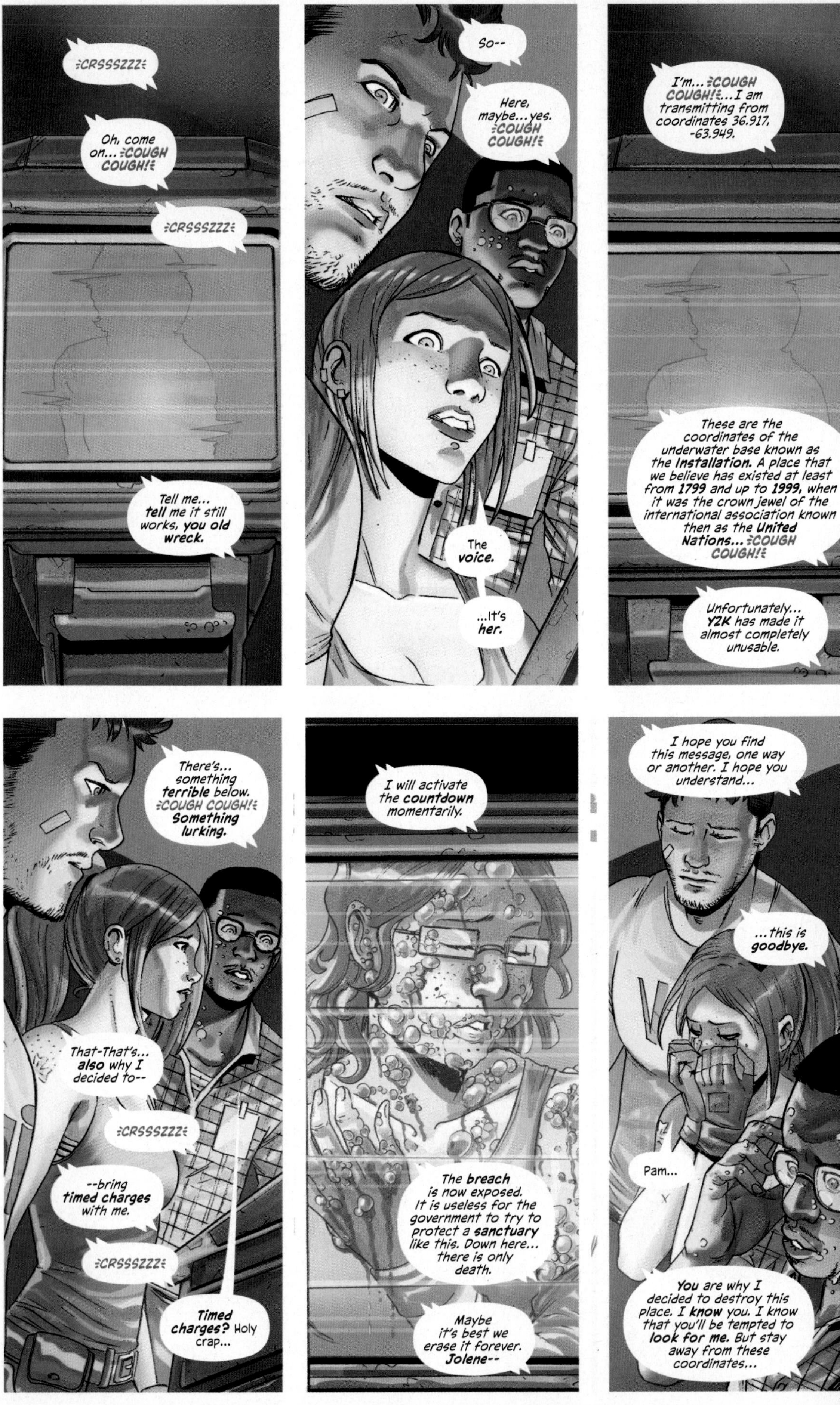

CRSSSZZZ
Oh, come on... COUGH COUGH!
CRSSSZZZ
Tell me... tell me it still works, you old wreck.
So--
Here, maybe... yes. COUGH COUGH!
The voice.
...It's her.
I'm... COUGH COUGH!... I am transmitting from coordinates 36.917, -63.949.
These are the coordinates of the underwater base known as the Installation. A place that we believe has existed at least from 1799 and up to 1999, when it was the crown jewel of the international association known then as the United Nations... COUGH COUGH!
Unfortunately... Y2K has made it almost completely unusable.
There's... something terrible below. COUGH COUGH! Something lurking.
That-That's... also why I decided to--
CRSSSZZZ
--bring timed charges with me.
CRSSSZZZ
Timed charges? Holy crap...
I will activate the countdown momentarily.
The breach is now exposed. It is useless for the government to try to protect a sanctuary like this. Down here... there is only death.
Maybe it's best we erase it forever. Jolene--
I hope you find this message, one way or another. I hope you understand...
...this is goodbye.
Pam...
You are why I decided to destroy this place. I know you. I know that you'll be tempted to look for me. But stay away from these coordinates...

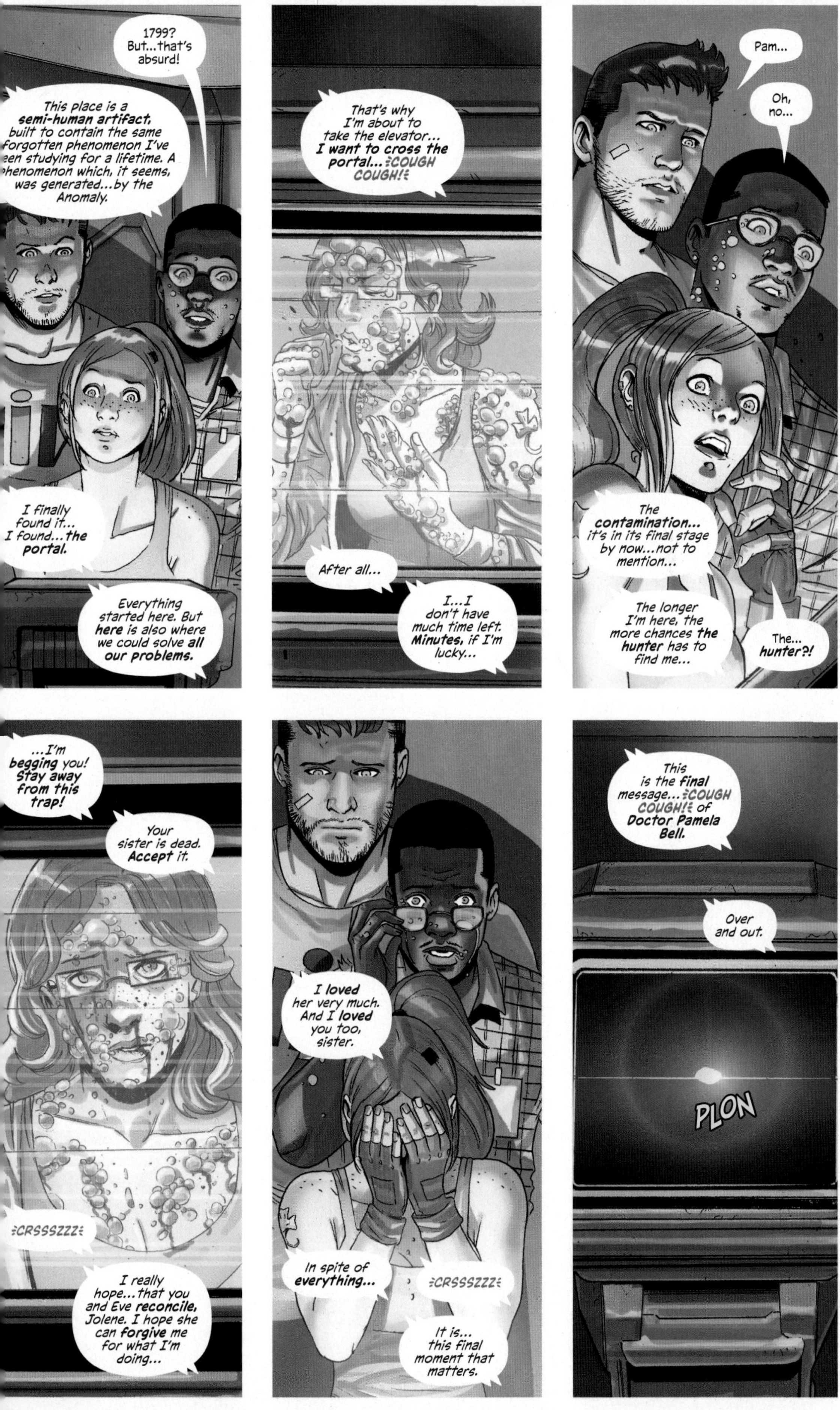
1799? But...that's absurd!
This place is a semi-human artifact, built to contain the same forgotten phenomenon I've een studying for a lifetime. A henomenon which, it seems, was generated...by the Anomaly.
I finally found it... I found...the portal.
Everything started here. But here is also where we could solve all our problems.
That's why I'm about to take the elevator... I want to cross the portal... COUGH COUGH!
After all...
I...I don't have much time left. Minutes, if I'm lucky...
Pam...
Oh, no...
The contamination... it's in its final stage by now...not to mention...
The longer I'm here, the more chances the hunter has to find me...
The... hunter?!
...I'm begging you! Stay away from this trap!
Your sister is dead. Accept it.
CRSSSZZZ
I really hope...that you and Eve reconcile, Jolene. I hope she can forgive me for what I'm doing...
I loved her very much. And I loved you too, sister.
In spite of everything...
CRSSSZZZ
It is... this final moment that matters.
This is the final message... COUGH COUGH! of Doctor Pamela Bell.
Over and out.
PLON

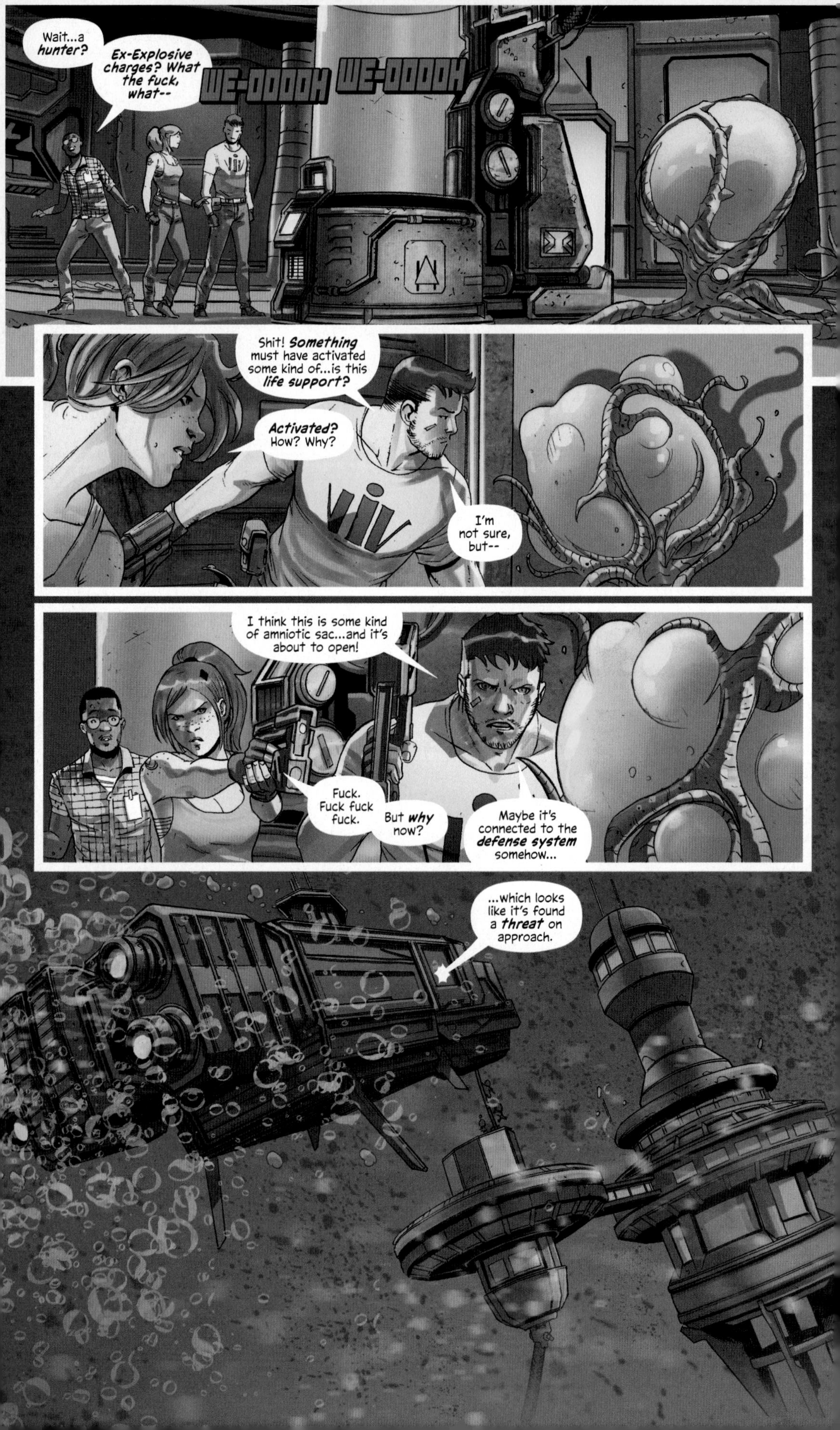

Wait...a hunter?
Ex-Explosive charges? What the fuck, what--
WE-OOOOH WE-OOOOH
Shit! Something must have activated some kind of...is this life support?
Activated? How? Why?
I'm not sure, but--
I think this is some kind of amniotic sac...and it's about to open!
Fuck. Fuck fuck fuck.
But why now?
Maybe it's connected to the defense system somehow...
...which looks like it's found a threat on approach.

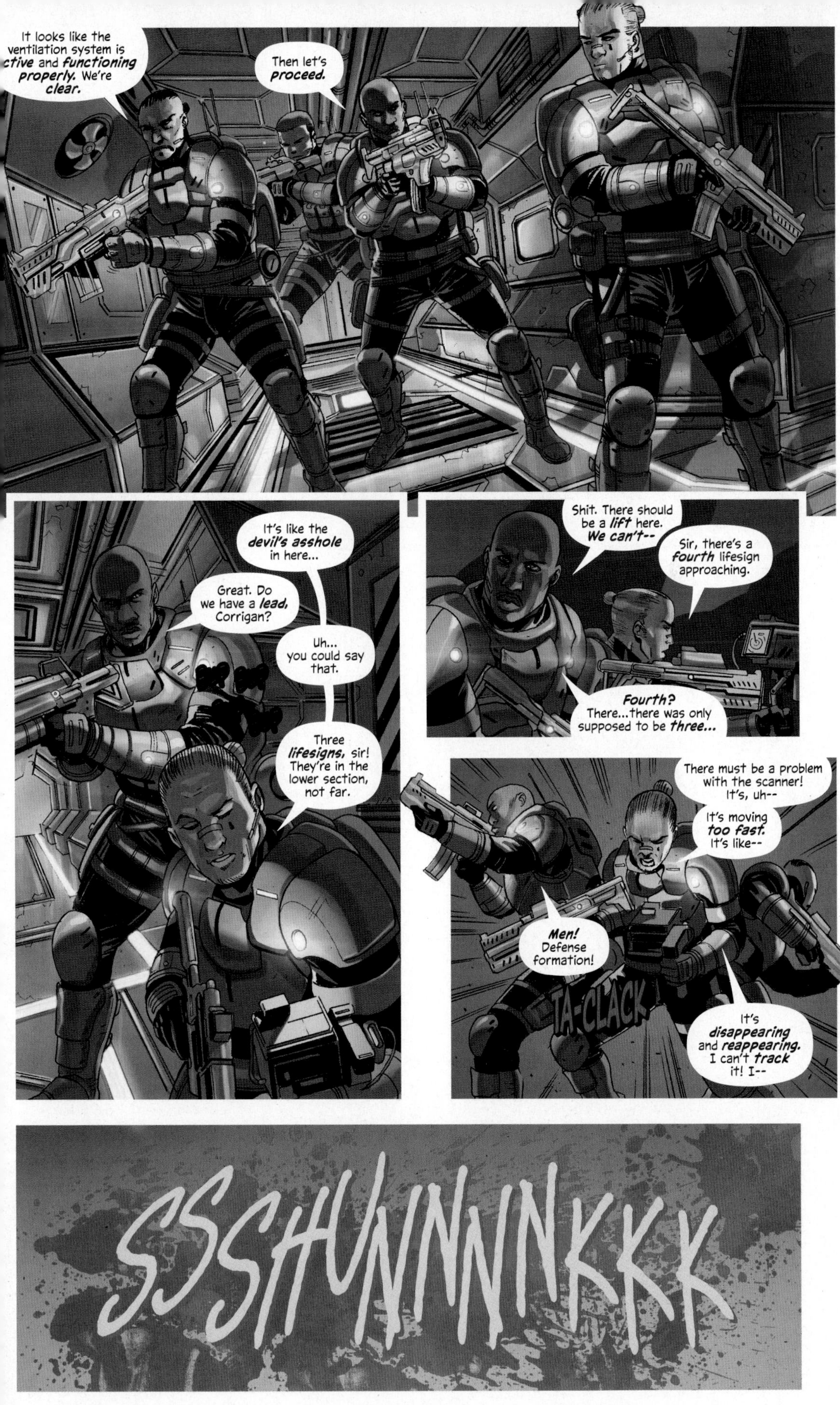

It looks like the ventilation system is ctive and functioning properly. We're clear.
Then let's proceed.
It's like the devil's asshole in here...
Great. Do we have a lead, Corrigan?
Uh... you could say that.
Three lifesigns, sir! They're in the lower section, not far.
Shit. There should be a lift here. We can't--
Sir, there's a fourth lifesign approaching.
Fourth? There...there was only supposed to be three...
There must be a problem with the scanner! It's, uh--
It's moving too fast. It's like--
Men! Defense formation!
TA-CLACK
It's disappearing and reappearing. I can't track it! I--
SSSHUNNNNKKK

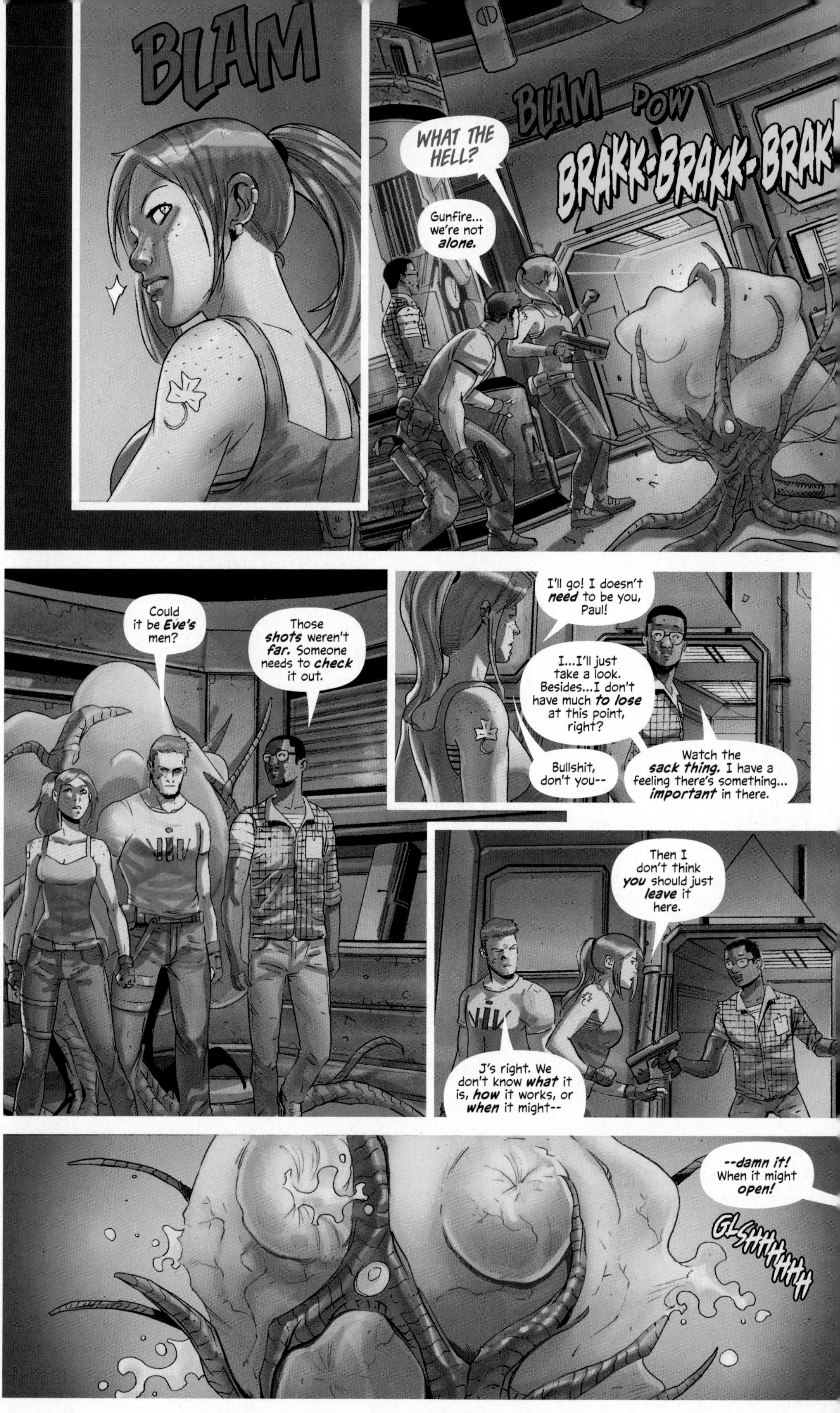
BLAM
BLAM
POW
BRAKK-BRAKK-BRAK
WHAT THE HELL?
Gunfire... we're not alone.
Could it be Eve's men?
Those shots weren't far. Someone needs to check it out.
I'll go! I doesn't need to be you, Paul!
I...I'll just take a look. Besides...I don't have much to lose at this point, right?
Bullshit, don't you--
Watch the sack thing. I have a feeling there's something... important in there.
Then I don't think you should just leave it here.
J's right. We don't know what it is, how it works, or when it might--
--damn it! When it might open!
GLSHHHHHH

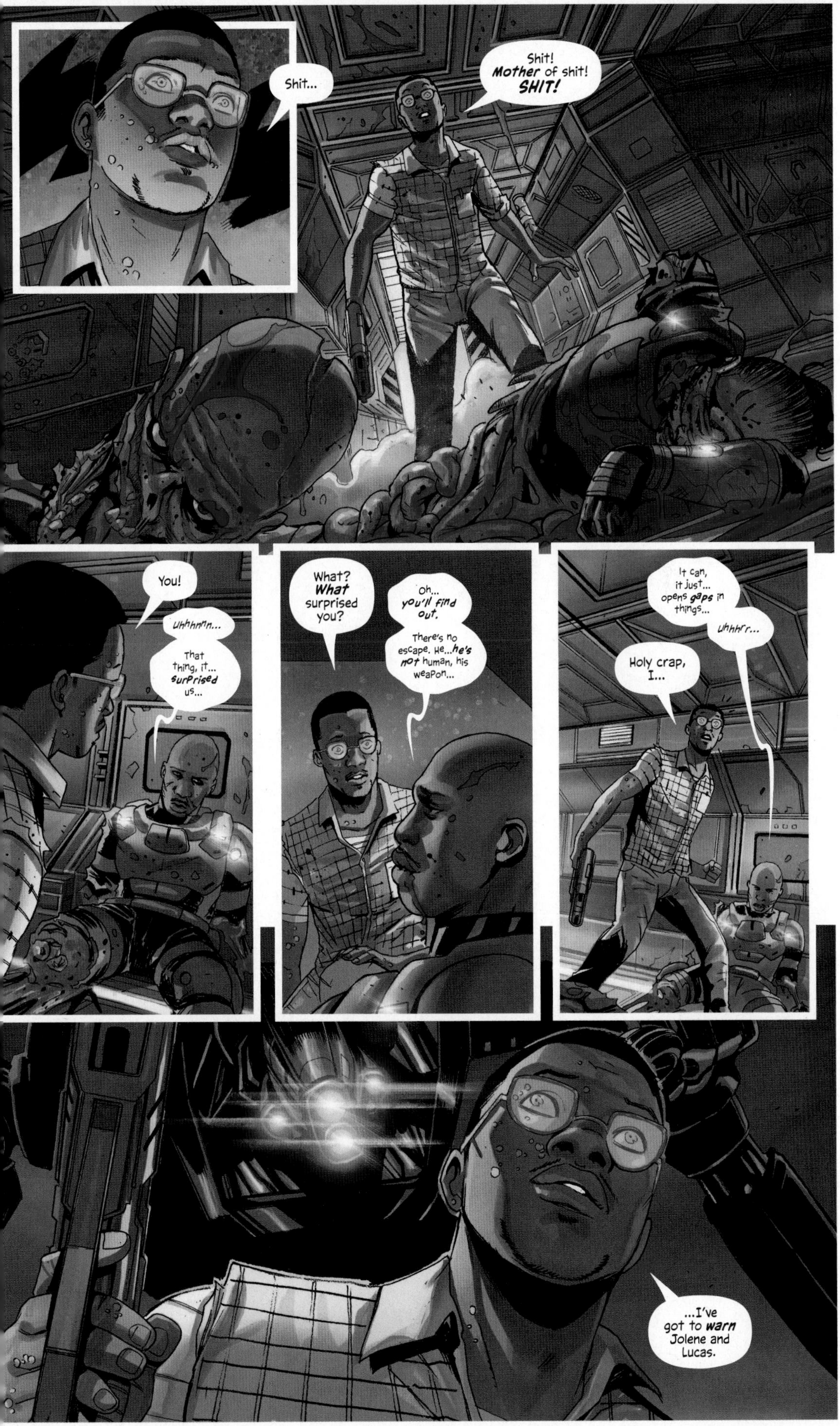
Shit...
Shit! Mother of shit! SHIT!
You!
Uhhhnnn...
That thing, it... surprised us...
What? What surprised you?
Oh... you'll find out.
There's no escape. He...he's not human, his weapon...
It can, it just... opens gaps in things...
Uhhhrr...
Holy crap, I...
...I've got to warn Jolene and Lucas.

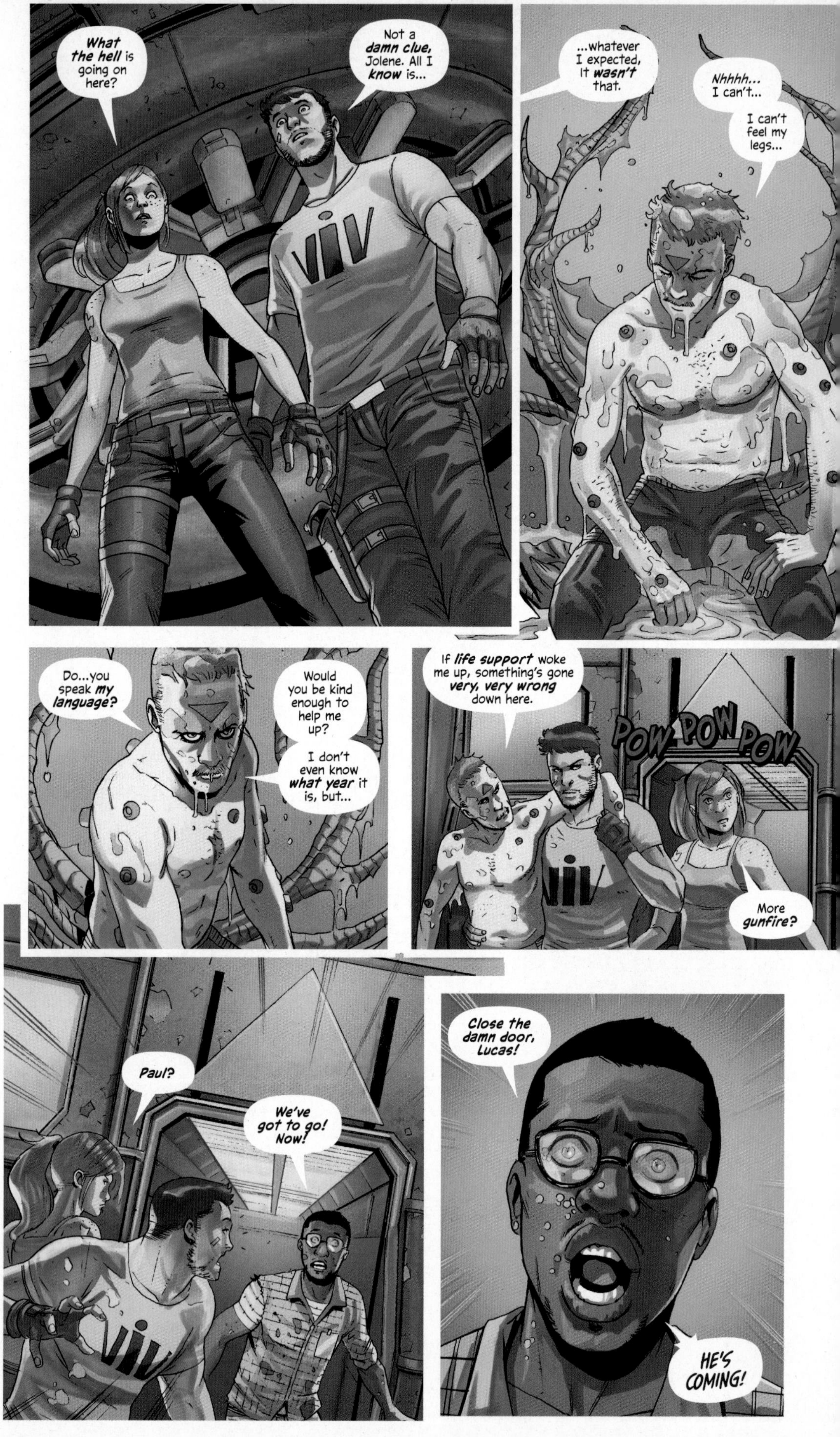
What the hell is going on here?
Not a damn clue, Jolene. All I know is...
...whatever I expected, it wasn't that.
Nhhhh... I can't...
I can't feel my legs...
Do...you speak my language?
Would you be kind enough to help me up?
I don't even know what year it is, but...
If life support woke me up, something's gone very, very wrong down here.
POW POW POW
More gunfire?
Paul?
We've got to go! Now!
Close the damn door, Lucas!
HE'S COMING!

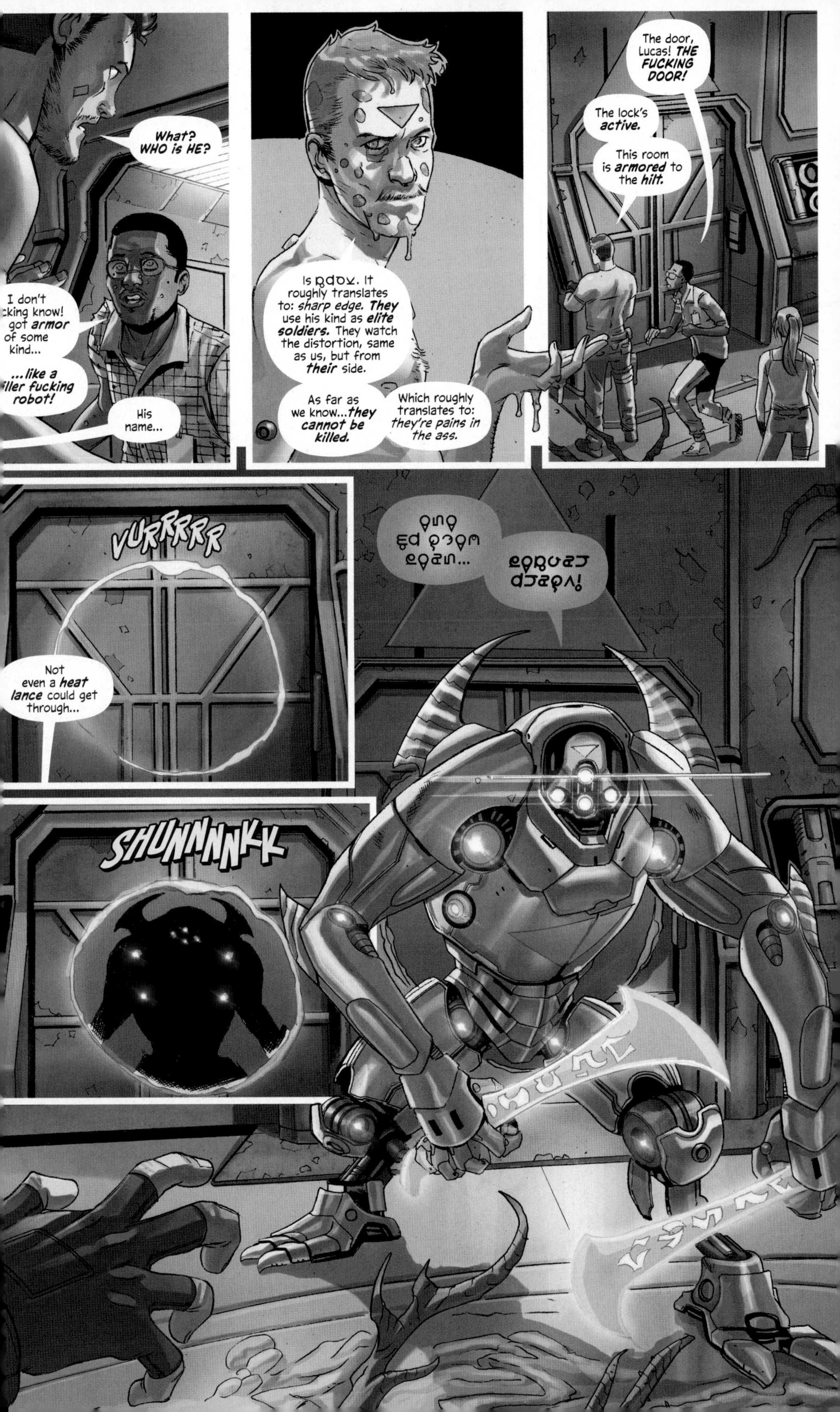
What? WHO is HE?
I don't
cking know!
got armor
of some
kind...
...like a
iller fucking
robot!
His name...
Is . It roughly translates to: sharp edge. They use his kind as elite soldiers. They watch the distortion, same as us, but from their side.
As far as we know...they cannot be killed.
Which roughly translates to: they're pains in the ass.
The door, Lucas! THE FUCKING DOOR!
The lock's active.
This room is armored to the hilt.
VURRRRR
Not even a heat lance could get through...
SHUNNNNKK

JOLENE!

BRRTTTTT

BRRTTTT

By God... would you stop?

SHUNNNN!

Don't you know *anything?* Have you been *trained* at all?

The ΠΔΦΥ are equipped with *spatial distortion rods.* They can displace physical space and its contents elsewhere. There is *no human technology* that can even scratch them.

ΧΡϹϽ!

ΟϽΛИϽ

Uh--but you...can you *communicate* with that... *thing?*

I hope so, boy... I *hope.*

But I'm a *physicist,* not a linguist. *If he kills us...* we'll *know* I've gotten the words wrong. Otherwise, *he'll* know...

"...we're not a threat."

BEEEEP

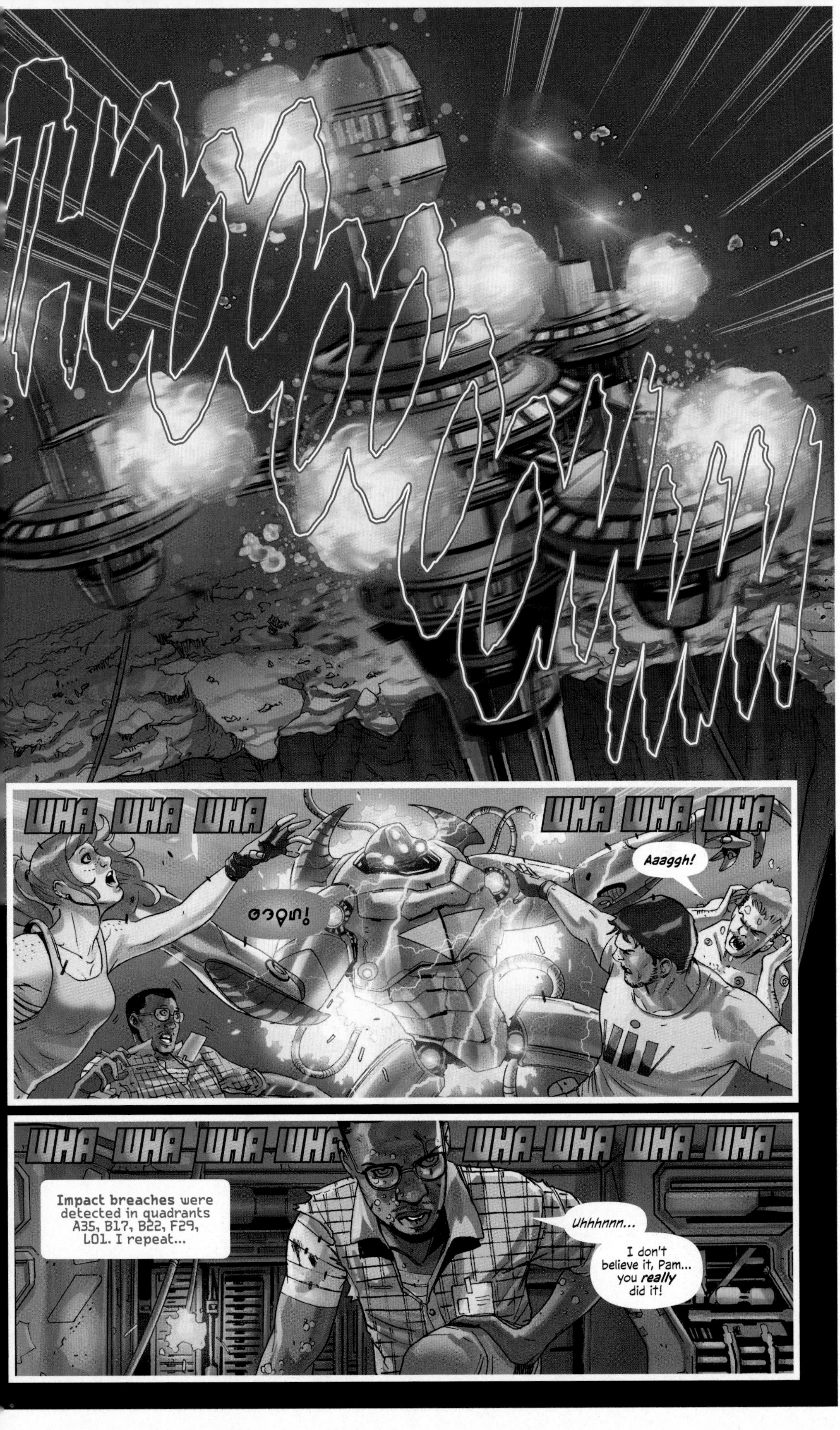
WHA WHA WHA
WHA WHA WHA
Aaaggh!
WHA WHA WHA WHA
WHA WHA WHA WHA
Impact breaches were detected in quadrants A35, B17, B22, F29, L01. I repeat...
Uhhhnnn...
I don't believe it, Pam... you *really* did it!

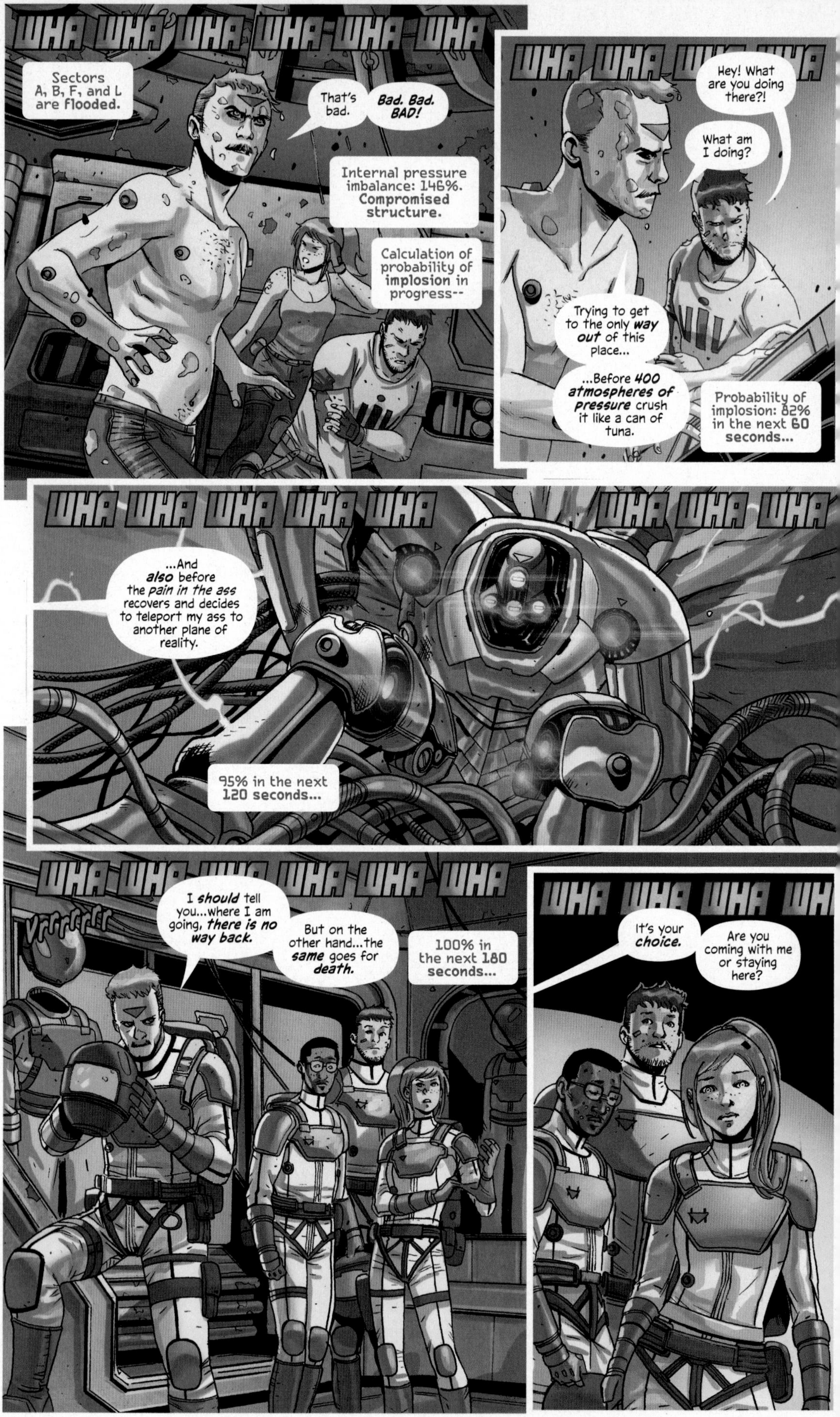
WHA WHA WHA WHA WHA WHA
Sectors A, B, F, and L are flooded.
That's bad.
Bad. Bad. BAD!
Internal pressure imbalance: 146%. Compromised structure.
Calculation of probability of implosion in progress--
WHA WHA WHA
Hey! What are you doing there?!
What am I doing?
Trying to get to the only way out of this place...
...Before 400 atmospheres of pressure crush it like a can of tuna.
Probability of implosion: 82% in the next 60 seconds...
WHA WHA WHA WHA WHA
WHA WHA WHA
...And also before the pain in the ass recovers and decides to teleport my ass to another plane of reality.
95% in the next 120 seconds...
WHA WHA WHA WHA WHA WHA
Vrrrrrrr
I should tell you...where I am going, there is no way back.
But on the other hand...the same goes for death.
100% in the next 180 seconds...
WHA WHA WHA
It's your choice.
Are you coming with me or staying here?

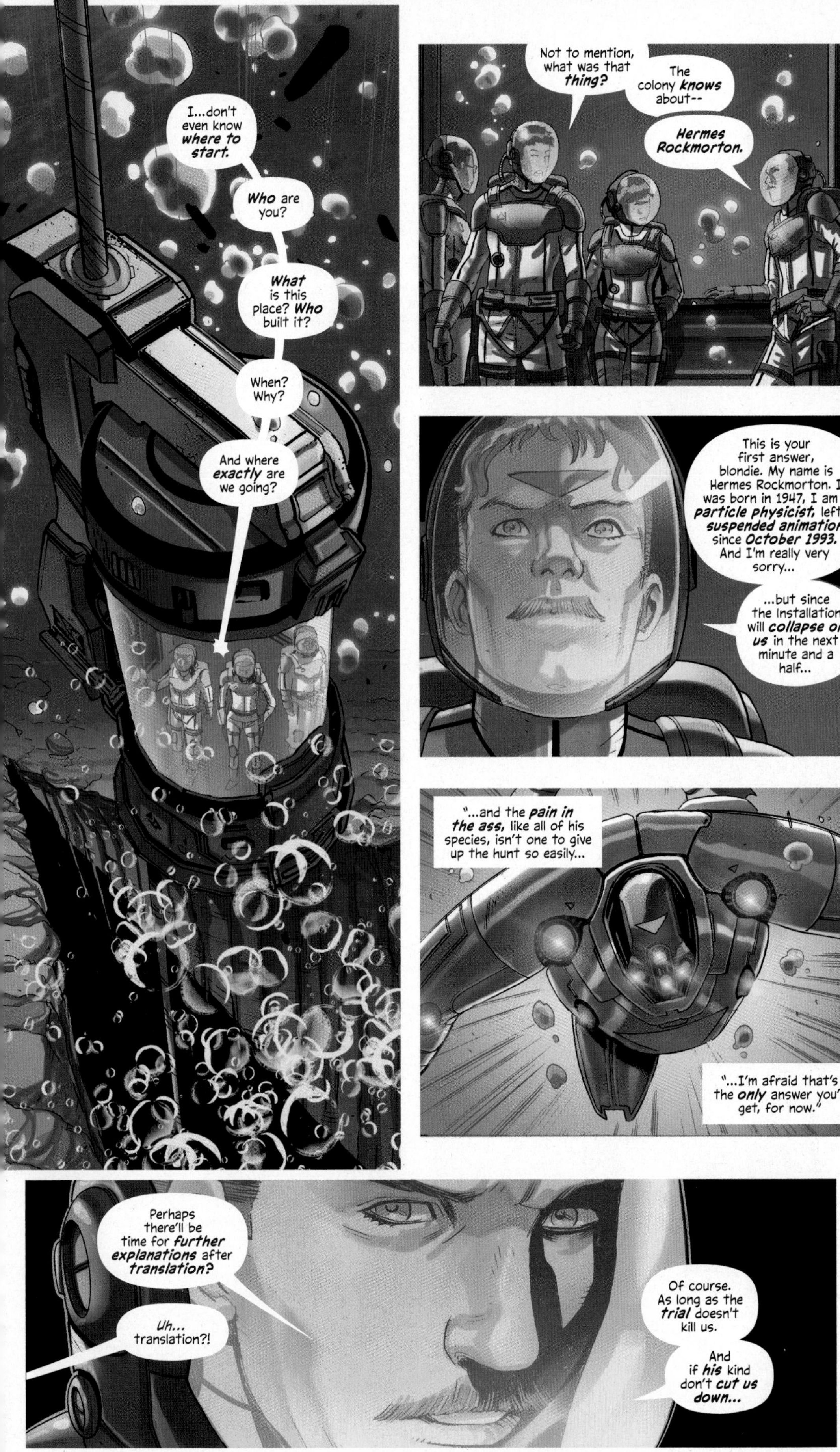

I...don't even know *where to start.*
Who are you?
What is this place? *Who* built it?
When? Why?
And where *exactly* are we going?
Not to mention, what was that *thing?*
The colony *knows* about--
Hermes Rockmorton.
This is your first answer, blondie. My name is Hermes Rockmorton. I was born in 1947, I am a *particle physicist,* left in *suspended animation* since *October 1993.* And I'm really very sorry...
...but since the Installation will *collapse on us* in the next minute and a half...
"...and the *pain in the ass,* like all of his species, isn't one to give up the hunt so easily...
"...I'm afraid that's the *only* answer you'll get, for now."
Perhaps there'll be time for *further explanations* after *translation?*
Uh... translation?!
Of course. As long as the *trial* doesn't kill us.
And if *his* kind don't *cut us down...*

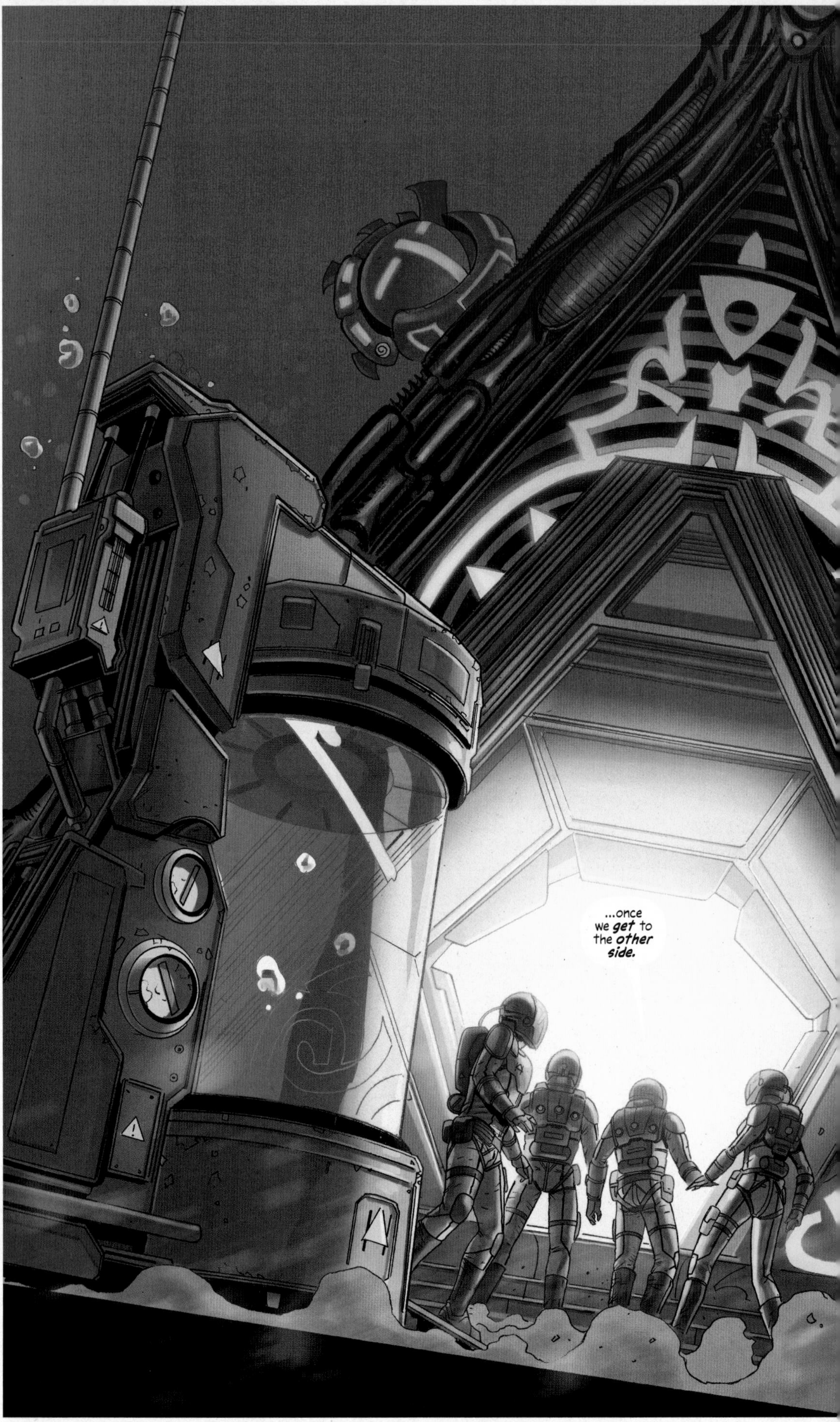
...once we get to the other side.

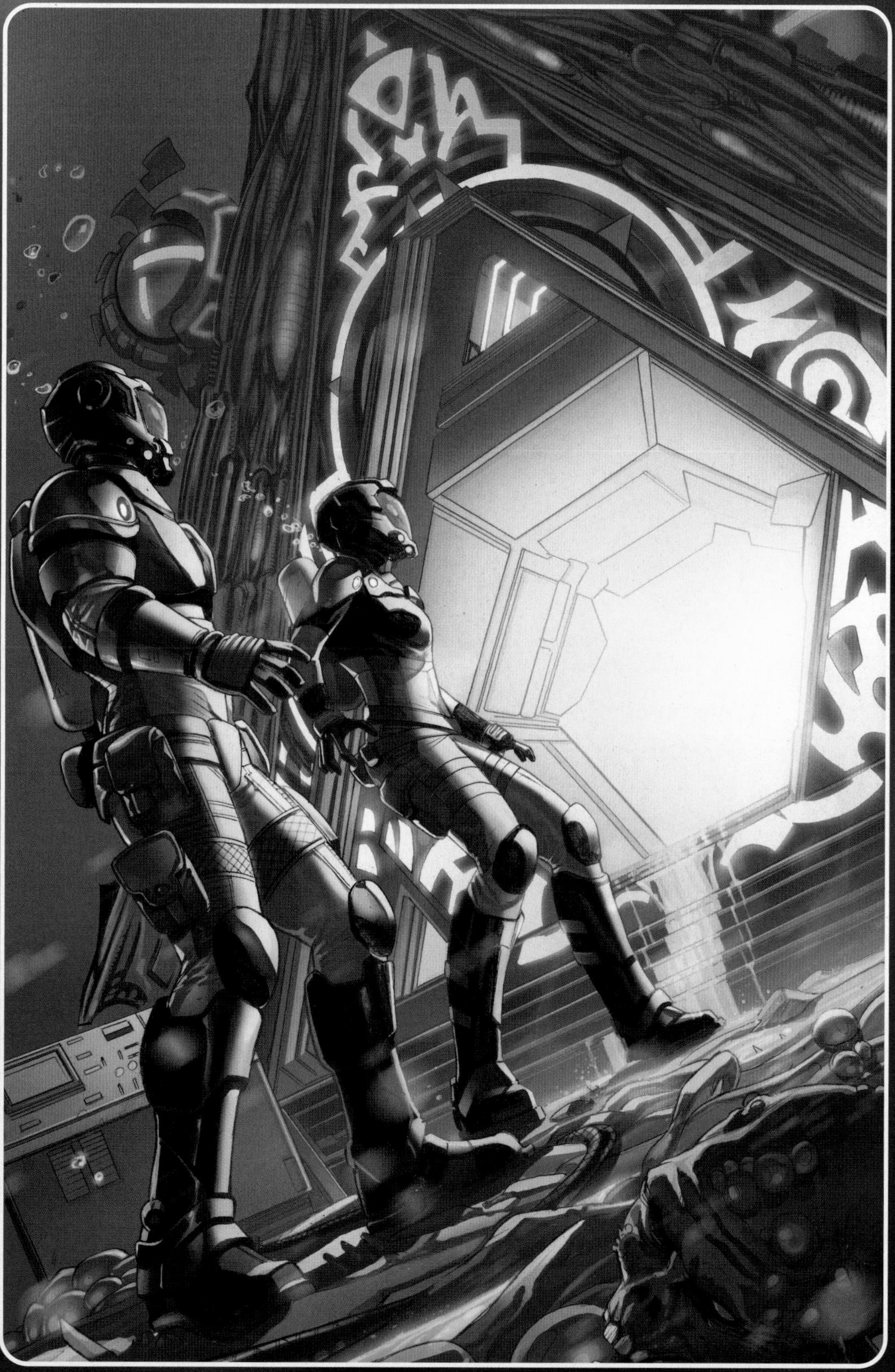

CHAPTER 05

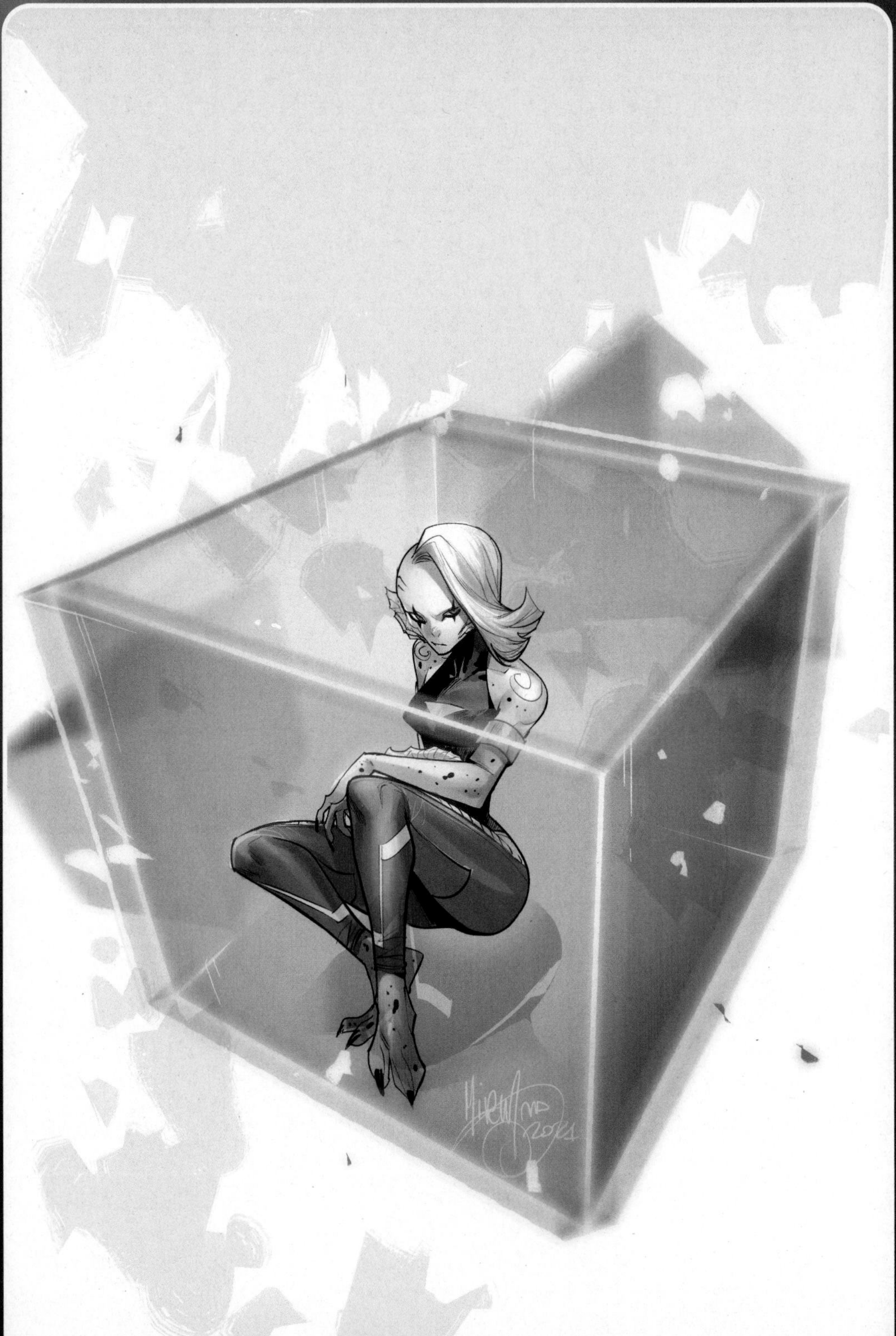

Let's take stock...

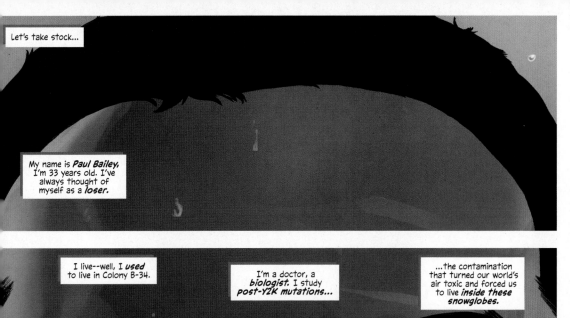

My name is *Paul Bailey*, I'm 33 years old. I've always thought of myself as a *loser*.

I live--well, I *used* to live in Colony B-34.

I'm a doctor, a *biologist*. I study *post-Y2K mutations*...

...the contamination that turned our world's air toxic and forced us to live *inside these snowglobes*.

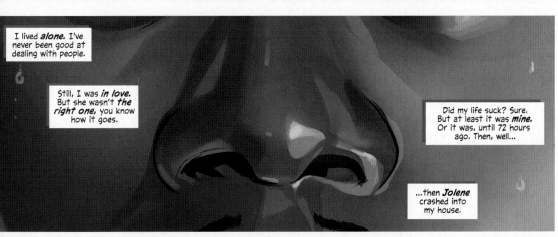

I lived *alone*. I've never been good at dealing with people.

Still, I was *in love*. But she wasn't *the right one*, you know how it goes.

Did my life suck? Sure. But at least it was *mine*. Or it was, until 72 hours ago. Then, well...

...then *Jolene* crashed into my house.

And now I'm... here. *Where* is here? *When* is it? No idea. I don't know what else to say...

...or I wouldn't, if I could speak, if I still had lungs to breathe. Man...I'm so *thirsty*.

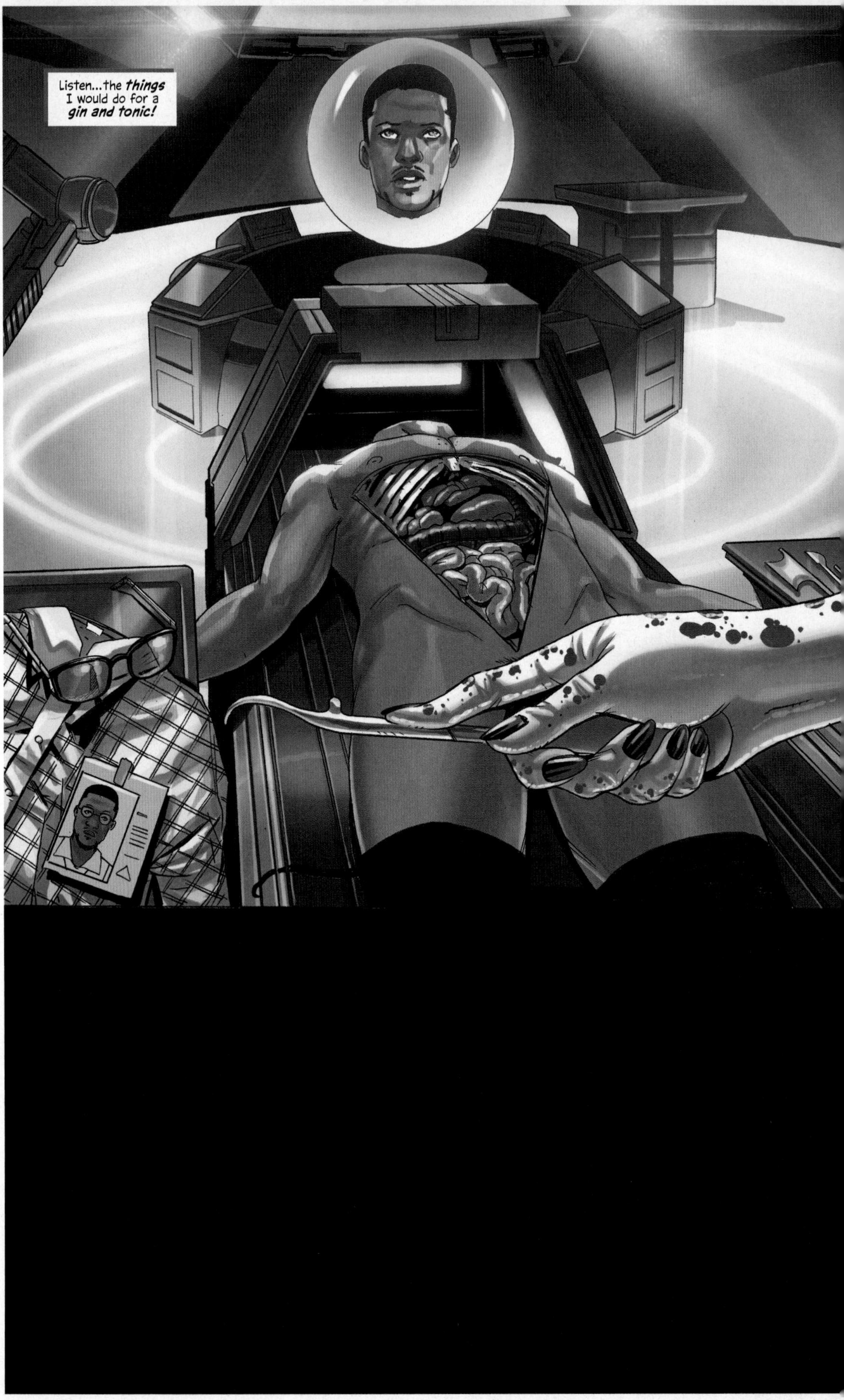
Listen...the *things* I would do for a *gin and tonic!*

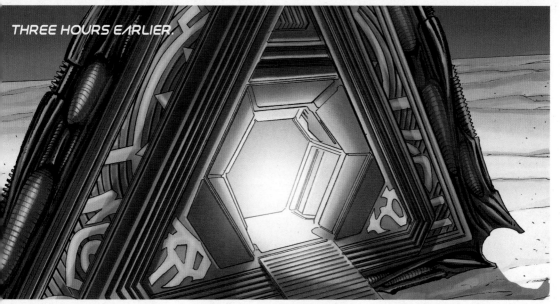

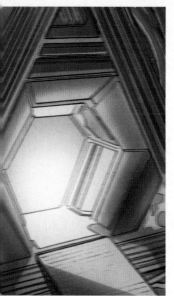

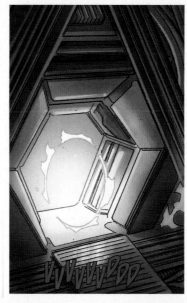

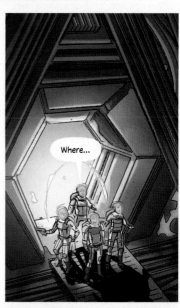

THREE HOURS EARLIER.
VVVVVVVDDD
Where...
...Where the hell?
On the other side, blondie.
Through the looking glass...if you're up on your Carroll.
Seems like we've made it.
Welcome, my friends...to the Land of the Pains in the Ass!

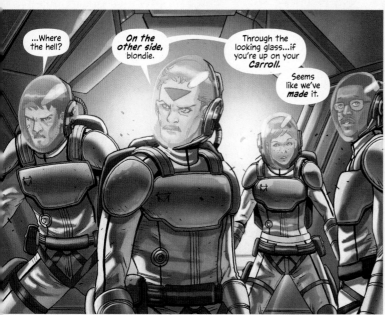

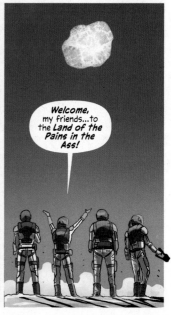

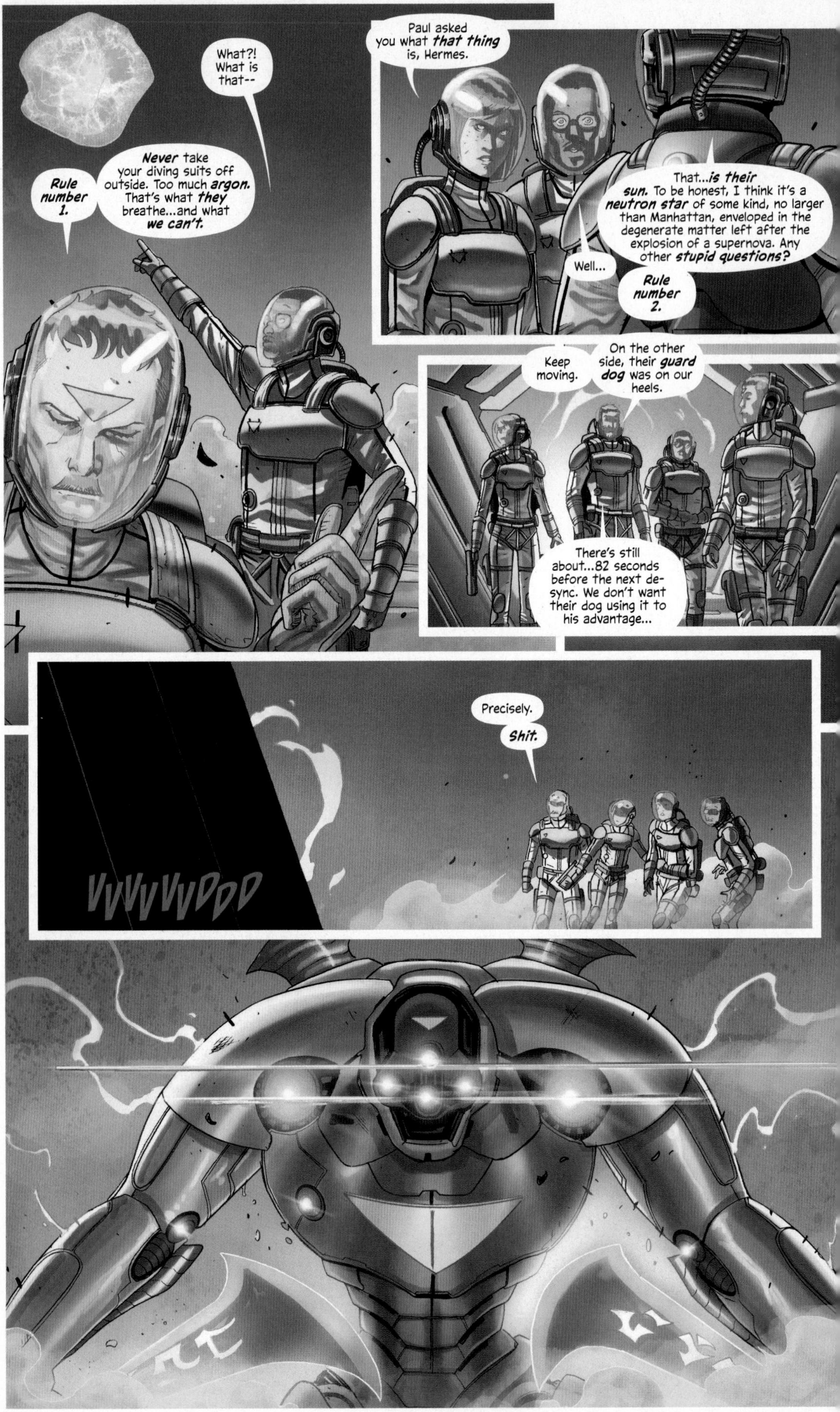
What?! What is that--
Never take your diving suits off outside. Too much argon. That's what they breathe...and what we can't.
Rule number 1.
Paul asked you what that thing is, Hermes.
Well...
That...is their sun. To be honest, I think it's a neutron star of some kind, no larger than Manhattan, enveloped in the degenerate matter left after the explosion of a supernova. Any other stupid questions?
Rule number 2.
Keep moving.
On the other side, their guard dog was on our heels.
There's still about...82 seconds before the next de-sync. We don't want their dog using it to his advantage...
Precisely.
Shit.
VVVVVVVDDD

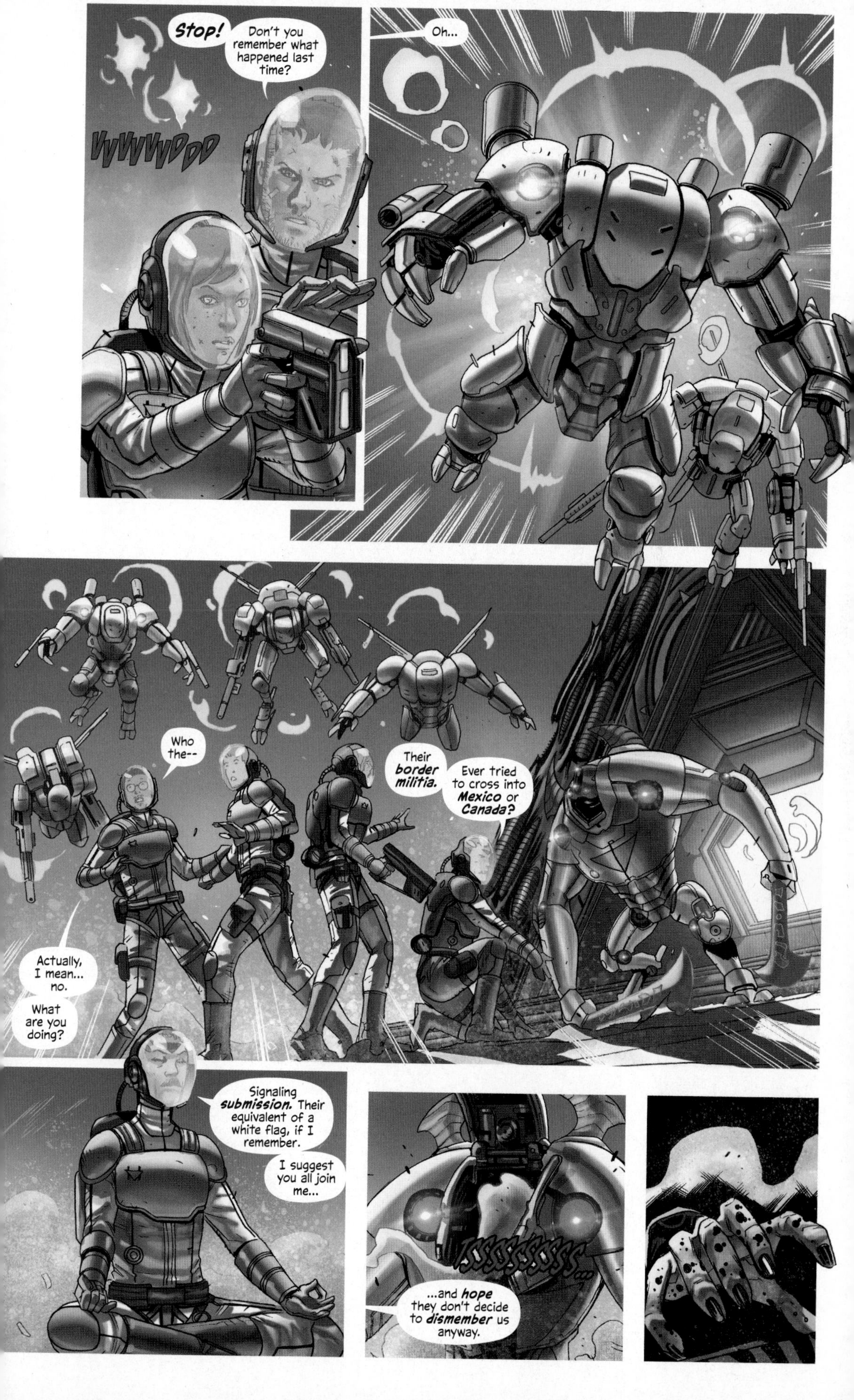
Stop!
Don't you remember what happened last time?
VVVVVVDDD
Oh...
Who the--
Their border militia.
Ever tried to cross into Mexico or Canada?
Actually, I mean... no.
What are you doing?
Signaling submission. Their equivalent of a white flag, if I remember.
I suggest you all join me...
TSSSSSSSSS...
...and hope they don't decide to dismember us anyway.

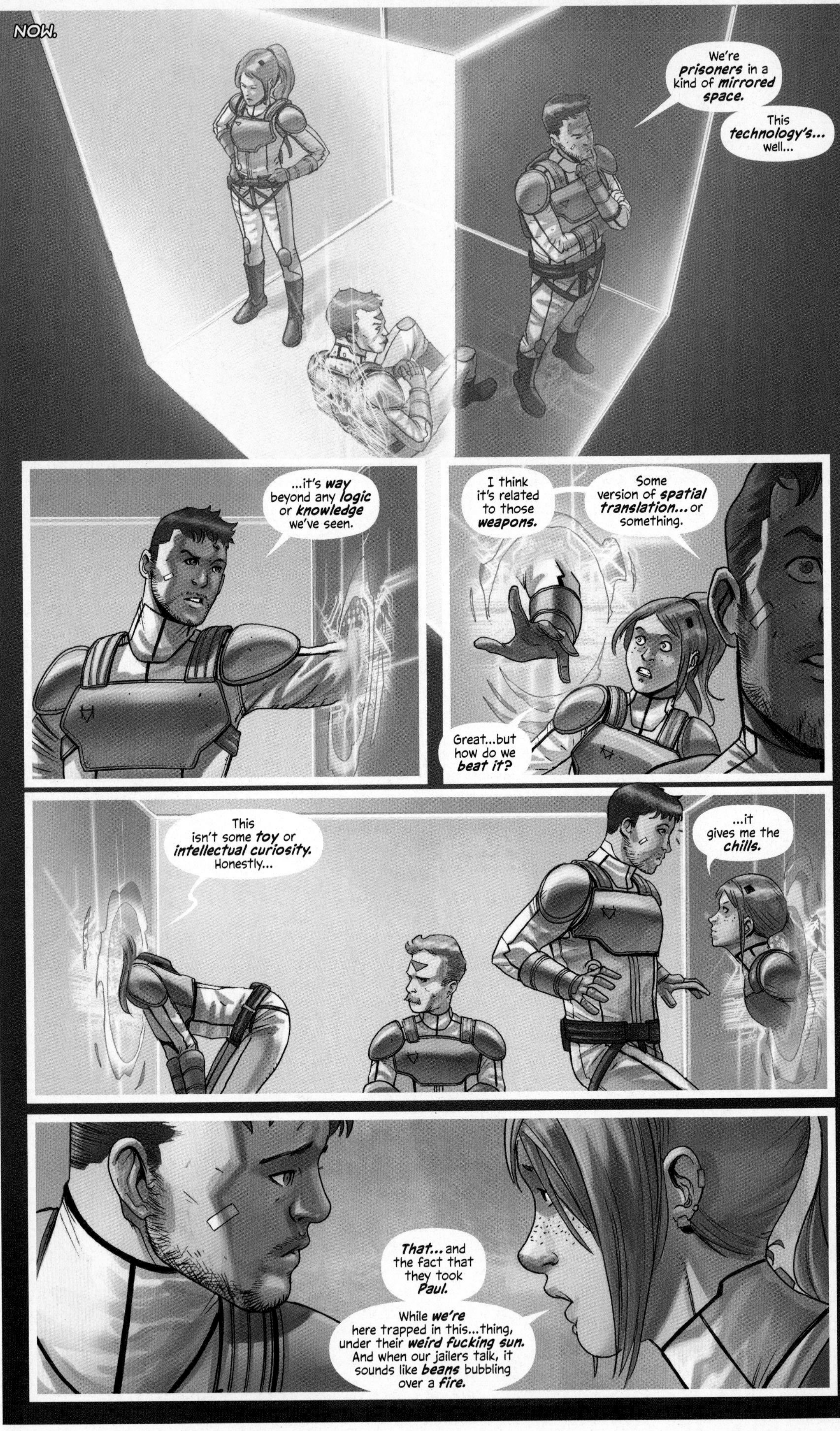
NOW.
We're prisoners in a kind of mirrored space.
This technology's... well...
...it's way beyond any logic or knowledge we've seen.
I think it's related to those weapons.
Some version of spatial translation... or something.
Great...but how do we beat it?
This isn't some toy or intellectual curiosity. Honestly...
...it gives me the chills.
That... and the fact that they took Paul.
While we're here trapped in this...thing, under their weird fucking sun. And when our jailers talk, it sounds like beans bubbling over a fire.

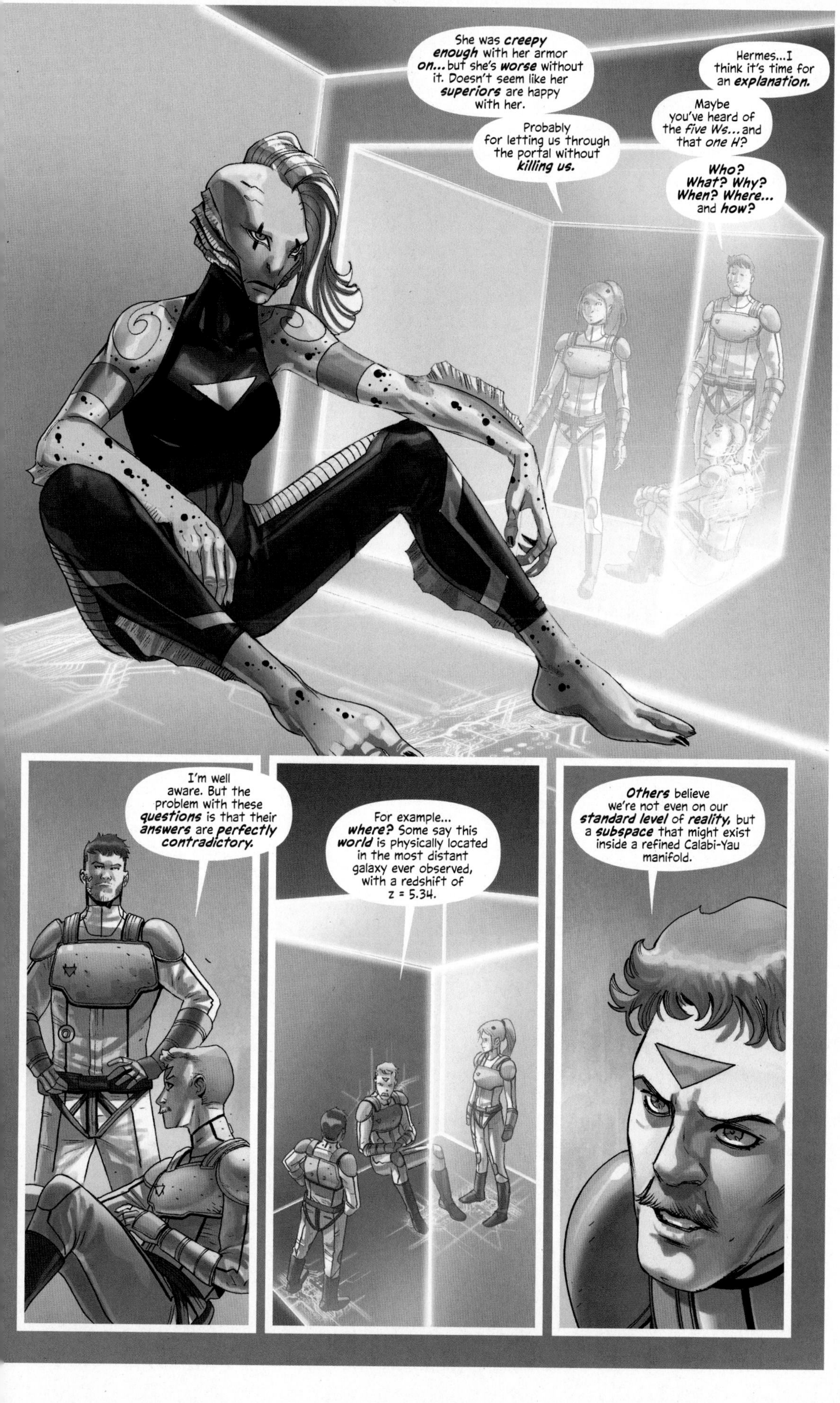
She was creepy enough with her armor on... but she's worse without it. Doesn't seem like her superiors are happy with her.
Probably for letting us through the portal without killing us.
Hermes...I think it's time for an explanation.
Maybe you've heard of the five Ws...and that one H?
Who? What? Why? When? Where... and how?
I'm well aware. But the problem with these questions is that their answers are perfectly contradictory.
For example... where? Some say this world is physically located in the most distant galaxy ever observed, with a redshift of z = 5.34.
Others believe we're not even on our standard level of reality, but a subspace that might exist inside a refined Calabi-Yau manifold.

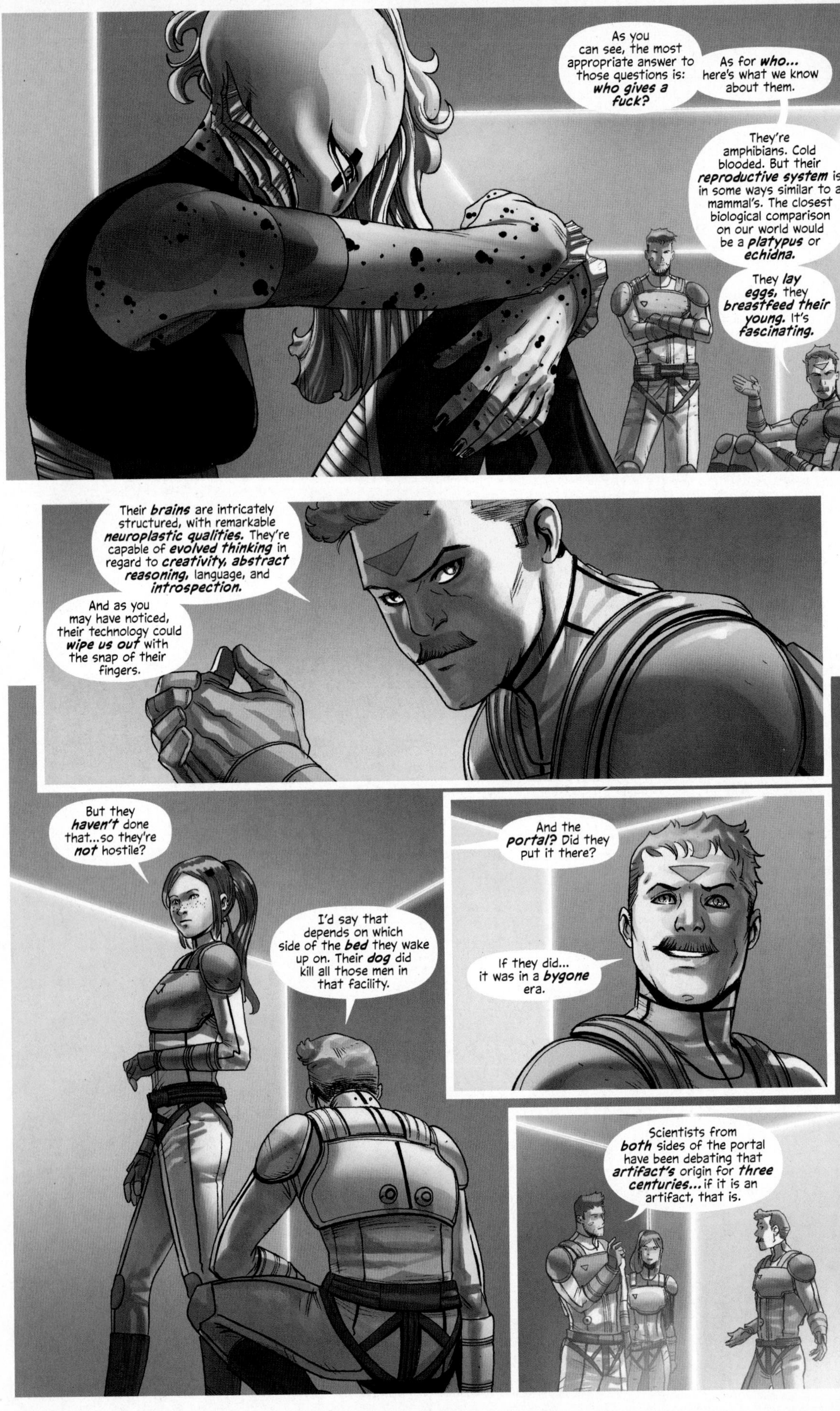

As you can see, the most appropriate answer to those questions is: ***who gives a fuck?***
As for ***who...*** here's what we know about them.
They're amphibians. Cold blooded. But their ***reproductive system*** is in some ways similar to a mammal's. The closest biological comparison on our world would be a ***platypus*** or ***echidna.***
They ***lay eggs,*** they ***breastfeed their young.*** It's ***fascinating.***
Their ***brains*** are intricately structured, with remarkable ***neuroplastic qualities.*** They're capable of ***evolved thinking*** in regard to ***creativity, abstract reasoning,*** language, and ***introspection.***
And as you may have noticed, their technology could ***wipe us out*** with the snap of their fingers.
But they ***haven't*** done that...so they're ***not*** hostile?
I'd say that depends on which side of the ***bed*** they wake up on. Their ***dog*** did kill all those men in that facility.
And the ***portal?*** Did they put it there?
If they did... it was in a ***bygone*** era.
Scientists from ***both*** sides of the portal have been debating that ***artifact's*** origin for ***three centuries...*** if it is an artifact, that is.

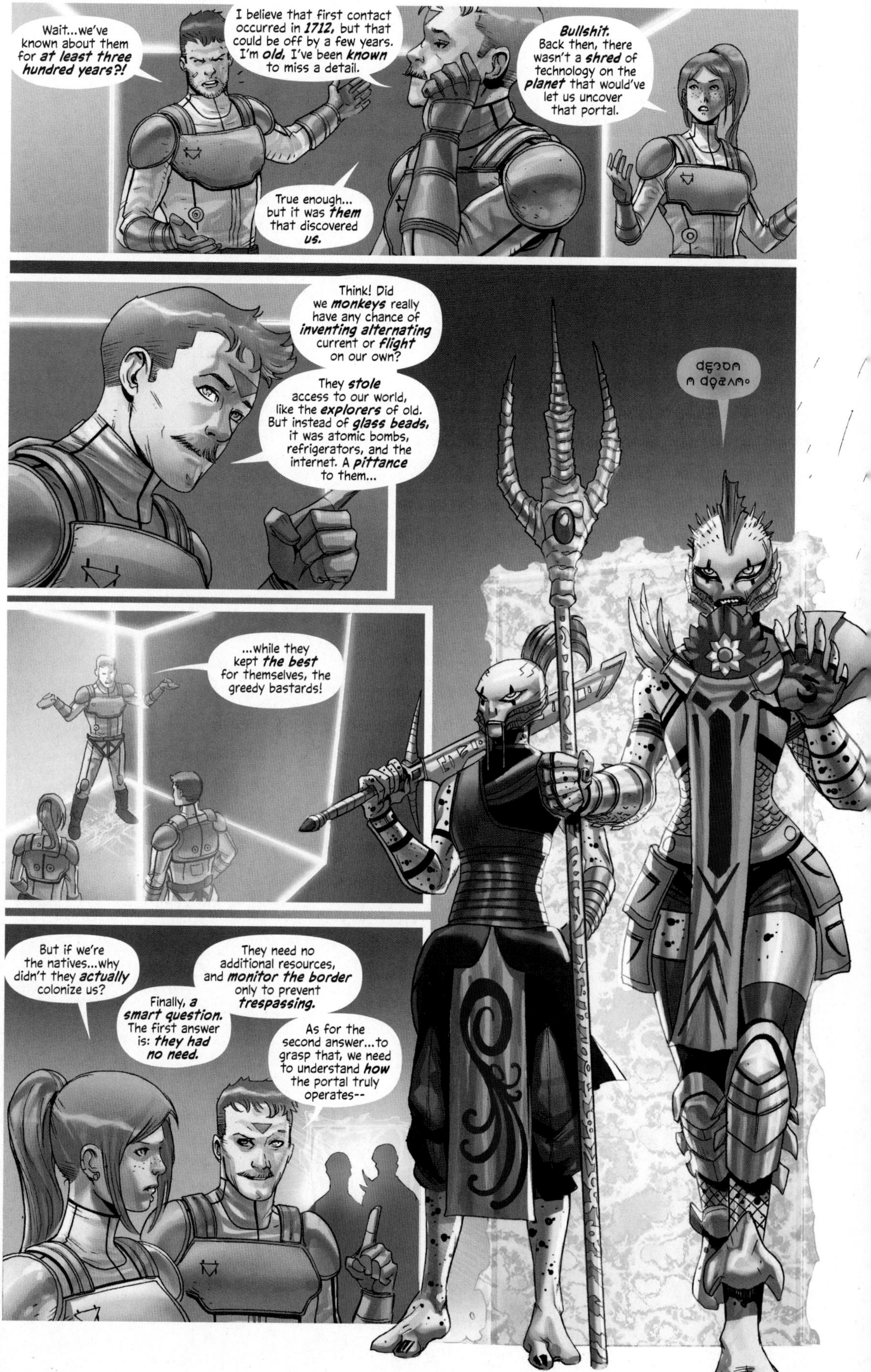
Wait...we've known about them for at least three hundred years?!
I believe that first contact occurred in 1712, but that could be off by a few years. I'm old, I've been known to miss a detail.
Bullshit. Back then, there wasn't a shred of technology on the planet that would've let us uncover that portal.
True enough... but it was them that discovered us.
Think! Did we monkeys really have any chance of inventing alternating current or flight on our own?
They stole access to our world, like the explorers of old. But instead of glass beads, it was atomic bombs, refrigerators, and the internet. A pittance to them...
...while they kept the best for themselves, the greedy bastards!
But if we're the natives...why didn't they actually colonize us?
They need no additional resources, and monitor the border only to prevent trespassing.
Finally, a smart question. The first answer is: they had no need.
As for the second answer...to grasp that, we need to understand how the portal truly operates--

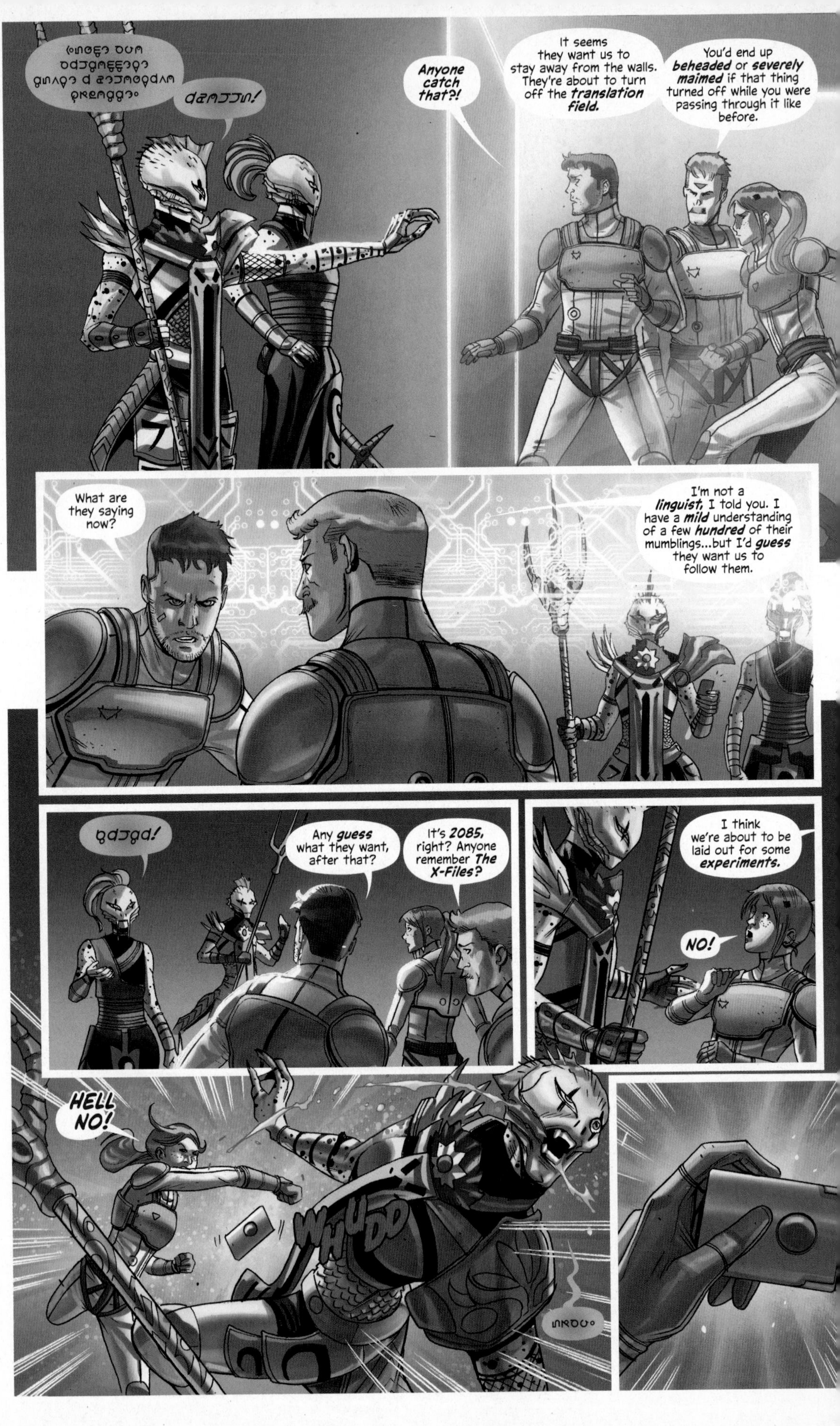
Anyone catch that?!
It seems they want us to stay away from the walls. They're about to turn off the translation field.
You'd end up beheaded or severely maimed if that thing turned off while you were passing through it like before.
What are they saying now?
I'm not a linguist, I told you. I have a mild understanding of a few hundred of their mumblings...but I'd guess they want us to follow them.
Any guess what they want, after that?
It's 2085, right? Anyone remember The X-Files?
I think we're about to be laid out for some experiments.
NO!
HELL NO!
WHUDD

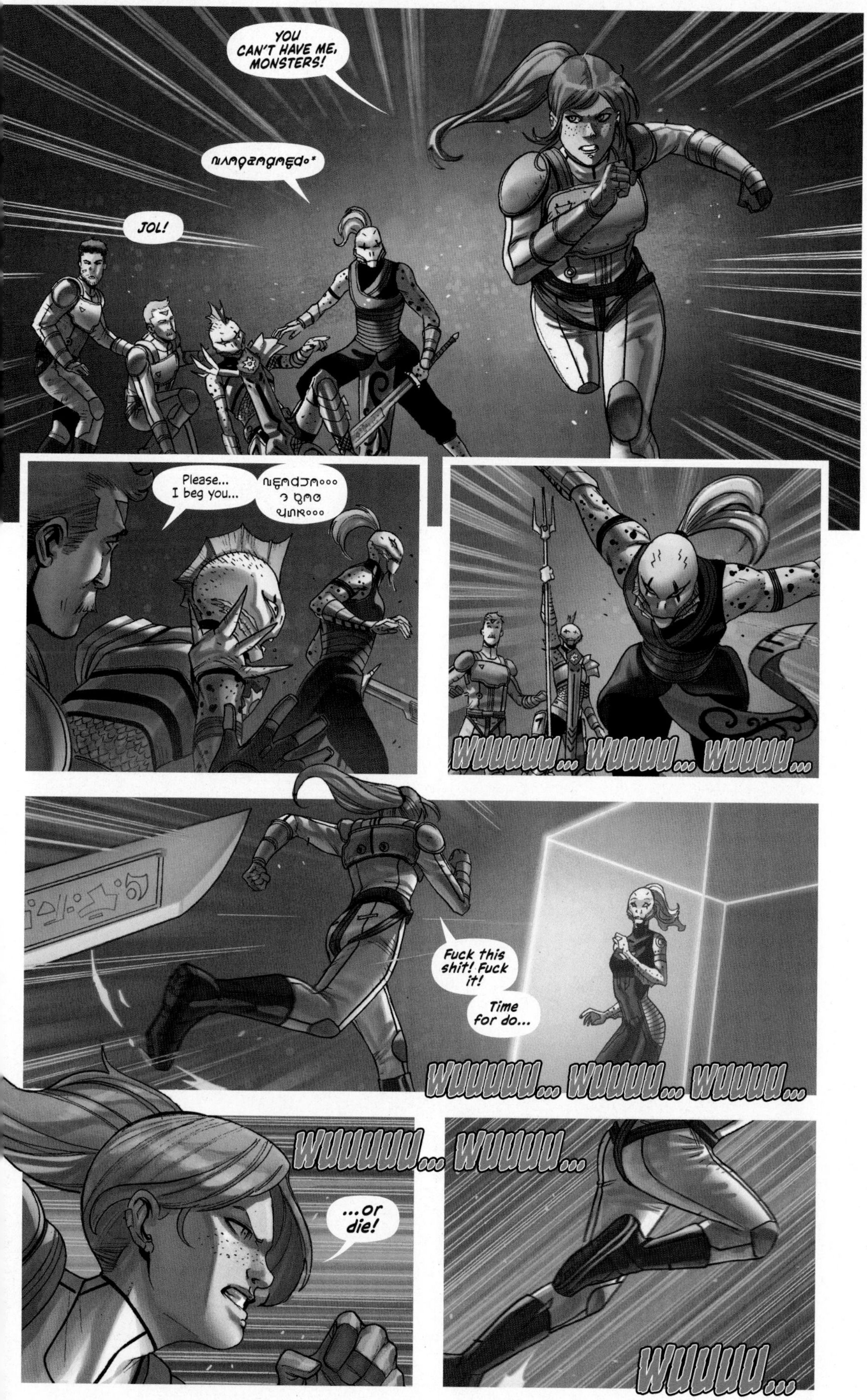
YOU CAN'T HAVE ME, MONSTERS!
JOL!
Please... I beg you...
WUUUUU... WUUUU... WUUUU...
Fuck this shit! Fuck it!
Time for do...
WUUUUU... WUUUU... WUUUU...
WUUUUU... WUUUU...
...or die!
WUUUU...

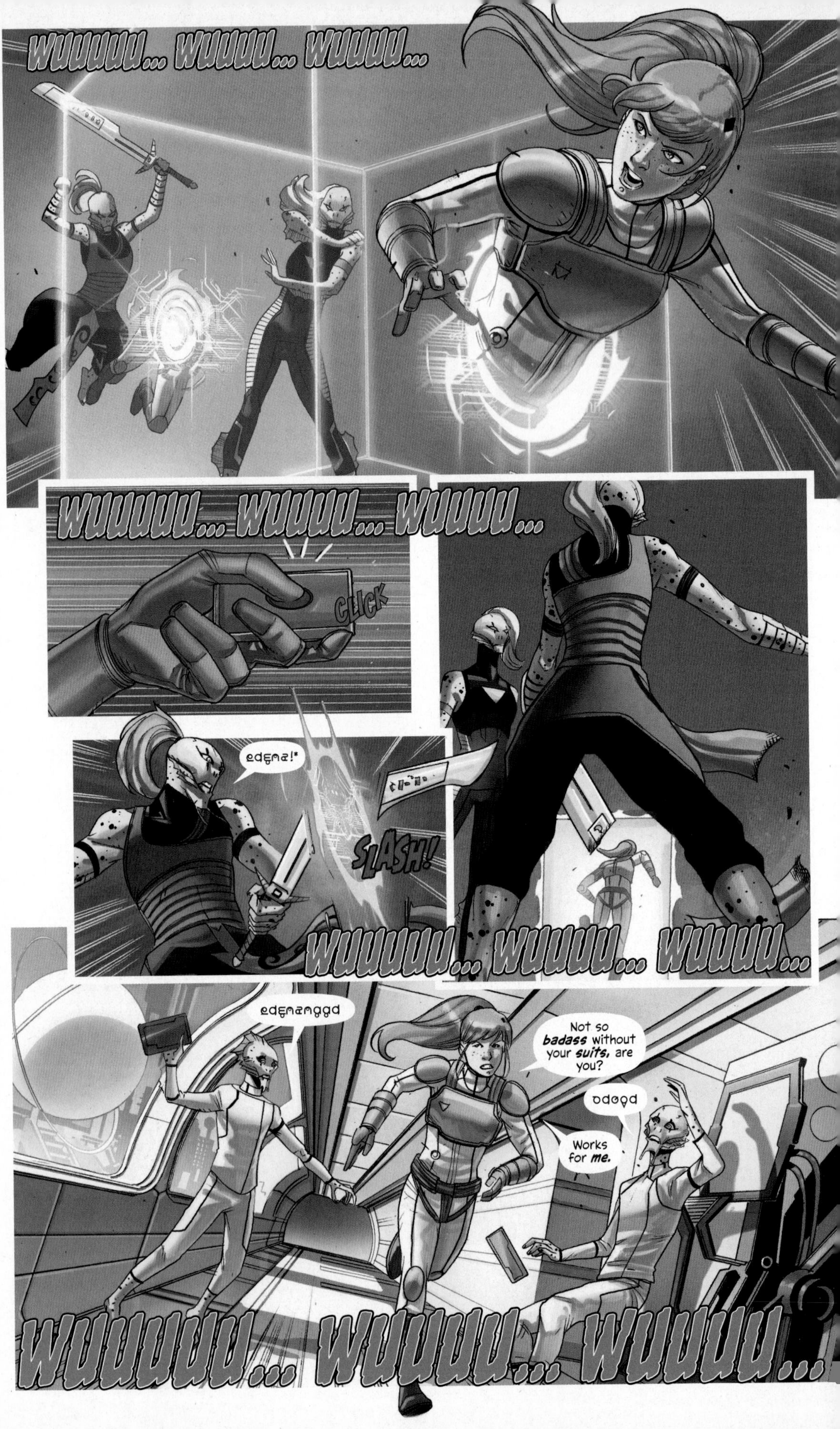

WUUUUU... WUUUU... WUUUU...
WUUUUU... WUUUU... WUUUU...
CLICK
SLASH!
WUUUUU... WUUUU... WUUUU...
Not so *badass* without your *suits,* are you?
Works for *me.*
WUUUUU... WUUUU... WUUUU...

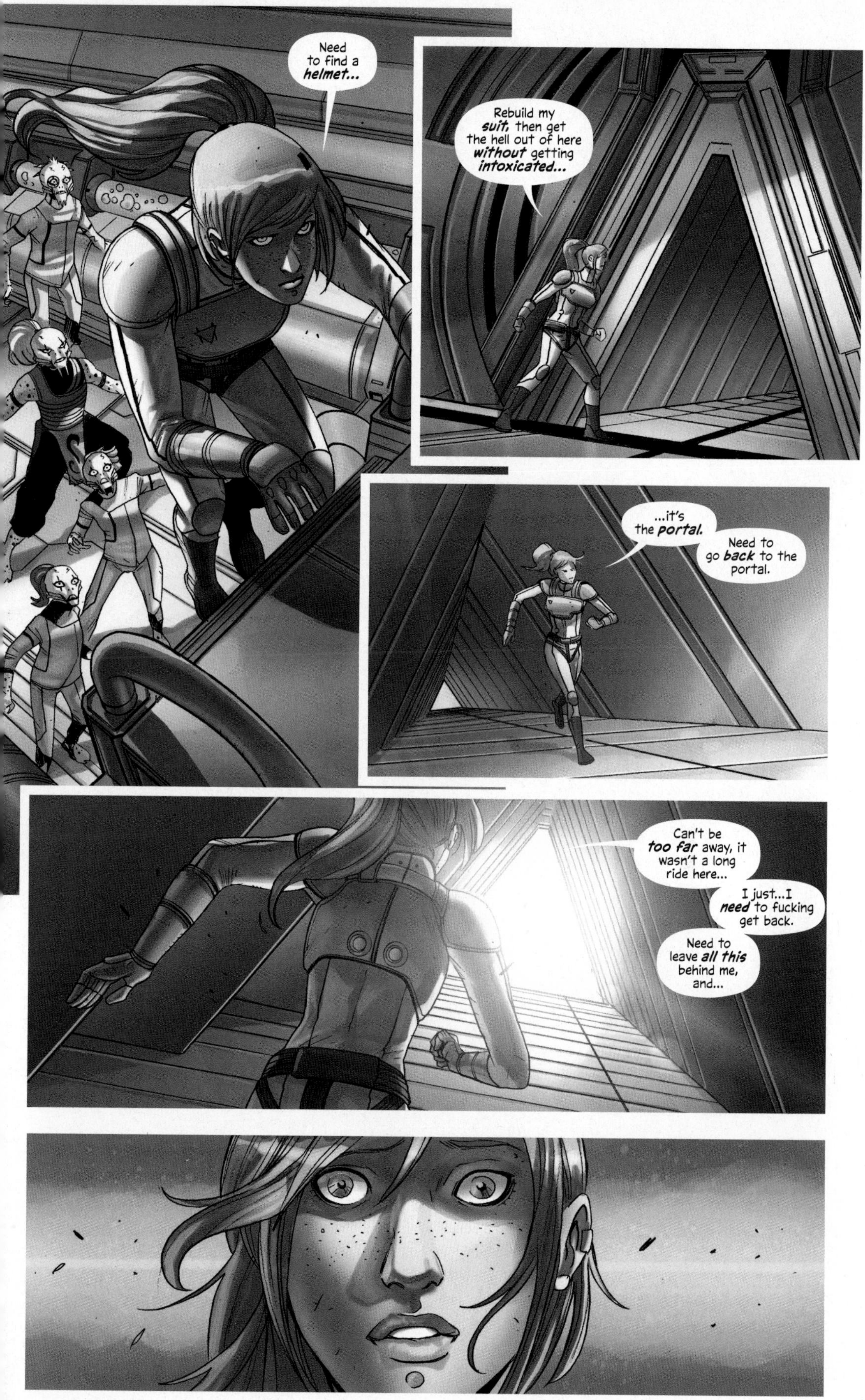
Need to find a *helmet...*
Rebuild my *suit,* then get the hell out of here *without* getting *intoxicated...*
...it's the *portal.*
Need to go *back* to the portal.
Can't be *too far* away, it wasn't a long ride here...
I just...I *need* to fucking get back.
Need to leave *all this* behind me, and...

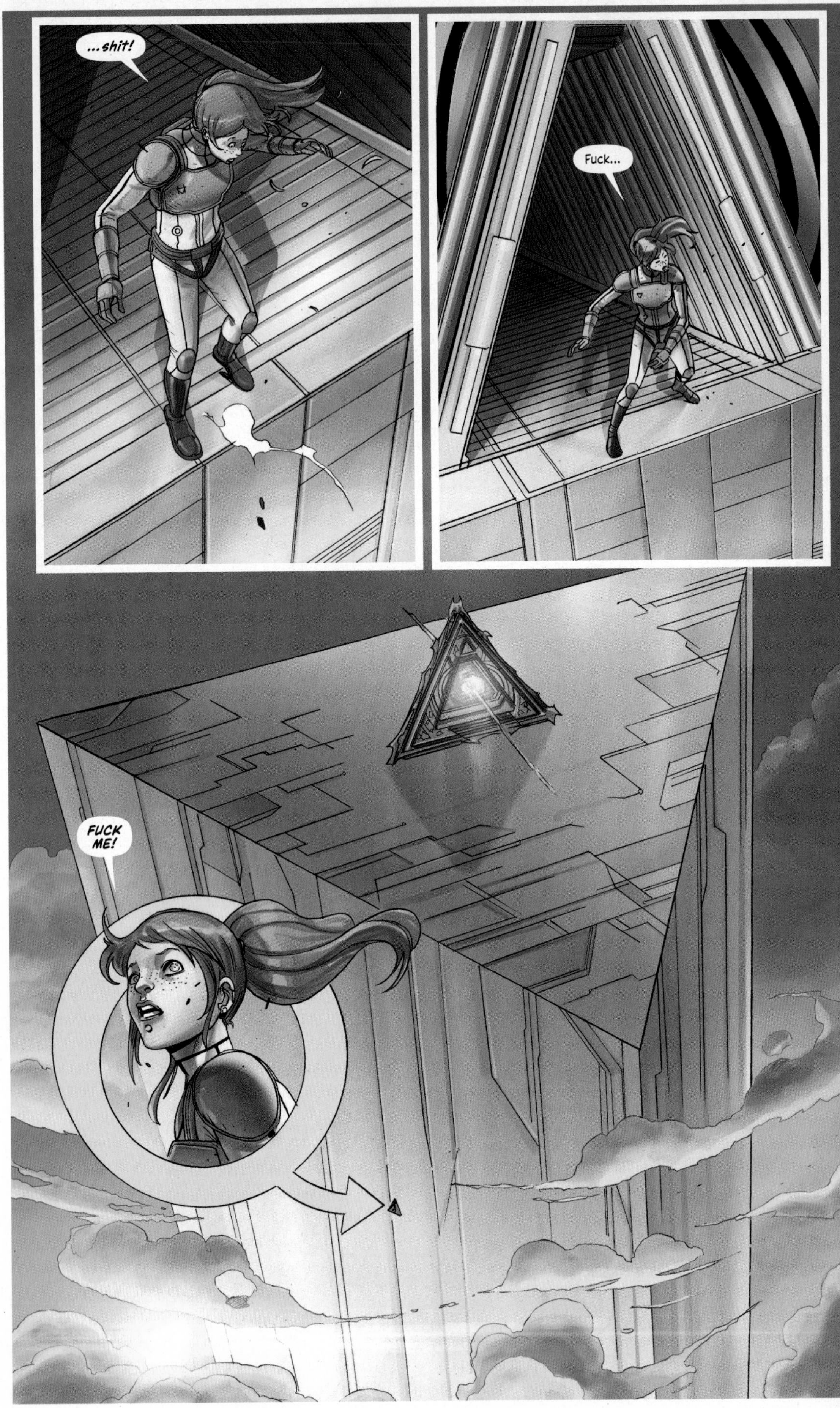
...shit!
Fuck...
FUCK ME!

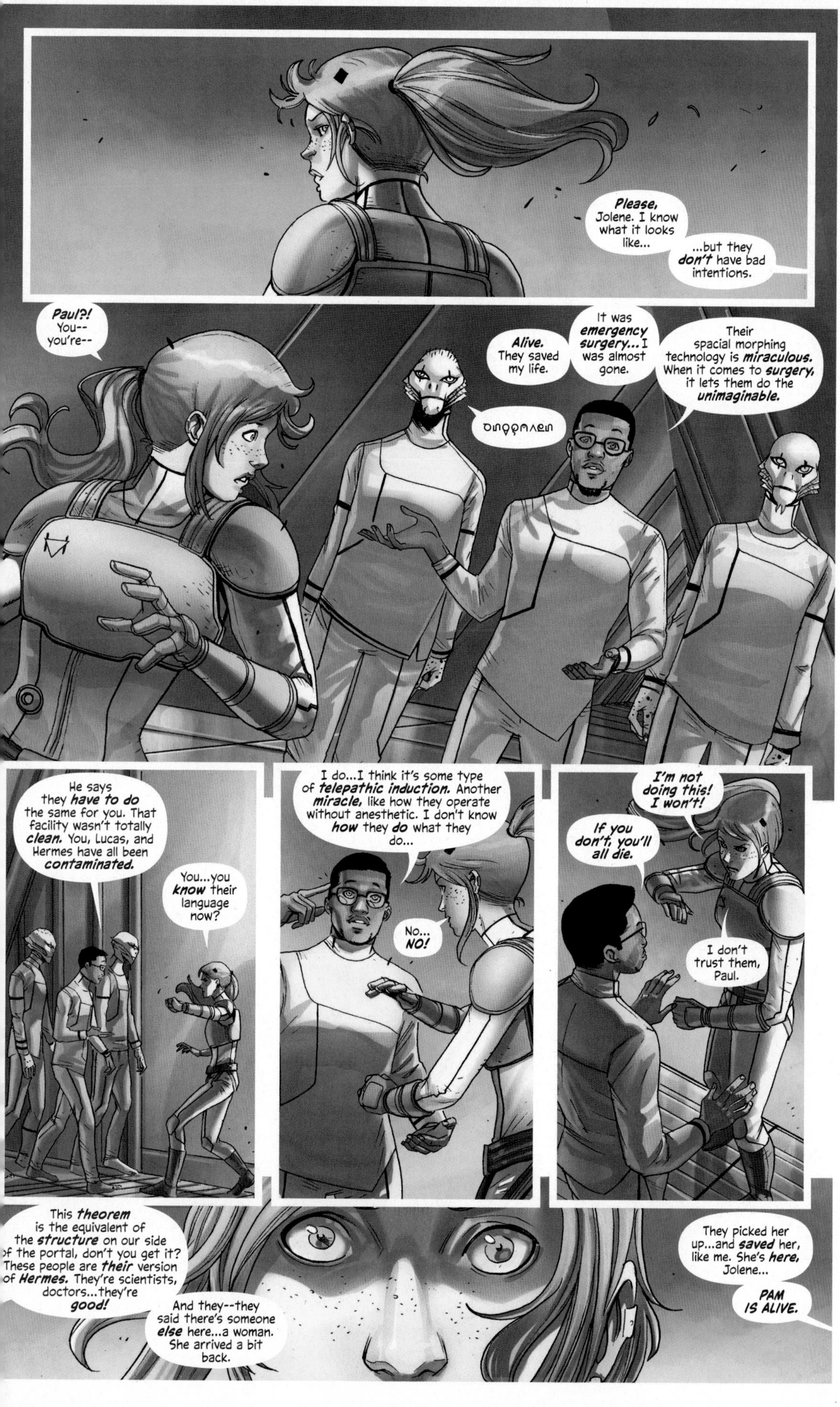
Please, Jolene. I know what it looks like...
...but they don't have bad intentions.
Paul?! You-- you're--
Alive. They saved my life.
It was emergency surgery... I was almost gone.
Their spacial morphing technology is miraculous. When it comes to surgery, it lets them do the unimaginable.
He says they have to do the same for you. That facility wasn't totally clean. You, Lucas, and Hermes have all been contaminated.
You...you know their language now?
I do...I think it's some type of telepathic induction. Another miracle, like how they operate without anesthetic. I don't know how they do what they do...
No... NO!
I'm not doing this! I won't!
If you don't, you'll all die.
I don't trust them, Paul.
This theorem is the equivalent of the structure on our side of the portal, don't you get it? These people are their version of Hermes. They're scientists, doctors...they're good!
And they--they said there's someone else here...a woman. She arrived a bit back.
They picked her up...and saved her, like me. She's here, Jolene...
PAM IS ALIVE.

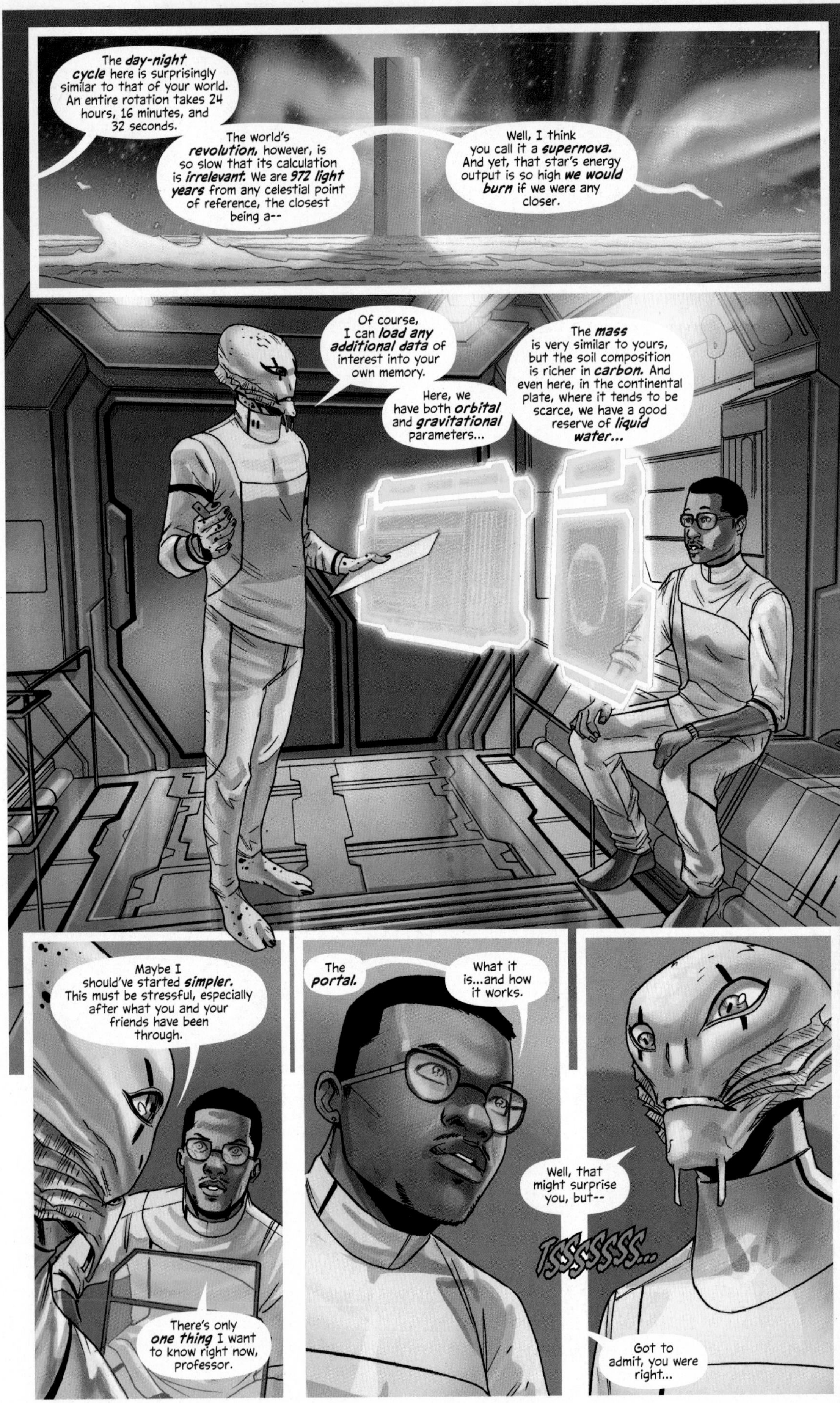
The day-night cycle here is surprisingly similar to that of your world. An entire rotation takes 24 hours, 16 minutes, and 32 seconds.
The world's revolution, however, is so slow that its calculation is irrelevant. We are 972 light years from any celestial point of reference, the closest being a--
Well, I think you call it a supernova. And yet, that star's energy output is so high we would burn if we were any closer.
Of course, I can load any additional data of interest into your own memory.
Here, we have both orbital and gravitational parameters...
The mass is very similar to yours, but the soil composition is richer in carbon. And even here, in the continental plate, where it tends to be scarce, we have a good reserve of liquid water...
Maybe I should've started simpler. This must be stressful, especially after what you and your friends have been through.
There's only one thing I want to know right now, professor.
The portal.
What it is...and how it works.
Well, that might surprise you, but--
TSSSSSS...
Got to admit, you were right...

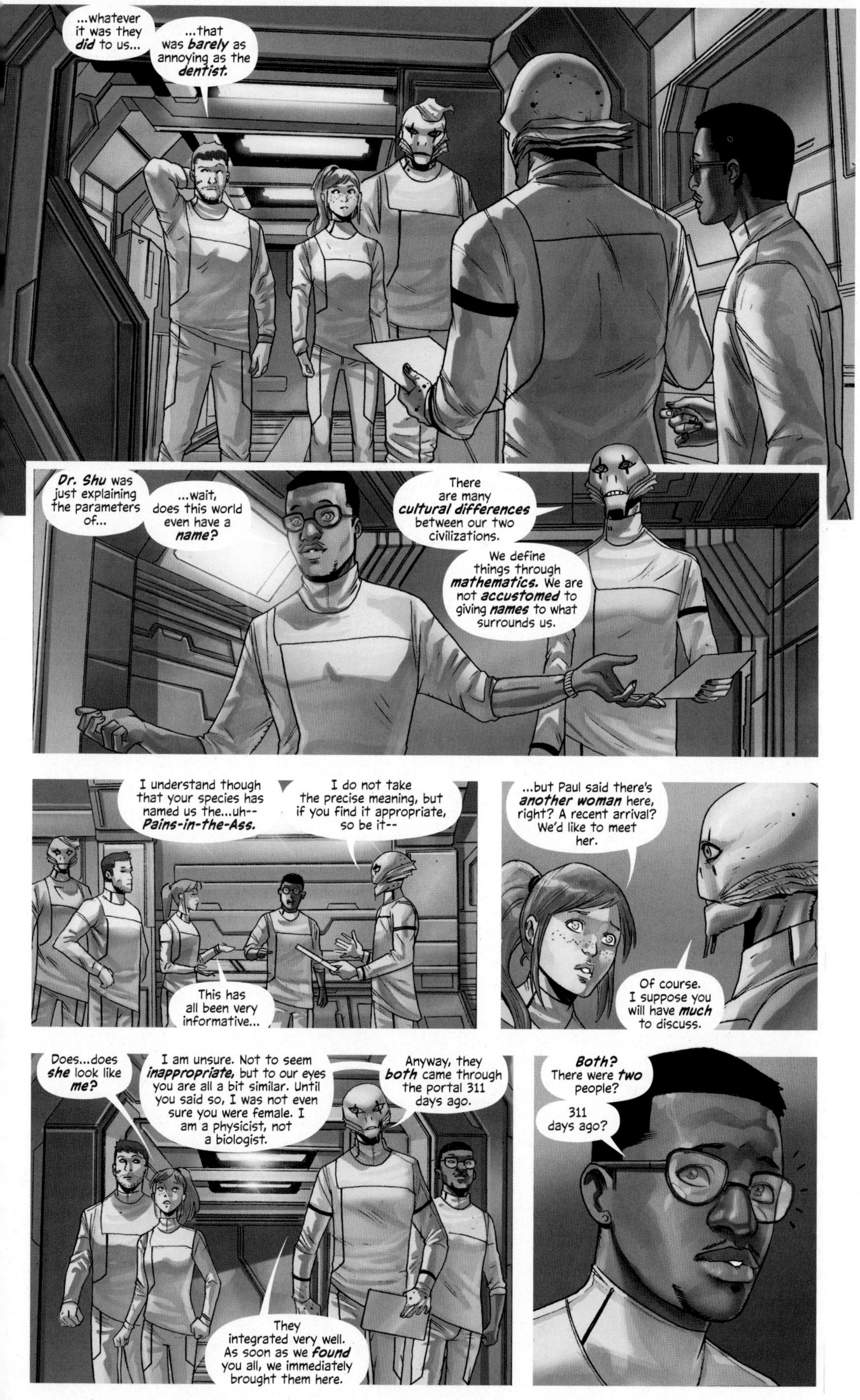

...whatever it was they did to us...
...that was barely as annoying as the dentist.
Dr. Shu was just explaining the parameters of...
...wait, does this world even have a name?
There are many cultural differences between our two civilizations.
We define things through mathematics. We are not accustomed to giving names to what surrounds us.
I understand though that your species has named us the...uh-- Pains-in-the-Ass.
I do not take the precise meaning, but if you find it appropriate, so be it--
This has all been very informative...
...but Paul said there's another woman here, right? A recent arrival? We'd like to meet her.
Of course. I suppose you will have much to discuss.
Does...does she look like me?
I am unsure. Not to seem inappropriate, but to our eyes you are all a bit similar. Until you said so, I was not even sure you were female. I am a physicist, not a biologist.
Anyway, they both came through the portal 311 days ago.
They integrated very well. As soon as we found you all, we immediately brought them here.
Both? There were two people?
311 days ago?

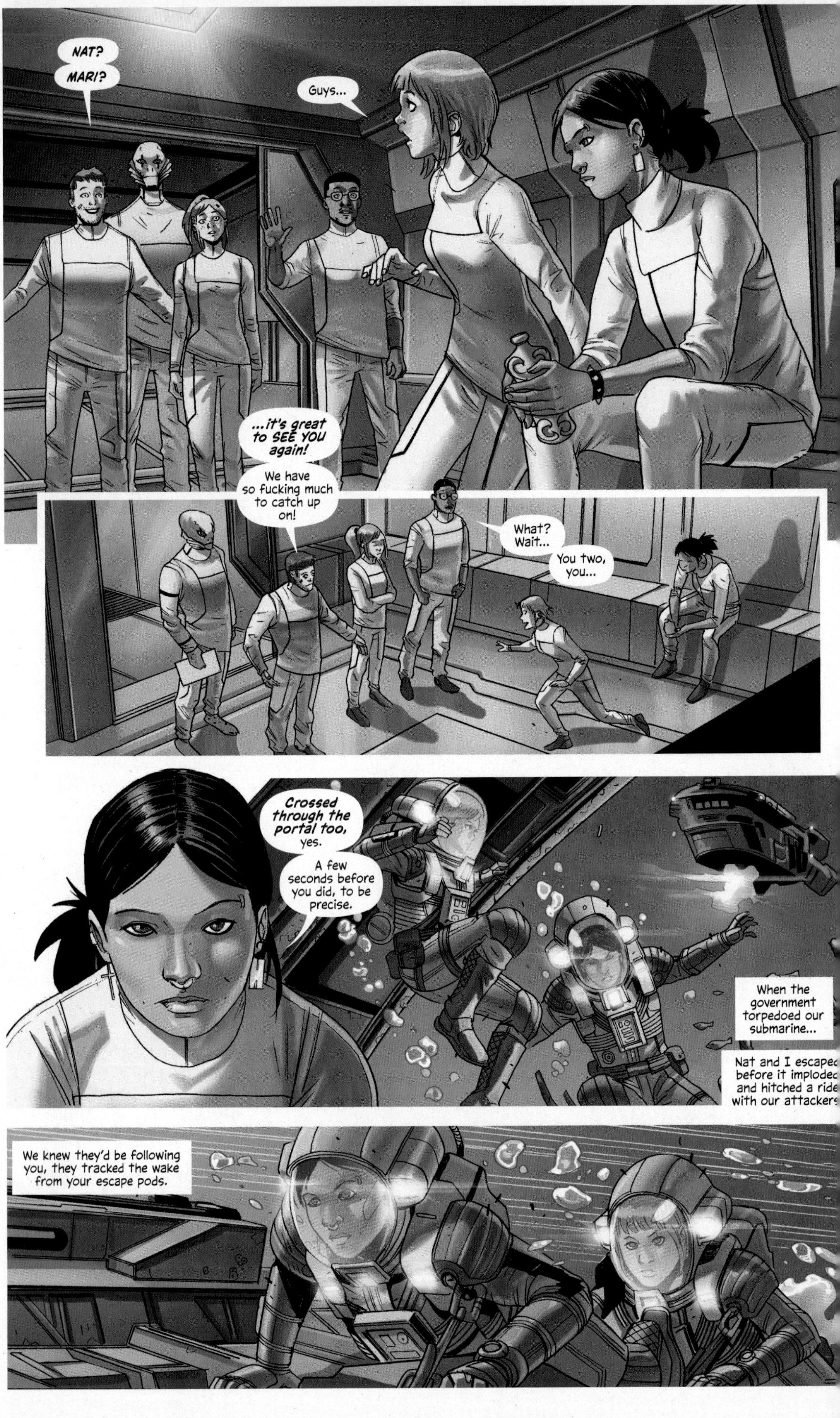
NAT?
MARI?
Guys...
...it's great to SEE YOU again!
We have so fucking much to catch up on!
What? Wait...
You two, you...
Crossed through the portal too, yes.
A few seconds before you did, to be precise.
When the government torpedoed our submarine...
Nat and I escaped before it imploded and hitched a ride with our attackers.
We knew they'd be following you, they tracked the wake from your escape pods.

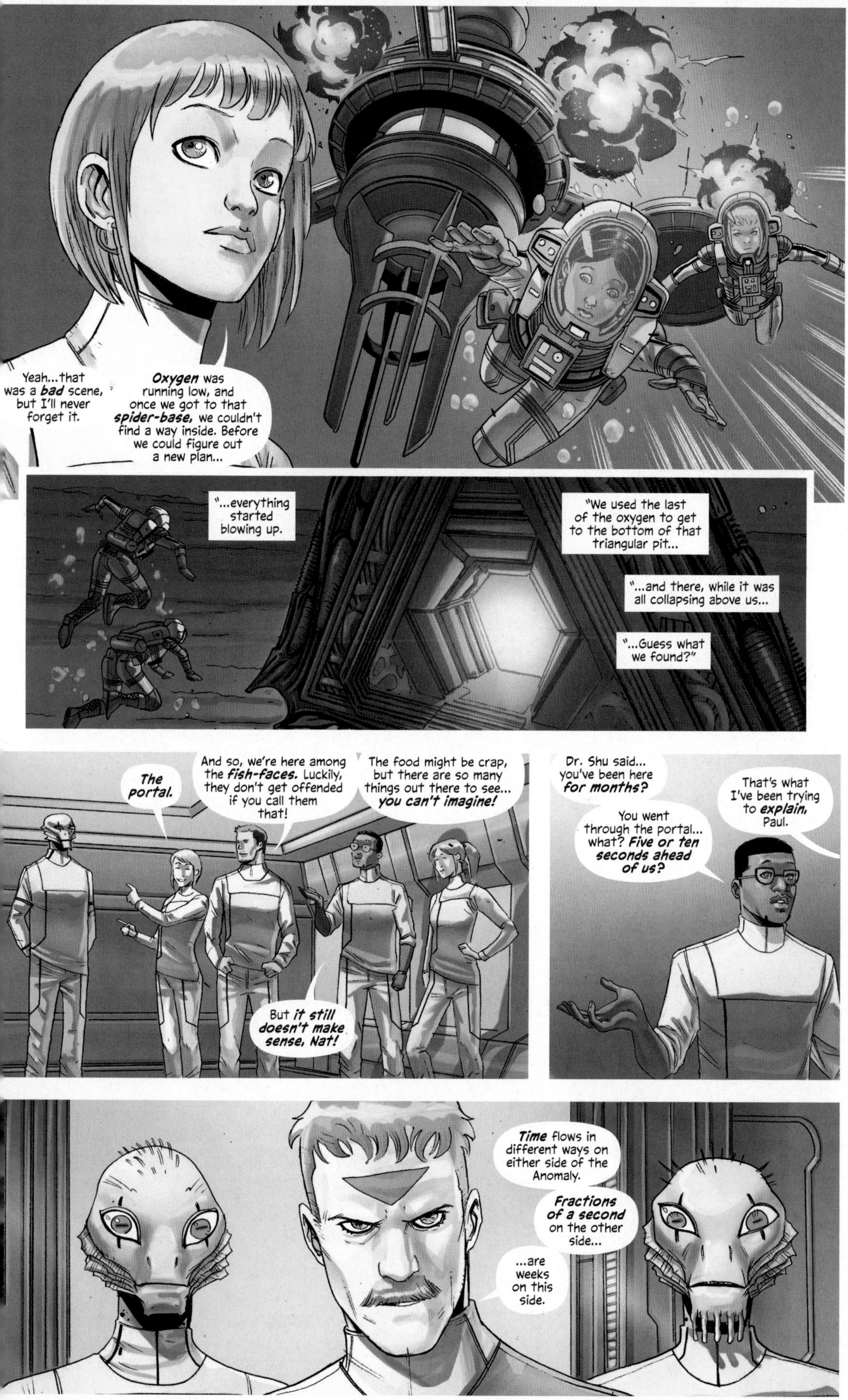

Yeah...that was a *bad* scene, but I'll never forget it.
Oxygen was running low, and once we got to that *spider-base,* we couldn't find a way inside. Before we could figure out a new plan...
"...everything started blowing up.
"We used the last of the oxygen to get to the bottom of that triangular pit...
"...and there, while it was all collapsing above us...
"...Guess what we found?"
The portal.
And so, we're here among the *fish-faces.* Luckily, they don't get offended if you call them that!
The food might be crap, but there are so many things out there to see... *you can't imagine!*
But *it still doesn't make sense, Nat!*
Dr. Shu said... you've been here *for months?*
You went through the portal... what? *Five or ten seconds ahead of us?*
That's what I've been trying to *explain,* Paul.
Time flows in different ways on either side of the Anomaly.
Fractions of a second on the other side...
...are weeks on this side.

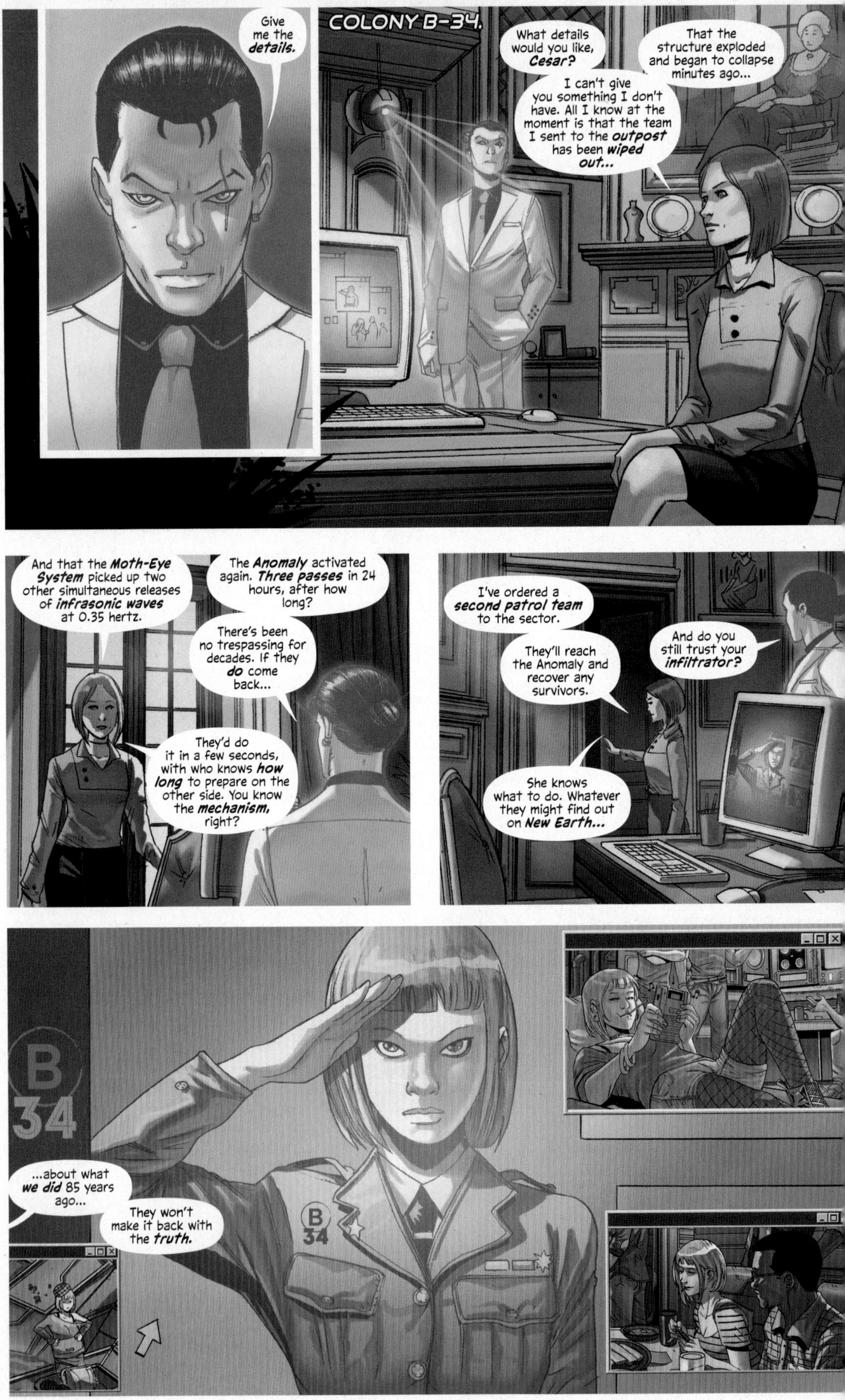
Give me the details.
COLONY B-34.
What details would you like, Cesar?
I can't give you something I don't have. All I know at the moment is that the team I sent to the outpost has been wiped out...
That the structure exploded and began to collapse minutes ago...
And that the Moth-Eye System picked up two other simultaneous releases of infrasonic waves at 0.35 hertz.
The Anomaly activated again. Three passes in 24 hours, after how long?
There's been no trespassing for decades. If they do come back...
They'd do it in a few seconds, with who knows how long to prepare on the other side. You know the mechanism, right?
I've ordered a second patrol team to the sector.
They'll reach the Anomaly and recover any survivors.
And do you still trust your infiltrator?
She knows what to do. Whatever they might find out on New Earth...
B 34
...about what we did 85 years ago...
They won't make it back with the truth.

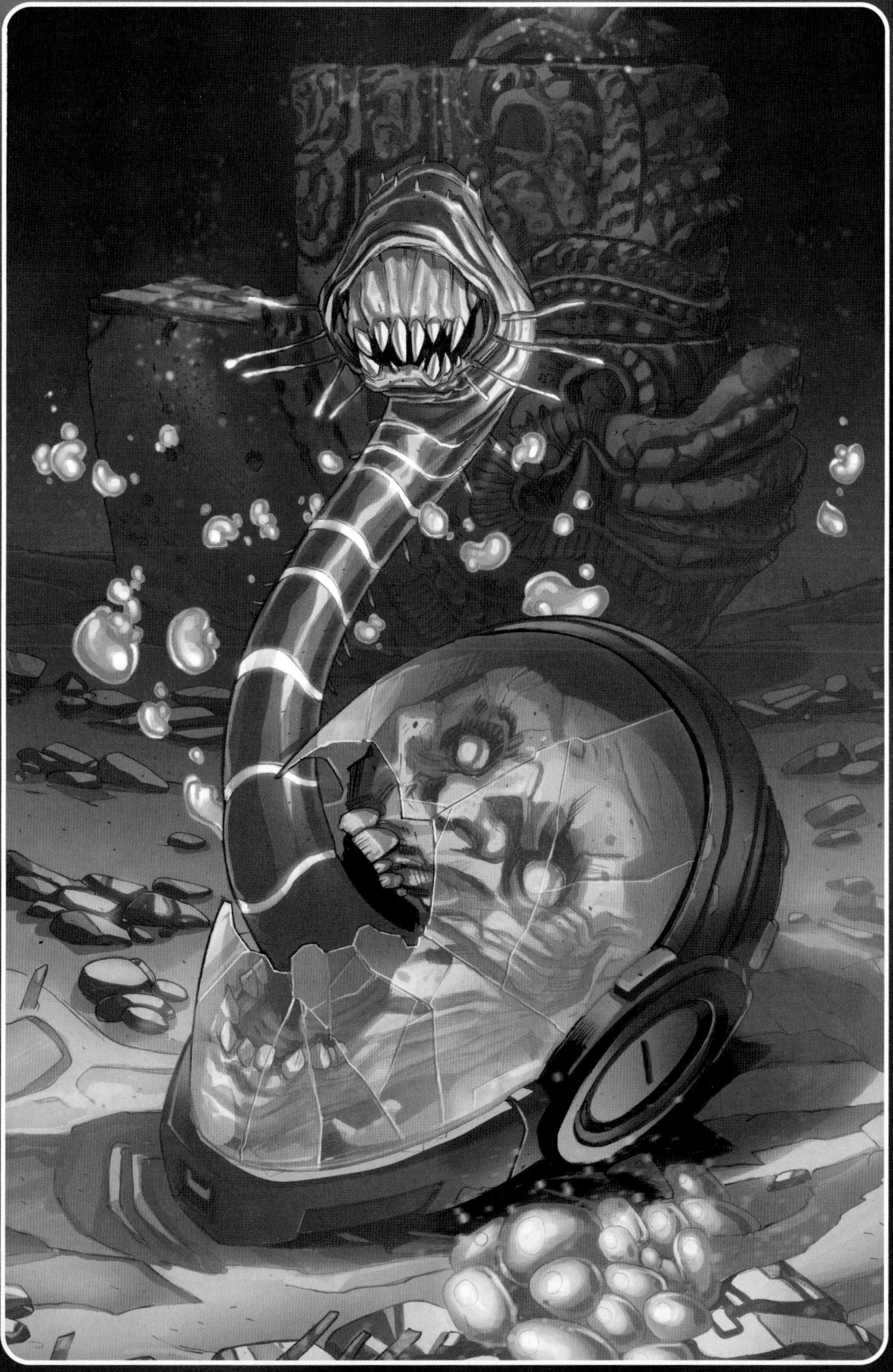

CHAPTER 06

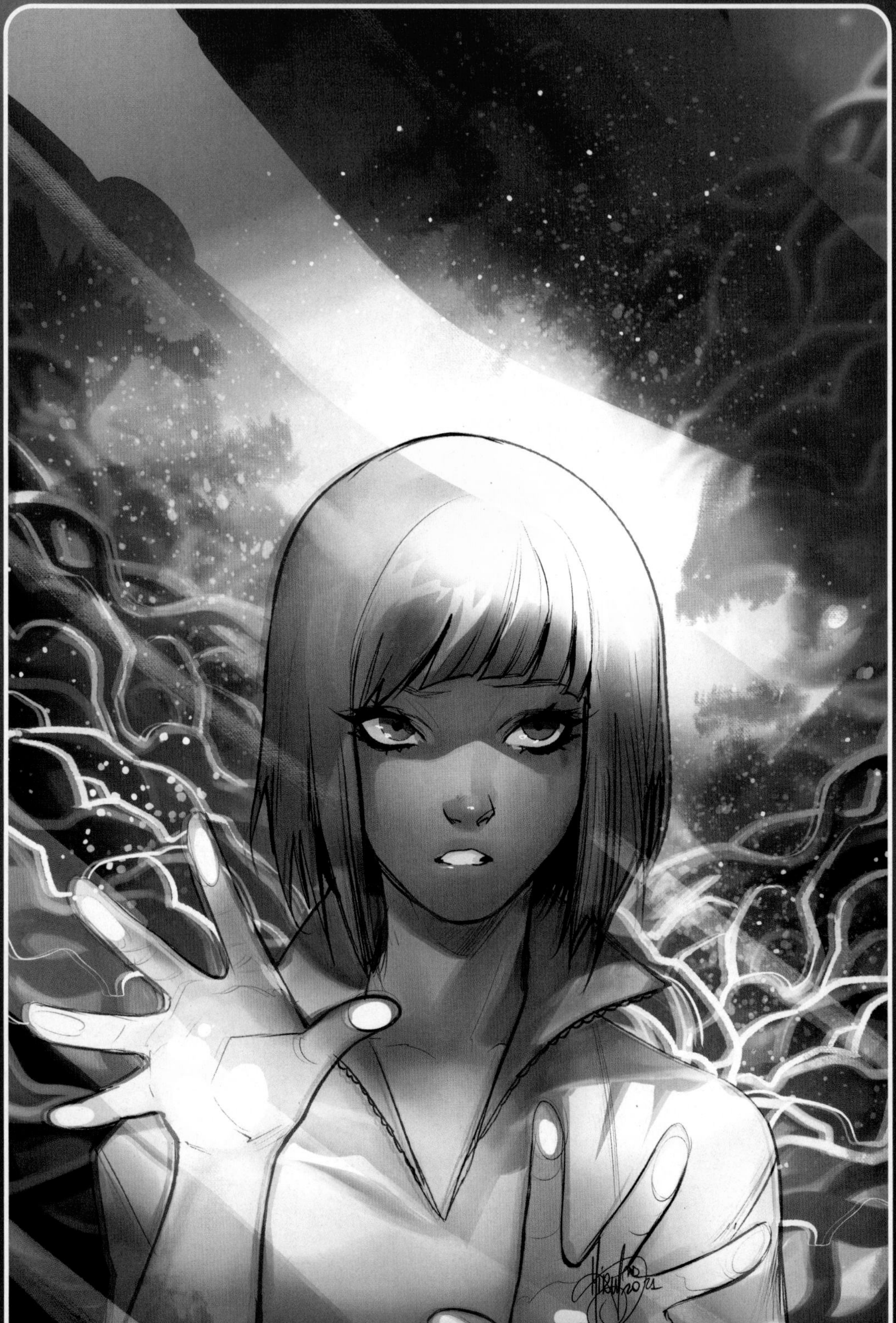

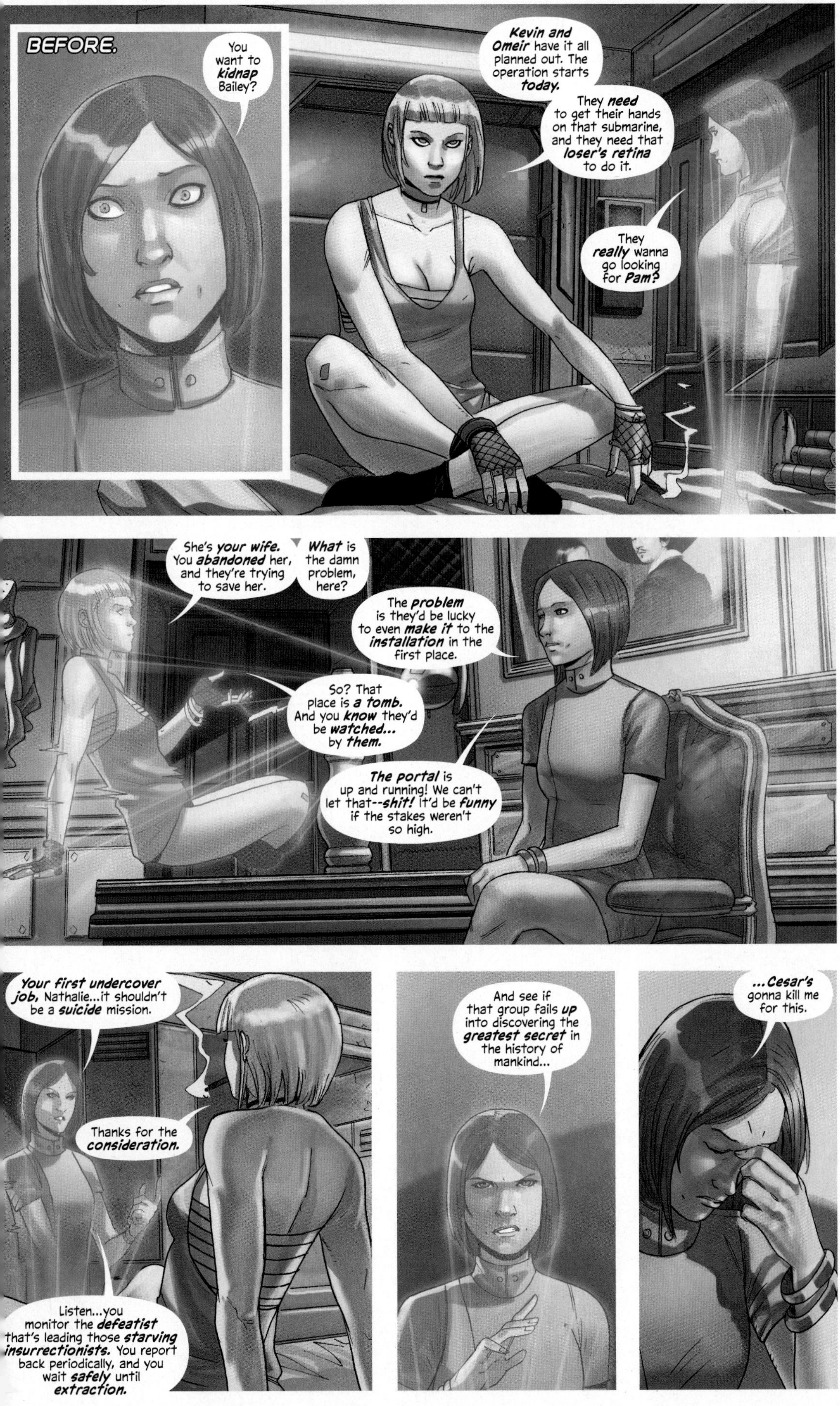

BEFORE.
You want to kidnap Bailey?
Kevin and Omeir have it all planned out. The operation starts today.
They need to get their hands on that submarine, and they need that loser's retina to do it.
They really wanna go looking for Pam?
She's your wife. You abandoned her, and they're trying to save her.
What is the damn problem, here?
The problem is they'd be lucky to even make it to the installation in the first place.
So? That place is a tomb. And you know they'd be watched... by them.
The portal is up and running! We can't let that--shit! It'd be funny if the stakes weren't so high.
Your first undercover job, Nathalie...it shouldn't be a suicide mission.
Thanks for the consideration.
Listen...you monitor the defeatist that's leading those starving insurrectionists. You report back periodically, and you wait safely until extraction.
And see if that group fails up into discovering the greatest secret in the history of mankind...
...Cesar's gonna kill me for this.

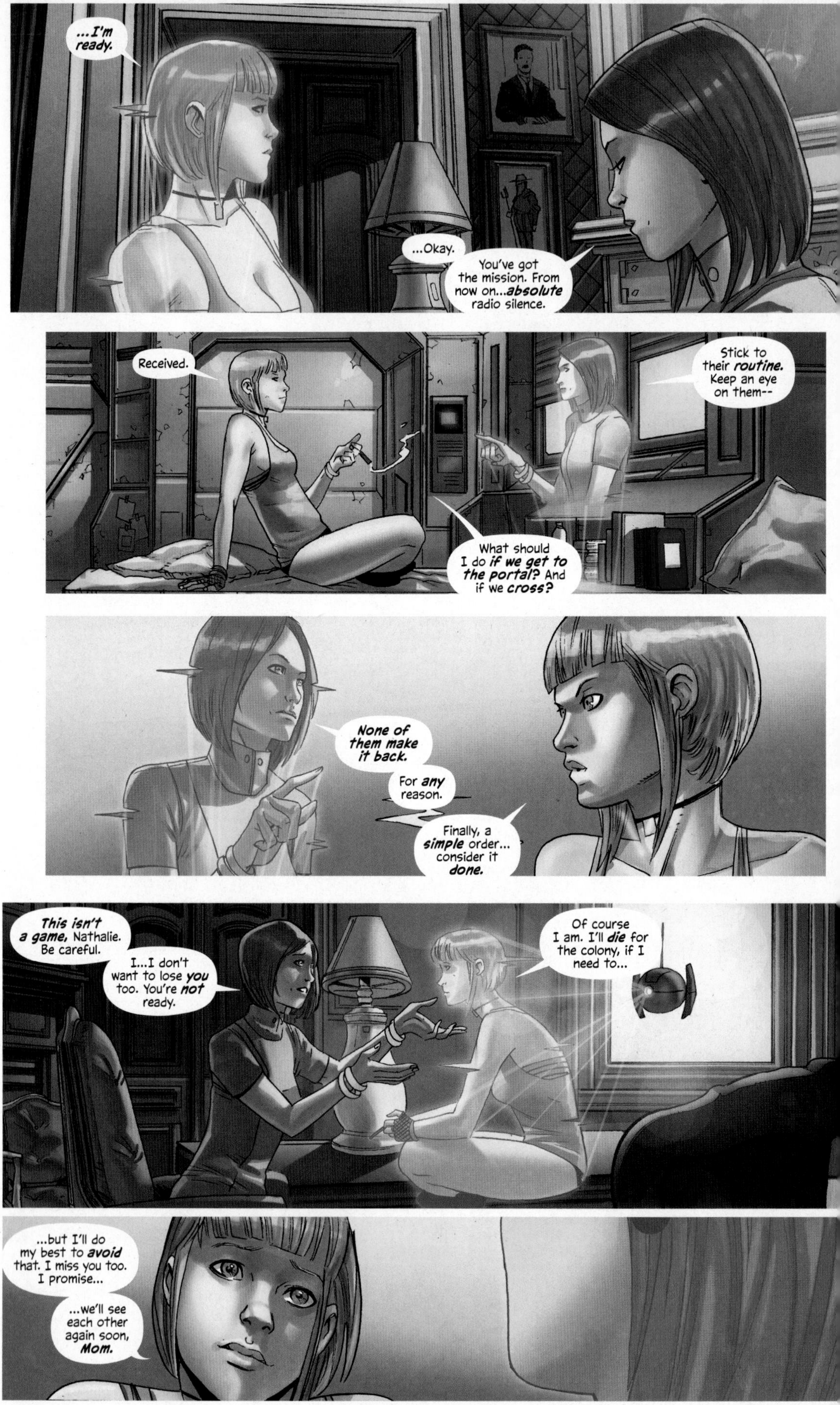
...I'm ready.
...Okay.
You've got the mission. From now on...absolute radio silence.
Received.
Stick to their routine. Keep an eye on them--
What should I do if we get to the portal? And if we cross?
None of them make it back.
For any reason.
Finally, a simple order... consider it done.
This isn't a game, Nathalie. Be careful.
I...I don't want to lose you too. You're not ready.
Of course I am. I'll die for the colony, if I need to...
...but I'll do my best to avoid that. I miss you too. I promise...
...we'll see each other again soon, Mom.

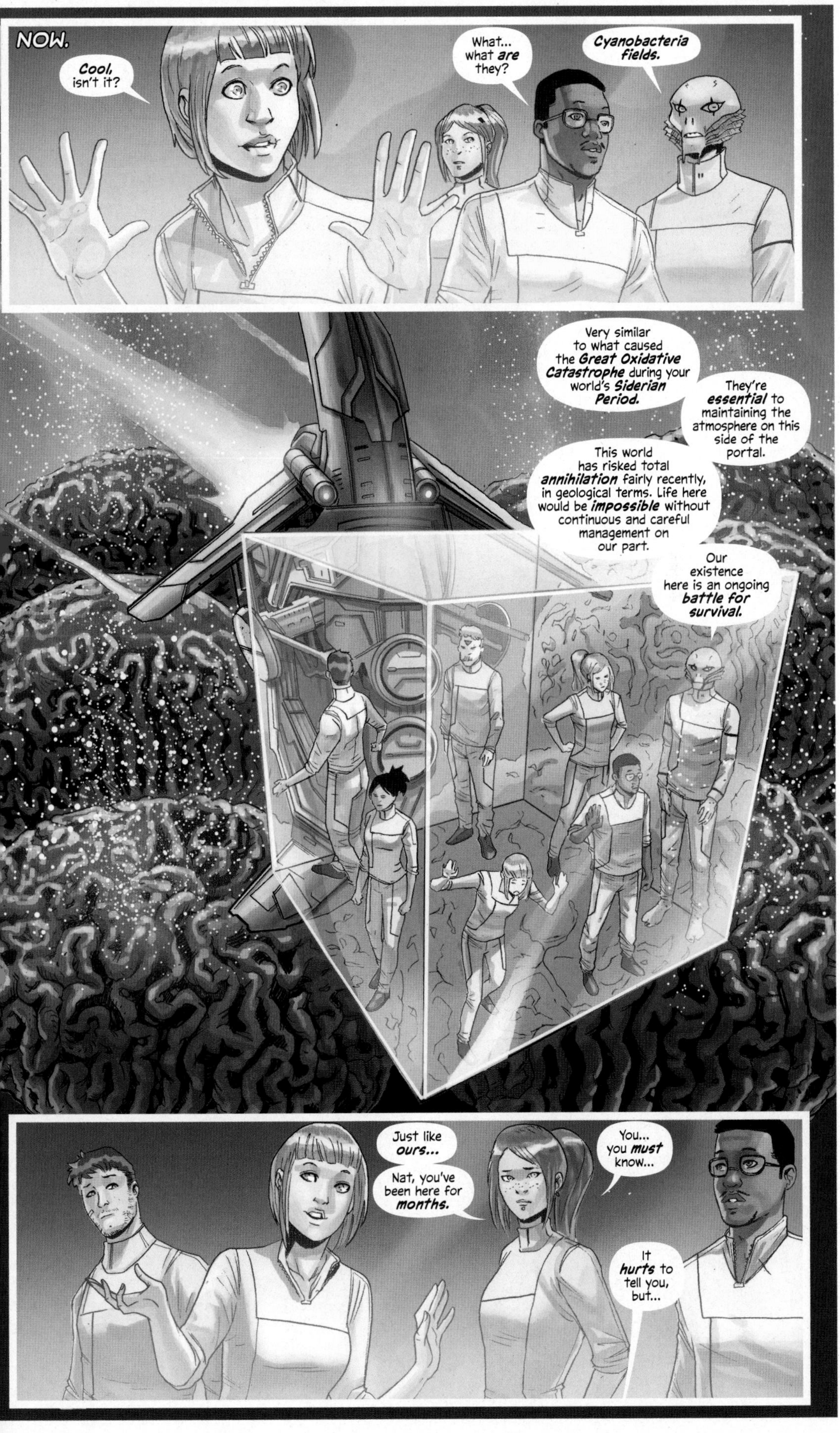
NOW.
Cool, isn't it?
What... what are they?
Cyanobacteria fields.
Very similar to what caused the Great Oxidative Catastrophe during your world's Siderian Period.
They're essential to maintaining the atmosphere on this side of the portal.
This world has risked total annihilation fairly recently, in geological terms. Life here would be impossible without continuous and careful management on our part.
Our existence here is an ongoing battle for survival.
Just like ours...
Nat, you've been here for months.
You... you must know...
It hurts to tell you, but...

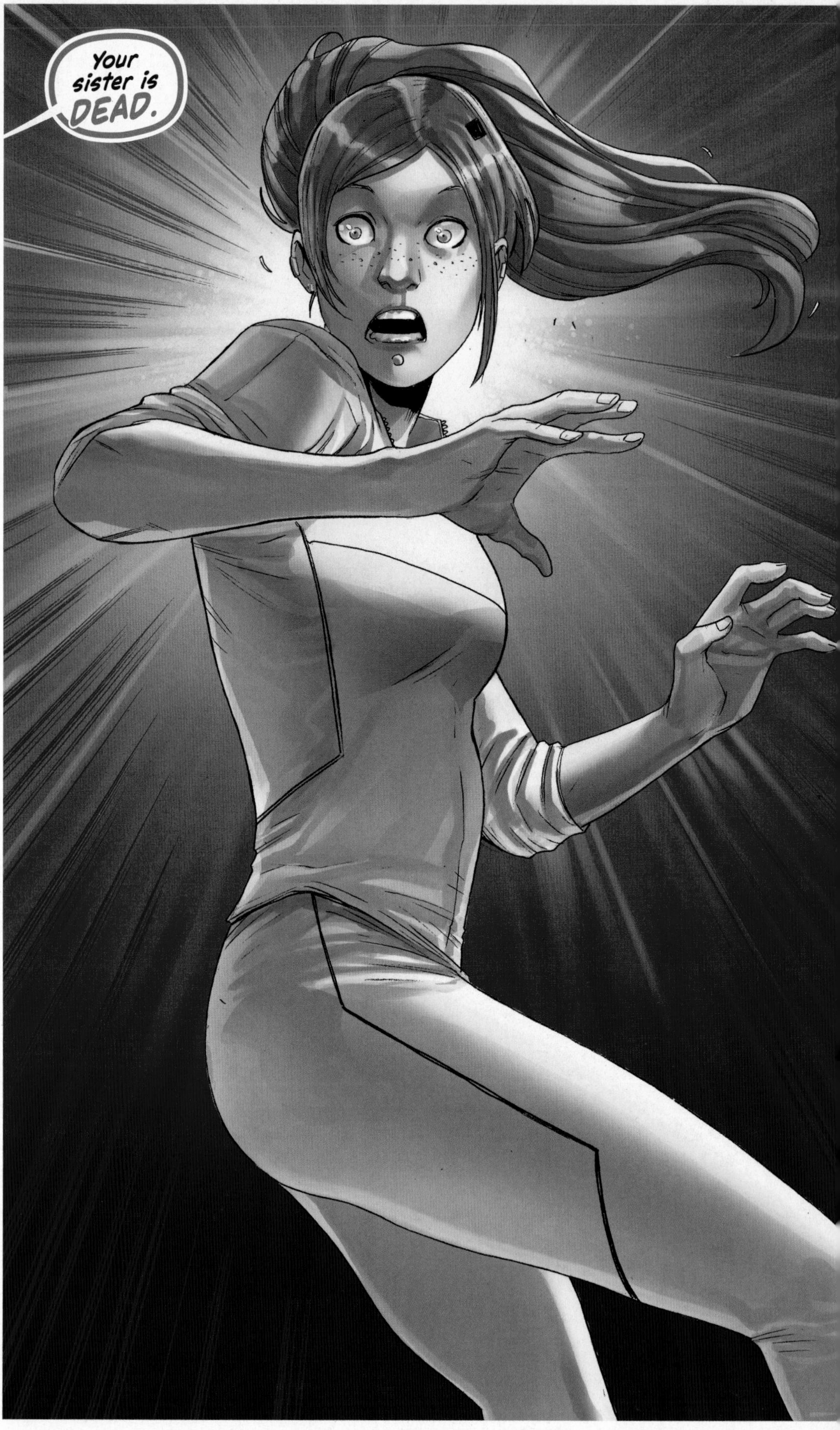
Your sister is DEAD.

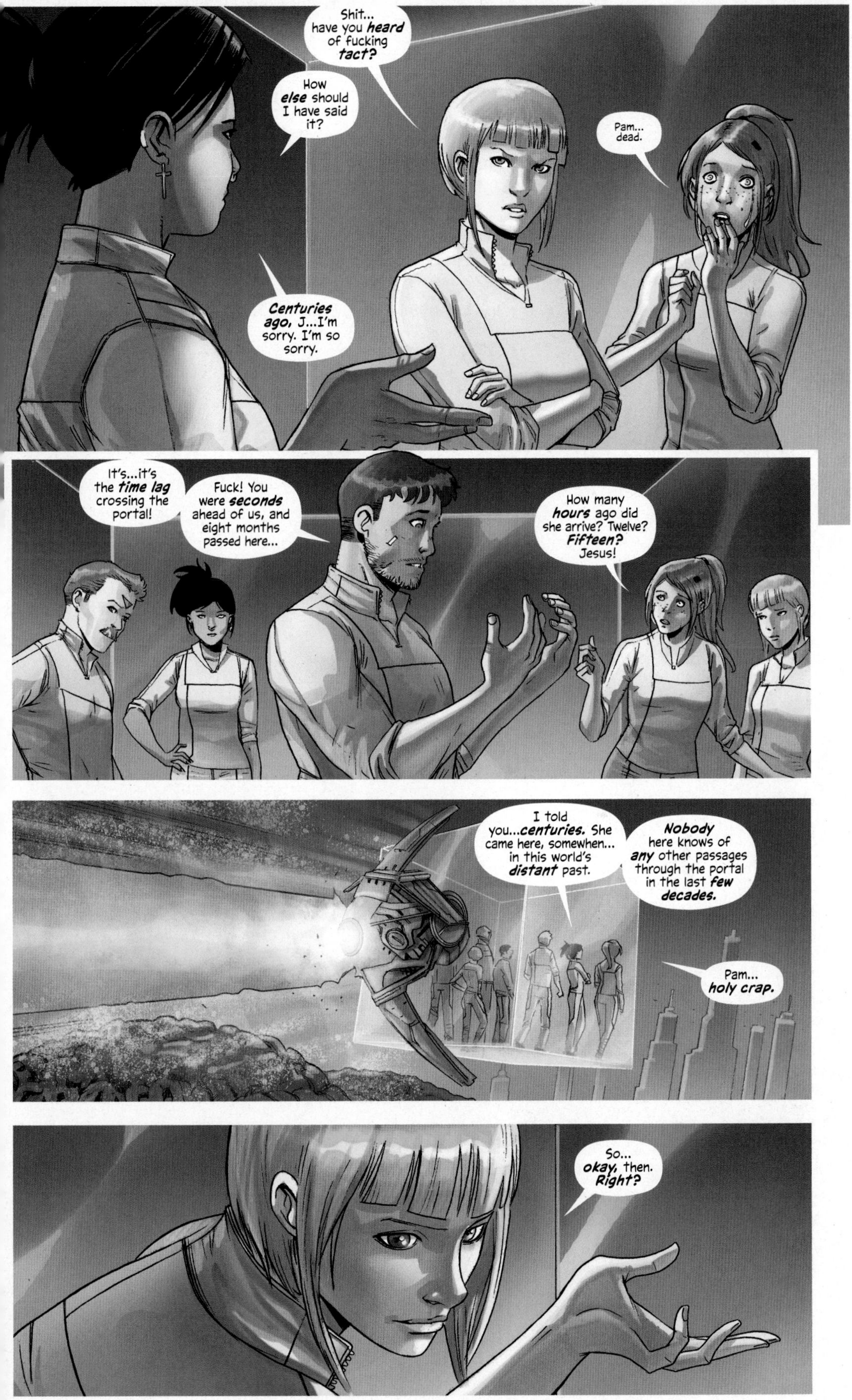
Shit... have you *heard* of fucking *tact?*
How *else* should I have said it?
Pam... dead.
Centuries ago, J...I'm sorry. I'm so sorry.
It's...it's the *time lag* crossing the portal!
Fuck! You were *seconds* ahead of us, and eight months passed here...
How many *hours* ago did she arrive? Twelve? *Fifteen?* Jesus!
I told you...*centuries.* She came here, somewhen... in this world's *distant* past.
Nobody here knows of *any* other passages through the portal in the last *few decades.*
Pam... *holy crap.*
So... *okay,* then. *Right?*

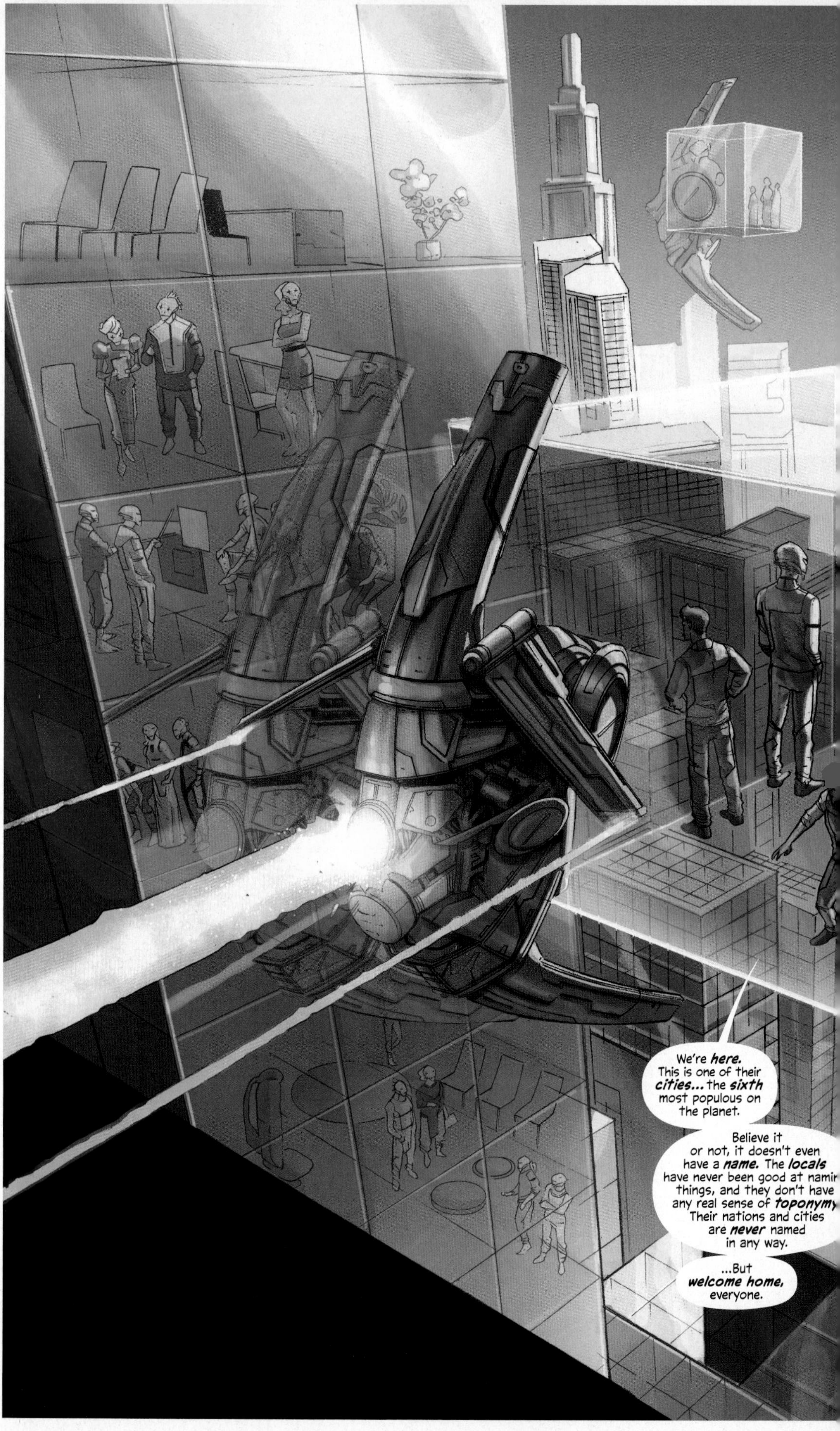
We're here. This is one of their cities... the sixth most populous on the planet.
Believe it or not, it doesn't even have a name. The locals have never been good at namir things, and they don't have any real sense of toponymy Their nations and cities are never named in any way.
...But welcome home, everyone.

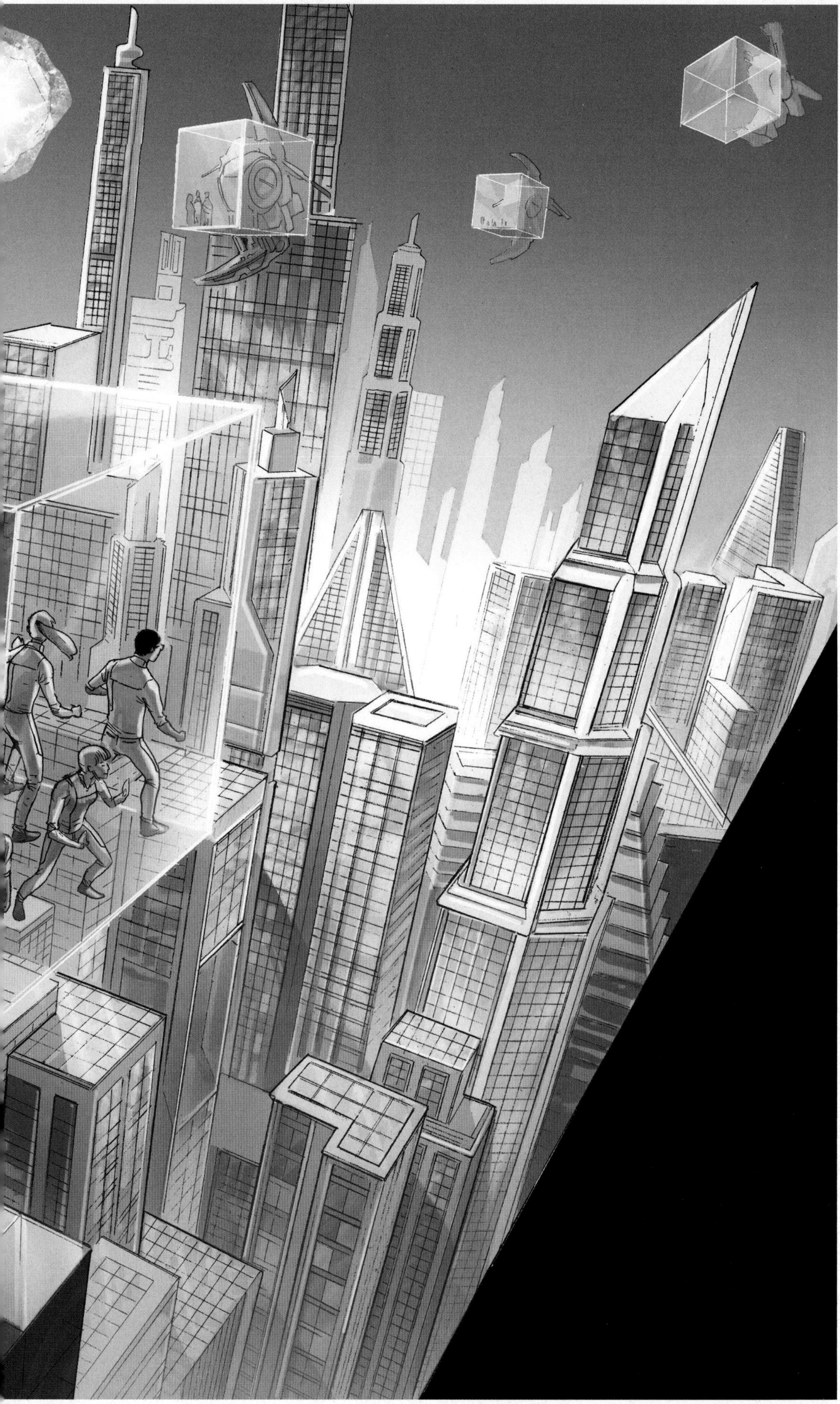

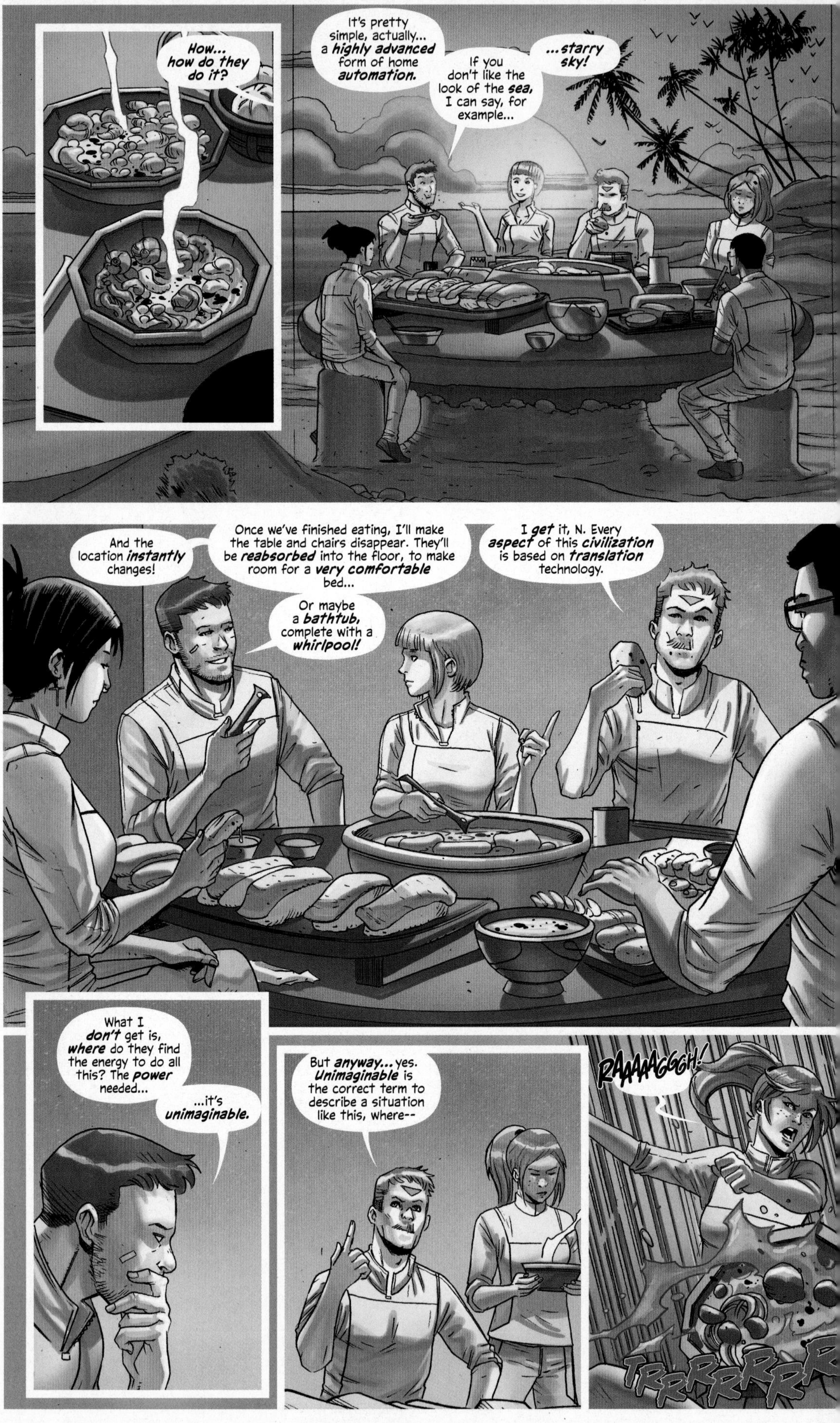
How... how do they do it?
It's pretty simple, actually... a highly advanced form of home automation.
If you don't like the look of the sea, I can say, for example...
...starry sky!
And the location instantly changes!
Once we've finished eating, I'll make the table and chairs disappear. They'll be reabsorbed into the floor, to make room for a very comfortable bed...
Or maybe a bathtub, complete with a whirlpool!
I get it, N. Every aspect of this civilization is based on translation technology.
What I don't get is, where do they find the energy to do all this? The power needed...
...it's unimaginable.
But anyway... yes. Unimaginable is the correct term to describe a situation like this, where--
RAAAAAGGGH!
TRRRRRRR

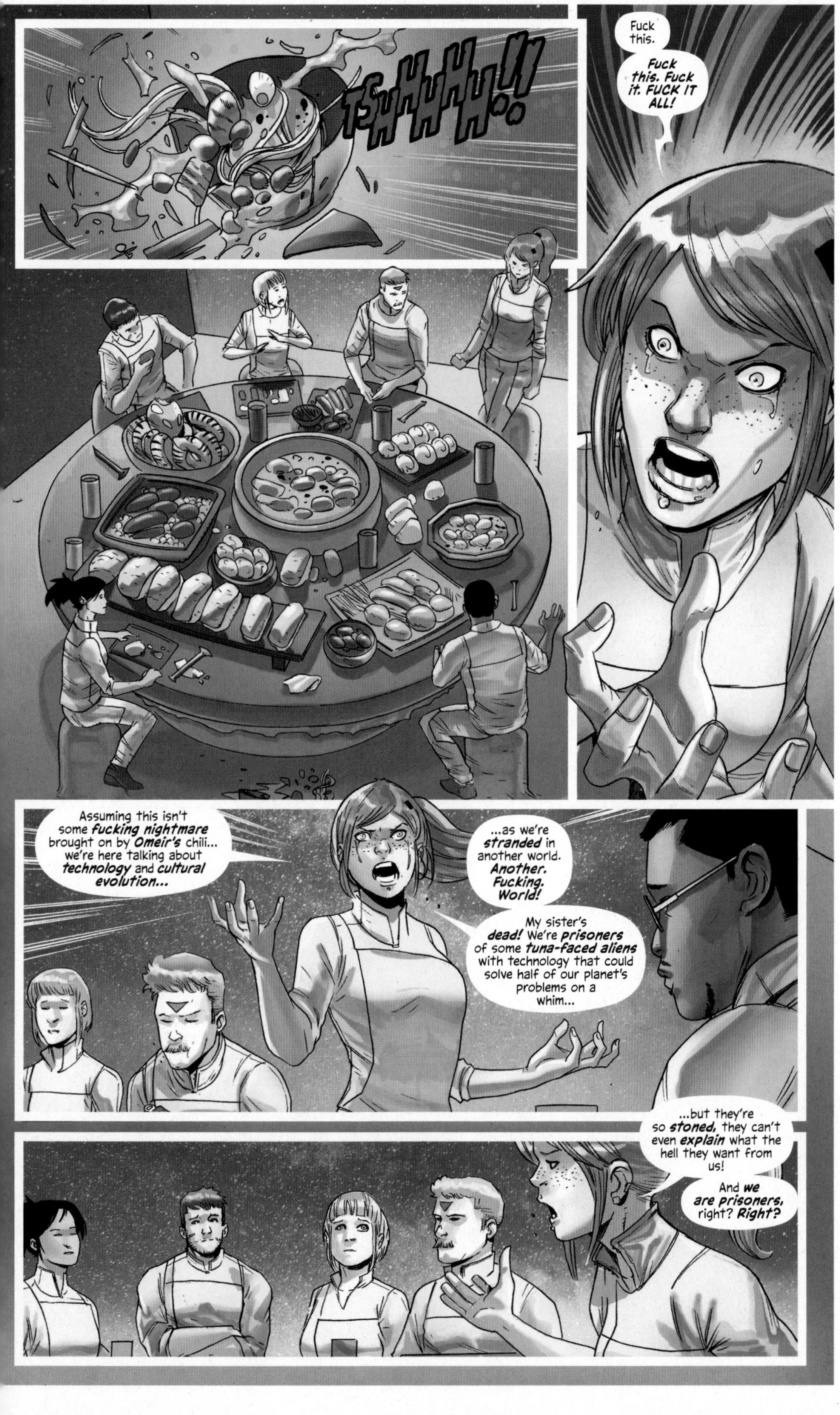
TSHHHHH..!!
Fuck this.
Fuck this. Fuck it. FUCK IT ALL!
Assuming this isn't some fucking nightmare brought on by Omeir's chili... we're here talking about technology and cultural evolution...
...as we're stranded in another world. Another. Fucking. World!
My sister's dead! We're prisoners of some tuna-faced aliens with technology that could solve half of our planet's problems on a whim...
...but they're so stoned, they can't even explain what the hell they want from us!
And we are prisoners, right? Right?

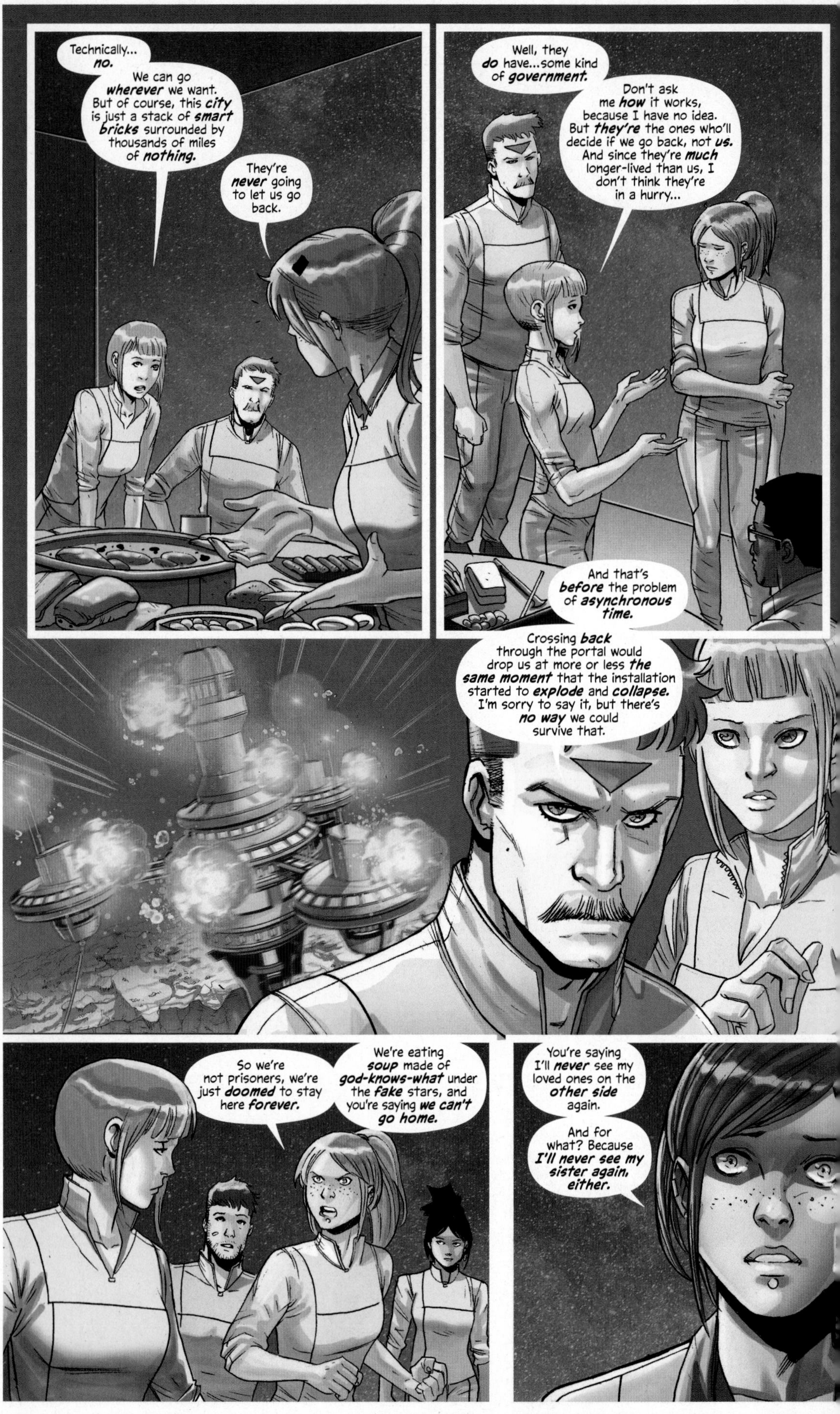
Technically... no.
We can go wherever we want. But of course, this city is just a stack of smart bricks surrounded by thousands of miles of nothing.
They're never going to let us go back.
Well, they do have...some kind of government.
Don't ask me how it works, because I have no idea. But they're the ones who'll decide if we go back, not us. And since they're much longer-lived than us, I don't think they're in a hurry...
And that's before the problem of asynchronous time.
Crossing back through the portal would drop us at more or less the same moment that the installation started to explode and collapse. I'm sorry to say it, but there's no way we could survive that.
So we're not prisoners, we're just doomed to stay here forever.
We're eating soup made of god-knows-what under the fake stars, and you're saying we can't go home.
You're saying I'll never see my loved ones on the other side again.
And for what? Because I'll never see my sister again, either.

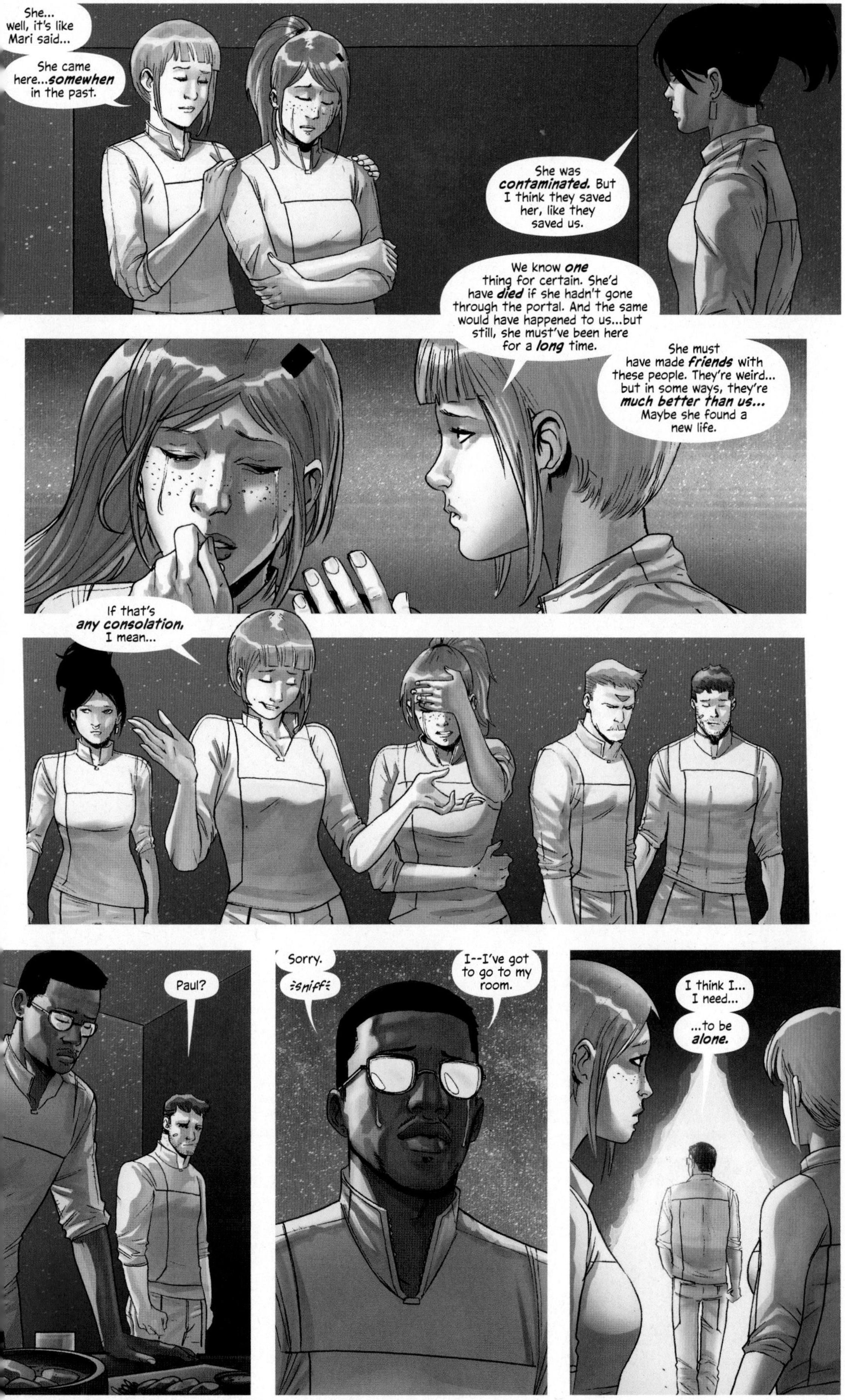

She... well, it's like Mari said...
She came here...*somewhen* in the past.
She was *contaminated.* But I think they saved her, like they saved us.
We know *one* thing for certain. She'd have *died* if she hadn't gone through the portal. And the same would have happened to us...but still, she must've been here for a *long* time.
She must have made *friends* with these people. They're weird... but in some ways, they're *much better than us...* Maybe she found a new life.
If that's *any consolation,* I mean...
Paul?
Sorry.
sniff
I--I've got to go to my room.
I think I... I need...
...to be *alone.*

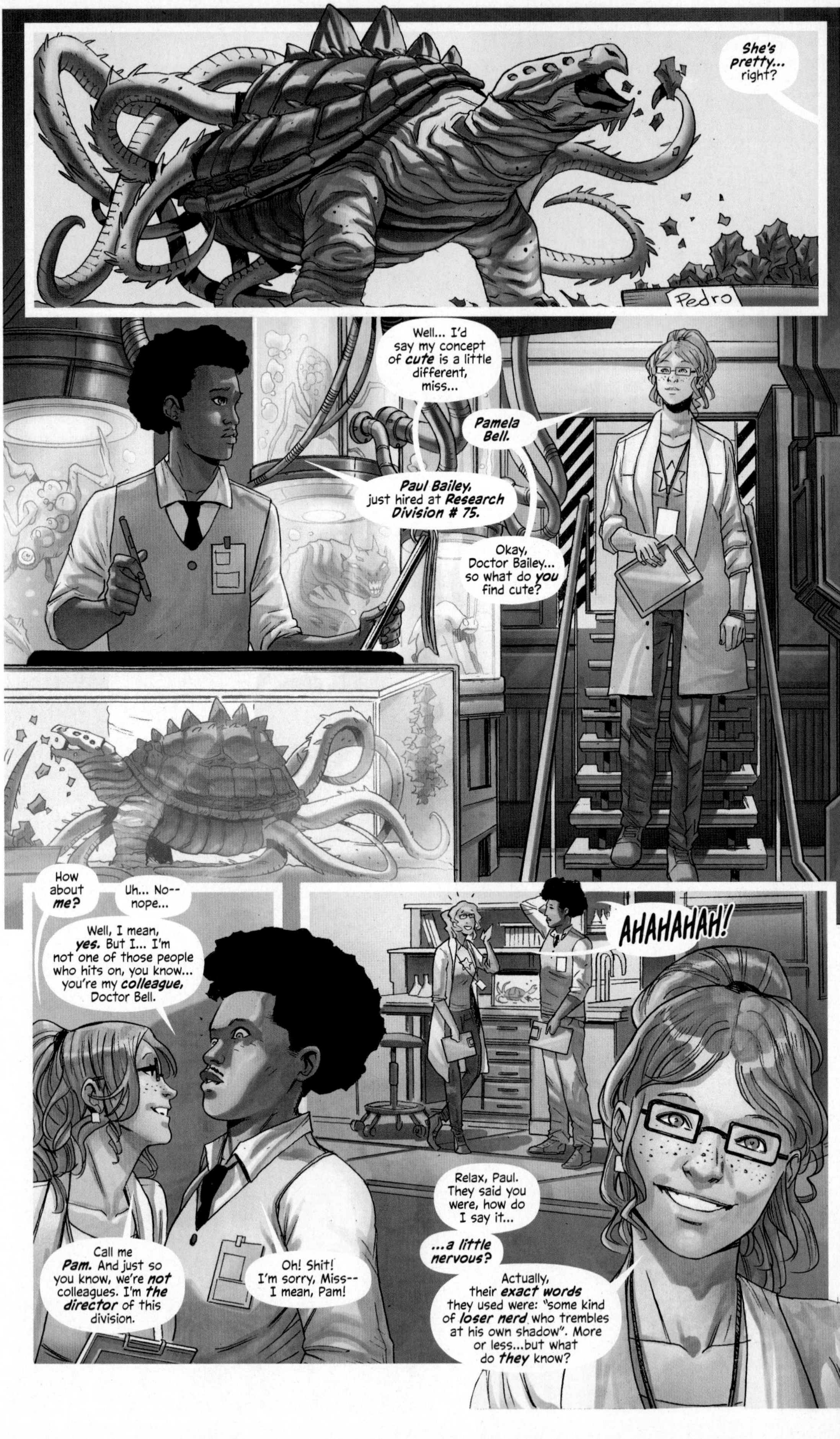

She's pretty... right?
Pedro
Well... I'd say my concept of cute is a little different, miss...
Pamela Bell.
Paul Bailey, just hired at Research Division # 75.
Okay, Doctor Bailey... so what do you find cute?
How about me?
Uh... No-- nope...
Well, I mean, yes. But I... I'm not one of those people who hits on, you know... you're my colleague, Doctor Bell.
Call me Pam. And just so you know, we're not colleagues. I'm the director of this division.
Oh! Shit! I'm sorry, Miss-- I mean, Pam!
AHAHAHAH!
Relax, Paul. They said you were, how do I say it...
...a little nervous?
Actually, their exact words they used were: "some kind of loser nerd who trembles at his own shadow". More or less...but what do they know?

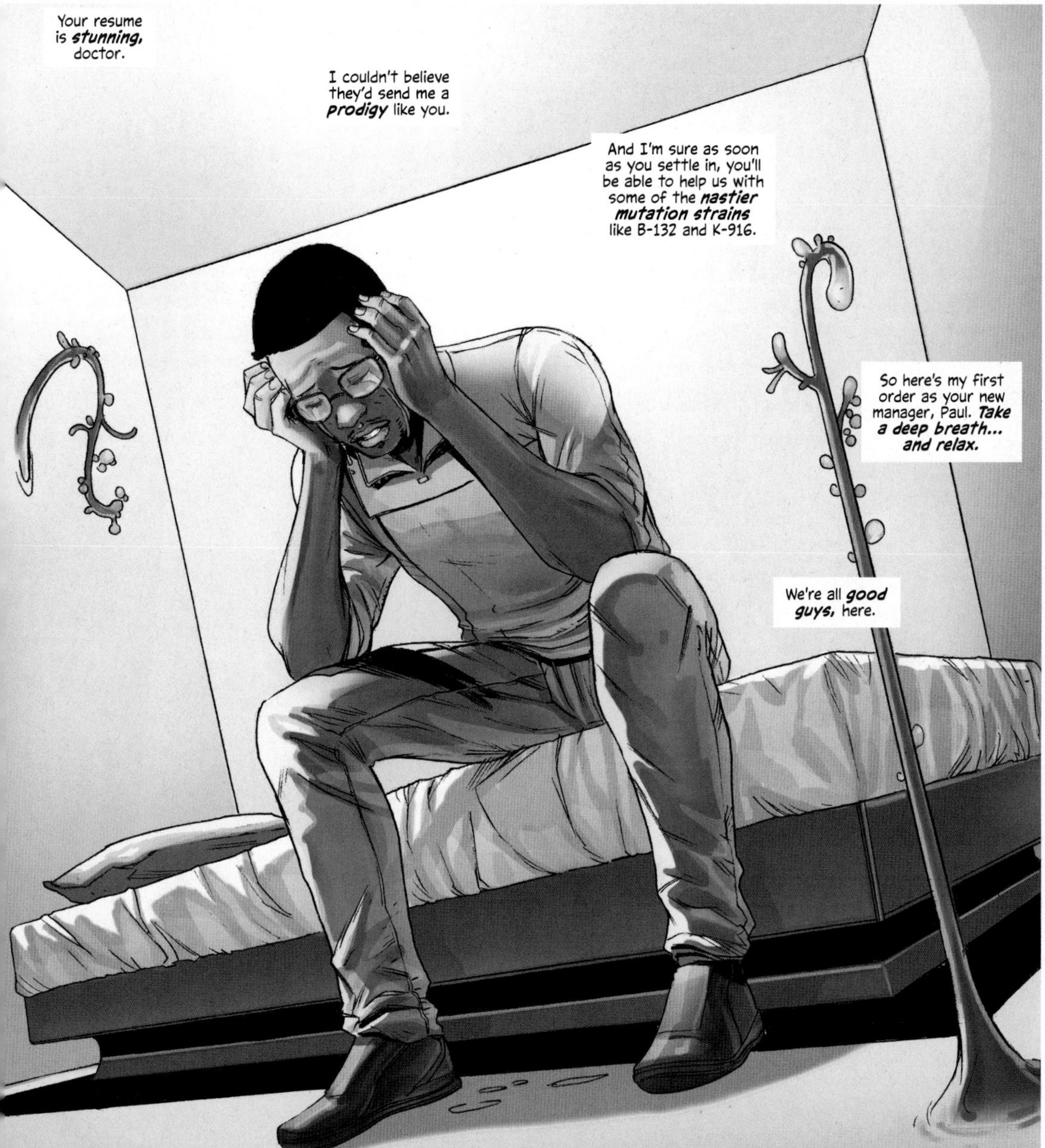
Your resume is ***stunning,*** doctor.
I couldn't believe they'd send me a ***prodigy*** like you.
And I'm sure as soon as you settle in, you'll be able to help us with some of the ***nastier mutation strains*** like B-132 and K-916.
So here's my first order as your new manager, Paul. ***Take a deep breath... and relax.***
We're all ***good guys,*** here.

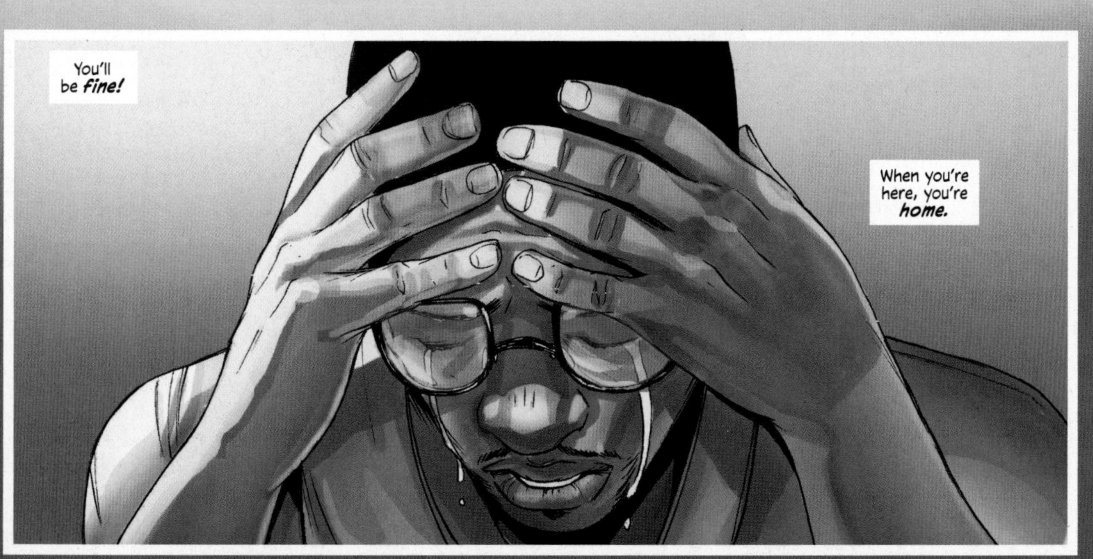
You'll be ***fine!***
When you're here, you're ***home.***

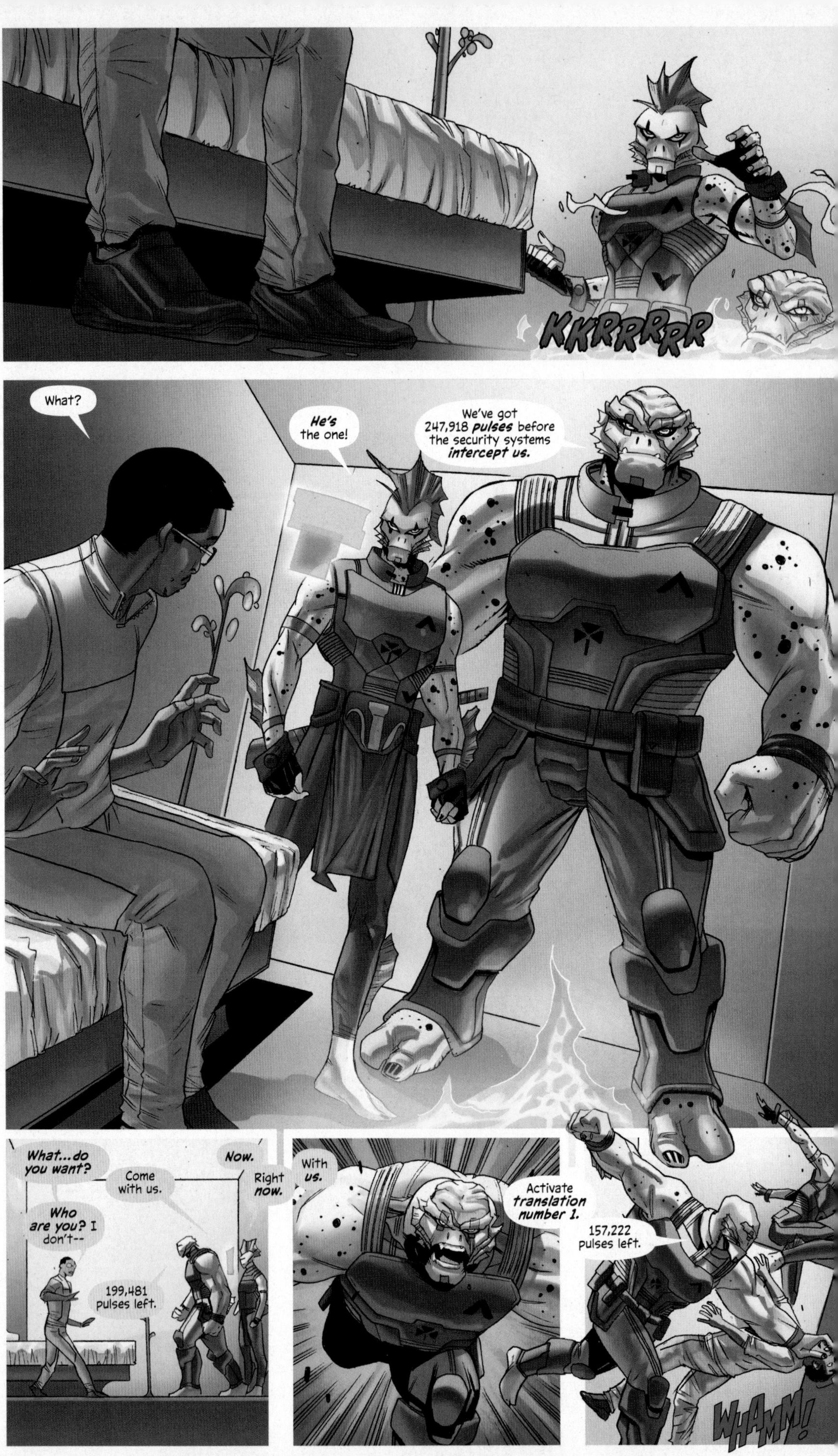
KKRRRRRR
What?
He's the one!
We've got 247,918 pulses before the security systems intercept us.
What...do you want?
Come with us.
Who are you? I don't--
199,481 pulses left.
Now.
Right now.
With us.
Activate translation number 1.
157,222 pulses left.
WHAMM!

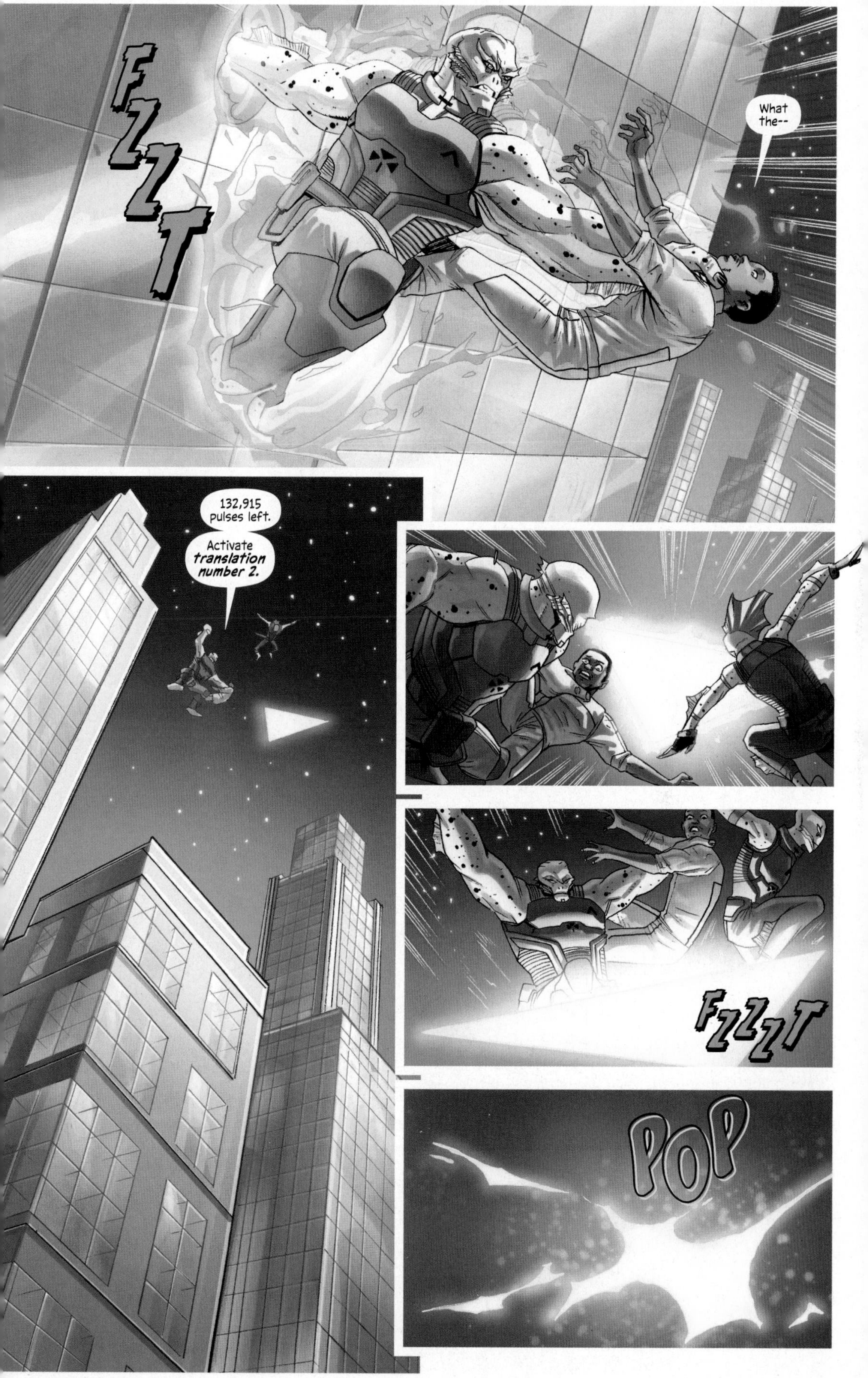
FZZZT
What the--
132,915 pulses left.
Activate *translation number 2.*
FZZZT
POP

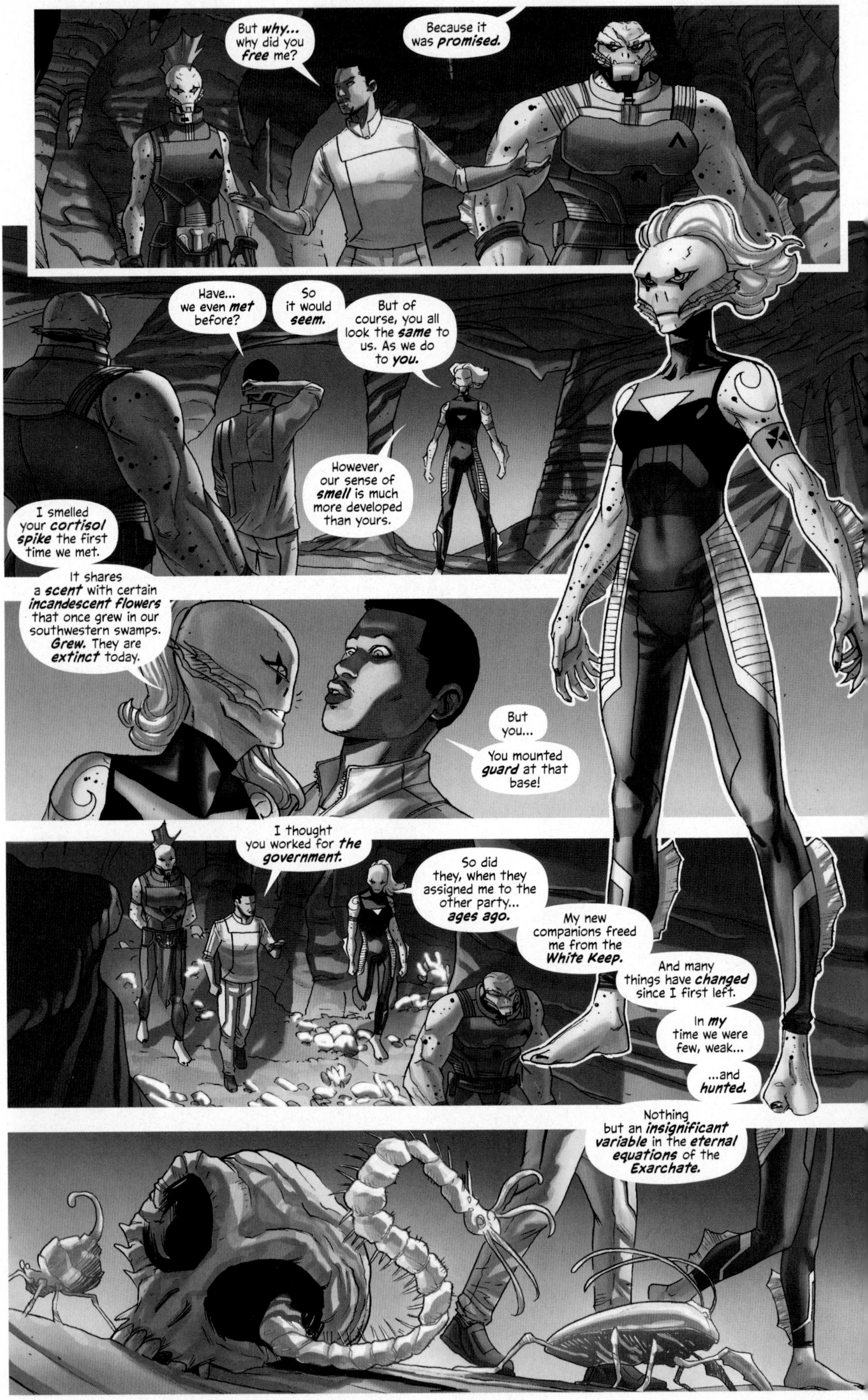

But ***why...*** why did you ***free*** me?
Because it was ***promised.***
Have... we even ***met*** before?
So it would ***seem.***
But of course, you all look the ***same*** to us. As we do to ***you.***
However, our sense of ***smell*** is much more developed than yours.
I smelled your ***cortisol spike*** the first time we met.
It shares a ***scent*** with certain ***incandescent flowers*** that once grew in our southwestern swamps. ***Grew.*** They are ***extinct*** today.
But you...
You mounted ***guard*** at that base!
I thought you worked for ***the government.***
So did they, when they assigned me to the other party... ***ages ago.***
My new companions freed me from the ***White Keep.***
And many things have ***changed*** since I first left.
In ***my*** time we were few, weak...
...and ***hunted.***
Nothing but an ***insignificant variable*** in the ***eternal equations*** of the ***Exarchate.***

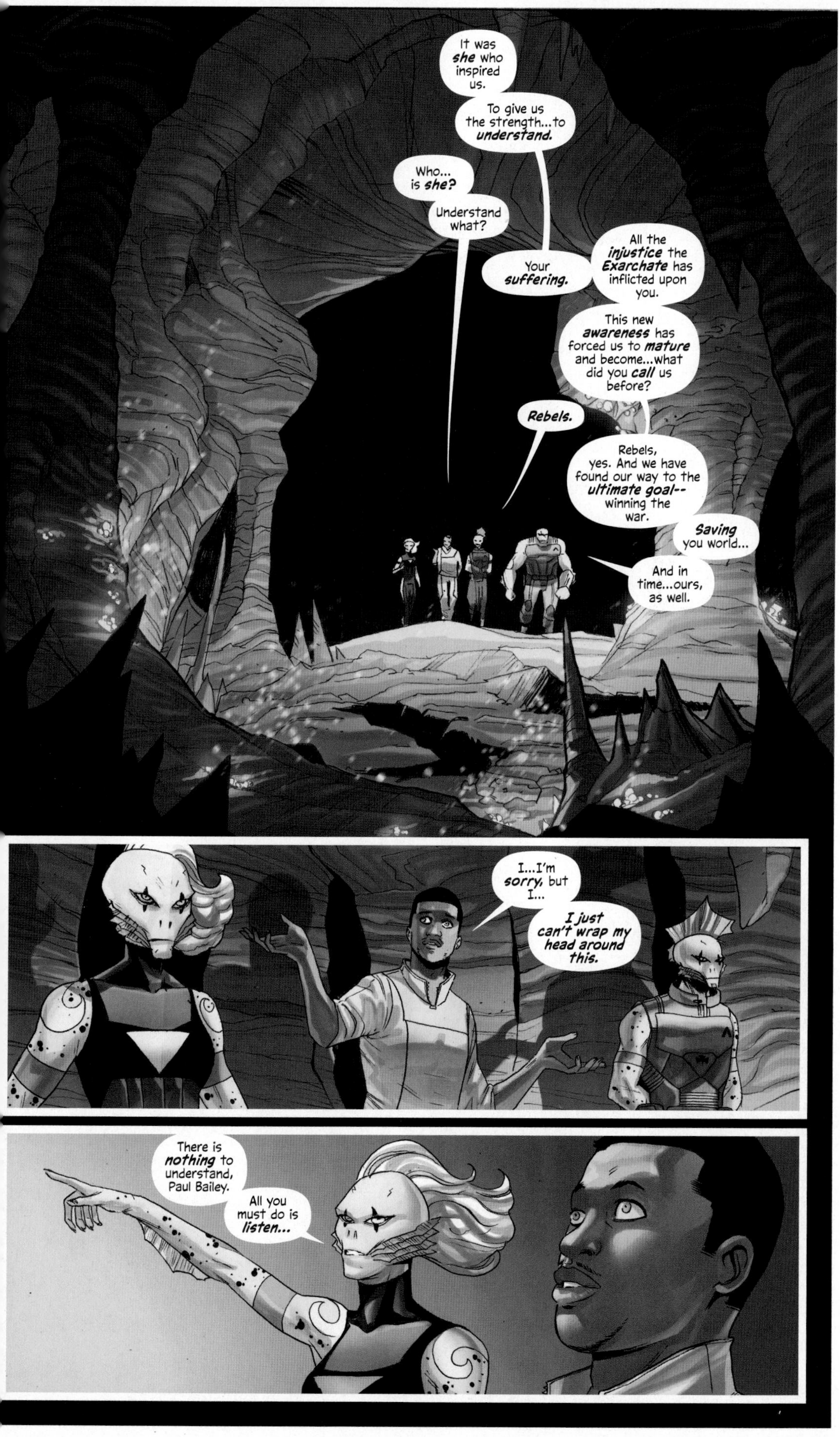

It was *she* who inspired us.
To give us the strength...to *understand.*
Who... is *she?*
Understand what?
Your *suffering.*
All the *injustice* the *Exarchate* has inflicted upon you.
This new *awareness* has forced us to *mature* and become...what did you *call* us before?
Rebels.
Rebels, yes. And we have found our way to the *ultimate goal--* winning the war.
Saving you world...
And in time...ours, as well.
I...I'm *sorry,* but I...
I just can't wrap my head around this.
There is *nothing* to understand, Paul Bailey.
All you must do is *listen...*

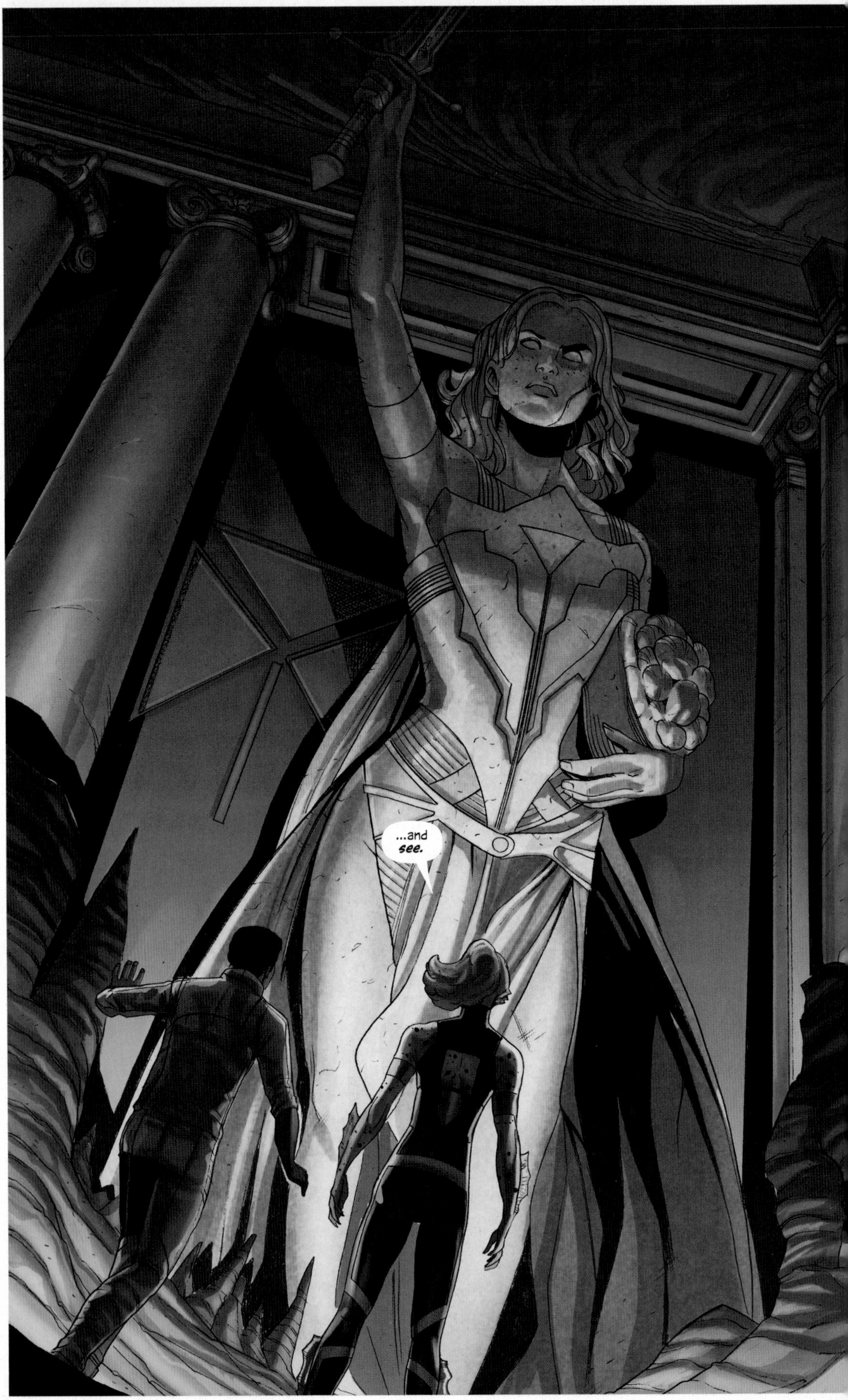
...and see.

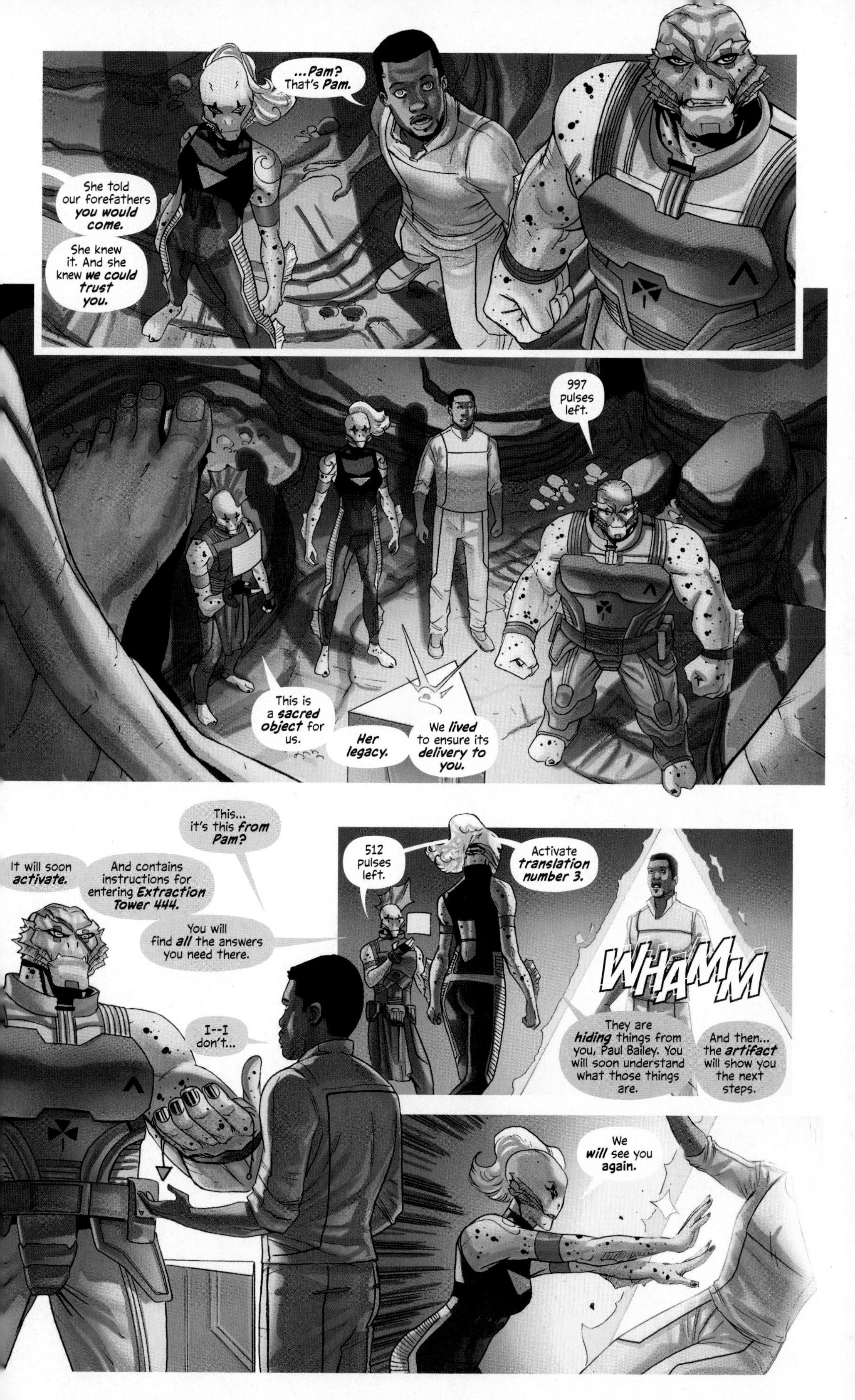
...Pam? That's Pam.
She told our forefathers you would come.
She knew it. And she knew we could trust you.
997 pulses left.
This is a sacred object for us.
Her legacy.
We lived to ensure its delivery to you.
This... it's this from Pam?
It will soon activate.
And contains instructions for entering Extraction Tower 444.
You will find all the answers you need there.
I--I don't...
512 pulses left.
Activate translation number 3.
WHAMM
They are hiding things from you, Paul Bailey. You will soon understand what those things are.
And then... the artifact will show you the next steps.
We will see you again.

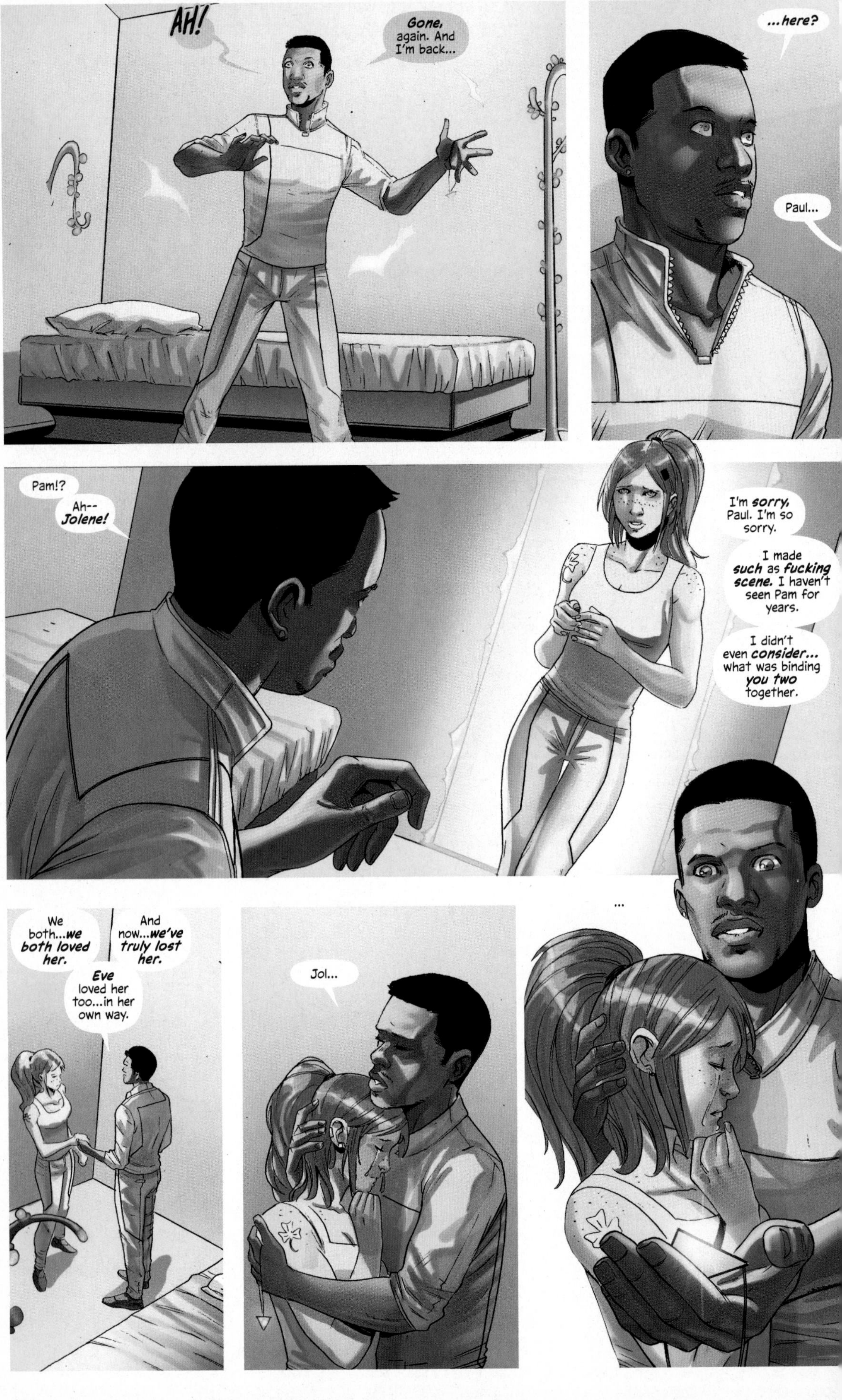
AH!
Gone, again. And I'm back...
...here?
Paul...
Pam!? Ah-- Jolene!
I'm sorry, Paul. I'm so sorry.
I made such as fucking scene. I haven't seen Pam for years.
I didn't even consider... what was binding you two together.
We both...we both loved her.
And now...we've truly lost her.
Eve loved her too...in her own way.
Jol...
...

COVER GALLERY

`-,-`

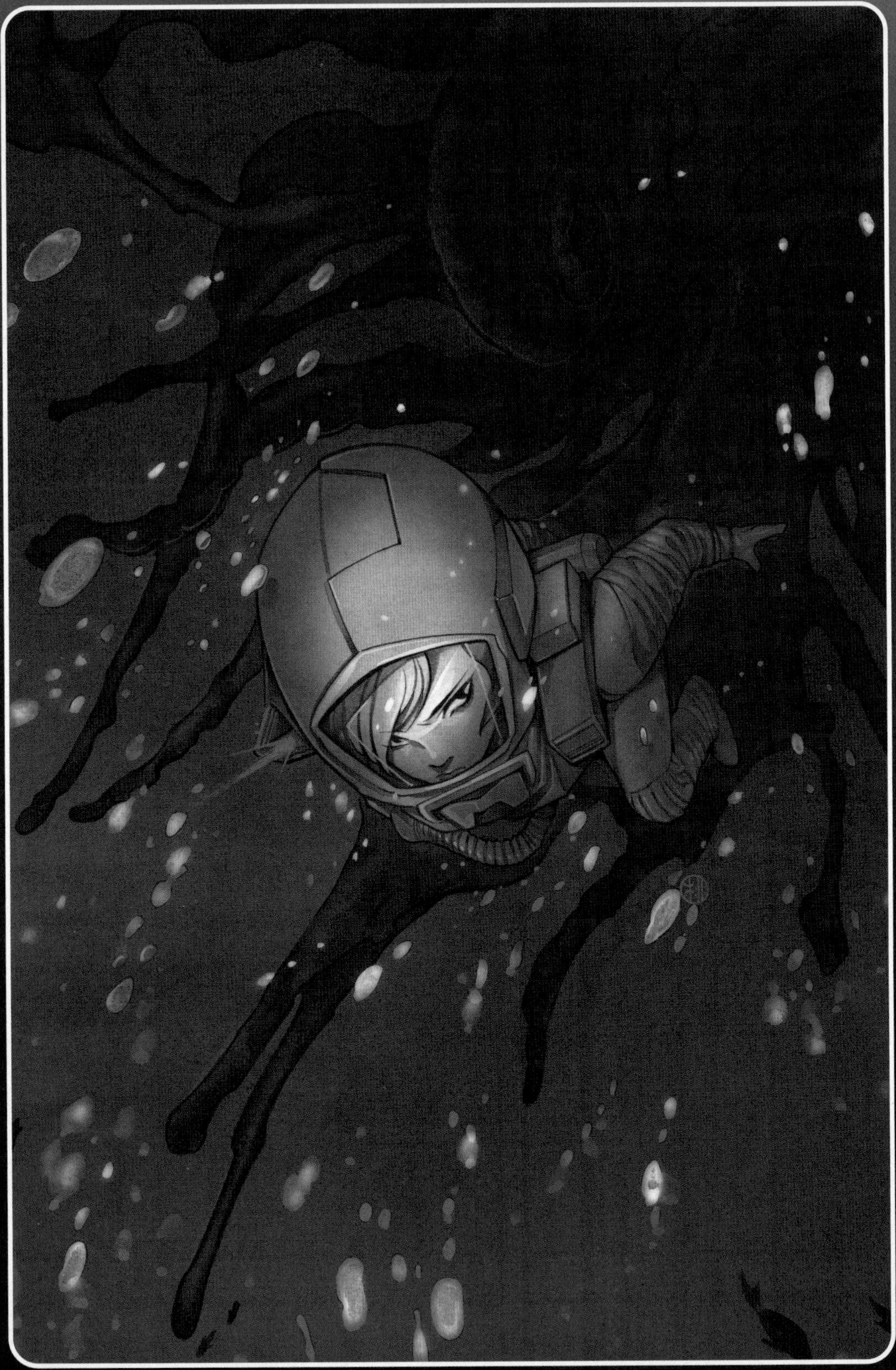

PEACH MOMOKO

ISSUE 01

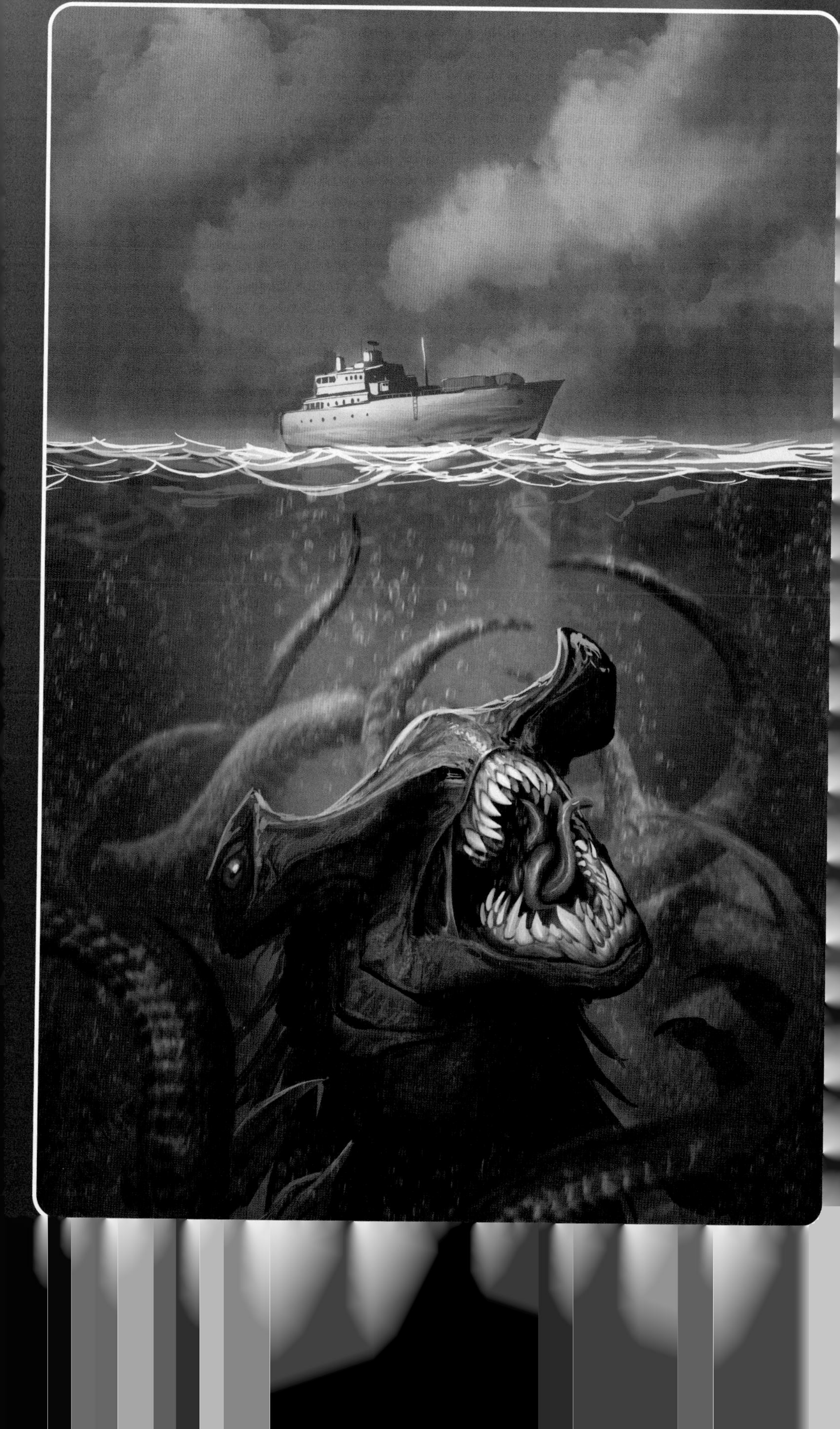

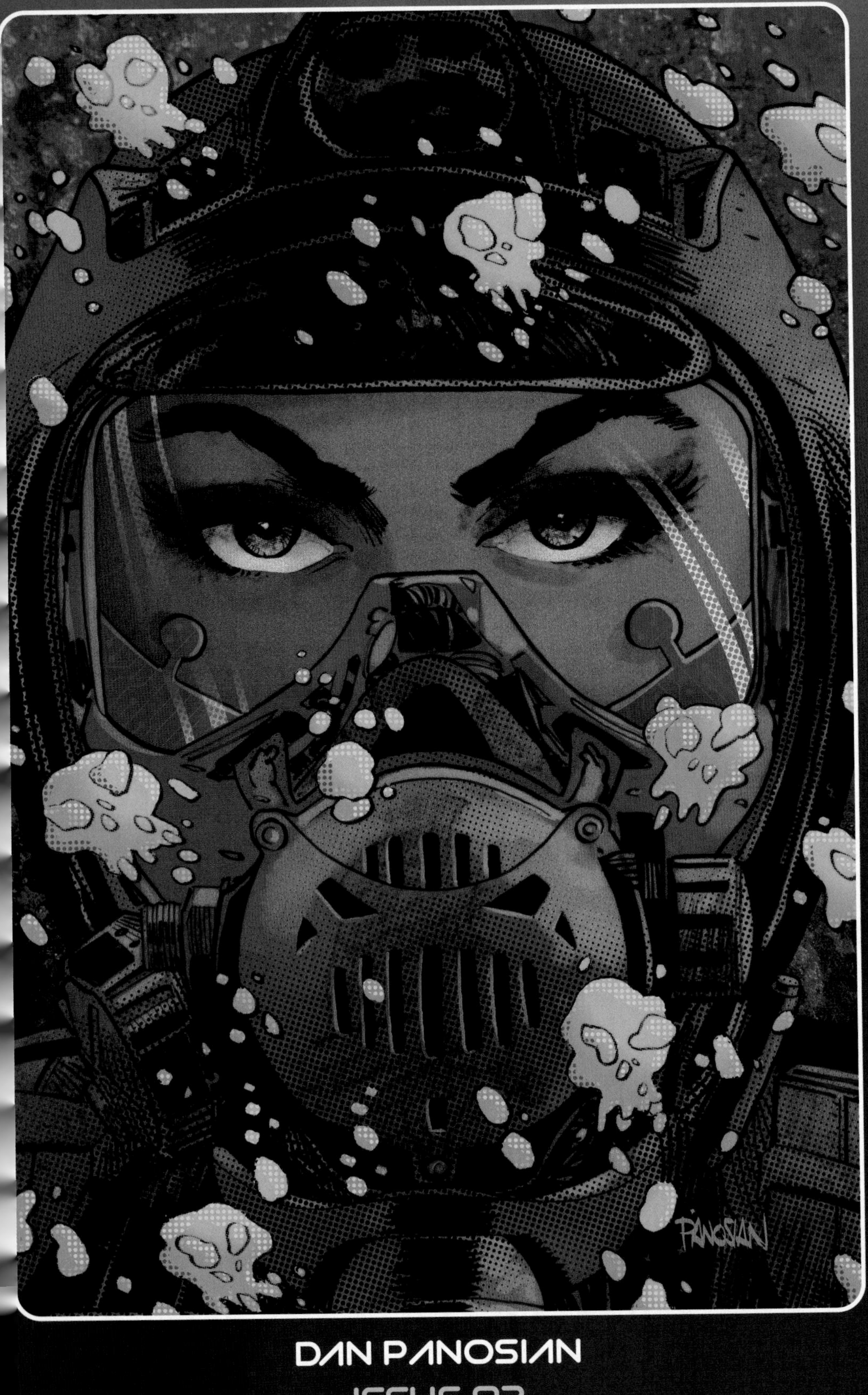
PANOSIAN

DAN PANOSIAN

ISSUE 02

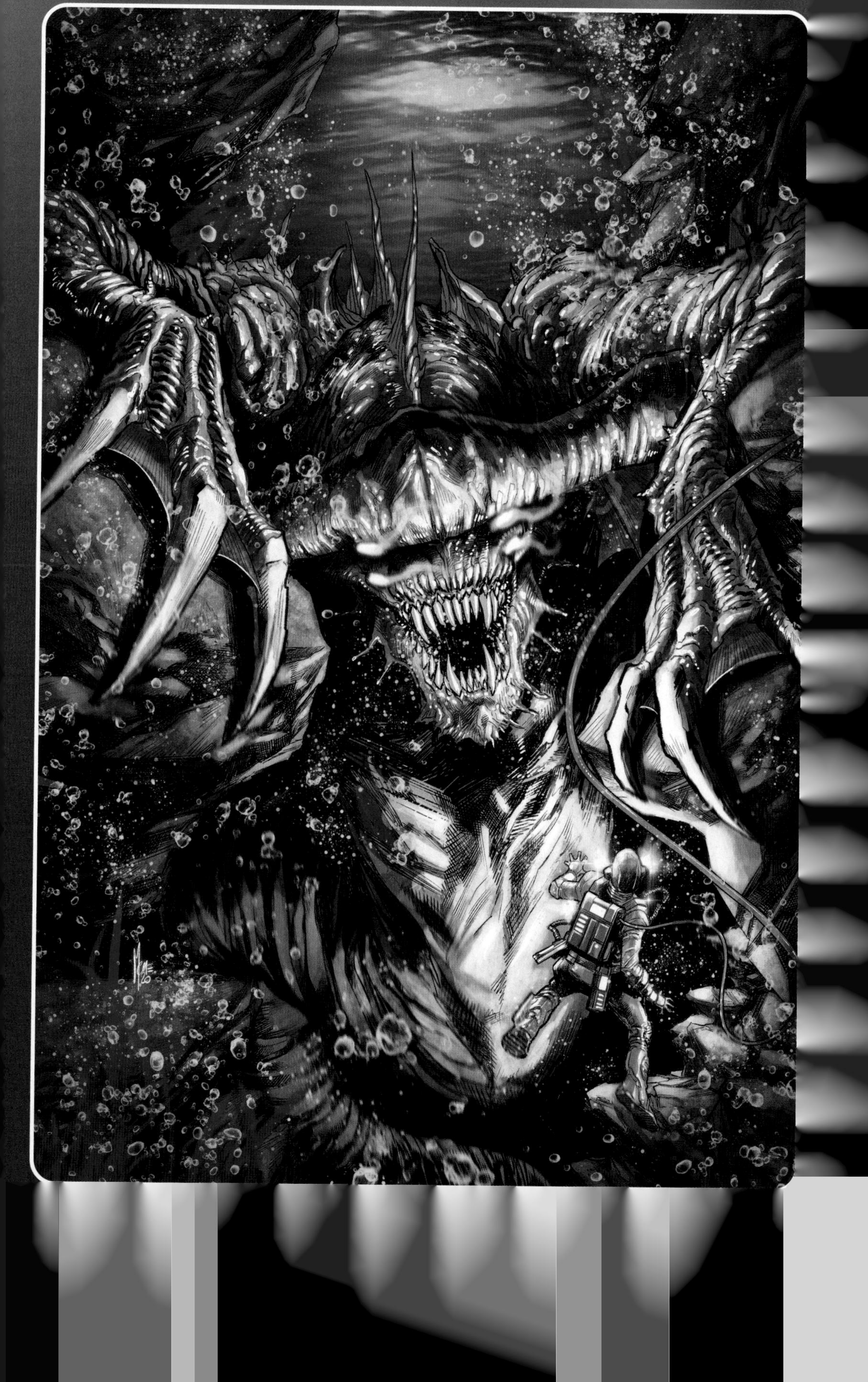

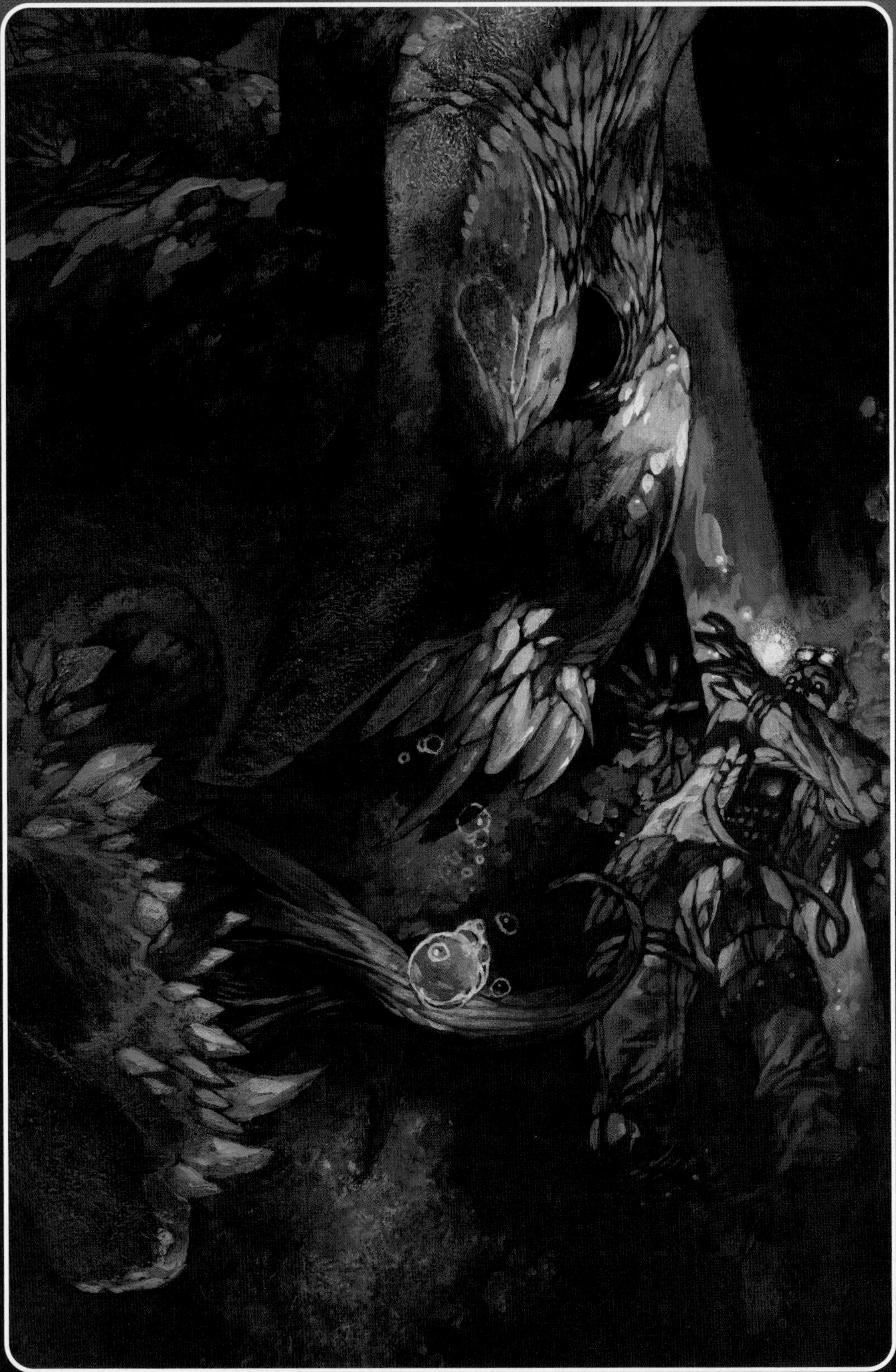

SIMONE BIANCHI
ISSUE 03

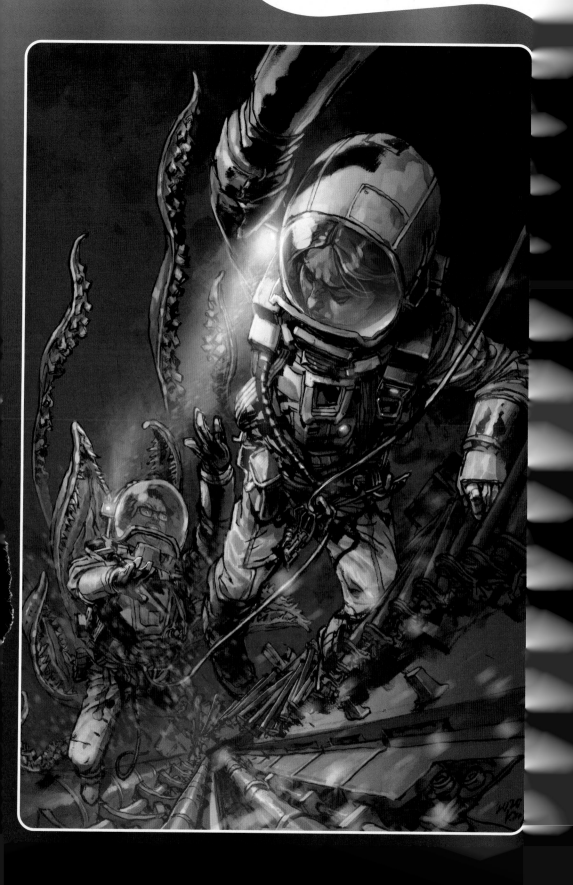

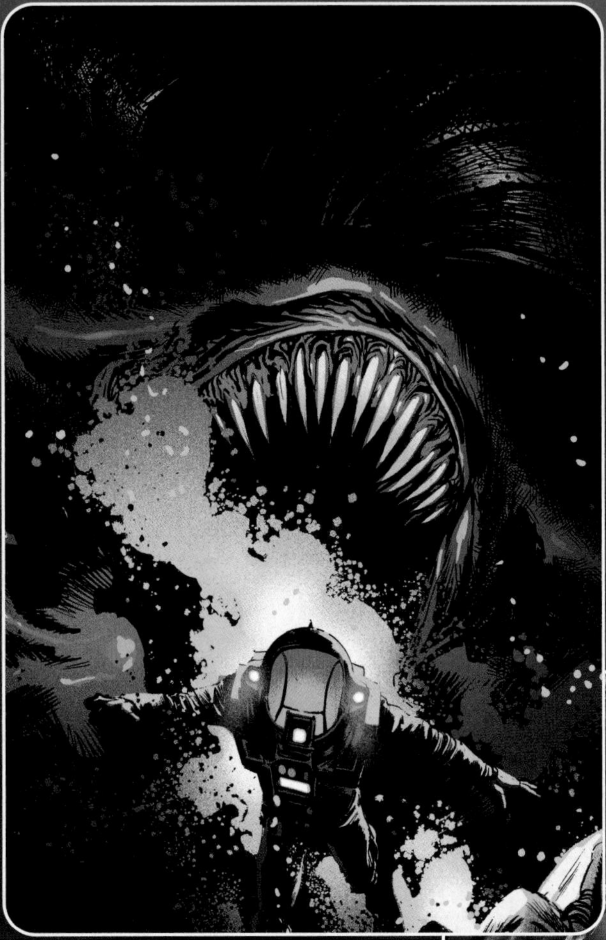

RAFAEL
ALBUQUERQUE

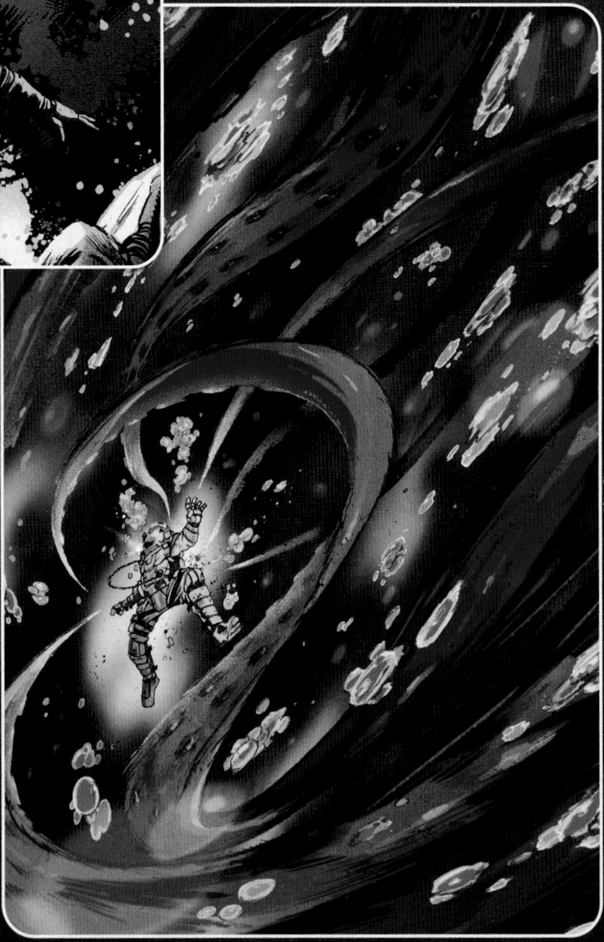

RICARDO
LOPEZ ORTIZ

ISSUE 04

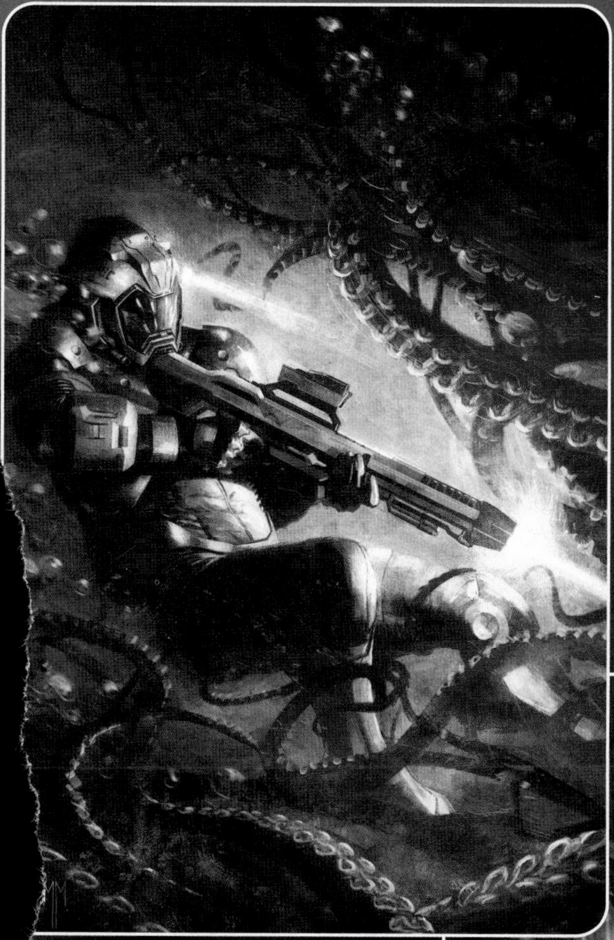

MARCO MASTRAZZO

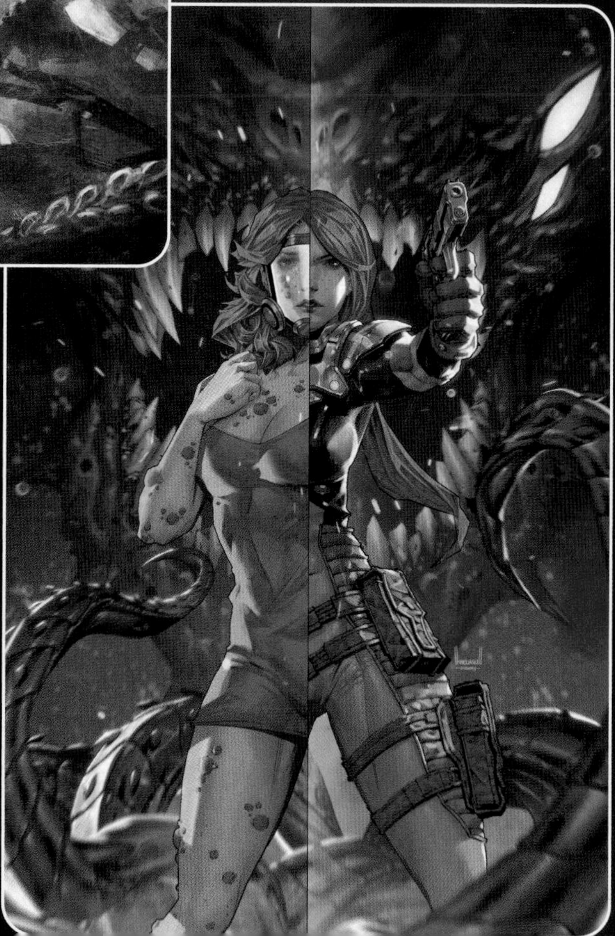

KAEL NGU

DARKO LAFUENTE
(COLORS: KIKE J. DIAZ)

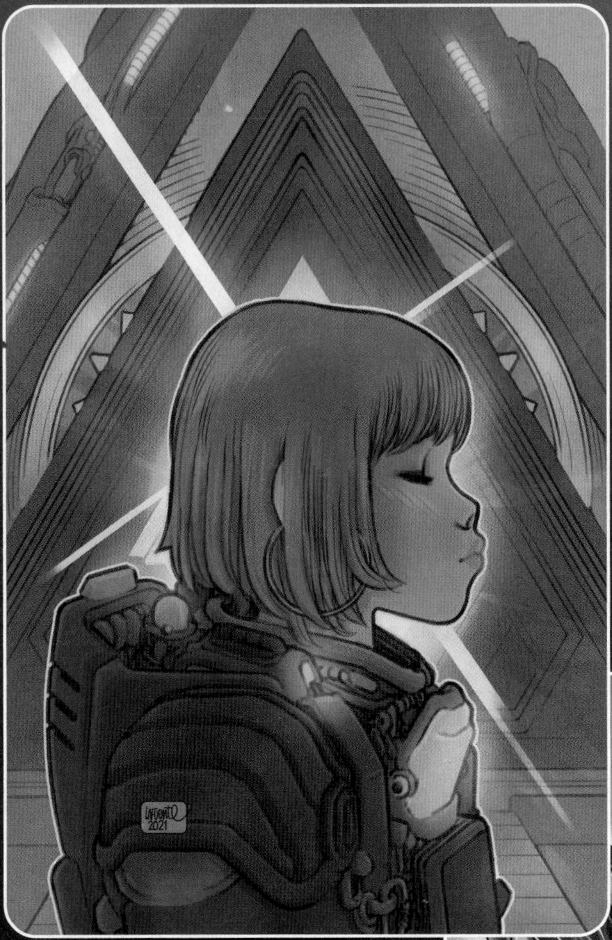

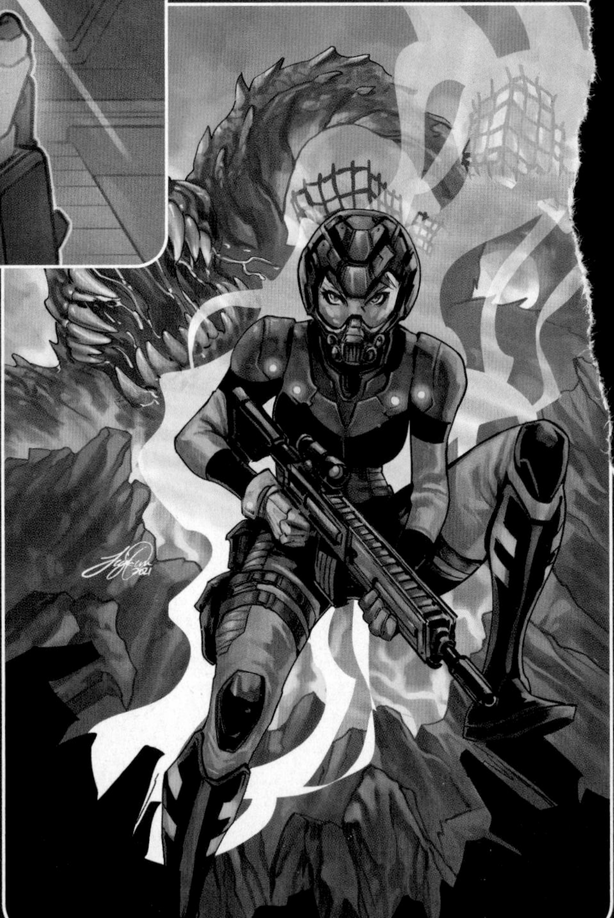

SIYA OUM

ISSUE 06